GOAL LINE

Boston Rebels
Book 4

JULIA CONNORS

For anyone who ever felt like what you wanted was just out of reach—please know, you deserve every happy ending, especially the ones you have to work hard for.

Author's Note

Goal Line deals with topics that may be sensitive for some readers, including accidental pregnancy, and an emotionally abusive parent. For a full list of content warnings, please visit my website: juliaconnors.com/goal-line

Please note that, for the sake of the story, some liberties were taken with the timing of the playoffs and the Olympic qualifiers.

Chapter One

LUKE

"We've played six games against St. Louis. We've won half, and they've won half." Coach pauses, looks around the locker room on the eve of Game 7 of the Stanley Cup Final, and then says, "I don't need to go over their strengths or their weaknesses—you already know them. What I do want to tell you before you take the ice tonight is that you are the better team. You deserve this win. But it'll only happen if every single one of you goes out there and gives it your all for the next sixty minutes of play. No distractions. No mistakes. Do. Your. Job."

Do your job. It seems so simple, but each time you take the ice, you face the reality that the game could go either way. On our journey to the finals, we beat teams that were better than us and lost to teams who weren't as good. So much can go right, and so much can go wrong, during those three periods.

Colt's the starting goalie tonight, so the pressure's off me —though I still feel the heightened nerves and adrenaline coursing through the locker room. But as I stand here moments before Game 7, surrounded by my new teammates who've welcomed me onto this team in a way I wasn't expecting, gratitude overrides all my other emotions.

Next to me, Colt digs his elbow into my side with a subtle nod, as if reminding me that my only job tonight is to watch him do his. Despite his reputation as an immature playboy, Colt's actually a great mentor; he's quick to provide suggestions, but in a way that feels helpful rather than condescending. He's made no secret of the fact that he plans to retire after his contract is up at the end of next season, and he wants me to be ready to step into his spot. Whether I will be, or not, remains to be seen.

Coach claps his hand against his clipboard, then glances at his phone. He leans in and says something to our assistant coach before telling us to line up, and then turns and heads out the door.

"That's weird," Colt mumbles. Coach never leaves the locker room before the team.

"Huh. Yeah." I'm not sure why, but I have an uneasy sense that something's not right. When I glance over at our general manager, AJ, I see the worry on her face, too. Whatever's going on, she knows this isn't normal.

"You heard him," our goalie coach, Evan Knight, says as he steps up to us.

Colt and I take our spots at the back of the line, and as we follow our teammates out the door and down the hallway toward the ice, I notice Coach off to the side, watching us walk by.

"Okay. Keep me posted," he says into the phone as we pass. "I love you too."

Behind me, AJ asks him, "Everything okay?"

I shouldn't be listening to their conversation. I should be focused on the game ahead. But the uneasy feeling gripping my belly and sending a nervous shiver up my spine won't let me ignore it.

"Eva was just sent to the hospital. Helene is flying to New York—"

I hear my best friend's name coming off her father's lips, and I stop in my tracks. *No. No, no, no.* This can't be happening.

I spin around, practically plowing over Coach Knight as I do. "Wait! What's wrong with Evie?" I can hear the panic in my voice, but I can't control it. I need to know what they know.

"We don't know yet. She was rushed to the ER during the layover on her flight back from Europe. I'm sure everything's going to be fine. Now get out there."

Swallowing past a sudden lump in my throat, I nod, hoping that he really does believe everything is fine, while also knowing that I need to warn Eva that her mother's on her way. *Shit.* I'm headed out to the ice for warmups, and my phone is in the locker room.

I slowly turn to face the line of my teammates. My shoulders are so tense that my pads are practically at my ears, and my hand is clenching my goalie stick so hard that I'm half afraid I might break it.

You need to fucking relax, I tell myself. Nothing terrible can be wrong with her because her dad doesn't seem that worried. But if her parents find out her secret, things will be very, very bad. So while I'm walking out to take the ice, in the back of my mind, I'm doing the math. Eva's mom is flying to New York, but it doesn't sound like she's at the hospital yet.

Maybe Eva already knows, and I'm worried for no reason. But maybe not—and I might be the only one who can save her right now. Even though "saving her" is only temporary. Eventually, her parents will find out. For now, at least I can warn her of her mother's imminent arrival.

———

"Are you even fucking paying attention out there?" Colt grumbles as we make our way back to the visiting team's locker room after warmups. I wish we were playing the last game of the Stanley Cup Final at home, in Boston, instead of in St. Louis. We never should've let it get to Game 7.

"Dude, my stomach's a mess," I say, and it's not quite a lie.

It's reasonable that I might need to take a shit before the biggest game of my life. But what I actually need is the privacy of a bathroom stall to text Eva—something my teammates, and especially my coach, can't know.

"You're acting like a damn rookie," Colt says, but the insult doesn't reach his eyes, which are full of sympathy. Nerves are a very real part of playing, and I certainly wouldn't be the first player to camp out in a bathroom stall before a game. Even the fifteen-year veteran goalie has probably been there once or twice in his life. "You're not even playing tonight."

"I just need to use the bathroom, then I'll be fine." I shrug.

When he looks at me like *Are you fucking kidding me?*, I add for good measure, "Unless you can't cut it out there, old man." I jab him with my elbow, and Colt lets out a choked laugh. He's old by professional hockey standards, but given that he's at the top of his game and a finalist for the Goalie of the Year award, which he's previously won three times, he knows I'm just giving him shit.

"The day *you* come in to replace *me*," he says with an eye roll, "is the day they take me out on a stretcher."

My eyes widen. Hockey players are superstitious as hell, and we don't say shit like that.

"Colt," I say, my voice full of warning. "What the fuck?"

He just laughs it off, like he's impervious to injury despite the fact that his knees are almost always killing him these days.

When we get back into the locker room, I dump my gear at my stall and grab my phone off the shelf, lifting my jersey and tucking it into the front of my hockey pants.

"You need your phone to take a shit?" Colt mumbles, side-eyeing me from where he stands at the locker next to mine.

"I might be in there a while." I turn and head into the bathroom.

LUKE

Evie, are you okay???

Also, heads-up that your mom is on her way to NYC to see you.

I get the alert that she has her notifications silenced, so I click "Notify anyway." I wait for the read receipt to pop up, but it doesn't. Gritting my teeth and taking a deep breath, I stand there, waiting . . . and waiting.

Then I call, but it goes straight to voicemail. *Fuck me.*

My mind's darting in a million directions, trying to figure out how to get a hold of her, but the only option I can think of is the nuclear one. The one my pride can barely allow me to choose.

A few moments later, as I hear Coach starting to give us our final instructions before the game, I realize my chance to contact Eva is coming to an end.

I pull up the contact I have saved only in case of emergency. It's a number I never wanted to have to use: Christopher Fucking Steele.

That's how he's saved in my contacts, and the only way I'll ever refer to Eva's skating partner. But given that I'm sure he's with her, and given that this whole situation is pretty much his fault, I text him anyway.

LUKE

> I hope you're with Eva right now, because her mom's on her way to the hospital, and she can't find out the truth until Eva's ready to tell her. My game is about to start. Take care of her until I can get there.

Even though we've never exchanged messages, I don't bother telling him it's me, because I know Eva gave him my number for emergencies, too.

And now, I just hope that he's with her. It's not something I've *ever* wished for before. Because whatever's wrong with her, and hopefully it's not any of the worst-case scenarios that my mind is considering, I'm guessing she doesn't have her phone and I need him to deliver that message.

As I listen to the guys getting rowdy, I know we're about to head back to the ice for the start of the game. I don't have time to wait around for Christopher Fucking Steele's response. I just have to pray everything works out.

Heading back into the locker room, I set my phone on the shelf and gather my gear, feeling like my heart is lodged in my throat. For the next two and a half hours, I'm going to be watching the game, knees bouncing, desperately wanting my team to win, but lacking the focus to stay fully engaged.

All I want to do is hop onto my father's private jet and fly to New York to make sure Evie's okay. I'm definitely not in the ideal mental space as I head into Game 7.

Let's hope I'm not needed on the ice tonight.

Chapter Two

EVA

"The good news, Evangeline," the doctor says, standing next to my hospital bed surrounded by three young residents, "is that both you and the baby are fine."

I breathe out a long sigh of relief and slump back against the raised mattress.

The older doctor nods toward one of the residents, and she explains how my body gave out on me, thanks to a combination of dehydration, low electrolytes, low iron, and exhaustion. "After we've finished giving you IV fluids and iron, you'll be fine to go home. But you need to start taking iron and some additional supplements, and you definitely need a few days of rest. You really shouldn't push yourself so hard while you're pregnant."

"I'm a figure skater trying to qualify for the Olympics," I remind them, my voice tight with the frustration I'm feeling. "Pushing myself is part of the job."

I'm not being flippant. I know what my body is capable of. Or what it *was* capable of, apparently, since pregnancy seems to be changing me daily, and what I could easily do three days ago might be challenging today.

That's precisely what happened in our last international competition, when I had to downgrade a difficult jump that Christopher and I had executed perfectly dozens of times. That competition should have been a first-place finish and the crowning glory at the end of a season fraught with personal challenges. Instead, we dropped from being the top-ranked US pairs team to third place.

"For the next few months, you're going to need to take it easy," the older doctor says. Christopher's hand tightens around mine in response to the way I squeeze his, while he sits rigidly beside me.

"Define taking it easy," I say, annoyance ringing out in my tone.

I'm fine. I don't know why they even brought me to the hospital. I'd slept on the plane from Paris to New York, which meant I hadn't eaten or drunk anything, and when I stood up too quickly after landing, I passed out. Christopher caught me, it's not like I even hit my head or anything. But despite assuring everyone I was okay, I was taken off the plane by EMTs.

I couldn't tell them in front of our coach, Jessie, that I was pregnant. As of right now, the only two people who know are my skating partner, Christopher, and my best friend, Luke. And I'd like to keep it that way until I'm ready to start sharing the news.

So, here we are—wasting time at the hospital, having

missed my connecting flight to Boston, and Christopher missing his flight back to LA.

"You're pregnant," the young female resident says with a sigh, as if I don't understand this fact or that she somehow knows my body better than I do. "You shouldn't even be skating when you're this far along."

I've been incredibly proud of myself to have continued at this level despite battling queasiness and fatigue for months on end. My coach and some of the other skaters we train with have noticed a difference in my energy levels, but only Christopher knows why. Pretty soon, though, I'm going to start showing. And from what I understand, that's the point at which I'll need to slow down in order to avoid injuring the baby.

But we're not there yet.

I needed to finish this season strong, and I did the best I could. Now, we're headed into our month-long summer break, which is the only time of year that I'm in Boston to see my parents. Then, in the late summer, we normally start our hardcore training in preparation for the competitions in the fall.

Even though I won't be able to go all out this summer, I'll still need to push myself. I have to be in the best physical condition possible during this pregnancy or I won't be in good enough shape afterward to pick up where I left off with my training.

After I have this baby, there will be one more chance to qualify for the Olympics—a goal that was handed down to me at birth, by virtue of being the child of two Olympians. There's no way I'm going to be the only person in my family not to achieve that.

I know it'll be that much harder with a newborn. But I'm determined to qualify for the Games *and* to be the best mom humanly possible.

"I'll talk to my OB about it when I'm back in Boston," I say, hoping that ends this conversation so I don't have to mention that I don't actually have an obstetrician in Boston. Mine is in LA, and I won't be back there for a month, which means I probably need to find someone to see in the interim.

"We'll give you some discharge paperwork to share with your doctor," the resident says. "You'll be out of here later tonight."

Next to me, Christopher slides his phone out of his pocket, and when I glance over at him, I can't read his expression. This is a recent phenomenon. After years of being completely in tune with one another, recognizing and experiencing every emotion together, there have been a few moments lately when he's felt a bit distant, almost like a stranger.

I exchange pleasantries with the care team as they leave, because that's what I've been trained to do my whole life. Performance Eva knows how to put on the "everything is great" front, no matter what I'm actually feeling.

When they're gone, I turn to Christopher. "What's wrong?"

He hands his phone to me. A single text from Luke. The only one he's ever sent to Christopher, apparently.

I quickly scan through the message. *Oh, shit.*

My eyes lock with Christopher's and, finally, I can tell exactly what he's thinking. My mom showing up is *bad*. But Luke showing up here would be *worse*.

"Where's my phone?" I ask, trying, but failing, to quell the panic.

He walks to the end of my bed and fishes through my belongings that were placed in a blue plastic bag when I was brought to the ER. My phone is in the pocket of my jacket, silenced like it always is.

And on the screen is a series of text messages from my mom, starting hours ago, telling me that Jessie called her and she's catching a flight from Boston to New York. *Fucking Jessie.*

And then there are messages from Luke, asking if I'm okay and warning me that my mom is on her way. Thank god he also texted Christopher, or I might not have gotten the news before she arrives.

"You have to go tell the doctors not to say anything in front of my mom," I plead, looking over at him. With his dark hair and nearly black eyes, we could be siblings. Instead, the whole world is convinced we're lovers. And for too long, I let myself hope for that as well.

"Eva," he sighs. "You're going to have to tell your parents eventually."

"Yes. On *my* terms, and *my* timeline. And that time isn't now."

Another sigh. "Fine," he says, all six feet of him rising from his chair. Wearing broken-in jeans and a tight black T-shirt beneath his trademark leather jacket, I can already envision the way heads will turn as he walks through the hallway. He's got a classically refined bone structure, with smooth skin and smoldering eyes, plus a cool indifference that makes women, and occasionally men, swoon.

"Thank you," I say, clicking back to my text thread with Luke as Christopher heads out the door.

I'm about to respond to my best friend's text when I hear my mother's voice, her faint British accent that lingers even after decades of living in the States. "I can't believe you didn't tell me you were in the hospital."

She sweeps into the small ER room. Her Hermès sunglasses sit atop her head, holding back her dark hair with her trademark silver streak that starts at her side part and sweeps across her forehead. *God, she's beautiful.* Severe, but beautiful. "You didn't even answer my calls or respond to my texts . . ."

"I just saw them two seconds ago and was about to call you." The second part is a lie, but she doesn't need to know that.

"What happened?" she asks as she sinks into the seat Christopher vacated a minute ago. "Are you okay?"

"Yeah, I just got dehydrated and passed out. It's really no big deal. I wish you hadn't come all this way—"

"You're in the hospital. *Of course* I was going to come!" The genuine worry in her tone puts me at ease. I expected her to blow in here mad. She's got a big personality and big emotions, with a knack for making everything about herself.

"I'm sorry I didn't tell you sooner and save you the trip. I'm fine, really."

Letting out a relieved sigh, she pulls her glasses off her head and tucks them into the large bag she always carries. "Thank god."

I don't miss that she doesn't say the thing most moms in this situation probably would: *you're pushing yourself too hard.* There's no such thing as pushing yourself "too hard" in

Helene Wilcott's book—at least not when an Olympic medal is the goal.

I nod toward the IV in my arm and tell her, "They're just giving me some fluids, and they're going to add in some iron because mine is low, and then I'll be good to go."

"Your iron is low? I'll talk to your nutritionist about adding in more red meat."

Closing my eyes briefly, I will myself to remain calm. I'm twenty-six years old and my mom still acts like she needs to make all my decisions for me, even what and how often I eat.

"I've got it under control, Mom."

"Clearly not." Folding her arms across her chest, she sits back in the chair and assesses me with her cool, impervious gaze. Is she worried? Disappointed? Upset? It's impossible to tell.

The only person in the world who can read her, who can handle her and her big emotions, is my stoic father. Dad's so different from Mom, so gentle and soft.

I'm instantly reminded of what happens every year. I always look forward to coming home for the summer, but within minutes of being around my mom, I struggle emotionally. Still, the quiet moments with my dad, enjoying a cup of tea on the deck each morning and quality time with Luke almost every day, are what keep me coming back summer after summer.

A nurse knocks twice on the door before entering the room with Christopher on her heels. "I'm just going to add this to your IV, and we'll start getting your discharge paper-work in order," she tells me, ignoring my mom where she sits next to my bed.

Mom opens her mouth, but I cut her off before she can

say anything. "Thank you so much," I say to the nurse. "Do you have a sense of how long that'll be, so we can reschedule our flights?"

"My guess is that you'll be out of here in the next two hours, tops."

"Thank you." I turn toward my mother. "Mom, maybe you can work on getting us flights back to Boston tonight? And Christopher, is there a chance you can make it to LA tonight?"

"There's a flight that leaves at 8 p.m. and has a few seats open. But I wasn't sure," he says, his eyes darting to my mom quickly, "if you needed me to stay."

"No, it's fine," I assure him. "You should go back to LA, and we'll go to Boston, as planned."

"All right," he says, glancing down at his phone. "I'll book that now."

Is it my imagination, or does he seem relieved?

Chapter Three

LUKE

I glance at the countdown clock on the wall of the locker room. We have four minutes until the third period starts, and I haven't had a chance to check my phone since sending Christopher Fucking Steele that text after warmups.

I have no idea if Eva's okay. I have no idea if she got my warning before Helene showed up. And I have no idea how the hell I'm supposed to focus on what Coach is saying while I'm this worried about his daughter.

I'm watching his lips move, but my own thoughts are all I hear. He must tell us to get ready to take the ice, because my teammates are gathering up their gloves and helmets and moving toward the door.

I look down at my skates, and that's when I feel a hand on my shoulder. "Son," Coach Wilcott says. "I know you're worried about her, but I need you to focus on the game."

As a late season trade, I've only played for him for a few

months, but I've known him my whole life. The rumors about him are true: he's the kind of coach you dream about playing for. He's supportive without giving you room to fuck up. He'll bring you to task, but without making you feel small. He doesn't hold anything over your head, and he treats you like the professional he expects you to be. He couldn't be more different than my last head coach, and it has nothing to do with how long I've known him.

I want to ask him how I could possibly focus on the game right now with Eva in the hospital. But she's his daughter, and he's still able to do his job, so what the hell would my excuse be?

"Helene's at the hospital with her now," he tells me when I glance up at him. I know he means that to ease my mind, but it has the exact opposite effect.

I still don't know if she's okay, and now I'm panicked that her mother may have found out that she's been keeping a secret that could wreck her chances of achieving the one thing her parents have always prioritized: an Olympic medal.

Giving him a curt nod, I stand. With my skates on, I'm a full head taller than him, and it's weird to look down at this man I've spent my whole life looking up to.

When I was a kid, Charlie Wilcott was the hockey player I aspired to be. He gave me some private lessons to get me started and helped me find my first hockey team. When I was eleven, he was the one who suggested I give being a goalie a chance. When I was getting recruited to play in college, he guided me. He even introduced me to my agent, Carson Kaplan.

My dad may own the team, but Charlie's been my hockey mentor my whole life. Playing for him never felt like it would be in the cards until I was traded mid-season and wound up back in my hometown.

"I need you to stop worrying about Eva," he says.

"Am I that obvious?" I mumble as I reach down to pick up my blocker.

"I know how protective you are of her," he says, his own version of *yes*. "But there's nothing you can do for her from here. So get your head back in the game."

"Understood," I say, nerves still thrumming, as he turns to head toward the locker room door.

"This vacant look you've had on your face all game is because of Wilcott's daughter?" my goalie coach, Evan Knight, asks. With everything that's on the line in this game, I understand the judgmental tone.

I clear my throat. "I haven't had a vacant look on my face all game."

"Yeah, you have. As your coach, let me give you a piece of advice: no girl is worth being *this* distracted over. You're a professional, act like one."

"I haven't been distracted," I grumble, but we both know it's bullshit.

He's stood next to me for the last two periods, pointing out everything I should notice about St. Louis's offense, Colt's reactions to each play, and the strengths and weaknesses of our defense—who honestly aren't playing as well as they could be. And all I've been able to manage in response are grunts of acknowledgement. I should be focused, because even though I'm the backup goalie tonight, there's always the chance I could have to play.

My coaches are both right: I need to get my head back in

this game. The problem is, I've always put Eva's well-being before my own. It's just never been an issue before.

So when I take my spot on the bench and watch the third period start, I'm determined to refocus. But I can't quiet the part of my mind that's picturing Eva in her hospital room and Helene finding out that she's pregnant. After everything Eva's parents have sacrificed for her and her skating career, I can't even predict what Helene's reaction would be, but I know it wouldn't be good.

Now, it's like I'm watching that scene—her mother's judgment and displeasure, and Eva shriveling in her mother's presence, like she always does—playing out side by side with the game I'm watching right in front of me.

And maybe I'm too focused on the imaginary scene in my head, because I don't even notice Colt fall to the ice until the crowd collectively gasps. I glance up at the Jumbotron, hoping for a replay, but right now, the camera is zooming in on Colt, lying on the ice, his face twisted in pain behind his goalie mask.

"Get ready," Coach Knight barks at me. "You may be going in."

My stomach drops as I grab my helmet, prepared to throw it on if needed. I glance back up at the screen in time to watch the replay of Colt butterflying down to block a shot, getting faked out as a St. Louis player moves left and sets up his shot. Realizing his mistake, Colt plants his skate and dives in the opposite direction, somehow managing a glove save. But then, he doesn't get up.

Adrenaline pumping, I glance back at the ice as our trainers and team doctor surround him, then over to the bench, where

Coach Wilcott has his gaze focused on Colt before it shifts to me. He gives me a nod, so I slip on my helmet, then my glove, and slide my blocker over my right hand so I can grab my stick.

Fuck. Focus . . . What was Evan saying about St. Louis's left winger?

Colt struggles to his feet, his arms over the shoulders of two of our trainers as they help him off the ice. Evan swings open the door so I can step out, and I skate over to the crease, where the referee asks if I want a warm up.

I should say yes, but I tell him I'm good, even while our team captain, Ronan McCabe, skates up and asks if I'm sure. "I'm fine," I say, confident that the surest way for me to get my head in the game is for the game to actually start up.

We're up 3-2, and there are fewer than ten minutes left.

All you have to do, I tell myself while watching McCabe pass to Drew Jenkins as they make their way toward St. Louis's goal, *is hold them off for the rest of the period. How many shots can they possibly take in that time?*

It's a question I shouldn't have risked asking myself, because apparently there's no limit. It's like our team has forgotten how to play offense, so it feels like the puck is always near our goal. We've also clearly forgotten how to play defense, if the number of shots on me is any indication.

I stop the first two, barely, but the third shot gets past me. My teammates tell me to shake it off and say they're going to step it up. All we need is one more goal and we can retake the lead.

St. Louis wins the face-off, and the puck is headed back toward me. The left winger Coach Knight mentioned earlier is moving with such fancy footwork he looks like a goddamn figure skater. *God, I hope Eva is okay.*

I don't even notice the shot until it's sailing toward me, and I raise my blocker, hoping to bat it off, but it sails right between my arm and my body.

Fuck.

"What the hell is wrong with you?" Zach asks. Unlike my teammates, he doesn't look pissed that we're down by a point. Instead, his face is full of concern for me.

"I don't know," I say, shaking my head to clear away the thoughts of Eva—but I can't. They're intrusive. Images of her flood my mind until I feel like I'm going crazy with worry. Worry that overwhelms me and clouds my judgement and allows yet another goal to get by me.

"All right, boys," Drew says with a definitive nod. "Now it's our turn."

Somehow, we manage to keep the puck down at the other net for the next two minutes, and when we score, it feels like maybe we can retake the lead, or at least tie it up and then fix this mess in overtime. We're only down by one now, and Drew's goal seems to have rallied the guys. With renewed energy, we control the puck and remain on offense . . . until one of their forwards snags it and makes a breakaway.

He's headed right toward me, and with renewed focus, I crouch into position, ready for the shot. As he pulls his stick back, I butterfly down to my left to block it, but the shot doesn't come. Instead, he takes the puck behind the net, and I don't react fast enough when he comes around the other side. Behind me, the lamp lights up with the signal that St. Louis has slid the puck into the goal. Again.

The buzzer sounds, and St. Louis's players jump the boards and flood the ice to celebrate winning the Stanley

Cup. And as I hang my head, knowing that this is at least half my fault, I still can't think about anything but Eva.

Chapter Four

EVA

I stare at my text that Luke hasn't responded to as we exit the narrow highway that winds up Boston's North Shore to our small coastal town. Winters can be bleak up here, but tourists flood the area in the summer, thanks to our beautiful beaches, local farms, and the abundance of coastal restaurants.

No matter what you're looking for, summer in Newbury Falls will most likely have it.

"You look tired," Mom says, and when I glance over at her, she turns her head forward and lets off the brake, moving us through the intersection mobbed with people out enjoying this warm summer night.

Another wave of nausea rolls through me, and I focus on

the road ahead. I get car sick easily, and pregnancy only makes it worse.

"Shocker, given that I was just hospitalized for exhaustion."

Of course I'm fucking tired, I want to scream. I just survived fifteen hours on three different flights, with a short ER visit before the last leg of travel, only to arrive back in Boston and have to hunt down my luggage at baggage claim, since it had arrived on my original flight.

In addition, I've been working overtime to keep my body in shape while ensuring I could hide this pregnancy from the world until the season ended, and yeah . . . the deep circles under my eyes don't lie.

"Don't be a smartass," she says.

I glance back down at my phone, wishing Luke would reply. I know the game ended an hour ago. They announced the loss on the radio, saying, "Hartmann choked so bad, someone should have given him the Heimlich." I immediately searched online to see what the hell they were talking about.

Luke is an amazing goalie. He's still fairly early in his career, but he's good, and one day, he's going to be great. Tonight, though? According to the brief clips I watched on my phone as Mom drove, tonight he was awful.

I don't know what the hell happened, but he looked like an amateur—like someone who'd only played goalie in juniors had somehow found himself between the pipes in the NHL. His reaction time was sluggish and his ability to anticipate where a shot would go—which has always been a sixth sense for him—completely failed him tonight.

In short, he was as terrible as the radio announcer had made him out to be.

Luke's always prepared. He goes into every game utterly focused, knowing exactly what he needs to do. I know he wasn't the starting goalie tonight, but he's a professional, and I can't understand why he wasn't ready when he was sent in.

That goalie I just saw clips of . . . that wasn't my best friend—there has to be something else going on.

As I sit here, trying to tune out my mother while she lectures me about taking better care of myself, I'm imagining what's going through Luke's mind. He exhibits the happy-go-lucky personality of a golden retriever, but he feels things deeply. Maybe too deeply, sometimes.

Getting traded to Boston, playing for the team his family owns and my dad coaches . . . this is the most genuinely happy I've *ever* seen him. I don't want him to feel like that's in jeopardy—but after the way he played tonight, it could be. And that has me terrified for him.

"So, *are you?*" The sharpness of my mother's tone snaps me out of my own head.

"Sorry, am I what?"

Her sigh fills the entire car. "I asked if you're getting enough protein."

"I think you'll have to ask the nutritionist and personal chef you hired, since they keep track of that." I try to make my reply sound less irritated than I feel, but Mom's low *hmmm* indicates that I've failed.

My personal chef works with my nutritionist to plan all my meals and snacks. Whether I'm home in Los Angeles, or competing somewhere else, the meals are always delivered perfectly proportioned, ready to heat and eat.

Mom claims it's because I hate to cook, but how would I know? I've never been given the opportunity. Since I was a teenager, my food has been selected for me, without regard to what I feel like eating. For the first few years after I moved out on my own, I didn't mind it—not having to think about what to eat or make something for myself gave me more time to focus on skating.

But eight years later, I'm tired of this life. Tired of every decision being made *for* me. I'm about to become a mom, and I don't even have any agency over my own life.

I know Mom making things easy for me wherever she can is her way of showing that she cares. And I'd never want her to think I don't appreciate everything she and Dad are doing to help me achieve this dream.

"I'll do that," she says, flicking her blinker on with a bit more force than necessary as she slows to turn into our driveway. And like it always does when I arrive home after being away for so long, the scene in front of me takes my breath away.

The moon shines brightly, illuminating the white cottage where it sits on the cliff with nothing beyond it but the waves of the Atlantic Ocean. It's a cloudless night and the stars are just starting to appear, but the moonlight is already making the waves sparkle.

My parents' small house is in an idyllic setting, far enough from the winding road that we seldom hear the cars headed to the beach, and with an expansive and unencumbered ocean view. The cliffs behind the house are too steep to access the private neighborhood beach below, but they protect us from storms, and we can follow a winding path down the hillside at the end of the street to get to the water.

"Will Dad be home in the morning?" I ask, wishing I was walking into his comforting hug.

"No, the team's not leaving St. Louis until tomorrow," Mom says as she pulls into the garage. "I'm sure they'd hoped to be celebrating tonight. He'll be home sometime in the afternoon."

"What do you have going on tomorrow?" I ask her.

"Some riding lessons in the morning, and then I need to go see about a horse in the afternoon," she says. Mom is forever going "to see about a horse." Buying and training show horses is a huge part of how she's helped Luke's mom, Elise Hartmann, build a world-class equestrian center and show park at their home here in Newbury Falls. Elise owns the center, but my mom is the lead trainer. "Want to grab lunch somewhere? You can come see the horse with me afterward if you want?"

"I'm not sure I'll feel up to it," I say, and a look of disappointment crosses my mom's face. Horses are her first love—even ahead of her family—but I never developed the same passion she did. She loves the outdoors and the wind on her face as she rides. I love the crisp air of the rink and the sound of my skates carving across the ice. "Lunch sounds good, though."

Does it? I used to do this thing growing up where I'd keep track of how many times a day I did or said something in pursuit of keeping my mom happy. As a kid, I thought the higher the daily tally, the better a daughter I was. It wasn't until I grew up and moved away that I realized monitoring my behavior like that actually made me feel worse, not better.

My mom isn't negative, per se; it's just her nature to search for ways to improve. She wants to motivate me, but sometimes I just feel like I can never live up to her increasingly rising expectations. Honestly, at this point, I'm not even sure an Olympic medal would result in a "Good job, I'm so proud of you," without an additional comment on how my performance could have been better.

She helps me unload my bags from the back of the car, and as we carry them through the breezeway into the mudroom, I glance toward the oval window on the far wall. It's too small and high up to showcase the entire view from the house, but as a kid, I loved to stand on the bench beneath it and look out at the water, pretending it was the window in a castle tower I was trapped in.

It's amazing how returning home every summer dredges up memories I haven't thought about in forever—both the good and the bad.

Mom hangs her purse on a wall hook and kicks her flats beneath the window bench.

"Let me help you get these to your room," she says, picking up a suitcase in one hand and swinging a large duffle bag over the other shoulder. She's used to maneuvering fifteen-hundred-pound horses, so her strength never surprises me.

I *am* surprised, however, when she sets my bags in my room and tells me she'll give me some space to unpack and get some sleep, before leaving me standing there alone. It's late, and she probably just wants to head to bed after her unplanned trip to New York. And living by myself in LA, I'm used to having my own space. So why do I suddenly feel so lonely?

As if the universe knows I need a lifeline to quell my erratic emotions, my phone buzzes in my pocket. I pull it out to see that my best friend has finally responded.

LUKE

Yeah, not a game to be proud of, for sure.

I'm relieved you're okay. Are you around tomorrow night?

EVA

Yeah, want to do something?

LUKE

With you? No thanks.

EVA

You're an ass.

LUKE

I don't know what you're talking about. I'm a fucking saint.

Good, at least his sarcasm is firmly intact. That's got to be a good sign, right?

EVA

Hold, please. I'm busy building my shrine to St. Luke.

He sends back a GIF of a kid rolling his eyes so hard he falls over backward in his chair.

EVA

Dinner tomorrow? I haven't had sushi in forever and I'm craving it.

Three dots appear, then disappear and, as usual, I know exactly what he's thinking.

EVA

Yes, I'm allowed to have raw fish. The worst that can happen is food poisoning, and it doesn't cross the placenta. So it's no more dangerous than having sushi when you're not pregnant.

LUKE

I didn't want to ask . . .

EVA

Am I really *that* sensitive now?

LUKE

I plead the fifth.

EVA

The asshole genes are working just fine tonight, I see.

I smile as I type and send the message, because Luke is the furthest thing from an actual asshole. His kindness sets him apart from his older brothers, who all share that trait. Fortunately, Luke got the lovable teddy bear side of his dad's personality, while his three brothers inherited the shrewd business sense, which grew the family business into a billion-dollar company.

LUKE

Am I picking you up tomorrow night? Or are you driving into the city?

EVA

You mind coming up here? We could go to that seafood place with the deck over the ocean? It shouldn't be a problem to get a reservation on a weeknight.

Mostly, I don't want to go into the city, because my car sickness hasn't fully dissipated, and the thought of making the same drive there and back again tomorrow just isn't appealing.

LUKE

Pretty sure reservations won't be a problem.
You know Tucker bought that place, right?

EVA

Your brother bought a restaurant??? Isn't he busy enough with his fancy new job with your team?

I can't remember his exact title, but earlier this year, Tucker started working some high-level position with the Boston Rebels, so he'll be poised to take over the organization once Luke's dad, Frank, is ready to step back. Everyone thinks of Frank Hartmann as the sole owner, but technically the entire Hartmann Family owns the team.

LUKE

He likes to stay busy.

The story is probably way more complicated, given that Tucker went through a nasty breakup of his engagement earlier this year. I don't know many details, but as curious as I am, I try not to pry. Despite being the focus of constant media attention, the Hartmanns are very private.

EVA

So what you're saying is you'll take care of getting a table?

LUKE

Sure. Pick you up at seven.

Chapter Five

LUKE

The sun's still high in the sky as I drive up the winding coastal road in Newbury Falls, my small hometown on the North Shore of Massachusetts. An hour outside of Boston, it's a land of beaches, horses, and quaint New England farms—an idyllic place to have grown up.

And if your last name is Hartmann, the expectation is that you'll return and raise a family here, as generations of our family have done.

My dad has wanted grandchildren for a decade, and with brothers who are all significantly older than me, I was pretty sure I'd be an uncle by now. Turns out, my brothers have all excelled at dodging this particular expectation in the same way that Hartmanns typically excel at whatever they put their minds to.

With my hockey career, I've always assumed that I'd be the last one to get married and have kids, but at this point, I could very well be the first—and I've never even had a serious girlfriend. *That's* how allergic to commitment my brothers are, especially after seeing Tucker's engagement blow up so spectacularly.

I speed past the huge brick pillars and the iron gates that mark the entrance to Wellington Manor, feeling no guilt about steering clear of my parents, since they both witnessed my unforgettably terrible Game 7 in St. Louis yesterday.

The text message I received this afternoon from my general manager, AJ, asking me to meet her at her office in the Rebels' practice facility early next week, is weighing heavily on my mind. I can't help but wonder if my dad knows I'm being called in like this, and if so, what his thoughts are. Playing for a team my family owns has been complicated.

I take the curve in the road and head toward Eva's childhood home, thinking maybe I should have offered to bring dinner and we could have eaten on the beach while watching the sunset instead. The beach at golden hour is our favorite, and I'm having second thoughts about seeing my brother at his restaurant tonight.

I've been fielding calls and texts from my parents and brothers for the last twenty-four hours. They all want to make sure I'm okay, and I just want to pretend like yesterday never happened—like I'm not singularly responsible for robbing my team of the championship they'd worked toward all season.

The Rebels had been well on their way to making the playoffs even *before* I was traded to them. This was their chance, and I showed up as the new guy on the team and lost it for them.

Even worse? Since my family owns the team, I've not only let the fans and my teammates down, but my parents and brothers as well.

My stomach roils as I replay the last ten minutes of the game in my mind. The only thing that prevents me from turning around, driving back to Boston, hiding out in my luxury condo, and shutting the whole world out is Eva. She needs a friend who knows what she's going through and can be there to support her.

I park in her driveway, amazed as always by the spectacular view beyond the small house.

The property I grew up on, just down the road, is the former summer estate of a New York steel tycoon. Despite its acres of rolling hills, fenced-in pastures, world-class riding facility, and classically inspired pool area, it doesn't hold a candle to this view.

The ocean was my first love until I found hockey . . . and Eva.

I'm out of my car and heading toward the front door when I hear voices from the back of the house. So I follow the stone path along the blue hydrangeas that line the side of the house and take the stairs up to the deck, where I see Charlie and Eva. Her arms are spread on the deck railing, her back to me as she looks out at the ocean. She has her head thrown back, laughing at something her father has said, and her dark hair sways across her bare shoulders in the breeze.

She's so serious by nature—so focused and driven—that it's a relief to see her relaxed, even for a moment. I'm about to announce myself when she glances over her shoulder and her eyes widen in surprise before a huge grin splits her face.

"Luke!" And then she's sprinting across the deck in her flip-flops.

She wraps me in a hug, and I want to close my eyes and breathe in the peach scent of her hair as I curl my arms around her lower back and dig my fingertips into her sides until she screams with laughter because she's so ticklish. But I don't. I keep my eyes open as I return her hug, nodding toward Charlie where he watches us.

"How are you doing?" Charlie asks once Eva steps back. The concern is evident in his tone, and I appreciate that his caring and thoughtful nature always outweighs the shrewd wisdom he displays as a coach.

"I've been better, honestly."

He nods, an acknowledgement that neither conveys disappointment nor indicates that he thinks this will be okay.

"Hopefully, dinner tonight will be what you both need after a rough day yesterday," he says, smiling fondly at his daughter.

"I suspect it will be," I say, relieved that everything seems normal between Charlie and me. "You ready, Evie?"

She laughs the same way she always does when I use that nickname—the one she proclaimed she hated once she hit middle school, and will allow no one but me to use.

"Sure am. Bye, Dad, have a good dinner with Mom," she says as she grabs her purse and jean jacket off a deck chair.

"I have some peach rings for you in my car," I tell her, chuckling when she bounds down the path. It's hard to tell if she's in a rush to leave or excited about her favorite candy.

"Take care of her," Charlie says to me quietly as we watch

her take the path toward the driveway. "I'm not sure she's as okay as she's pretending she is."

I wait, hoping he'll say more. When he doesn't, I give him a nod. "I will."

Then I turn and follow his daughter down the driveway —letting her lead, like I always do.

———

"Can I interest you in some wine or a cocktail?" the waitress asks Eva after taking our appetizer order.

"Water's fine," she says, her brow furrowing as she sets the drink menu on the table.

The waitress turns her head toward me. "And for you?"

"Uh . . ." I was going to get a beer, but given Eva's pregnancy, I would feel bad drinking in front of her.

"He'd like whatever IPA you have on draft," Eva chimes in. "Preferably something hoppy."

The waitress runs through a few options, and I choose one. "You didn't need to order for me," I say once the waitress has left.

"Seemed like you weren't sure if you should order a drink since I can't drink, and I was shutting down that nonsense."

My head tilts as I look at her curiously. "Why is that *nonsense?*"

"Because it's not like you have any responsibility for my condition—"

"And if I had? Would you have wanted me to stop drinking through your pregnancy?" I'm relieved that we have a table in the corner of the overwater deck, so no one can overhear us. The ocean is calmer on this side of the peninsula than on the other side, where Eva's house is, so instead of crashing waves, we have water lapping at the rocks below the deck to muffle our conversation.

Eva rolls her eyes, and I'm not sure if it's at the ridiculous notion that I could be responsible for her pregnancy—which, given our circumstances, is quite impossible—or at the idea that I wouldn't drink during those nine months.

"Not drinking while his significant other is pregnant seems like the least a guy could do," she says with a slight shrug.

Yes, it's the absolute least. And more than anything, I hate that she's conditioned to expect the least from guys.

"Yeah, well, since that guy's not here—"

Eva's snort stops me. "Please"—she rolls her eyes—"let's not do this. I'm *not* going to try to find him. I don't have anything to go on except that he's German. I don't even remember his name. Just because *that* was a mistake, doesn't mean *this* is." She glances down meaningfully at her belly, which is hidden under the table. Not that there's anything to see.

She still has the toned body of a competitive athlete, and the singular sign that she's pregnant—which you'd only notice if you were paying close attention—is that her breasts are bigger. I mean, not that I look at them enough to know what size they were before pregnancy, or now. No, I definitely don't have that information burned into my brain.

"I was *not* implying that your baby is a mistake, Evie."

She sits back, crossing her arms, and suddenly her body language is borderline hostile. "You don't have to. Everyone else will."

I fold my arms on the table in front of me and lean

toward her, wanting to make sure she understands my words. "Fuck everyone else. Their opinions don't matter."

"Do you honestly believe that?" she asks, and I hate the way everyone else's opinions matter so much to her.

"Of course I do."

"Even about yourself? Even about last night's game?"

"That's different." I glance out at the water as the setting sun casts orange and purple rays over the rippling waves.

"You going to tell me what happened?"

I look back at her, noting the way her dark hair contrasts with her porcelain skin, the way her dark eyes, framed in long lashes, focus on me, searching for any sign that I'm not actually okay.

As I consider how in the world I can explain what happened without making her feel responsible, a light flush creeps across her cheeks, making me wonder if she interprets my pause as annoyance over the question.

"Yeah. I choked. I wasn't expecting to play, and I guess I wasn't in the right headspace."

"You didn't look like yourself out there," she says. "At all."

"Didn't feel like myself."

"Luke," she says with a sigh. "Was it because you were worried about me?"

"Pfft. You flatter yourself." I roll my eyes as I use the phrase we both constantly employ to remind each other that this is a friendship, and no one is catching feelings. It started as a joke before our senior prom, and it's stuck with us all these years.

"Do I? I'd hate to think I was the cause of you losing that game."

"Then don't. Because you weren't." The only thing more

horrifying than her thinking that I lost the game because I wasn't prepared to play would be her knowing the truth: I was so busy worrying about her that I didn't take care of my team. It's not a fact I'm proud of and it's not something I can share with her or anyone else, especially not my family or teammates.

From how her shoulders tense, I can tell she's frustrated that I won't say more. I'm wondering if I should give in and at least tell her how worried I was when the waitress returns with my beer and Eva's water. "Do you, by any chance, have any decent mocktails?" I ask.

"Not on the menu," she says, "but I can ask the bartender if he can make something. What were you thinking?"

I glance at Eva and raise an eyebrow. "What sounds good?"

She shakes her head, but her lips part in a small smile. "Something fruity? I don't know, surprise me."

"See," I say as the waitress heads inside to the bar, "that wasn't so hard."

"That's what she said," Eva says with a little smirk. I roll my eyes, refusing to dignify the barb with a response—because talking about how hard my dick gets is *not* something I do with my best friend.

"I *meant* that asking for what you want isn't hard."

Eva licks her lower lip, pulling it between her teeth. I witness her face changing as multiple thoughts travel through her head. "I'm working on it, okay?"

I've always given Eva shit for not being demanding enough. While the world may take one look at her cool exterior and assume she's a diva, that couldn't be further from the truth. Eva knows her job is to perform at an elite level, and she's been so busy doing that since high school that I frequently worry she's forgotten how to actually *live.*

"Hey!" Tucker's booming voice comes from behind our table. "If it isn't Baby Hartmann and his sidekick." I groan at the nickname I'll never grow out of.

"Hey, boss," I say as I stand to give my brother a one-armed hug—the kind that says *Hey, I like you, but we're not that close.* It's the same greeting my brothers and I have always given each other, but out of all of them, I like Tucker the most.

For nine years before I came along, he played the part of the amiable middle child who knew how to placate our rigid and demanding oldest brother, Preston, and keep his little brother, Tristan, in line. By the time I was born, my brothers were already the Hartmann legacy triumvirate, and I became Baby Hartmann.

"Don't be a dick to Eva," I mutter to Tucker. He pulls back and gives me that lazy smile, as if to say *I'm never a dick.* It's amazing the conversations we can have without uttering a word.

"Hey, gorgeous," he says, turning toward Eva and bending down to give her a kiss on the cheek.

I have to remind myself that, of course, he's going to kiss her hello—she's practically family. He's not doing it to piss me off. Or at least, I don't think he is.

"So," Tucker says, reaching behind him to pull up an empty chair to our table. "What are you kids up to?" And when he plops down in that seat, leaning back and crossing an ankle over his opposite knee, I know that our private dinner—our chance to catch up—just ended.

Next time, I'm insisting we get out of our hometown.

Chapter Six

EVA

Sitting on the top level of the Boston Rebels parking garage in my dad's Jeep with the top down, I soak up the late-afternoon sun. It's shockingly pleasant for mid-June—not dry heat like Los Angeles has, but not oppressively humid like Boston can get once July rolls around.

Normally, that's when I'd head back to LA to start training again. Now, I have no idea what my summer will look like. I glance at my phone again.

CHRISTOPHER

Are you sure you'll want to continue training when you get back to LA? I don't want you to push yourself too hard or do anything that might jeopardize your health or the baby's.

EVA

I'll be fine. Remember, my OB said I could keep skating until I had a pronounced bump. And even then, she said we could train off-ice. I need to stay in shape or our chances of qualifying after I have the baby are SLIM.

We've already met one of the requirements for the Olympics—we placed in the top three at nationals this spring. But we narrowly missed the second requirement—meeting the minimum technical elements score at the international competition a couple of weeks ago. First, I downgraded our jump, and then Christopher made a small error that cost us another few tenths of a point. Suddenly, our spot on the US Olympic team, which had previously seemed like a sure thing, was in question.

In ordinary circumstances, we'd still have two more shots at qualifying in an international competition. But one of them is in October, not even a month after I'm due, so I won't be cleared to compete. That leaves a final opportunity in December.

My careless one-night stand has put our careers in jeopardy.

CHRISTOPHER

We'll figure it out, Eva, but we'll do it in a way that's not going to risk your health. And we need to talk to Jessie. If we're truly determined not to work with her anymore, we need to find a new coach . . . yesterday!

Jessie hasn't even reached out to see if I'm okay after watching the EMTs take me off an airplane a week ago. *Some coach she is.*

Neither Christopher nor I have particularly liked working with her. At first, we chalked it up to the fact that we'd had the same coach for many seasons, and we just needed to acclimate to someone new. Now, at the end of our second year with her, I'm dreading the idea of working with her again.

I don't shy away from hard work. I'll put in the time, do whatever I need to do to get better. Christopher always calls me his "little workhorse," and he's not wrong. I keep up with him in every regard, pushing myself much harder physically than he has to push himself.

I want that Olympic medal, not just so I can hang it on the empty hook in the display box that showcases Mom's medal for show jumping and Dad's medal for hockey, but because I've trained too hard and come too far to give up now. Pregnant or not, I need to qualify for the Olympics by the end of the year or, come February, Christopher and I will be watching the Games instead of participating in them. Again.

Last time, we were sidelined when Christopher blew out his knee during warmups for our first Olympic competition. The alternate pair took the ice, and we watched from a TV in the hospital before we flew home for his surgery. This time, if we don't make it, it'll be entirely on me.

The problem with Jessie, though, is that we don't trust her. There's no end to how hard she works us, and it doesn't seem to be helping us improve. If anything, we've stagnated while working with her and she blames that on us. Nothing we do is ever good enough . . . and honestly, I have enough of that with my mom; I don't need it from my coach, too.

Jessie was actually Mom's choice after our last coach died

in a tragic car accident. Christopher and I were so distraught over the tragedy and devastated to lose a coach we loved and had worked with for our entire careers that we let Mom lead the search. We weren't in a position, mentally or emotionally, to be more involved in the process, and so we only met Jessie for a brief skating session before Mom hired her.

"Hey, pumpkin," Dad says as he walks up to the car.

I slip my phone into my bag, hoping that I don't look as guilty as I feel about my plan to fire Jessie and find a new coach. I'd like to stay in my parents' good graces.

"Hey, thanks for letting me use the car."

"You get everything done you wanted to do?"

"Yeah." I'd come into the city with Dad late this morning, and while he attended some meetings at the practice rink, I drove into the Back Bay and visited some of my favorite shops. Not only did I feel like I needed a few new items of clothing since most of my clothes aren't quite fitting right anymore, but after being home for a week now, I'm climbing the walls. There's only so many times I can sleep in, go to the beach, visit Mom at the stables, or catch up on TV shows and movies I've been meaning to see before my days start to feel pointless.

In past years when I've come home for the summer, Luke's been home at Wellington Manor, and we'd spend our days at his pool, or at the beach. We'd take trips into Boston, or we'd drive north along the coast to explore the seaside towns, always in search of the best ice cream shops. Luke's an ice cream connoisseur and still in search of the best flavors in New England.

But that was when Luke played for Calgary and planned his summer visit home to coincide with mine. Now that he plays in Boston, he bought a place downtown. Having him an hour away instead of just down the road has made everything about this trip feel different.

Even though I still keep in touch with my other high school friends, most of them have moved on. They either got jobs wherever they went to college, or they live in the city now and have made new friends—ones who are around for more than a month a year. Seeing them when I'm home is a coffee date or meeting up for drinks, not long days of catching up on what we missed in the last year since we saw each other. It all feels a bit . . . superficial.

Not with Luke, though. Maybe it's because we still text each other fifty times a day and tell each other everything—or almost everything—but when the two of us are together, it's like no time has passed.

"Good," Dad says. "Am I dropping you off at Luke's place?"

"No, he's going to be here to get me any minute."

"Okay. How are you getting home?"

I know Dad's just being a dad and making sure his baby girl is taken care of, but I've lived on my own since I graduated from high school and moved to LA to work with a new coach and a new skating partner. I can take care of myself.

"We're going to watch *Pride and Prejudice* after we get something to eat, so I'm going to stay at his place tonight. He has ice time in the morning and wants me to skate with him. I'll text you and let you know when I'll be back tomorrow."

Dad looks uneasy at the idea of me spending the night at a guy's house. I figured this would be his response, which is why I snuck my skating bag and a backpack into the back of the Jeep this morning before we left Newbury Falls. It's such a teenage avoidance tactic, but I just didn't want it to turn into a big discussion.

"Dad," I say with a laugh, "*it's Luke.*" Luke, who I've had a million sleepovers with, starting when we were little kids and stopping . . . never. He's visited me in LA, I've visited him in Calgary, and every summer, we practically live at each other's houses.

"I know," he says, relaxing his shoulders as he folds his arms across the door of the Jeep and leans in. "How's he doing, by the way?"

I've only seen Luke once since our dinner nearly a week ago. "You know Luke," I say, worried that if I say too much, it'll influence my dad's opinion of him as a player. "Things just roll off him. But, if I'm being honest, I think the constant sports commentary about his performance in the game is probably affecting him more than he's letting on."

"He needs to turn that shit off," Dad says with a sigh.

If only it were that easy.

"Sometimes other people's voices just get in your head. We've all been there, it sucks."

"I hope the skills work he's doing with Evan helps with his headspace," Dad says. "I'm far more worried about *that* than his actual skill level. He's going to be fine, as long as he doesn't let that one game get to him."

"Have you told him that?"

Dad twists his lips together, his classic thinking face. "Not sure if I have."

"Might be good for him to hear it. You know how much he hates disappointing people."

"Does he think we're disappointed in him?"

"Dad," I say, my voice flat, as though to indicate the

answer is beyond obvious. "*Clearly,* the fans and his team-mates are upset about the loss, and most of all, he's disappointed in himself. There are no two ways about it; *he* is the reason the Rebels lost Game 7."

By now, I've watched the replay of the end of the game dozens of times, trying to figure out what the hell happened. His head wasn't in the game, obviously. And given the panicked texts he had sent me and Christopher right before the game started, I'm worried that he was too focused on me, too afraid something was wrong with me or the baby, or that my mom would find out I was pregnant when she got to the hospital.

Damn it, I need to tell my parents. There's a little voice in the back of my head that reminds me that he probably could have focused more on the game if he hadn't been worried about whether my secret would be exposed before I was ready.

"Things were falling apart before he came in. Plus, people have shit games," my dad says. "It happened to Colt during the second round of the playoffs a few years ago. Sometimes the pressure gets to people. Sometimes they just have a bad day. There are a hundred reasons his game could have been off. The point is, he needs to figure out why it happened, and fix *that.*"

It's good advice, but if Luke knows what happened that day, he hasn't admitted it to me. "You guys have a team psychologist or something?"

"No, not officially. But Zach has someone he swears by, and I think he's gotten some of the other guys to talk to her. I'll see if he can mention it to Luke."

I'm about to suggest that maybe the team should invest in

having a sports psychologist on staff when Luke's car takes the turn onto the top level of the garage, the sound of his engine signaling his arrival before I even see the sleek black Mercedes pull up beside us.

Once my bags are packed into the back of his car and we say goodbye to my dad, Luke asks, "You see the text from Amy earlier?"

"Yeah." Amy was my best girlfriend in high school, and while we've kept in touch over the years, we're not nearly as close now as we were before. She lives in Boston now, and apparently she's going out to celebrate her birthday tonight with a group that includes some of our other high school friends. Since Luke and I are both in town, she invited us to come out.

"Any interest?" he asks, taking turn after turn to reach the exit of the parking garage.

I roll my head back against the padded leather headrest, thinking about how I'm starving, even though I got myself lunch earlier. I'm always starving now, and I've never been able to make decisions on an empty stomach. "I don't know. You?"

"On the one hand, we can stay in with Mr. Darcy and Lizzie, and on the other hand, we can go out with our friends. *How could we ever choose?*"

I'd expected that Luke would want to hide out in his condo, licking his wounds out of the public eye. Maybe now that it's been a week since the playoffs ended, he's finally ready to reemerge?

Generally, Luke's always up for going out and making sure everyone has a good time. It's probably one of the reasons our friendship has worked so well over the years—

he keeps me from being too serious, and I keep him from being too wild.

So maybe after a week of being a hermit, a night out is exactly what he needs?

"I can't make decisions like this when I'm hungry," I tell him. "Feed me, and then we can decide what we want to do tonight."

———

"So what's the game plan?" Luke asks as I enter his living room. When his eyes flick up from his phone and he sees me standing there, he presses his lips together and raises his eyebrows. "You look . . . nice."

"I just spent an hour getting ready," I say, my voice teasing as I think about how long it took me to curl my hair and try on multiple different outfits before settling on this sundress I bought today. The scoop neck and empire waist keep the focus on my upper body, and the short skirt highlights my muscular legs. "And all I get is *nice?*"

He stands and takes two steps toward me, coming so close that I have to lean my head back to look at him. Instantly, I wish I hadn't. He's too damn perfect, with his light brown hair falling in effortless waves, bright blue eyes, flawless skin that always looks sun-kissed, and a mischievous smile.

Luke is too cute for his own good, too down to earth when he has every reason to be conceited, and too kind and thoughtful in an otherwise harsh and competitive world.

"Were you looking for a different response, Evie?" His voice is quiet, husky even, as he looks down at me.

He doesn't sound like *my* Luke. He sounds like the compulsive flirt I so often see when we're out in large groups, and I have to remind myself that this is the version of him I'll also see tonight . . . with other women. It's a version I'm very familiar with, because Luke has a constant stream of women rotating in and out of his life, or more accurately, his bed. He claims he doesn't date during the season, but in truth, he's just never had a relationship last long enough to bother mentioning it to me.

I swat at his stomach with the back of my hand, pushing him away. "You flatter yourself."

At this point, that phrase is like a safe word for me. When I get even the smallest inkling that Luke might be flirting with me, it immediately pops out. Self-preservation and all that.

"And ewww." I roll my eyes for good measure, wondering if it's the pregnancy hormones that have me wishing—for the first time in a long time—that he actually *was* flirting with me. "Don't use that seductive voice you use with *other women.*"

He lets out a small, sharp laugh. "I don't know what voice you're talking about."

Glancing up at him, I smirk and drop my voice low, letting it flow out like his, thick and smooth. "Were you looking for a different response, Evie?"

His laugh is genuine this time. "You do a terrible impression of me."

"I'm pretty sure that's exactly what you sounded like, so maybe your game with women is just not as good as you think it is?"

"Or maybe," he says, shoving his hands into his pockets, "it was never as good as *you* thought it was?"

I'm trying to figure out his meaning when he turns and grabs a hat from where it sits on the back of the chair and slips it on, brushing his hair off his face. His hair is his most notable feature, and when it isn't falling on either side of his forehead, he looks like a different person—young and carefree without the weight of a Stanley Cup loss on his shoulders. I'm sure that's the point. With the hat covering his hair and casting a shadow across his face, he'll be less recognizable while we're out tonight.

He steps closer, resting his hand on my lower back as he guides me toward the front door with a gruff, "Let's go. Don't want to keep the birthday girl waiting."

The nighttime air is still warm when we exit his building, and my long hair hangs down my back, tickling my bare shoulder blades. Luke's fingertips remain on my lower back, guiding me around people who aren't going at the same fast pace as we walk the few blocks to the bar where we're meeting Amy.

"So what's our story for why you aren't drinking?" he asks.

"I have to practice in the morning." I glance up at him over my shoulder. "That's believable, right?"

His jaw tics, but he nods, and I focus back on the sidewalk in front of me.

"You know you're going to have to tell people eventually, right?" he asks. "Or they'll start figuring it out."

"How the hell would they figure it out? I'm not even showing," I say, and when I look up at him, I can't help but notice that his gaze is focused on my chest. Which, to be fair, is pretty hard to miss in my scoop-neck black tank dress. It's not like he's checking *me* out or anything.

As his eyes meet mine, he clears his throat. "But you will be soon. How many weeks are you now?"

"Twenty-four."

"Holy shit, Evie." The words are whispered. "Over half-way? Already?"

"Well, I didn't figure it out until I was nineteen weeks along." Because of my intense exercise and skating regimen and the strict diet I'm on during training, my period has never been regular. It wasn't until I'd missed it for several months in a row that I got worried and took a pregnancy test.

He slips his hand around to my hip and snuggles me into his side. "I know. Guess I just forgot how far along you are, especially because you're still not really showing."

"You're right, though," I say as I lean my head to the side, resting it in the space between his chest and shoulder. "Now that I'm not training, and given how far along I am, it'll become obvious soon. I'm already noticing the difference in how my clothes fit. My belly's getting hard, and it's definitely bigger. That's why I had to go shopping today . . . to find things that fit but don't make me look pregnant."

"You did good with this dress," he says, and he's right. Because it's tight on my chest and loose below it, the fabric hides my belly. "What else did you get?"

"Tons of stuff. You saw the shopping bags we unloaded from your car, right?" I'd brought them all with me instead of having my dad take them home because I wasn't sure what I'd want to wear tonight.

His chest shakes with laughter. "I thought those were all gifts for me."

I reach across my body to poke him in the side. "Sure, you did. Even *you're* not that vain."

"You'd be shocked," he says, humor in his voice as he drops his arm from my back and reaches forward to pull open the door to the bar.

Chapter Seven

LUKE

"Hartmannnnnnn." Amy drags out my name, like she can't quite figure out how to make her mouth form proper sounds. Given the number of birthday shots she's already done, and the way she's double-fisting some shot glass concoction with whipped cream on top, I'm hardly surprised. "Do another birthday shot with me?"

My eyes lock on Eva's, and the performative smile she's struggling to maintain indicates she's ready to go. Not that anyone else would be able to tell. She's been happy and enthusiastic the entire time we've been here, nursing her soda and dancing with our high school friends. But social situations are always taxing for her—she can be extroverted for a while, but then she needs some alone time to recharge.

Although I can't fully relate to this characteristic of hers, I've known her for long enough to understand and appreciate her limits, so I'm already mentally working out our escape plan.

"Can't," I tell Amy. "I have to skate tomorrow."

"Oh, come on." Her lips vibrate as she exhales through her pout. "That was Eva's excuse too. She's not drinking at all!"

"She doesn't drink during training and has a low tolerance anyway," I say. "And with the dangerous spins and jumps she does, she can't risk being hungover."

"Eva!" Amy shouts, motioning her over. When she steps up to us, Amy tells her, "Hartmann was just telling me you're a lightweight."

Her lips quirk up in amusement. "Was he now?"

"That's not what I said."

Eva taps her pointer finger against her lips, looking like she's trying to make a decision. "Should I tell them about the Elf on the Shelf, so she can see who is *actually* the lightweight in this friendship?"

The laugh bursts out of me. "What?" I have no idea what she's talking about, but I get ready to hear a ridiculous and totally fictional story—the kind we used to tell all the time in high school as part of an ongoing quest to see how far we could spin out a tale before people called bullshit. The issue is, our friends have always been incredibly gullible.

"Yeah, that time you had too many spiked eggnogs and dressed up as the Elf on the Shelf at your family Christmas Party?" Eva's yelling over the music, and she's caught the attention of a few of our friends.

Anyone who knows me well enough knows I hate eggnog. Apparently, it's not something my high school friends remember, because Hannah, Jonathan, and Reese are all egging her on to tell the story.

"Sure." I shrug, already laughing because her smile is finally genuine, and I can't wait for her to start spinning the tale.

"So a few years ago," Eva says, her dark eyes scanning the small circle of our friends, "Luke enjoyed a bit too much eggnog with brandy—"

"That shit is *toxic*," Reese interjects, as he seems to recall some of his own bad decisions.

"Sure is," Eva agrees with a laugh. "And in his inebriated state, Luke decided that he was going to dress up as the Elf on the Shelf."

"Only because I was saving you after Preston dared *you* to do it." I glance at my friends, roll my eyes, and say, "Terrible example of a truth or dare game gone astray."

"Yes, well," Eva says, "I was sober enough to decline. So, the Hartmanns have their own set of Santa and Mrs. Claus costumes, and the Santa costume was in use because of the holiday party. All the Rebels families were there, and the kids were taking turns sitting on Santa's lap." At least that part of the story is true . . . we do have an annual Christmas party, and the Rebels team members always come with their families.

"Oh god." Hannah chuckles. "Please tell me you put on the Mrs. Claus costume, Hartmann."

I raise my arms in a shrug, giving them my best guilty-as-charged face. "Eva refused to wear it because she said it was too frumpy, and she'd only be dressing up as Mrs. Claus if it was a slutty Halloween costume."

Eva barks out a laugh. "Well, on Luke's frame, the costume was perfectly . . . indecent. That red velvet skirt that would have gone to my knees barely covered his"—her eyes are full of mirth—"junk. He couldn't even get the shirt on, and the bib part of the dress wasn't doing a great job of covering his chest. But the best part was the tights."

"Don't tell them about the tights," I groan. "Or the bells."

"Oh my god, the bells!" Eva's peals of laughter ring out, and the way she's so delighted has me practically glowing. Not sure there's anything I wouldn't do to make this girl happy, including embarrassing myself. "So yes, he was wearing these red thigh-high tights that barely went above his knees, and the Mrs. Claus slippers, which barely fit over the front half of his feet. And the toes of the slippers had bells on them"—she pauses to laugh—"which he thought was hysterical, so he was prancing around to make the bells ring."

"Prancing?" Amy asks, halfway doubled over with laughter.

"You know," I say as I do a little jig to demonstrate, which has everyone laughing even harder.

"Oh my god!" Hannah shrieks through her laughter, with her hand pressed to her chest.

"Dude," Reese says, shaking his head but laughing. The two of us played hockey together all four years of high school, and against each other twice a year in college. "Just hand over your man card already."

"Very secure in my manhood, my friend." I punch his shoulder extra hard for good measure, because fuck that sexist shit. There's nothing even remotely normal about *anyone*, of any gender, dressing up in a too-small Mrs. Claus costume and prancing around with bells on their feet.

"So, how was this an Elf on the Shelf situation?" Jonathan asks.

"Oh!" Eva says. "Because he decided that he looked more

like the Elf than Mrs. Claus, so he started freaking perching on everything. The piano, the back of the couch, the post at the bottom of the stairs—"

"My ass still hurts from that one," I say. I think that if Eva hadn't pursued figure skating like she did, she'd be an author —probably penning smutty rom-coms like the ones she reads on long trips and in between training sessions— because she can always weave a funny story out of thin air.

"When he decided he was going to try to sit at the top of the twelve-foot Christmas tree, his brothers finally put a stop to the nonsense."

"Please tell me you took photos?" Hannah asks. "I need to see this with my own eyes."

Eva rolls her eyes. "I would never let someone document my best friend's drunken escapades."

"I wish I'd taken a selfie or something," I say, "because I'd love to see what I looked like. I barely remember any of this happening, but I'm sure I looked hot doing it."

"Man, to embarrass yourself like that in front of your future teammates. You have balls of steel," Reese says, apparently changing his mind and deciding that this behavior somehow makes me more manly?

"Nah, they were all gone by then. It was just family and close friends left."

I'm sure most of my current teammates would totally believe this story. Not because I get drunk and do stupid things often, but because—outside of hockey—I generally don't really care what people think of me.

Eva says it's the confidence of growing up secure in the knowledge that I was completely loved, never feeling like I had to prove myself in any way. And maybe she's right . . . maybe my parents' unwavering support, and her parents' endless pressure, is why we have such different perspectives on other people's opinions.

"Speaking of drinking too much, I think I need to get this lightweight home," Eva says, nodding her head at me. "We're on the ice in, like, six hours, and I have a feeling I'll be skating circles around him."

With promises of "getting together again soon," Eva and I turn and leave our high school friends behind. As we head to the door, I snake my arm around her hip, pulling her to my side. "The fucking Elf of the Shelf, Evie?" I laugh into her hair as I press a kiss to the top of her head. "You're too much."

"Pretty sure I'm just right, actually." She tilts her head up and grins at me with a bright smile that pushes her cheeks up and scrunches her eyes. It's the kind of smile that makes my whole axis tilt, forcing me to hold on to her tighter so I don't stumble.

Because when Eva Wilcott smiles at me like that, I temporarily forget that she friend-zoned me a decade ago, fell in love with someone else, and is pregnant with a stranger's baby. Because all I want—all I've ever wanted—is her.

Chapter Eight

EVA

"I told you I'd be skating circles around you this morning," I call out as I skate past Luke. Setting myself up for a double lutz with a long glide on my left back outside edge, I plant my right toe pick and use my left leg to propel me into the air with a quick double rotation, before landing on my right back outside edge.

"Holy shit, Evie," he says, barely audibly. "How is that safe?"

"It was only a double," I tell him. I could do any type of double jump in my sleep. Triples are a stretch, and I've never been able to do a quad. It's a big part of the reason that I switched from singles skating to pairs when I was a teenager —not only do I prefer the more artistic and emotional nature of a pairs performance, but the expectations for jumps aren't as stringent.

I've been a nationally ranked pairs skater since I started

with Christopher right after high school, and I was never going to make it that far in singles. My mother was right about one thing: it was the logical choice.

I cross my right foot over my left as I approach him again, then swivel toward center ice, where I go into an upright spin. But I'm only a few rotations in, just starting to really pick up speed, when a wave of nausea hits me. *Oh shit.*

Uncrossing my legs, I set my outside skate on the ice to slow myself down, and then I lower my body to sit. My ass hits the ice harder than I expect, and I let out a yelp in response to the pain that shoots up the left side of my back.

Luke's skates come to a skidding stop right next to me, and he drops to his knees, gripping each of my shoulders. "Shit, Evie, what happened?"

I close my eyes, breathing through my nose to keep the nausea at bay. The familiar scent of the ice is mixed with Luke's scent—he always smells a little musky and a little sweet, like if you crossed sandalwood and vanilla ice cream. "Just got dizzy."

"Is that . . . normal, now?"

"No. I never really got morning sickness or anything," I tell him. It's one of the reasons that I didn't realize I was pregnant until I was so far along—though maybe the food aversions and low-level queasiness should have clued me in.

His voice is soft, and his palm moves from my shoulder to cup the side of my face. I lean into him as he asks, "Do you feel okay otherwise?"

"I don't know. That was . . . weird?" *Scary* is more like it. My heart is still racing as I remember going into a spin I've done thousands of times and feeling sick from the motion. It makes me doubt my ability to train in this condition and, to be honest, doubt myself as well.

"Maybe you need to see a doctor? Do you even *have* a doctor here?"

"I need to find one. My obstetrician is in LA, but the doctors at the ER in New York told me to follow up with my OB."

"That was a week ago," he admonishes. "You haven't even made an appointment yet?"

I rest my upper body against his chest, letting my cheek fall onto his shoulder. "I will. I just haven't looked for someone yet. It honestly feels like it'd be easier to go back to LA for a few days and see my doctor there. Or just wait until I go back at the end of the month for a commercial I have to film."

"How is flying across the country and back easier than just finding a new doctor?" He doesn't sound skeptical, just confused.

"I don't know. Lots of things feel overwhelming right now . . ." The lump forming in my throat and the tears suddenly filling my eyes have me pressing my lips together. *Why am I so freaking emotional?*

Wrapping his arms around my shoulders and holding me to him, he stays quiet, giving me the space to process my own thoughts and formulate what to say next.

"I think maybe . . . it's some combination of not having a routine now that skating season is over, feeling like I have no day-to-day plan or purpose, hating that you're in Boston instead of Newbury Falls and we're not getting to spend as much time together as we normally do during the summers, worrying about what life will be like after the baby . . ." I gulp, unable to continue speaking because the lump is so thick in my throat, I think I might choke.

He smooths his hand along my back, waiting for me to say more. And as it always happens when he does that, my emotions continue pouring out.

"I thought I could handle it on my own, but right now, everything feels so overwhelming. Instead of identifying what I need to do and then doing it, I'm paralyzed by indecision. The way my whole life is about to change feels almost too big to deal with. I don't know how I'm going to tell my parents. I don't know what's going to happen with my skating career. Christopher and I need to find a new coach, and I need to break that news to my parents too. And how the hell did I think I was going to be able to train and compete with a new baby? I'll need childcare and—"

Luke moves his hand to my chin, gently guiding my head off his chest so he can look at me. I hate the painful expression he has as he gazes down at me, as though seeing me weak like this actually hurts him.

He uses his thumbs to wipe away the tears streaming down my cheeks. "One thing at a time, Evie. Let's start with getting you an obstetrician in Boston. Let me take care of that for you so you can get the prenatal care you need, and then we'll worry about the next steps."

"Luke." My body shakes as I laugh out his name and tears continue escaping. *What is wrong with me?* I don't cry. "You don't need to do that."

"I know, but I *want* to. There's so little I can do to help you right now. Let me do *this*."

I nod, then bring the sleeve of my sweatshirt up to wipe

my face, and his hands fall away from my face. I miss his touch more than I should, but it's better this way.

"Think you can stand?" he asks.

"I think so." I move onto my knees, and as Luke's hands grasp my waist, I put one skate under me and stand. I'm still a tad dizzy, but nothing like before. Still, I'm glad he's holding on to my hips and keeping me steady, just in case. "Thank god, no one else is here to see me like this."

"Fuck everyone else, Evie. Remember: their opinions don't matter."

But they do. "My parents' opinions matter . . . and they are going to be beyond disappointed. I can already hear my mom going on and on about me throwing away my skating career because I was careless." And, my god, the stupid amounts of money they've spent to help make my dreams come true. The coaches, the travel, the nutritionist and private chef . . . they've poured everything into this dream, even when it meant forsaking things they might have wanted, like a bigger house or a family vacation that didn't include a skating competition. "And my dad will just do that thing he does . . ." I let out a watery laugh.

"What thing?"

"The thing where he nods vigorously and says, 'Okay, okay . . . this is a new challenge, but we'll find a way through it.'"

Luke bursts out laughing, and the deep rumble resonates through my soul, dredging up memories of happier times that have me smiling now, too.

"Yep, he'd totally say that," Luke agrees. "Which makes you pretty lucky, all things considered. The circumstances may not be ideal, but at least you know your parents will still be there for you."

"But not like yours." I take a deep breath, then sigh. "Your dad would be over the moon, and your mom would already be designing the nursery. They wouldn't be upset about it. They'd be thrilled."

"So true," he says with a laugh. "But just because your parents may not react the same way doesn't mean that they're not going to be happy to welcome this baby into their lives. *And* to help you figure out how to keep training and competing so you can qualify for the Olympics."

I can feel my lips turn down at the corners as I shake my head.

"What?" By the way his eyebrows draw together as he looks at me, I can tell he sees the sadness seeping across my face.

"I don't know. Having to go to the hospital last week shook my confidence in my ability to do this. I think . . ." I start to push off my back skate, planning to continue this conversation as we skate back to the door that will lead us off the rink and into the stands, but my back spasms, and I double over in pain.

"Evie!" Luke lunges for me.

I'm afraid he's going to pull me up to standing and that it'll hurt worse, so I say, "Don't!" right before he touches me. With my hands resting on my knees so I can keep my lower back stretched out, I tell him, "Just, give me a minute."

"What happened?"

"My back seized up."

"You probably hurt it when you landed on your ass."

"I didn't *land* on my ass. I sat down because I was dizzy."

"Sure looked to me like you fell."

I note his teasing tone and recognize this as a distraction technique. "If you remember, before the dizziness got in the way, I was skating circles around you."

"Sure you were. Do I need to carry you off the ice?"

I take a deep breath, knowing that it's going to hurt like hell to stand back up, but that I can't exactly go about the rest of my day bent over like this. "Could you just give me your hand for balance?"

He extends his hand in front of me, and I gingerly take it, first with one hand, and then with the other, before he raises it slowly so I can bring myself up to standing.

"You need me to help you off the ice?" he asks.

I nod. "Just . . . slowly pull me along, please. I think the backward motion of pushing off my left skate messed me up, and I don't want to risk it by trying again."

He gets me over to the door, and then steps over the ledge onto the rubber mats that line the walkway in front of the stands. I stand on the ice, trying to figure out which will hurt less: lifting and stepping up with my left leg, or leading with my right, and then bringing my left along after.

"How about if I just lift you over it?" Luke asks. Before I can even respond, he brings his hands under my armpits, lifts me straight up, steps backward, and sets me on the rubber flooring.

I try to ignore the way his wrists graze my breasts as he lets me go, but that's the most action I've seen in five months, and my body definitely takes note.

No, I tell myself. *I'm not going there with Luke. Ever.*

I know it's just the pregnancy hormones. I feel like I've been raring to go for months now—a more than moderate disappointment, given that I don't have anyone in my life to fulfill those needs. And there's no reason to get my body's hopes up because I already know Luke doesn't feel that way about me. Not at all.

He clears his throat, like he can tell I'm imagining what his hands would feel like on me, and my cheeks and neck grow hot in response. "Need some help getting your skates off?"

Chapter Nine

LUKE

"I'm fine, Dad, really," Eva says into the phone. She has her finger pressed against her other ear, like there's some background noise she's trying to block out, but the TV's currently muted for her phone call. "It just hurts to sit directly on my butt, so I don't want to make the drive home today. I'm fine here at Luke's for another night. He'll just bring me home tomorrow."

She pauses and reaches over to the coffee table and plucks a peach ring out of the package I left there for her.

"Yep, it's fine," she says. "He has a meeting in the morning with AJ—" She stops suddenly, and it seems like Charlie has interrupted her, but her eyes widen as she glances over at me. I glance down quickly, stirring her favorite drink—mint tea with a splash of lemonade—hoping she didn't just catch me staring at her.

I love having her around, especially since so much time passes between visits. But I didn't consider what it would be like to have her in my space like this. Past summers, we've spent tons of time together, but it was always at one of our childhood homes, surrounded by *childhood* memories. There were almost always other people around, and now, I'm painfully aware of how *together* the two of us are.

Last night, when she walked out into my living room, looking so damn gorgeous in that dress, I almost made a fucking fool of myself. I don't think she realizes how her body's already changing . . . but I do. Her hair is longer and glossier than before. Her skin glows, her breasts are bigger, and her hips are curvier.

She's always been pretty, but that's never been the thing I loved about her. It's the way she's stronger than she realizes, determined without being stubborn, a perfect mixture of grace and athleticism, and funny as hell. Even though her exterior persona can come across as cool and indifferent, she's got an amazing heart and makes me smile like nobody else can.

I bring the mug of tea around the kitchen island and walk over to where she's lying on my couch, propped up with pillows and a heating pad across her lower back.

"My dad wants to talk to you," she says, handing me the phone while rolling her eyes and mouthing *Sorry.*

Handing her the mug, I take her phone. "Hey, Coach." My whole life I've called Eva's dad by his first name—Uncle Charlie when I was a kid, then Charlie when I was older. But since I started playing for him, it feels weird to call him anything but Coach, even when we're not doing something hockey related.

"Hey, son," he says, and I swallow down the guilt at how I was just thinking about his daughter's body. If he had any idea how I feel about her, he *definitely* wouldn't trust me the way he does. "You sure you don't mind Eva staying another night? I can come and pick her up if you need some space?"

"I'm positive," I say, laughing to myself at how much I *don't* want her to leave. *Ever.*

Is it hard having her here as a friend, when I have always wanted so much more than that with her? Obviously. Would I trade the moments I get to spend with her for . . . anything? Not a chance.

"All right. So tell me about this meeting with AJ." The way he says it, as an invitation instead of a demand, makes me comfortable opening up.

"You didn't know she wanted to meet with me?"

"No, but she meets with players all the time, and there's no reason I would need to know. The general manager's job is not the coach's purview. Are you worried?"

I glance at Eva, not really wanting to admit in front of her how nervous I am about this meeting. But I don't want to lie. "Yeah, a bit."

"I wouldn't be, if I were you," he says. "I've talked to her about the game, and the only thing she's concerned about is your well-being. That was a tough loss. It was a shit way to end the game and the season—for you, and for the team. Everyone is disappointed that we didn't win the Cup, but Luke, no one is *mad* at you about it. Least of all, AJ."

I snort out a laugh. "I have a hard time believing that." Especially since I haven't heard from any of my teammates since we got off the plane in Boston over a week ago. Not one text. Not one call.

After the amount of time we spent together these last few months—not just practicing and playing together, but hanging out off the ice too—their silence is a concerning change.

"Be that as it may, I'm telling you the god's honest truth, son. So lick your wounds in private if you need to, but go into that meeting tomorrow with your head held high. AJ didn't bring you onto this team because she thought you were already the best player you could be. She did it because she knows you've got a lot of growth ahead of you. Show her you still do."

"How do I do that?" I mutter.

"You figure out how to put that game in the past and *move on*. You *learn* from what happened without dwelling on it. Believe it or not, every player's been where you are at some point in their career. Those who can't move past it, generally don't keep playing. I *want* you to keep playing, and I'm assuming you want that too?"

"Yeah." I let out a deep breath, because that might be the first time I've actually admitted that to myself. I've been playing the end of that game back in my mind, over and over, thinking there's no way AJ would want to keep me on the team after that. No way Charlie would still want me to play for him. No way my teammates would be able to forgive me. But maybe . . . maybe the first thing that needs to happen is forgiving myself? And then I can prove to myself, my teammates, Charlie, and AJ that I still deserve a place on this team.

"Good," Charlie says. "So let's move on, then."

———

"What do you think Lizzie would have done if Darcy had come out of that pond with no clothes on?" Eva laughs, her head shaking the pillows on my lap. It's taking all my focus not to let my body react—her head's basically on my dick and her laughter is sending vibrations through the pillows. If she doesn't stop that, she's going to be resting her head on my hard-on.

Goddamn, this is like being right back in high school again with the way I'm lusting after her nonstop. Back then, I had to watch her flirt with just about every guy *but* me. At least now, I don't have to see that shit in real time . . . though the evidence of her "Italian affair" is growing more apparent every day.

"Honestly? Her poor little virgin heart probably would've had a heart attack at the sight, and she'd be buried at Pemberley," I say. "Darcy would secretly visit her grave every day, leaving her flowers and pining after a life that could have been if he hadn't been such a snob."

Eva turns her head and looks up at me, laughing—but that smile quickly turns to a wince as she reaches behind her and presses the heel of her hand into her lower back. "Shit."

"Muscle spasm?" I ask, moving her hand out of the way. I dig my thumb into the tense cord of muscle, moving along it like I did throughout the first episode of *Pride and Prejudice* hours ago.

She sighs, her lips parting and her eyes closing, and fuck me if she doesn't look like she's having a sexual experience. The groan she releases has me even more on edge.

I glance out the floor-to-ceiling windows of my high-rise condo and realize that it's almost fully dark. I'm about to suggest we order dinner when Eva says, "I feel so fucking helpless right now. I couldn't even take my own skates off today, and I can barely move without my back spasming—all because I did a spin I've done a thousand times before and got dizzy. Is this going to happen every time I skate? How are Christopher and I going to train?"

"It was just unlucky timing. You probably had low blood sugar because you didn't eat anything before we skated. We'll ask the doctor tomorrow."

I hadn't really known where to start in terms of helping Eva find an OB, so I'd texted our team doctor because I figured she'd have a recommendation. Not that recommending obstetricians is a normal part of being a doctor in the NHL, but I couldn't exactly ask one of my teammates who has kids, and I figured Dr. D'Angelis was bound by HIPAA not to tell anyone else about my request.

She'd texted me back, letting me know her best friend was an OB and asked if I needed her to get me an appointment quickly. Lo and behold, we have something scheduled for lunchtime tomorrow. I don't even want to guess what she thinks of my request.

"We?" Eva asks.

"Or you, if you don't want me to come with you."

It's totally understandable if she doesn't want you at that appointment with her, I remind myself. I don't know why I even want to be there—it's not *my* baby. But it's Evie's, and I want to be there for her.

"I do," she says, her voice sounding small and quiet. "Want you there, I mean. Suddenly, this all feels . . . too much. I thought I could handle this . . . skating, competing, being a mom. And now I'm worried that it's too big of a challenge. What if I let him down?"

"Let who down? Christopher?" I ask, trying to soften the hard edge in my voice that reveals exactly how I feel about him. But I hear it, and I'm sure she does too.

"Yeah. He's my *partner*, Luke. This affects him as much as it affects me."

"You wouldn't be *in* this situation if it weren't for *him*."

Am I mad about that? Or just mad that he's basically replaced me as the person she's closest to? It's been torture, watching them grow closer over the years—the way their skating became so in sync and intimate, that it was like watching two people with one soul.

That's probably why half the internet thought they were in a relationship for the past few years. The video compilations that constantly show up on social media—the two of them staring into each other's eyes as they glide across the ice, their bodies wrapped together as they do some death-defying spin, him picking her up and kissing her forehead every time they finish their routine. It all makes it seem like they're in a serious relationship.

Which they are, but it's a professional one. Something Eva started to forget, leading her straight into this mess.

"Luke." She says my name as a warning to not pit myself against him.

I grit my teeth together. "He should have been looking out for you."

"He *was* looking out for me. That's why he didn't let anything happen between us." She sighs and looks down at her lap. "It's not his fault that I let all those crazy fans who were shipping us convince me that there was something more."

I notice her full pink lips turn down at the corners while

her eyebrows dip together with an adorable crease between them, and it takes all my willpower to avoid wrapping her in my arms and telling her it's all going to be okay.

"I know you got caught up in everything," I say, still angry at how Christopher Fucking Steele played into the fan's narrative: kissing and hugging her to give the fans something to talk about, basking in the limelight as people speculated that something was developing between them. And he was so damn convincing, she fell for it. "But he's guilty too."

"The only thing he's guilty of is insisting we keep things professional."

"*Nooo*, he's guilty of convincing everyone—you included—that he had feelings he didn't really have."

"So much of pairs skating is about the chemistry between the two skaters," she reminds me. "All he did was fulfill that part of the performance particularly well."

My free hand flexes against my thigh as I try to keep myself from responding about how he led her on for *years*. How could a man spend that much time with her, touch nearly every part of her body, and convince everyone he was falling for her . . . but not actually fall?

Meanwhile, all she has to do is smile at me and I can hardly breathe.

"And that night in Italy?" I ask, hoping she'll finally tell me everything.

"What about it?"

"When you told him how you felt? What actually happened?"

"I already told you. I decided to lick my wounds with alcohol and get over him with some guy I met at the bar, then ended up figuring out I was pregnant months later."

There are so many questions I still have about that night. Was it her first one-night stand? Why didn't she get the guy's name? How could she have failed to protect herself against the possibility of pregnancy? Or worse, an STI?

"Did it help you get over Christopher, at least?" I ask instead.

Her full, glossy lips turn up at the corner. "Actually, yeah. I think I felt . . . I don't know. Embarrassed, for sure, that he didn't return those feelings. But also, maybe a little . . . relieved?"

Well, this is new information. "Relieved? Why?"

"Once I knew that it was all just a performance for him, I was able to look at my own feelings a bit more critically as well. It made me realize that everyone calling us the 'Perfect Pair'"—she makes air quotes as she references the moniker fans gave them after they took home their first gold at US Nationals—"made me think that things actually *would* be perfect if we were together. That *I* would be perfect."

You already are perfect, just the way you are. I desperately want to convince her of this, but that goes way beyond best friend territory.

"And you got all that from having sex with a stranger?" I tease. Maybe it's something I should try? Maybe having sex would help me get over Eva? It's not like I haven't considered the possibility before.

She reaches up and bonks my forehead with the heel of her hand. "No, dumbass," she says with a laugh as I grab her hand and bring it down to the pillow, keeping my own hand wrapped around hers. "It wasn't having sex with someone else that made me realize my own feelings weren't that strong, it was knowing that he didn't have those feelings for me at all."

Well shit, that's no help. I've known since our senior year of high school that Eva was never going to see me as more than a friend. Eight years later, my own feelings haven't changed. Unfortunately, neither have hers.

Chapter Ten

LUKE

I turn the corner and head down the hallway in the Rebels' practice facility that will lead me to AJ's office. It's late morning and most people's office doors are open, but everyone appears to be too busy working to notice me pass by.

When I get to the alcove off the hallway where AJ's assistant, Colleen, normally sits, her desk is empty. The door to AJ's office is cracked open, and I glance at my watch to see that I'm still a few minutes early. I'm about to take a seat in one of the chairs in the waiting area, when my father's voice carries through the crack in the door.

". . . and after that loss? *This* is why I didn't want you to bring Luke onto this team. You've put me in a really tough position."

My jaw drops open. *What the hell?*

Like it generally happens, I didn't know I was going to be traded to the Rebels until after the deal was done. I came to practice one day and my general manager in Calgary let me know that I was expected to join the Rebels in Dallas, where they were playing the next night. I wasn't even two years into a four-year contract and thought I had been playing well, so the news of the trade was like a sucker punch to the gut.

I'd never expected to play for the Rebels. When I was first drafted, Dad and I talked, and we agreed that it could be seen as a conflict of interest or nepotism, given that our family owns the team. So I was shocked by the news of the trade, but also, kind of happy?

Dad wouldn't have risked possible negative media attention if he hadn't believed that I was truly a valuable addition to the team, would he? That negative attention never came, though. A few sports pundits commented on it, but nothing stuck. I settled into the team so easily, and it felt like such a good fit, that it never occurred to me to ask Dad why he'd had the change of heart.

Apparently . . . he hadn't. In fact, it sounds like he didn't want AJ to bring me to the Rebels at all.

I turn, realizing that I need to get out of this alcove before Colleen comes back and finds me eavesdropping, or worse— my dad walks out of that office and knows I overheard him.

Retreating quickly down the hallway, I walk all the way back to the elevators where I stand and give myself a moment. Could I have misunderstood his meaning? Is there any other interpretation?

I knew that my terrible performance in Game 7 would disappoint him. I just didn't realize he would take it as proof that I shouldn't have been brought onto the team in the first place. *Fuck*. How can I play for the Rebels when the team's owner, my own father, doesn't want me here? Is this why AJ wanted to meet with me today?

I'm pacing in front of the elevators, trying not to over-react to my dad's words, and contemplating my next move, when Colleen walks by. "Oh, Luke, are you here for your meeting with AJ?"

"Yep," I say, giving her the smile I know she'll expect from me. "I was just . . . checking my messages first." I pat my front pocket where my phone is, hoping she'll think I just put it away.

"All right, c'mon." She nods toward the hall for me to walk with her.

"So, that new husband of yours treating you right?" I ask as we walk along. "Because if he's not . . ."

She laughs and elbows me. "All right, you little flirt."

"I'm just saying, he better be treating you well." Do I *need* to flirt with my GM's assistant? Hell no. But did all the Hartmann brothers inherit some sort of compulsive need to flirt? Seems we did.

Word has it that Dad used to be like that too, until he met Mom. He's been devoted to her ever since. They're actually kind of sickeningly in love. I think that's why none of my brothers want to settle down. When the bar's that high, it's hard to find "the one."

"He is," Colleen assures me.

"Okay, well, next time I see him, I'm going to make sure." I narrow my eyes menacingly, and she bursts out laughing.

Her husband is a 6'4" former boxer, so I'm sure she knows I'm just joking around. "You do that," she says as we take the turn toward AJ's office and see my father walking out.

Then Tucker follows on his heels, and I feel like I was sucker punched—again. I must let out a heavy breath, because Colleen turns and looks at me. I give her what's probably a tight smile, then nod at my dad and brother. We always aim to keep things professional at work, so they treat me the same way they'd treat any other player.

"Hey, Hartmann, thanks for coming in," AJ says as she steps back, holding the door to her office open and motioning me in. After shutting the door, she tells me to take a seat on the couch.

Like I'm sure most people are, I was pretty surprised when I first walked into AJ's office. It's feminine in a way you wouldn't expect to find in the office of an NHL general manager with a reputation for being a complete ballbuster. But that's the thing about AJ—she defies convention. If she wants an office where the couch and side chairs sport frilly pillows and the coffee table looks like it came out of a Restoration Hardware photoshoot, she's going to have it. And she's not going to give a shit about whether you like it or not.

I like that about her, as does most of the team, it seems. Even our surly captain, McCabe, who used to hate her, is now absolutely devoted to her. I wouldn't be surprised if he's already ring shopping after only a few weeks of them being together.

"How are you doing?" she asks, once she's seated in one of the side chairs, her body turned toward where I sit to her right on the couch.

"I've been better."

"I figured. Listen, I'm sorry that I waited a week to talk to you. I just wanted to know where we stood with Colt first," she says.

Immediately, my mind goes to the worst-case scenario, because if Colt's going to be fine for next season, she's probably going to trade me. If he's not, she'll probably keep me around so she doesn't have to bring on two new goalies in the same season.

I don't know which option is worse: getting to stay because Colt's career is cut short, or having to go when I've found a team that feels like such a good fit?

I was supposed to replace Colt as the first-string goalie when he retires at the end of next season. But after the way I absolutely choked in the most crucial moment of the playoffs, there's no way she'd think I'm ready to replace one of the best goalies of all time.

I nod. "Understandable."

In my head, I keep hearing my dad's voice: *This is why I didn't want you to bring Luke onto this team.*

This.

This . . . loss.

The way I fucking froze out there, unable to think of anything but Eva . . . it's unpardonable. Even *I* can't forgive myself for it, and clearly, my dad can't either.

"Amazingly"—she shakes her head and smiles—"he's going to be fine. A couple weeks on crutches, and then a bit of rehab, but he should be fine by the beginning of the season."

My shoulders sag. "That's a relief."

"Right? So, I hear you're going to be doing some skills sessions with Evan. I'll ask Colt to sit in on those. I know you guys have a good rapport, and I think he might have some tips for how to handle games like the one you just had."

"What?" My voice squeaks, sounding like I just inhaled helium.

AJ reacts with her trademark professionalism, but I feel like she's holding in laughter. "What part of that wasn't clear?" She speaks slowly, recognizing my stunned expression.

"I–I'm not being traded?"

"You've played seventeen games for us. That's not exactly enough data to know yet whether this is a good fit. But from my perspective, you had sixteen pretty good games, and one terrible one."

"It wasn't just *a game*. It was Game 7 of the finals!" Why am I reminding her of this? Why am I arguing, quite passionately, against myself?

"Yeah, it was pretty awful timing to have a bad game. But our defense fell apart before you even came onto the ice. Then you fell apart. We've got work to do to be ready for next season, and I'm going to need you to train harder this summer than you're probably used to in the off season—"

"I'm ready." The words jump out, ignited by the tiny spark of hope that flares to life in my chest. It's the first time in a week I've felt like maybe things will be okay.

I'll do whatever I need to do. Work harder than I've ever worked. Anything she asks.

"Good. And I want you to start talking to a sports psychologist."

Anything but that.

"You have someone in mind?" I ask.

"Talk to Zach. Charlie says he has someone great."

This is new information. Is this why Zach is so fucking chill?

"I'll look into it."

She narrows her eyes at me in a way that reminds me she's a shrewd businesswoman, in addition to knowing more about hockey than just about anyone I've ever met. "Make sure you do."

Well, that's fucking ominous. I almost say as much, but I press my lips together just in time and give her a nod. "Thanks for this second chance, AJ. It means a lot."

"It's not a second chance, Hartmann. You didn't ruin the first chance . . ."

I think she means that to be a supportive statement, but the way the sentence trails off makes me feel like she almost added "yet" at the end.

"Let me know when you've got that first meeting set up with the sports psychologist. And I'll have Evan keep me updated on the skills practices. I think he's also working with Lennington and Kotzu," she tells me. One of them is a goalie for Minnesota, and the other for Dallas, but both are from the Boston area and back for the off-season. I've practiced with them during the summers before, which is how I knew Coach Knight even before I was traded.

Hell, maybe that's *why* I was traded? Maybe he recommended me to AJ? It's nice to think that even if my own father doesn't want me on this team, both Charlie and Evan do.

Chapter Eleven

EVA

"Are you sure you're okay?" I ask, glancing over at Luke as we reach the top of the second flight of stairs. I better love this doctor after climbing this many stairs, while pregnant, to see her. And that elevator better be in working order by the next time I'm here, because my poor back is barely handling this, and if my current level of stamina is any indication, I'm tiring more easily every single day.

I need to start training again. A week off, and I'm already feeling weak.

"I'm fine," Luke says with a shrug. And while he sounds fine, he's been unusually quiet since he got back from his meeting with AJ.

He didn't say it, but I know he was nervous about the outcome of that meeting. I can always tell when he's worried —his eyebrows flatten into nearly straight lines, and he gets a

85

far-off look in his eyes. I saw both of those expressions a few times yesterday.

But according to him, everything went well. AJ wants him to do some skills work with his goalie coach throughout the summer, which he was planning to do anyway, and it doesn't sound like there was any other fallout from Game 7. It all sounded positive, but something's still . . . off. I wish he'd open up and tell me what it is. Even if there's nothing I can do to fix it, I can listen and be supportive.

"Just glad you let me come with you for this," he says, his voice light but sounding a little strained.

"You can come in *only* if we do an ultrasound," I remind him. The thought of Luke sitting next to me while I'm draped in a gown with my feet up in stirrups . . . I shudder to think about how absolutely unsexy that would be. Not that Luke sees me like that, but I also don't need him to see me getting a pelvic exam.

"I hope we get to see that little squash," he says, glancing down at my stomach.

The laugh erupts from the back of my throat right as Luke reaches for the door to the doctor's office. "Do you mean little squish?" I've heard people call babies *squish* before, but never *squash*.

"No. Right now the baby is as big as a squash."

"How do you know that?"

"There's this app . . ." He stops speaking when it registers that I've stopped walking and am staring at him with my lips parted but unable to form words.

"You . . .?"

Putting his hand on my lower back, his thumb pressing across my tightened muscles there, he guides me toward the reception desk and whispers, "A couple days ago, you said you were twenty-four weeks along, so I downloaded an app to see what that meant for the baby's development. It's pretty cool. It showed me everything that's happened so far. Like, did you know he or she is eleven inches long and over a pound at this point? And the app will show me updates every week."

I don't know why my eyes are watering like this . . . again.

Maybe it's because there's one, and only one, perfect man in this world, and he's standing right next to me—but he's only ever wanted to be my best friend.

Missing out on the last Olympics because Christopher was injured, our coach's tragic death, internet shippers getting into my psyche and convincing me I felt things I didn't feel, getting pregnant and not even knowing the name of the baby's father—I've had my share of recent disap-pointments.

But *nothing* is as heartbreaking as this single fact: *Luke Hartmann will never be anything more than my best friend.*

Even after living with that knowledge since I first fell for him in high school . . . time has not dulled the ache. Because he's only gotten better—in every single way—with age.

Still, I'd rather have him as a best friend than not have him in my life at all. So, I'll just have to keep setting up boundaries to prevent myself from getting my hopes up and imagining us as more than friends.

Taking care of people he loves is just what Luke does. And I know he loves me, just not in the way I wish he did.

"Can I help you?" the woman at the reception desk asks as she slides the glass panel open.

Swallowing the lump in my throat and blinking away my

watery eyes, I turn toward her. "Hi. I'm Evangeline Wilcott. I have an appointment with Dr. Lowery."

"Of course. Can I get a copy of your insurance card?"

I fish it out of my wallet, remembering that I need to look into what happens if I stop skating. Currently, my insurance is provided by the national skating organization, but if Christopher and I have to take a break for something other than a skating-related injury, I don't know what happens to my insurance.

"Hey." Luke's voice is quiet as he steps in next to me, cradling me against his side as he places his hand on my lower back and rubs circles along my spine with his thumb. "You good?"

I release my lower lip, which I'd been holding tightly between my teeth. "Yep."

"You sure?"

"Yep." I don't think I can say more than that. I don't know why this visit feels more intense than the first, and only, visit I had with my obstetrician in LA just over a month ago. Maybe because I was still holding out hope that I wasn't pregnant when I showed up for that appointment? And now that I know for certain, it feels more real? I was able to compartmentalize this entire situation while we were still training and competing. It was something I didn't have to deal with until "later."

My ability to focus only on what's in front of me, without feeling anxious about things that might happen down the road, has always served me well as a competitive figure skater.

But now, "later" has arrived. This pregnancy isn't something I can ignore. Now that I'm not training, my body is changing rapidly, and my breasts feel like they're heavier every day. Things that used to be easy, like walking up two flights of stairs, are getting more challenging. With nothing else to steal my attention or focus, this situation is now *real* and it's *here*.

Luke's fingers curl around my side as he hugs me to him and drops a kiss on the top of my head. And that's when the hot tears of disappointment start falling. As Luke stands beside me, comforting and supporting me, I have to wonder if there's anything worse than having exactly what you've always wanted dangling right in front of your face, but lacking the ability to make it yours?

I wipe the tears away with the heel of my hand, right as the woman turns back toward me with my insurance card in hand. She takes one look at me and says quietly, "Let's get you into a room."

"Thanks," I mumble as I step toward the door that will lead back to the patient rooms.

When she opens the door from the other side, she tells Luke, "I need you to wait out here."

I glance up at him and give him a watery smile, but he just looks at me with worried eyes before he nods and turns back toward the waiting room.

"I'm Val, Dr. Lowery's nurse," the woman from the reception desk says. "I'm going to get you into a room. We'll go over a few questions, and then I'll get your height and weight."

"Okay," I say, following her down the hallway.

As soon as the door shuts behind me in the small room, Val sits on the rolling stool across from the exam table she gestures to. I take a seat, then she looks at me with concern in her eyes and asks, "Are you okay?"

"Yeah, I'm just emotional."

"Are you safe?" she asks.

My eyebrows dip together, and I'm sure there's confusion written across my face.

"Sometimes when women come in and they're upset," Val says, "and they've got a big guy towering over them protectively . . . it can be a sign that there's something not quite right about the relationship."

My shoulders shake with laughter. "I'm sorry, there's nothing funny about that. But that guy"—I tilt my head in the direction of the waiting room—"is my best friend, and the biggest teddy bear you'll ever meet. He's just here to support me."

"Okay." Val nods, not even trying to hide her look of relief. "I'm glad to hear that. So he's not the father of your baby?"

I wish.

"No."

"So, why are you crying?"

How can I tell her I'm crying because Luke is *so* perfect, but will never be mine? I can't. So instead, I say, "The reality of this pregnancy is just setting in, I guess. Everything I say here is confidential, right?"

"As long as you're not a danger to yourself or others, yes."

I nod. "I'm a competitive figure skater. My season just ended, and I'm feeling very overwhelmed as I think about what this pregnancy means for me personally, and for my career. Given the timeline of when I'll give birth, there will only be one qualifier my partner and I can compete in before the Olympics. And we won't have long to train to get ready for it after the baby is born."

"You'll need to talk to Dr. Lowery about when you'll be cleared to start training again," Val says. "There's a period of time, postpartum, where you're supposed to take it easy because your body will need time to heal. But first things first. What was the first day of your last period?"

I explain to her why I don't know a precise date, but I give her the date of conception and explain the due date that my doctor back in Los Angeles gave me.

"Okay," she says as she eyes my abdomen. "We'll do an ultrasound to check the baby's growth and confirm the due date."

"I know I don't look like I'm that far along," I say.

"That sometimes happens when people are training like you must be. But we'll just double-check that everything is progressing normally—"

"Because you're concerned that it isn't?"

She shakes her head. "No, but because you're a new patient, we want to establish a baseline of where you are right now, so we check your progress at future visits against that baseline. There's nothing to worry about."

Clearly, I'm not doing a good job of hiding my anxiety. It's not like I wanted *this* pregnancy in *these* circumstances. But as soon as I found out I was pregnant—as soon as I realized I was going to be a mom—I knew it was meant to be. I'm not sure how or why, but I just knew that loving this baby was what I was put on Earth to do.

After running through some initial questions and getting my height and weight, Val has me change into a fabric gown and tells me Dr. Lowery will be in shortly.

When she walks into the room, I know I'm going to like her. She's wearing sleek grey slacks and killer high heels, with a form-fitting tank top under her white lab coat. Her honey-colored hair is back in a sleek ponytail and her face is free of makeup except for some mascara and bright pink lipstick. She's confident and friendly, and from the minute she opens her mouth, she exudes competence and warmth.

After my exam, she answers my questions about my pregnancy and when I might need to stop on-ice training, and then says, "You can put your clothes back on, and we'll move you to the room next door so I can do a quick ultrasound and we can see your baby."

"My friend is in the waiting room. Can he come in for the ultrasound, too?"

"Sure. What's his name? I'll have Val call him in."

"Luke," I say.

"Ooohhh." She nods. "That's right. Olivia told me about you guys."

"Olivia?"

"Olivia D'Angelis. She's the team doctor for the Rebels. I fit you in as a favor to her," she says, and some things start clicking together: the empty waiting room, a nurse at the reception desk, the fact that we breezed right into this appointment. She's fitting us in on her lunch break. "You can meet me right in here," she says, stepping backward into the hallway and pointing to another door, "as soon as you're dressed."

I don't expect to find Luke already sitting in the ultrasound room, chatting away amiably with Dr. Lowery, when I get there. But of course he's already made her his newest friend. He's always so at ease with everyone, so confident in who he is, I guess, that he doesn't need to worry about impressing people. And they're always drawn to him anyway, just like I am.

When he sees me standing in the doorway, he smiles and pats the exam chair, saying, "Hop up, Evie. Let's see this baby."

Chapter Twelve

LUKE

I try not to watch as Dr. Lowery preps for the ultrasound by tucking Eva's shirt up into her bra and pushing the waistband of her skirt down so low it's practically indecent—but it's kind of a nice distraction from the way my dad's voice has been on replay in my head the whole time I sat in the waiting room: *This is why I didn't want you to bring Luke onto this team.*

Eva's got her eyes screwed tightly shut, so my hand finds hers where it's curled into a fist by her side. Given what she's told me about the circumstances of this pregnancy, and how afraid she is of disappointing her parents and Christopher Fucking Steele, I'm not surprised she's so tense.

The tips of her fingers curl into my palm, and she squeezes, then lets her head fall to the side so she's looking at me.

You're good. I mouth the words, not wanting to interrupt the silence as the doctor gets ready. Instead, I take the opportunity to reach out and sweep back the strand of hair that's fallen onto her forehead and tuck it behind her ear as I whisper, "We got this."

Eva gives me a small nod and takes a deep breath.

"This is going to feel cool," the doctor says, squirting some clear gel onto Eva's belly. We both look up at the screen above her feet. It's black with some grayish spots at first, but as Dr. Lowery moves the transponder around, a large bubble appears in the center of the screen. We watch in awe as the shape of a baby emerges—the head, followed by the curved body, and tiny legs and arms.

"Oh my god," I whisper, my eyes getting watery as I'm struck by the magic of what we're seeing. It was one thing to see drawings of a fetus side by side with various fruits and vegetables in the app while reading about each week's development. It's another entirely to see the shape of an actual baby, to watch it move, to imagine what it will look like.

Eva's hand is squeezing mine so tightly I'm pretty sure I'll have a permanent imprint of her nails in my palm. I glance at her, noticing how her breaths are shallow as her eyes remain fixed on the screen, unblinking. I can't tell how she's feeling —is this awe, or the beginning of a freak-out? Or is it just reality setting in even further?

She closes her eyes and a tear leaks down the side of her face. Reaching up, I wipe it away with my thumb, then lean forward and kiss her forehead. All I want to do at this moment is make sure she knows she's not alone. I'll do whatever I can to help her—always have, always will.

Dr. Lowery explains some of the measurements she's taking, confirms that the baby is perfectly healthy and growing right along schedule. "One thing to note is that you have a retroverted uterus, which means it's slightly tilted backward. That might be another reason you're barely showing at this point. It shouldn't impact your labor or delivery, but we'll keep an eye on it to make sure that it rights itself as the pregnancy progresses."

Eva nods, and then Dr. Lowery asks, "Do you already know the sex of the baby? Or do you want to know?"

Yes. It's on the tip of my tongue, but I have the good sense to hold that in. It's not my place to have an opinion here, no matter how curious I am.

"No," Eva says. "Maybe eventually . . . but not yet."

Dr. Lowery just nods and touches the screen. The whirling sound of a printer fills the room, and she reaches down to rip off a five-inch-wide strip of photo paper that curls as she hands it to Eva. "Here are some photos for you," she says, but Eva doesn't take them, she just looks over at me.

"Thanks," I say as I reach out my hand for them.

I don't miss the way Dr. Lowery looks at Eva with concern as she wipes the gel off her abdomen. "We're done for today. On your way out, you can make your next appointment. Take all the time you need getting out of here." She gives Eva's shoulder a squeeze, making me wonder how much Eva told her about the circumstances of her pregnancy, and then heads out the door.

Eva swings her legs over the edge of the table, sitting up to face me. But she makes no move to fix her clothing or stand up.

"Did you ask her about skating?" I ask her.

"Yeah, she said I'm fine to keep going until I've more significantly *popped.* She said I also need to eat more protein and religiously take my vitamins and supplements so I don't let my iron get low again. I don't know . . . all this makes me wonder if I shouldn't hop on a plane back to LA so Christopher and I can get some more training in before I can't anymore. Losing this time on the ice seems . . . irresponsible, given that I'll get to a point where I'll be forced to stop skating. Shouldn't I take advantage of every moment I *do* have to train?"

Noooooo. The thought erupts from my soul and reverberates through every part of my being. I thought she'd be here for *at least* a month and hoped maybe she'd stay through her whole pregnancy. I don't want to lose one second with her.

"I also need to figure out my health insurance. If I stop skating, will I still have insurance?" She shakes her head. "And really, how am I going to tell my parents? I can't even get myself to come up with a solid plan for that because I can't figure out a way to not disappoint them. Just thinking about it makes me want to throw up. God, I've fucked everything up so badly!"

"Hey," I say, standing and stepping between her legs so I can gather her up in my arms. She leans her head against my chest and her arms come around my lower back as she clings to me. Her shoulders shake with sobs, and I want to do something, *anything*, to make this better.

"What if we got married?" The suggestion is out of my mouth before the thought even fully forms in my head.

Holy shit. I did not just say that.

She freezes, then pulls back, looking up at me with her eyebrows raised into high peaks above her swollen eyes. Head tilting, she coughs out a laugh. "What?"

I swallow so deeply I can feel the muscles ripple along my neck, and I watch her eyes track the movement before her gaze returns to my face. And even though I didn't intend to suggest marriage, even though I didn't think it through before making that offer, now that it's out there—the one thing I've always wanted but thought I could never have—I don't want to take it back.

"Think about it, Evie," I say, bringing my hands up to cup her shoulders. "It could be a mutually beneficial solution to both of our problems."

"How so?"

The fact that she didn't laugh in my face and say, "you flatter yourself," has to be a good sign, right? She didn't push me away or immediately put up barriers, like she normally does the moment she senses us inching beyond "just friends."

"Well, if we got married, and then told everyone we were expecting a baby together, I think both our families would be thrilled. Plus, once the world knows about your pregnancy, it would make your change in the routine at the last competition more explicable, and fans would finally lose interest in you and Christopher being a couple. Plus, it would help explain my performance in Game 7."

Her eyes widen the slightest bit as she gazes up at me, and that's when I realize I've said too much. Now she *has* to know that the way I played that night was because I was worried sick about her. And fuck, now if she says yes, it's probably going to be out of guilt.

"So you'd be painted as the father-to-be who was distraught when he found out the mother of his child was rushed to the hospital," she says slowly, working out the story we could tell. "I'd be painted as someone who pushed herself too hard, given my condition, because I didn't want to let my partner down."

I nod. "Mutually beneficial. No one needs to know how and why you got pregnant, and you wouldn't need to worry about insurance or childcare or anything else, really. I'll take care of you, Evie. Besides, our parents will be *thrilled.* Mine have been itching for grandchildren for years. Yours might still have concerns about your skating career and next year's Olympics, but if they thought this baby was *ours,* conceived after years of friendship that grew into something more . . ." I say as my fingertips slide across her shoulders and up the sides of her neck so I can cup her jaw in my hands. "I don't think anyone would question it."

Her cheeks push up as she smiles and lets out a bubbly laugh. "No, I agree. We could probably convince everyone that this is our love child."

I'm about to ask her if it's because the two of us are so good at making people believe our ridiculous stories, or if it's because our friends and family have always wondered whether there's more to our friendship than we've ever admitted, when she says, "But I feel like I'd be taking advantage of you."

"How so?" I run my thumbs along her cheekbones as I try to figure out why she looks sad all of a sudden.

"Because what do *I* bring to this marriage? *You* provide me with healthcare, and I live here with you. *You* make it so that I don't have to admit how I really got pregnant, which gives me cover from the fans who would otherwise suspect I had cheated on Christopher. Instead of looking like an irresponsible harlot, I'm a woman in a secret relationship with her best friend, not with her skating partner like everyone thought. My dad will be thrilled, and hopefully my mom will be a little less mad than she would've been otherwise. Aside from still having to figure out how to train and compete, this solves all *my* problems. What do *you* get out of it?"

You.

The thought of Eva hopping on a plane back to LA to start training again—with Christopher Fucking Steele, no less—makes me nauseous.

I *know* she's never going to feel the same way about me as I feel about her, but all good marriages are built on friendship. In fact, our long history and the way we've always been there for each other over the years—even when living on opposite coasts and sometimes in different countries—probably makes our marriage more likely to survive than most. Don't all marriages eventually just turn into deep, abiding friendships anyway, once that initial passion burns out?

"Besides making sure you're taken care of, I get the media off my back about Game 7. I give them a plausible story to explain my performance that night, and I give them something else to focus on. And most importantly"—I glance away so she won't see my shame—"a grandchild, here in Boston, gives my dad a reason to keep me on the team."

Her eyebrows pinch at that. "What? Why would your dad not keep you on the team?"

I wasn't planning on telling her what I'd overheard—not yet anyway. And I probably shouldn't say anything until I've had some time to process it. But I'm just desperate enough to find *anything* that will keep her here with me and, on the off chance this is it, I have to bring it up.

"This morning, I overheard him talking to AJ. He said the Game 7 loss was exactly why he didn't want her to bring me to Boston in the first place."

Eva's face falls and she leans forward, tightening her arms

around my back to pull me against her. My hands move to the nape of her neck as she rests her forehead against my chest. "Luke . . . I'm so sorry."

"Yeah. Me too," I tell her, staring at the gray wall behind her, my voice flat as I force myself not to give in to these emotions—otherwise, I'll probably end up fucking crying in this room with her.

She gives me another squeeze, then sits back and looks up at me. "I think we both need to think about this a little more. There are probably factors we're not considering."

"Like?"

"I don't think the doctor's office is the place to figure this out," she says, glancing at the door. "Dr. Lowery probably wants us out of here so she can take her lunch break. Why don't we go get something to eat, and then . . . we can think this through properly."

"Hungry already?" I ask with a chuckle. She'd been eating lunch—a grilled chicken sandwich that was stuffed so full it had lettuce, tomato, cheese, and avocado hanging out the sides—when I got back to my place after my meeting with AJ. I'd made myself a quick protein shake, and I'm not even remotely hungry yet.

"I'm *never* not hungry. This little . . ." She trails off as she gazes down at her bare belly, and then looks up at me with a small smile. ". . . squash must be consuming every calorie I eat."

"All right," I say, bringing my hands to her sides, where her shirt is tucked into her bra, and pulling it down to cover her abdomen. "Let's go feed you and Baby Squash."

Chapter Thirteen

EVA

"It can't possibly be this simple," I say to Luke as he sets the bowl with his large salad on the coffee table. I glance over, noting how my half-eaten burger and empty fry container is a stark contrast to his salad. But I'm eating for two, and the doctor said I needed more protein and iron, so the burger felt like a good choice.

"Why not?" he asks, grabbing his root beer off the table. "We can easily sneak away and get married when we're in Vegas next weekend for the NHL awards ceremony."

"Our parents will be so disappointed if they're not present when we get married." I know our dads, especially, will be devastated. Luke's like a son to my dad, and his parents are basically family to me. "What do we gain by not telling them our plan and letting them participate in it?"

"I think eloping is the most feasible option. If we let our parents know ahead of time, you know that our moms are going to want to plan a wedding. They'll make it a whole *thing*, and I think it's just easier to sell our story if we get married first. If the goal is to get you on my health insurance as quickly as possible, then waiting while they throw together a wedding doesn't help that." He shrugs, talking like the idea of us getting married is the most natural thing in the world. Like it's not everything I've ever wanted . . . but *not* the way I wanted it.

Being Luke Hartmann's wife might be the ending I've dreamed of for our friendship, but being his *fake wife* might just become the hardest thing I'll ever have to endure.

Luke is the standard I've always held other men up to . . . and no one *ever* measures up. If we're married, he'll be his normal, wonderful happy-go-lucky self, content with our friendship, while I'll be wishing for way more. And given how my pregnancy hormones have me raring to go, day and night, I'm worried that I'll be eyeing him like I can't wait to devour him, and that will make it weird and uncomfortable for him.

"Yeah," I say. "Plus, a real wedding would be awkward as hell, given that this is all fake."

As hard as it may be to marry Luke and pretend I don't have feelings for him, I think that walking down the aisle to him in front of our friends and family, knowing it doesn't mean anything, could be the thing to actually break me.

He swallows and his whole neck convulses with the movement. "I think all successful marriages are rooted in friendship and ultimately become even deeper friendships," he says, glancing out the floor-to-ceiling windows along the wall of the dining area, as he reaches over to set his root beer back on the coffee table. "Honestly, if I had to pick one person I was going to spend the rest of my life with"—he looks back at me, but his expression is unreadable—"it would be you, Evie."

Now I'm the one swallowing down the lump rising in my throat. If he *had* to pick . . . not if he *got* to pick one person, but if he was forced to. That one word tells me everything I need to know.

"Am I forcing you into this?" I ask, and the words come out strangled with worry. But as he opens his mouth to respond, I rush on. "I mean, I know *you* were the one who suggested it. But I don't want you to hitch yourself to me just because you feel bad for me and want to help. I appreciate that you're offering, but I . . . I worry that you're going to resent this choice down the road, that you're going to resent me and the baby—"

My rambling is interrupted as he reaches out, wrapping one arm around my back, pulling me across the couch cushion, and depositing me in his lap. He engulfs me in his arms and holds my side against his chest. Dipping his head so his lips brush across the top of my head, he whispers, "Shut up, Evie." His chest shakes against me, but I can't tell if it's his racing heart or silent laughter. "I could never resent you, or a child that is half you."

"Maybe so," I mumble against his T-shirt, wondering if I'm crazy to believe him. "But you may resent the situation. What if you meet someone else?"

"I won't," he says, without any hesitation.

I pull back, looking up at him. "How do you know that?"

"Because I'll be married. And I'm not going to go looking for anything outside of our relationship."

"What if . . ." I glance back down, wanting to ask about how we'll each fulfill whatever sexual needs we have. I'm sure it would be way too weird and awkward if we crossed that line with each other. No matter how many times I've pictured him while getting myself off, I know that's a one-way street. How mortifying would it be if I brought it up and he just looked at me and said, "you flatter yourself"?

He tilts my chin up and his gaze roams across my face, assessing. "What if *what*?"

"Nothing." It's way too embarrassing. I have an excellent sex toy collection; I just have to get it here from LA so I can satisfy myself when my hormones kick in. "I'm sure there will be lots of things we'll have to figure out as we go. Like, for example, when are we going to get my stuff from LA and move it here?"

"We can head to LA and pack you up after Vegas. Didn't you say you had a commercial to film for an endorsement? Maybe we can time those together. What about your training?"

"I'll have to work that out with Christopher," I say, and I don't miss the way his jaw clenches. I reach up and smooth my palm across it. "Hey, he's my partner and one of my best friends. You're going to have to get over whatever it is that you hate so much about him."

He tries to look away, but I wrap my thumb under his chin and steer him back so he's looking at me. Still, he says nothing.

"What *is* it you don't like about him, anyway?" If I didn't know better, I'd almost think Luke was jealous—but that makes no sense. Well, maybe it does, in the same way I'd be jealous if Luke had another best friend who was a girl. In fact, I'd be out of my mind with jealousy, even if I didn't have feelings for him. I like knowing that, out of the dozens of friends he has, I'm his *best* friend. There's a possessive side of me that never wants to share him, or that title, with anyone else.

He sighs, and his breath caresses my forehead. "I just don't feel like he has your best interests at heart."

"Why should he?" I ask. "I mean, obviously we care about each other, like friends do. But shouldn't each of us have our own *individual* best interests at heart?"

"I guess."

"Luke, the only time you'd put someone else's best interests before your own is if you loved that person with all your heart. And that's just not how Christopher and I feel about each other. I love him as a friend, nothing more. And he feels the same way."

After the emotional spiral I went through this year, convincing myself that we'd be perfect together, only to find myself shockingly relieved after I got over the initial embarrassment of Christopher not returning those feelings, it feels good to be at this point. I doubt my feelings for him were ever anything more than me wanting my life to seem perfect and convincing myself that if he and I were together, it would be.

"Okay. I just . . . I don't want any external speculation that our marriage isn't real," Luke says. "And if he continues to act the same way toward you once you're back to competing, there will be rumors."

"I'll talk to him about it."

"And all the social media videos of you guys practicing together, the stolen glances, the teasing and playfulness—you can't tell me your team wasn't trying to sell the lie."

He's right. We have our own social media account and his

cousin runs it. When she figured out that fans wanted to see those types of behind-the-scenes videos, she put more and more of them out . . . even going so far as to have us stage some of them.

"It won't be a problem," I say. "And the only way this skating thing is going to work is if Christopher will move out here—"

"Do you think he will?"

"Yes. If we can find a coach out here, I think he'll do it. It's only, what? Eight months until the Olympics? I've given him eight years of my life in LA, he can give me eight months in Boston."

"What do you mean, you *gave* him eight years of my life?" Luke's eyebrows dip as he studies me.

"Christopher took a risk partnering with me when his last partner stopped skating," I remind him. It can be incredibly difficult for female figure skaters to find a partner, because there are so many more women than men in our sport, and I knew how lucky I was that he offered to skate with me. "I worked overtime to prove myself and it's paid off for both of us. We're both much better together than either of us was before. And he wants this Olympic medal as much as I do. When he got hurt at the last Olympics, I was fielding calls from coaches and parents who wanted me to meet new potential partners. You wouldn't believe the way men were lining up to leave their current partners if I'd come skate with them instead." I roll my eyes. "Vultures. But I didn't leave him when he was hurt, and he's not going to leave me because I'm pregnant. That's not the partnership we've built."

Whatever hard look I saw in Luke's eyes before begins to soften. He hates talking about Christopher, so we rarely do.

But not talking about one of the most important people in my life with the other most important person in my life can be . . . difficult.

"See, though. You *do* have each other's best interests at heart, then."

I hear the unasked question. "Not because we're in love, Luke. Because we want the same end goal, and we're committed to achieving it together. We're a team. You, of all people, should understand that dynamic. It just happens that my team is smaller than yours."

"Okay," he says, pulling me back against him, and then leaning back so I'm lying against his chest. As I lie there, the carbs sink in, my body gives into the exhaustion of working overtime to grow a tiny human, and my eyelids grow heavy.

Just as I'm about to give in to sleep, I swear I hear him whisper, "But just so you know, I'm always going to have your best interests at heart."

Chapter Fourteen

LUKE

DREW

Audrey and I have a babysitter tonight. Who wants to go out and grab a drink with us after dinner?

COLT

Jules and I are in.

MCCABE

Sorry, we don't have childcare tonight.

COLT

"We" is still so weird.

DREW

So what you're saying is, AJ's there, and even though she could stay with Abby, you don't want to come out with us?

MCCABE

Hmmmm, choosing between getting drinks
with you guys or staying home with my
girlfriend? It's a real tough choice.

I laugh to myself at this exchange, because it *is* weird that
McCabe, who always seemed to hate our GM, is now dating
her. And it's so recent that none of us have had time to get
used to the idea.

WALSH

Marissa and I have plans, so another time!

ZACH

Ashleigh and I might be able to come. Neon
Cactus? Or are we branching out?

DREW

Audrey wants margaritas, so you know
where you'll find us.

COLT

Jules says she's inviting Lauren and
Morgan too.

I'm trying to keep up with this conversation. I know that
Lauren is Jules and Audrey's future sister-in-law, because
she's engaged to their brother, Jameson. I've met Morgan,
too, because she's my agent's daughter, but I can't remember
what the relationship is between her and these other
women.

DREW

The more the merrier. Hartmann, are you
in???

LUKE

I'm a maybe. I have plans with Eva so I'll see if she's up for it.

ZACH

Be careful with the coach's daughter, Lover Boy.

LUKE

Lifelong friends, guys. I have a picture of us together in diapers to prove it.

WALSH

Marissa and I started out as friends. Just saying.

LUKE

In diapers?

COLT

Need I remind you I've also known Jules since she was just a kid?

DREW

It sounds so wrong when you say that, old man. You were already an adult when you met her!

ZACH

He has a point.

COLT

I'm just saying, the friendship line can be crossed quite easily by two consenting adults.

WALSH

Sure can. So be careful, Hartmann. The last thing you need right now is to piss off Coach. And messing with his only child would be . . . a bad choice.

LUKE

You all are the worst.

Luke Hartmann renamed the group Assholes.

———

"So, do you think we need to establish some ground rules or something?" Eva asks as we walk through the Public Garden on our way to the Neon Cactus. "About tonight?" I ask, bringing my hand to her lower back to steer her around some tourists who stop right in front of us to take pictures of the swan boats on the lagoon. The Public Garden is beautiful this time of year. Nothing beats the late spring when the tulips are all in full bloom, but summer in the Garden is beautiful, too. Tonight, it's breezy and warm, and the hanging branches of the weeping willows sway above us as we take the path up to the footbridge that spans the narrowest part of the lagoon.

"I guess. Like, are we just acting normal? Or are we trying to play this off like we're interested in each other so they'll start to suspect something and not be shocked when we announce we're married?"

I have a feeling, based on the earlier text exchange I had with my teammates, that they already suspect something's going on and will be looking for any clues. Given how hard it is for me to keep my hands off Eva whenever she's around, I don't think we need to pretend. Eva's so used to how affectionate I am with her that I don't think she notices. But my teammates will.

"I think that the last thing we want to do is have my

teammates raising alarm bells that could get in the way of our plans."

I still can't quite believe that I convinced Eva Wilcott to marry me. And honestly, I'm still not quite sure how I feel about this.

On the one hand, it allows me to make sure she's taken care of and eliminates some potential obstacles to her achieving her dreams. She would never have been able to afford the kind of nanny who can both live with her and travel when she competes after the baby is born. I'd do that for her if I could, but I know she'd never let me give up my career for hers. However, I can afford the healthcare and childcare she'll need.

I'd be lying, though, if I didn't say I'm nervous as hell about how I'll manage my emotions and my physical response to her once she officially moves in. The thought of having her in my space all the time, but not being able to *have* her the way I've always wanted her? It'll be torture.

Still, I don't regret the offer. It might be torture for me, but it'll save her. Plus, I'm positive we'll make a great team when it comes to raising this baby.

"Okaaay," she says, dragging out the word. I wait, knowing there's something else she wants to say. "You know what we didn't decide yesterday?"

I think back to our conversation in my condo before I took her home to Newbury Falls. "No, what?"

"Are we putting an end date on this marriage?"

I try not to react physically, even though it feels like she just slapped me. "I didn't think we were?"

Grabbing the hem of my button-down, she stops walking and pulls me to the side of the bridge. We're right at the top, where people often stop to take pictures or enjoy the view, and as she steps back to the railing of the bridge, I rest my hands on either side of her, boxing her in.

"Luke." My name quietly rolling off her lips has a shot of longing traveling up my spine. "I don't want you to be *stuck* with me, and with a kid who isn't yours, just because you're a nice guy."

Using the fingertips of my right hand to push her hair behind her ear, and balancing my weight on my left, I lean down so I can quietly say, "I think I already told you, there's no one else in the world I'd want to do this with. I'm *choosing* to be stuck with you."

I glance down and don't miss the way the goose bumps spread across her cleavage. *Good.* I want her to be somewhat affected, given what she does to me.

She doesn't move her head, doesn't turn to look at me, where I'm frozen with my face right next to her cheek. Her voice is hollow when she asks, "What if you change your mind?"

"I'm not going to change my mind. But if something happens and either of us wants out, I guess we'll cross that bridge when we get there."

She sighs. "We could always tell people that we realized we were better off as friends." Glancing over then, she gives me a small smile—the kind that turns her lips up slightly but doesn't crinkle the corners of her eyes like a happy smile would—as I pull back slightly.

Even while I know that I shouldn't get my hopes up and that agreeing to be *just friends* is the safest option, there's no world in which I believe that. I'm not marrying her because I expect this to turn into more. But if somehow it did, I'm pretty sure my life would be complete.

"We're going to have a baby together, Evie," I say as I cup my hand and run it along her belly, feeling the slightest bump beginning to emerge. "And we're going to do what's best for this kid."

"And what's that?" she asks, a slight shiver racking her body.

"We're going to create a loving home to raise this Baby Squash in. We'll figure it out as we go, just like all couples do when they're first married or first become parents."

She leans forward, resting her forehead on my chest. "You're sure about this?"

"I'm sure."

"You're too good to me. You know that, right?"

"There's no such thing as too good when it comes to you, Evie." I dip my face to kiss the top of her head, and when the sweet peach scent of her shampoo hits me, I realize I'm close to being noticeably turned on. "Let's go."

Taking her hand, I lead her across the rest of the bridge and over into Beacon Hill. The Neon Cactus is a bit of a dive bar, and I'm not quite sure why the Rebels started hanging out here this season, but I can tell it's not what Eva expected when I pull open the door and guide her in.

Her gaze flicks back and forth across the space as we pause to let our eyes adjust to the darkness inside, and she lets out a low "hmmmm."

Shellacked wooden walls are plastered with neon signs and trimmed with Christmas lights. The back area of the bar has multiple pool tables, and the front has booths lining most of the perimeter, with a large bar occupying the center of the space.

My teammates have pushed together a long row of tables along one edge of the room, and it's still early enough that the bar is otherwise fairly empty. Just a few couples are scattered around, and a rowdy group of twenty-somethings play pool in the back.

"What's the *hmmmm* for?" I ask.

"I should have pictured it like this from the name," she says, "but somehow, I imagined it to be a bit more swanky."

"Are you disappointed?"

She lets out a genuine laugh as I guide her toward the table of my teammates. "It's perfect."

Colt, Jules, Audrey, and Drew are sitting along one side of the table, so I pull out the seat for Evie that's opposite them.

She's going to love Jules—they have the same tough exterior that hides a soft heart. She and Audrey have somewhat similar personalities, and if Evie and I weren't getting married and telling people this baby is mine, I'm sure she and Audrey would bond about the whole single mom thing. Audrey raised her son, Graham, alone for five years before his dad, Drew, came back into the picture. I still don't know the whole story, because it all happened before I was traded to Boston.

As I introduce Eva to my teammates, I'm shocked at how totally normal Drew and Colt are acting. I don't know what I expected hanging out with them this first time after we lost —but it wasn't the same easy camaraderie we always have. As I suspected, Eva hits it off with Audrey and Jules. Sometimes it can take her a bit of time to warm up to new people, especially in unfamiliar settings, but the three of them are instantly chatting away.

Excusing myself, I head to the bar to get us some drinks, and it's not until I rest my elbow on the long wooden bar top that I realize Drew's followed me.

"Glad you came out," he says as he steps up beside me. "We all wanted to give you some space after the last game. You doing okay?"

I'm tempted to ask why they thought I'd need space. I'm such an extrovert, such a people person, that "space" is the *worst* thing you could give me. But they may not know me well enough to understand that yet.

Although, I probably still would have spent more time than normal at home, licking my wounds and trying to block out the sportscasters' comments about my performance.

I've been a player long enough to know that a team can go radio silent for the week or two after playoffs end, as everyone is trying to catch up on their personal lives. We all miss out on a lot during the season, and lots of guys live in the city they play for during the year and then move "home" for the off-season. Even while I know this, it would have been nice to hear from my teammates sometime in the last two weeks and to know that they weren't all pissed at me.

"I'm fine."

Drew turns his head to look at me and pauses a beat before he says, "You sure?"

"Yep."

I've got almost decades of Hartmann family training ingrained in me:

Don't show weakness.

Maintain the family name and reputation at any cost.
Don't talk about your problems with anyone outside your family.

I already fucked up the first two of those three "family rules" during the last game. I let my one and only weakness—Evangeline Wilcott—get in the way of my game, and I tarnished my family's name in the process.

So I'd need a lot more drinks than I'm planning to have tonight in order to break the third rule and open up about how I'm *really* feeling.

"You know, if you ever want to talk about it, I have a sports psychologist who is . . . perfect."

I arch an eyebrow. I didn't realize this was a *thing* among my teammates. "Yeah?"

"Zach recommended her earlier in the season, and meeting with her made a huge difference in my performance, as well as my ability to balance my personal life and hockey."

Oh, so it's the same person AJ suggested I talk to. I'm not sure it makes me any more eager to set up that initial meeting, but it *is* interesting . . . especially because Drew almost never gets into fights anymore, after having a reputation as a brawler back in Denver. I wonder if it's because he's talking to this sports psychologist?

I'm considering whether I want to ask him more questions when the bartender walks up. "What can I get you guys?"

We both order for ourselves, before I ask, "Do you have any non-alcoholic drinks?"

"Yeah," he says, grabbing a menu from below the bar and

passing it over. "There's a mocktail section on the back. I'll give you a minute to look while I grab those other drinks."

"Eva doesn't drink?" Drew asks.

"She has to skate tomorrow morning, and she never drinks if she's going to be skating."

He huffs a laugh while I scan the menu. "Imagine if hockey players didn't drink the night before a practice? We'd never go out."

True. Our season is long, and we typically practice or have games six days a week. "Good thing you're not a figure skater, then," I say.

Not that Drew parties that much. From what I can tell, neither his fiancée, Audrey, nor her sister, Jules, ever have more than a couple of drinks. I think it's some sort of a family thing, because on the occasions that their older brother Jameson is out with us, he always orders a scotch that he barely touches.

The bartender returns with our drinks, and I order Eva a virgin peach coconut margarita.

"You know her drink order?" Drew asks, side-eyeing me.

"Have you never had a best friend?" I ask and roll my eyes. Why wouldn't I know my best friend's favorite things?

"Uhhhhh . . ." Drew just trails off and looks away. "I guess not since I was a kid."

"I know Eva as well as I know myself," I tell him. *Maybe better, actually.*

I seem to have no problem delving into what makes her tick—every single thing she loves, the things she doesn't like, her fears and her dreams. Why is it so difficult for me to dig that deeply within myself?

"That's how I feel about Audrey," he says and lifts his eyebrow again. "You *sure* you two are just friends?"

I give him a pointed look. "The fact that you can't believe that I could be friends with a girl without trying to sleep with her says more about you than it does about me."

That's the type of thing I always say when the topic of my friendship with Eva comes up, but it's also not true. I'd move our friendship across that line in a heartbeat, if that's what she wanted.

Still, I *can* and *have* maintained a platonic relationship with her my whole life and plan on continuing that trend moving forward.

"I wasn't talking about trying to sleep with her," Drew says. "I was talking about finding that person who makes you feel *whole*."

I press my lips together and remember how—only a few weeks ago—he and Colt gave McCabe similar advice about what it was like to be in love, while I sat by and pretended I had no clue what it felt like.

Slipping my card out of my wallet, I hand it to the bartender, asking him to keep a tab open for our table. Then I turn to Drew, determined to deflect his comment about Eva making me whole. I *know* it's true, but he doesn't need to.

"See, that's the thing," I say with a shrug and a smirk. "I already *am* the whole package."

Chapter Fifteen

EVA

I'm chatting with Audrey, Jules, and their future sister-in-law, Lauren, who just showed up with their brother, Jameson, when I hear Drew and Luke laughing behind me. Then, Luke leans down and places a drink on the table in front of me. When I glance at him, questioning why he's giving me a margarita, he whispers, "Virgin coconut peach margarita," before pulling out his chair next to mine.

"What are you guys laughing about?" Audrey asks Drew.

"Just Hartmann's enormous ego."

Colt rolls his eyes and grins, making me wonder what's going through his mind. I don't think Luke is super close with any of the guys yet, but I could see those two developing a bond as they continue playing together next season.

If they keep playing together, I correct myself. Is it really likely that AJ would trade Luke? Is that even what Frank wants? Hard to know for sure based on what Luke overheard, but at the same time, knowing that his dad didn't want him to play for the Rebels in the first place must be eating away at him.

The Hartmanns are a tight-knit family with a close bond that Luke's parents carefully cultivated his entire life. Even as everyone jokes about his brothers being assholes, the four of them are always there for each other. You cross one, and you're going to battle with all of them. What would his brothers think if they knew their dad's opinion on Luke playing for the team? Will our getting married and giving them a grandkid actually help smooth things over?

I still haven't fully come to terms with how I feel about Luke offering to say that he's the father of this baby. It's one thing to marry me to make sure I have healthcare and am taken care of. That's right in line with Luke's protective nature—the way he always wants to help everyone. But claiming this baby is his? I get why it's easier that way, but I worry about how our parents, or anyone else, would feel if they found out the truth.

"I always think that people with a huge ego are overcompensating for something," Jules says, lifting an eyebrow at Colt. The whole table erupts in a chorus of "Ooooooo," and she laughs and shakes her head. "No," she says, unable to contain her laughter. "Like, maybe the person is more sensitive or sweeter than they want to let on."

I'm so tempted to jump in and say that no one is sweeter than Luke. But I don't know these people yet. I don't know what he would like them to think or know about him. So I let him defend himself.

"I'm plenty sweet when I want to be," he says, leaning back and casually draping his arm across the back of my chair. I don't miss each pair of eyes following his arm. Does he notice?

Shit. I thought we were *not* trying to make them speculate. "C'mon, Evie," he chides, "tell them how sweet I can be."

"Pfft." I blow out the air between my lips and roll my eyes. "When we were seven, he superglued the ends of my braids together behind my back, because he was mad that I won rock, paper, scissors, and we got to watch the TV show I chose."

"Oh, come on!" he says with an exaggerated sigh. "That was almost twenty years ago!"

"You guys have known each other that long?" Audrey asks.

"Yeah," I say. "We've literally been best friends since we were in diapers."

"Oooooh," Audrey says with a small laugh. "Okay. I thought you two were together."

I don't miss the way Drew and Colt eye each other, then look back at us when Lauren adds, "So did I."

I glance at Luke, waiting for him to clear things up, but he just shakes his head, smiling.

"Happens all the time," I tell them. "We're just friends."

"Exactly," Luke adds, right as Jameson glances at Lauren and says, "I remember when we were *just friends.*"

"Just because you were obsessed with me," Lauren says as she digs her elbow into her fiancé's side, "doesn't mean that's what's going on with them."

He presses a kiss on her forehead, then tilts her chin up so he's gazing at her. None of us miss the heat in his eyes when he says, "I'm still obsessed with you."

"All right, you two," Jules says. "We get it, you don't need to eye-fuck each other in public."

"Jules!" Audrey says and glances at me. "Pardon my sister. She sometimes lacks a filter."

"I think it's sweet," I say with a shrug, wondering if anyone will ever feel the same way about me that Jameson so clearly feels about Lauren. "How did you two meet?"

Lauren launches into the story of their ill-fated years working together and a near miss with a relationship between the two of them. Instead, he introduced her to her late husband, and then they reunited after her husband died. While she talks, the rest of the table is chatting away, because they were all there as it unfolded. But Luke and I are hanging on her every word, and I can imagine there's so much more to their story—it sounds just like the romance novels I love to read when I travel—and I want to dig deeper and learn more.

Before I can ask any more questions, though, Luke says, "Wait, so you both worked at Kaplan?"

"Yeah," Jameson says. "I started there as an agent after I retired from the Rebels so I could stay home with Jules and Audrey. Lauren was there for a few years before she moved out to Park City, and then I stuck around until I started my own agency a few years ago."

"Huh. Carson's my agent."

"Sorry about that," Jameson says, but his voice is hard and lacks any actual sympathy.

Lauren elbows him. "Hey, he's still my uncle."

"Wait," Luke says with a laugh as he glances around the table. "This is all starting to feel very incestuous."

Lauren lifts one of her auburn eyebrows, her big blue eyes widening. "How so?"

"Just how you're all related. So you're Carson's niece and Jameson used to work for him." He fixes his gaze on Jameson. "Jules and Audrey are your siblings, and Jules is engaged to your best friend." He nods toward Colt. "And Audrey is engaged to one of your players." He nods toward Drew.

"That's not incest," Jameson growls. "That's just family."

"Why are we talking about incest?" The voice comes from a girl with strawberry-blonde hair and a light smattering of freckles across her nose and cheeks as she drops into the chair beside me.

"We're not." God, Jameson is so fucking growly. I wonder if he's like that with Lauren in private, too? It's kind of hot, actually.

Beside him, Lauren laughs. "Hartmann's just figuring out how we're all related."

"Oh," she laughs. "Hi, I'm Morgan. I'm Lauren's cousin." She reaches out to shake my hand and nods at Luke. Presumably, they've met before.

"She's also Carson's daughter," Jameson adds.

"Hi, I'm Eva Wilcott."

Morgan points to each of us in turn. "Coach's daughter . . . team owner's son. Got it. And you two are . . .?"

Luke and I look at each other and laugh, because clearly, she's trying to figure out if we're together. "Best friends," he says decisively.

Morgan presses her lips together with another nod. I get the feeling she's trying to hold something in . . . a laugh or a smirk, maybe?

Well, at least his teammates and their significant others

will have no trouble believing our backstory if we do go through with this marriage. It's a good thing they don't know that Luke's this affectionate and attentive with everyone.

That arm he has draped across the back of my chair? The way he looks over at me with an adoring smile? The way he leans in when he speaks to me? Even if I was a complete stranger, nothing about his behavior would be different—everyone is an instant friend to Luke Hartmann. Not that he lets many people get *super* close, but he's naturally charming and easygoing.

"So, do you live in Boston, Eva?" Morgan asks.

"I'm from Newbury Falls originally, that's how I know Luke—we grew up together. But I've lived in LA for the past eight years."

"Oh? I love LA. What do you do there?"

"Uh . . ." I don't know why it's hard for me to answer this question. On the one hand, I'm pretty used to people already knowing who I am when we meet, and I kind of like this rare anonymity. On the other hand, my level of performance for the second half of this season hasn't been what I wanted it to be, so I'm reluctant to explain on the off chance that she'll look me up.

"She's a pairs figure skater," Luke fills in as he glances over at me like he can't figure out why I just trailed off like that. "One of the best in the world, actually."

"Oh my god!" Lauren's whole face changes to one of complete shock. "Holy crap, how did I not put that together? Evangeline Wilcott? I freaking love how you skate! I've known your dad for over a year, and I never made the connection!"

"Oh," I say, drawing back. "You're a skating fan?"

"I watch my fair share of skating, yeah."

Jameson clears his throat and glances at Morgan, who has her eyebrows raised, staring at Lauren like she's waiting for her to say more.

"And?" Morgan prompts.

"And nothing," Lauren says with a laugh as she shakes her head. "I'm just a fan."

"I feel like there's a lot more to the story than that," I can't help but say.

Her cheeks turn pink, and she flinches as Morgan kicks her under the table. "Okay, fine, I used to skate."

I smile. "Oh yeah? Competitively?"

"Yeah. I was a singles skater, though. Honestly, I like watching pairs skating better. The emotion and artistry when there are two people so in sync just adds a whole other level to the performance."

"How long did you compete for?" I ask, trying to figure out why Jameson and Morgan are still staring at her expectantly.

"Uh . . . like . . . about ten years or so."

"Jesus," Jameson says, his voice low and gravelly. "Stop being like this."

"Hey!" she says, turning toward him and swatting his chest. "Maybe I don't want to talk about it."

"I'm sorry," I say, leaning back and feeling bad for asking so many questions. When I meet new people, it feels like things often go sideways. If I'm not friendly and talkative and don't ask questions, everyone thinks I'm some sort of ice queen. But when I do, I always seem to overdo it somehow. "I didn't mean to pry."

Luke's arm curls around my back, and he gives my

shoulder a supportive squeeze. Then Lauren glances at me, and her face softens into a sympathetic smile. "You didn't pry. You asked the questions anyone would ask when my fiancé and cousin are sitting here acting so weird."

Morgan turns toward me, also clearly feeling bad about this. "Lauren was a nationally ranked singles skater. She was expected to take first place in nationals—"

I gasp so loud the entire table turns to look at me. "No wayyyyyy." My lips are parted in shock, and I can't seem to make my mouth move, but then Luke squeezes my shoulder again. "I . . . Oh my god, I know exactly who you are. I can't believe I didn't realize it the minute you said you skated. You were, like, my idol when I was a kid."

Lauren laughs lightly. "Now I feel old."

"Oh my god, no. You're maybe, what, six years older than me? But when I was a kid, I was at some of the same competitions as you, and I used to love to watch the older girls compete. You were my favorite . . ." I shake my head, remembering how Lauren Manning's skating was the perfect combination of beauty and athleticism. Part of the reason I worked so hard was because I wanted to be her someday. I just didn't have the same strength. "Your jumps were so beautiful. I'm so sorry about how your skating career ended."

The fall she had at nationals completely knocked her out. I was watching it on TV, and it was scary as hell. She never returned to competitive skating after that.

"Eh." Lauren shrugs. "It sucked at the time, but I'm very over it."

"Do you still skate at all? Like for fun?" I ask, completely star-struck at meeting one of my childhood idols in person, and discovering that she's just as sweet and down to earth as she seemed back then.

"No," is all she says, and I can tell by the way she glances sideways at Jameson that there's still more to the story. But now, I have the good sense not to pry further. I don't know her, and I'm not entitled to the details of her past unless she feels comfortable sharing, which she clearly doesn't.

"Well," I say, leaning forward and resting my elbows on the table as I fold my arms in front of me. "It's so great to meet you in person. Really . . . ten-year-old me would be absolutely dying right now if she knew I would meet Lauren Manning someday."

I try to remember if I still have the hat I had her sign for me at a competition so long ago. I bet it's in the chest at the end of my bed at my parents' house. I'll have to look tomorrow when I get home.

She shakes her head. "It's a bit surreal for me, too. It's been a long time since anyone knew who I was because of skating."

"Well, if you ever want to skate together, you just let me know. That would be fun."

The look on her face tells me she thinks it would be anything *but* fun. "Maybe sometime."

"So, what do you do now?" I ask, hoping to steer the conversation to topics she's more comfortable with.

"I'm the director of marketing for the Rebels," she says, then tells me a little about how she got into marketing in the first place.

I take a sip of the drink I'd forgotten Luke set in front of me and marvel at how delicious it is. Why didn't I know before now that there are drinks this good without alcohol?

As all the chatter starts back up around the table, I lean my head back against Luke's arm to look up at him. "This is the best thing I've ever tasted."

"Sounded like something you'd like. Peach, and all that." He swipes his tongue across his lower lip, and I force myself not to wonder what it would feel like to kiss him.

Goddamn these pregnancy hormones. I long ago accepted that our friendship was only ever going to be that. Now, my body is drawn to him every time he's near. I need to get this under control if I'm going to live with him, or it's going to become *really* uncomfortable for both of us.

His eyes are focused on my lips when he says, "Can I taste?" and it takes me a second to realize he's talking about the drink in my hand. Man, I wish he wanted to taste it on my lips.

No. No, you don't! my brain screams at me.

I raise the glass toward him, and he glances down, bringing it slowly to his mouth. I force myself to look away, because I'm way more turned on than I have any reason to be. Even though Morgan looks away before my eyes can meet hers, I don't miss the way she was watching us closely.

"That *is* good," Luke says.

"I may need to come here daily for one of these," I joke as I take the glass back and lift my head to take another sip, hoping to distract myself. It's then that I notice how cozy we are, me leaning against him, him with his arm wrapped around me.

I sit forward in my seat, setting my glass back on the table and turning to chat with Morgan. Anything to forget about how unsettled I'm feeling about marrying this man who's only a friend, but who I wish could be so much more.

Chapter Sixteen

EVA

"That's the craziest, most asinine idea I've ever heard, Eva," Christopher says. Doubt and judgement twist his face on my phone screen, where it's propped against the mirror of the vanity in my childhood bedroom. "You *can't* be serious?"

I waited a few days after Luke first proposed the idea to tell Christopher because I wanted to be *sure.* If either Luke or I had any doubts or changed our minds, I didn't want anyone else to know about the plan in the first place.

We agreed that Christopher was the *only* person we'd tell about the arrangement because he already knew the circumstances of my pregnancy, and I didn't want to lie to him. It had taken some work to get Luke on board with the plan. I wish I understood why he hates Christopher so much.

"There are *way* worse outcomes to this situation than a marriage of convenience with my best friend. We love each other," I say, and when Christopher's eyebrows shoot up toward his hairline, I clarify, "as friends. We always have. And since we'll never be more than just friends, it's the perfect solution. Neither one of us will fall for the other, so we don't have to worry about this arrangement getting complicated."

I have a decade of experience hiding my true feelings for Luke, so this will just be more of the same. As long as I can keep these pregnancy hormones under control, I can do this —especially if it helps him stay on the Rebels and return to his father's good graces.

"And what about when one of you has . . . needs . . . that you want to satisfy outside the relationship? You know Luke's reputation."

I sigh and grab my curling iron off the countertop, hoping that if I focus on doing my hair, I'll be better able to hide my true feelings on the matter. Christopher doesn't need to know how much it hurts every time I see pictures of Luke with a new girl. At least he never lets things progress to relationship status. "I do, and that's something we still need to work out."

Christopher just shakes his head. When we first started skating together, I think he was almost jealous of my friendship with Luke. He always insisted that Luke must have feelings for me. *No guy puts as much effort into a girl as Luke puts into you, unless he has feelings for her,* Christopher once told me.

I've always insisted that guys and girls can be friends, as long as no one's feelings develop beyond that—something I've apparently failed to do with *both* of my best guy friends.

Or, maybe convincing myself I had feelings for Christopher was just a diversion, a way to pretend that I didn't *still* have feelings for Luke, a decade after he showed me that he wasn't interested in anything more than friendship.

"So if you plan to stay in Boston, what does that mean for us?"

"Okay, hear me out. There's this coach . . . " I tell him about a veteran coach who trained a Boston-based Olympian, Catarina Mosche, who retired after the last Games. Coincidentally, she had also trained Lauren, and her name had come up late into our visit at the Neon Cactus two nights ago. "She's currently taking on new skaters."

"Catarina was a singles skater, Eva," he reminds me. "What experience does she have training pairs?"

"So, I actually met her for coffee yesterday," I tell him, and watch his eyebrows raise again.

Christopher is extremely emotive, and his face has limitless expressions. It's something that's made him an excellent performer. If I'd only understood that the emotion he displays does not always correspond to how he actually feels, I could have saved myself a lot of heartache.

"She's trained pairs before," I tell him. "Never at the Olympic level, but she has plenty of experience with Olympic skating. Come out to Boston. Meet her. Let's figure out how this can work. *Please.*"

Christopher closes his eyes briefly, nodding before opening them again. "So . . . what? I'd move and we'd train there?"

"Just until the Olympics. Just eight months," I remind him, hoping he considers the fact that we've spent our entire adulthoods together, side-by-side, whatever the world threw at us—as a team.

"And you're still planning to retire after that?"

I don't know if it's the fear of the unknown that makes him unable to process this, but I first broached this idea before I even found out I was pregnant. Now that I am, how could I continue to train and compete with a baby? It will be hard enough to do for the short time leading up to the Olympics, but continuing at that pace afterward? It seems impossible.

It would be one thing if I had a husband or partner who could be home and could also travel to competitions with me and the baby. But that's not what I have, nor is it something I could ever ask of Luke.

He travels more during the season than I do in an entire year. And then the playoffs are totally unpredictable and have the potential to extend a season by a month or more. His suggestion of a nanny who could travel with me when needed is definitely the best solution.

But for the long term? I don't want my child raised by a nanny while his or her parents are gone all the time.

"This is my last shot at an Olympic medal. After that, I only get one shot at being a good mom—to be present and loving and supportive. I don't want to mess that up."

A *lot* happened between us this winter. I admitted that I was developing feelings for him while we were at a competition in Italy. He said we were better off as friends and skating partners. I ran out and got drunk to cope with the rejection and realization that he was right. I ended up pregnant as a result and needed him to overcompensate to make up for my inability to skate at the same level as I had before the pregnancy.

But despite *all* of that, he's always stood by my side. He's been my confidant and my closest friend, aside from Luke, for years.

"You're going to be a great mom, Eva. I just hate to see you give up your career. Plenty of people keep skating after they have a child." He's right, but their circumstances haven't been the same as mine. "I get why it would be harder, but that doesn't make it impossible."

How do I tell him that as great as our years of skating together have been, *I'm tired*? I'm tired of pushing myself so hard all the time, of the constant need to be perfect, of the strict exercise and eating regimen, of the travel and the competitions.

I've been skating my entire life, and I'm a little afraid I don't know who I am without that. I need to figure that out, because one thing I know for sure is that tying your entire identity to your sport, like my mom did with riding and horses, isn't going to help me be a good mom.

I want to be a good mom, and yet here I am, not even sure I know how to be good to myself.

Instead of saying all of that, I tell him, "No, it may not be impossible. But it's also not what I want. We'll close out our last season together with an Olympic appearance, and hopefully an Olympic medal, and then I'll help you choose a new partner if you want me to. But my days of competing are coming to an end."

When our season ended a few weeks ago, I still wasn't completely certain about retiring. But something changed in the OB's office last week. Until then, the pregnancy had been something I was aware of but hadn't fully accepted, probably because I had so few symptoms initially. Seeing the baby on the ultrasound changed that . . . as did the conversation with Luke afterward.

"So how do you see this working?" Christopher asks. "You want me to move out there so we can train together until you have the baby? And then what? I'll stay there through the Olympics?"

I nod as I twist another strand of hair around my curling iron. "The Hartmanns have a lot of properties in Boston. Luke said he can easily find one you can stay in while we finish out our last season together."

Christopher scoffs. "What's he getting out of all of this? I understand why this marriage benefits you, but aside from finally locking you down, how does it benefit him?"

"Besides taking the spotlight off how he lost Game 7 for his team, there's some family stuff going on too." I'm intentionally vague as I glance away to focus on the mirror and make sure I don't burn myself with the curling iron. "And this . . . would be good."

"So you're not going to tell me?" He lets out a dry laugh.

"I shared all my reasons, but that doesn't mean you're entitled to his. You already know more than anyone else ever will."

"You really think everyone's going to believe this? After half the internet has been shipping us for the past two seasons?"

"You and me? We're great performers," I say, throwing his exact words back at him, with a wink to hide the hurt I still feel from his insistence that all he had ever given fans was a performance.

Emotions always run high going into, and especially finishing, a competition routine. We always held hands stepping onto the ice and pressed our foreheads together as he whispered, "Let's kill it, Eva," before a routine. Then, after we finished, he always wrapped me up in an embrace and spun me around the ice, planting kisses on my forehead when we got our score. It was equal parts close friendship and performing for the fans. It was nothing more, even if I'd convinced myself otherwise for a few months this past winter.

"Fans will believe us when we assure them I've been with Luke all along, and you and I have been nothing but skating partners."

"All along, huh?" he asks with a quirked eyebrow. "Is that the story?"

"I think so," I say. "Luke's on his way over, and we're going to finalize the details tonight. We leave for Vegas on Friday. Is there any way you can squeeze in a quick trip to Boston so we can meet with our potential new coach before I go?"

"You mean sometime in the next *three days*?"

"I know. I'm sorry I didn't give you more notice. But she's free any time Wednesday or Thursday."

"You're lucky I love you," he says. It's something he says all the time, and I know he means he loves me in the same way Luke does—like a sibling. But as my door cracks open and Luke pops his head in, I'm still incredibly grateful for my AirPods, because I know that Luke wouldn't have taken his comment that way.

Luke still blames Christopher for my decisions that night . . . It's best if he *never* hears him say those words.

"Hey." Luke's deep voice cuts through my noise-canceling AirPods, and I don't miss the way Christopher's eyes track his movement as he bends to kiss the top of my head. "You ready?"

I take out one of my earbuds and glance up at him, nodding my chin toward my phone sitting on the vanity. "Say hi to Christopher," I say, with a *be nice* tone that you'd use with a petulant child.

"Well, if it isn't Christopher Fucking Steele," he mutters, quietly enough that I'm pretty sure he isn't heard on the other end. If he does hear him, Christopher does a remarkable job of not reacting. Luke snatches the AirPod out of my hand and sticks it in his ear. "Hey, man, sorry, I have to steal Eva away. We have plans."

"Hey!" I say when Luke reaches forward and taps the screen to disconnect the call. "What the hell?"

"I'll play nice with him when he's around, because he's your partner. But let's make sure he knows where he stands —because being your skating partner means next to nothing when you're about to be *my wife*."

My stomach shouldn't flip over when he calls me his wife. A shiver shouldn't streak down my spine as the thrill rushes through me.

He isn't jealous; he just doesn't like my skating partner— and I'd do well to remember that. There's no way I'm letting myself get caught up in the what-ifs with him like I did with Christopher. Especially because my friendship with Luke means more to me than any other relationship I've ever had in my life.

There's no way I'm risking that.

I roll my eyes, and then turn back to the mirror to curl my last piece of hair.

"You ready?" he asks.

I lock eyes with him in the mirror. "Do I look ready?" I have a big pink Velcro roller sitting at the top of my forehead and am holding a curling iron above me as I curl a lock of hair. I'm in a tank top and my pink striped pajama shorts.

"You always look great, Evie. You don't have to do all"—he waves his hand in a circle near my face—"this."

I want to tell him to stop saying things like that, but I don't want him to know how much his compliments affect me. He's a pro-level flirt and knows what to say to women to make them swoon. I'm sure he doesn't even mean it.

"I'll be ready in, like, five minutes. How'd you even get in?"

"Your dad let me in," he says.

"I didn't think my parents were back yet," I say, suddenly worried that my half of the conversation could have been overheard. My parents went to the farmers' market down near the harbor, and I didn't hear them return.

"I'm not sure if your mom is home, but your dad definitely is. He's got the baseball game on and asked if I wanted to grab a beer and watch it with him."

"I hope you let him down gently?" I say, feeling bad that Dad's just hanging out watching the game by himself, while Luke and I are about to head out to dinner. But we have important details to work out if this is all going to happen as planned.

I spent more time with my parents over this past week, knowing we're about to drop a major bomb on both our families this weekend. However they feel about the bomb, it *will* mean that I'm staying in Boston permanently. After nearly a decade of living on the opposite coast, I hope they'll be happy about that. Especially when this baby arrives. We'll have plenty of family time together for the first time in my adult life.

"I did," Luke says.

"All right, do you mind maybe watching the game with him for a few minutes while I get dressed?" I ask, hoping that the maxi dress I bought two weeks ago still fits okay.

Luke's chest shakes with silent laughter at my request that he leave while I change. "What do you think it'll be like when you move in with me? I don't always walk around fully clothed. Are you going to be weird if I'm hanging out in just my boxers?"

"Yes!" I practically screech, and then I throw in an "Ewww," so that he thinks I'm grossed out by the idea.

I haven't let myself think too much about the day-to-day experience of living with him. The thought of walking into the kitchen in the morning and finding him in his boxers, pouring a cup of coffee is . . . *not something you can think about right now*, my brain screams at me. But goddamn, now that the mental image is there, it's hard to get out of my head.

"Okay," Luke says with a dramatic sigh as he heads toward the door. "I'll try to stay fully clothed at all times so I don't gross you out."

I can tell he's teasing. He *knows* how good he looks, clothed or unclothed. But I'll keep pretending that I don't see the appeal. Maybe eventually, I'll even convince myself it's true.

Chapter Seventeen

LUKE

"There's something Christopher said to me a few days ago, and now I can't get it out of my head," Eva says, looking over at me from her lounge chair next to the hotel pool in Las Vegas.

"Oh yeah?" I ask casually, keeping my eyes focused on the pool as my shoulders stiffen. "What's that?"

If he said something that hurt her, I'm going to smash his fucking face. Seeing him a few days ago when he was in Boston was harder than I expected. The fact that she had feelings for him, even though nothing happened as a result, makes it impossible for me not to hate him.

How could someone be so stupid as to be offered Eva Wilcott's heart and not want it? Meanwhile, I'd give anything for her to feel more than friendship toward me.

She rolls onto her hip so she's facing me, and I turn to look at her. *Fuuuck.*

Even with her bikini on, you still can't really tell she's

pregnant. The high waist of her briefs covers any emerging bump, but the way she's practically spilling out of the top is proof that her body really is changing. The crease of cleavage between her breasts has my mind racing with possibility. I glance back up at her to find her eyebrows raised.

"Did you just check out my boobs?" she asks with an incredulous laugh.

Shit, I thought my sunglasses would hide that.

"I'm *sorry*, but are they growing exponentially? I think pretty soon they're going to need their own zip code." Hopefully if I joke around with her about it, she won't notice the bulge growing in my swim trunks. I may need to cover myself with a towel.

"Men," she mutters and shakes her head before sitting up and swinging her legs over the edge of the chair so she's facing me. She slips her arms into her coverup and pulls it closed in front of her as she says, "I need to head back up to my room, or I won't have time to get ready for the awards ceremony."

"I'll walk you up," I say, throwing on my T-shirt. I swipe my hat off the table and put it on backward to hold my sweaty hair out of my face. I'm pretty sure it's the same temperature here in Las Vegas as it is on the face of the sun. And all the people who walk around saying, "But it's a dry heat, so it doesn't feel as hot!" are out of their minds.

Once we're back inside the magnificently air-conditioned hotel and heading toward the elevators, I ask, "So what did Christopher say that you can't get out of your head?"

Eva glances around as a few people walk by. "I'll tell you when we're somewhere more private."

The first elevator that arrives is empty, so once the door

closes behind her and we've each tapped our key card to select our floors, I ask again. "So?"

"You know what." She gives her head a little shake with a roll of her eyes, and I can't miss how pink her cheeks are. I'm trying to figure out if it's because she's hot or embarrassed, but the way the skin along her arms and across her chest prickles with goose bumps makes me think it's the latter. "Never mind."

"Evie, you can tell me anything. You know that, right?"

"It's nothing." She rolls her eyes again and looks away. It's such a classic defense mechanism for her when she doesn't want to talk about something.

I step closer and she takes a slight step back until she's up against the wall of the elevator. "Evie," I say like it's a warning. "We don't keep secrets from each other. Especially not now."

She leans her head back against the mirrored wall as she looks up at me, and it presses her dark hair forward around her face and shoulders. "Fine." Her chest heaves with a deep breath, but I force myself not to take my gaze off her face. "He asked what we're going to do when one of us has *needs*. You know, since this marriage isn't going to be *like that*."

Why didn't she bring this up days ago when we worked through our agreement? I lift my hand and place it above her head, leaning in just a tad more. Since we've been planning this, I've never let myself hope that things would turn physical between us. "Seems simple enough. You have needs, you come to me."

Her lips part as she sucks in a breath. "And if *you* have needs?"

"I'll be fine." Celibacy sucks, but there's no way in hell I'd ever make a fool of her by sleeping with someone else while we're married.

She lets out a choked laugh. "Yeah, except I know your reputation. And I don't want to be blindsided by news that my *husband* is cheating."

"I would never go outside this marriage for *anything*. And I don't expect you to, either. So again, if you have needs, you come to me. It's that simple."

"But Luke," she says, and her short, shallow breaths make it seem like she's fucking panting. It's the first time in a very long time that I've wondered if she is—or could ever be—attracted to me. "That could ruin our friendship."

"Cheating is a hard no for me. So if you think you'd be happier with someone else, let's not do this." Behind me, the elevator dings to signal its arrival at my floor. "You've still got a few hours to think about it. The choice is yours."

With that, I push off the wall behind her, turn, and leave her standing there with her mouth agape. I don't, however, miss the way she whispers, "Holy shit," before the elevator doors close.

———

As I walk into the hotel event space where the NHL awards ceremony is being held, I'm not sure if I should be worried that I haven't heard from Eva since leaving her in the elevator hours ago.

I'm trying to take the "no news is good news" approach, but there's a very real possibility that she might show up to this event tonight and tell me she's changed her mind. Instead of sneaking off afterward to get married in the chapel I booked, then hopping on a flight to LA, we'd . . . what? Just head back to our separate hotel rooms and forget the whole thing?

Given how much time and care we put into planning all this out over the last couple of weeks, I never imagined myself returning to my condo in Boston by myself after this weekend. Now I realize how fucking lonely that would feel. I've gotten used to having Eva around, even though it's only been an occasional day or night here and there since she first came back to Boston three weeks ago.

I never seriously considered the possibility of her backing out of this arrangement at the last minute. What would that even mean for our friendship?

I glance around the room, looking for my teammates. Only McCabe and Colt are here. McCabe, because AJ is receiving her GM of the Year award, and Colt, because he's receiving the Goaltender of the Year award. I don't see Colt anywhere yet, but McCabe is standing in line at the bar, so I head in that direction.

"Remind me why you're here," McCabe's grumpy ass says as I come up next to him right after he orders. But the way he calls out to the bartender, "Make it two beers!" lets me know he's giving me shit rather than asking a legitimate question.

Anyone can attend the awards ceremony, and there are plenty of fans here in addition to players, coaches, team management, and the media.

"Perks of my family owning the team," I say with a shrug. Then I drop my voice, and say, "Listen, I'm sorry about how the last game went. It wasn't my best effort—"

"You need to stop fucking apologizing," he practically growls.

I did plenty of apologizing in the locker room immediately after the game, and my teammates and coaches all said the same thing . . . games are won and lost by teams, not by individuals. And while I *know* this to be true, I also know that a huge proportion of the blame rests solidly on my shoulders.

"Shit happens," he continues, his voice still low. "Shit games happen. All you can do is learn from them and move on. You keep living in the past like this and it's going to fuck with your game."

My laugh is practically a snort. "Could my game possibly be any more fucked? And how exactly is this in the past, when every time I turn around another sports pundit is analyzing that third period, and debating how I could possibly have sucked so bad?"

I've seen countless replays of me missing a shot in that third period. You'd think by now they'd have moved on to some other big sports story, but apparently my performance and that loss still warrant attention, even weeks later.

"You did suck," McCabe says, and I appreciate his brutal honesty. I don't want my teammates to feel like they need to sugarcoat things to spare my feelings, or—what I'm even more worried about—because my family owns the team. "But it was half a period, in one game. It doesn't mean you suck as a goalie—"

"Right, just Game 7 of the Stanley Cup Finals, no big deal."

"Listen, there's no two ways about it—it was a big deal. But you're still early in your career. You're still learning and growing as a player. Don't let it fuck with your head. Learn from it. Whatever had you so distracted, cut that shit right out of your life," he says, and I try not to flinch, knowing that I'm doing the absolute opposite. I'm not cutting Eva out of my life, I'm marrying her . . . if she's still up for it. "Or learn how to keep that shit off the ice. Everyone has bad games. I had two of them in the playoffs, and both were because I was too focused on AJ and Abby. I had to learn how to compartmentalize when I was on the ice."

Normally, I can do that. But there was something different about the utter panic I felt that night—that something could be wrong with Eva or the baby, or that Helene would discover Eva's secret before she was ready to tell her mom. I probably *should* talk to someone about that and figure out how to prevent it from happening again.

I glance over McCabe's shoulder before I respond, and that's when I see Eva walking in with her parents. I hadn't asked her, but I'd expected her to wear white tonight for our wedding. Should I be worried that she's in a dark green dress, with her hair in a high, slicked back ponytail? She looks gorgeous and sultry, which is not how I'd pictured her wanting to look on her wedding day. Is this her way of telling me the wedding's off?

"Dude. Wipe that look off your face. If Coach catches you looking at his daughter that way . . ."

My head snaps toward McCabe to find that he's followed my gaze. "I wasn't looking at her in *any* way."

"Uh-huh." He takes a sip of his beer as his eyes narrow. His face changes, like he's come to a certain realization. "You have feelings for this girl?"

My head rears back. "What? No. She's my best friend."

"You keep saying that, but Renaud's my best friend," he says, referring to one of our teammates I've never met because he's been on the IR with a broken hand all season, "and I sure as shit don't look at him the way you're looking at her. Was she the reason you were so distracted in Game 7? The fact that she was sick?"

I try not to let my surprise at how accurately he's assessed the situation register on my face. "How'd you know she was sick?"

"How do you think?"

Mentally, I put myself back in that hallway when I heard the news, realizing that the only other person in a position to hear Coach was AJ.

"I keep forgetting you're with AJ. That's still so . . . weird. How you hated her so much, until . . ."

"Until I didn't." His words are clipped, indicating the end of that discussion.

"You're staring at her again," he warns, turning his head to follow my gaze. AJ is now standing near the Wilcotts, chatting with them. "Let's go."

"Where?" I ask, even though I can tell by the tone of his voice that he can't wait to get over there to AJ.

"I'd like to meet your best friend, Lover Boy." His voice is pure sarcasm, like he's already concluded that she's more to me than a best friend.

"Dude, do not call me that in front of her or I'll never live it down."

"She doesn't know your reputation?" he asks as we make our way toward the entrance of the huge auditorium where they stand.

"She does," I groan. "But just because women flock to me doesn't mean I'm doing anything to earn that reputation."

"Huh." His single-word response is pensive, and I wonder if I've revealed too much.

When we reach the Wilcotts, McCabe slides his arm around AJ's waist and kisses the top of her head.

"Still not quite used to this," Coach says with an awkward laugh.

"You'll get there," AJ and McCabe say at the same time.

It makes me wonder if he's going to feel the same way about Eva and me if we get married. Will it be awkward for our parents? Is it wishful thinking that they might be totally thrilled for us?

Too afraid of what I might see on her face or what my expression might reveal, I've avoided meeting Eva's gaze. When I finally do, she gives me a small, reassuring smile that has some of the tightness in my chest loosening.

We chat for a minute, and then Charlie and Helene are off to talk to someone else, and it's just the four of us left standing there.

"I'm so sorry to hear you were sick a few weeks ago," AJ tells Eva. "You feeling better now?"

"Yeah, I was just exhausted and dehydrated," she says. "The end of competition season really did me in." She gives me a quick sideways glance, and I can tell she's not sure what to say or do next. Like most people when they first meet AJ, I think Eva's a bit intimidated.

"She's doing fine now," I say, bringing my hand to her lower back. "But—"

I'm interrupted by the announcement asking us to take our seats, and we part ways with AJ and McCabe who are sitting near the stage, while we head to the theater-style box seats that line the perimeter, facing the stage.

As we walk, my pinky brushes Eva's hand and relief floods through me. Not touching her is physically painful. She glances at me then, and her look is almost shy—nothing like the brazen girl I've known my whole life. It seems like this pregnancy has undermined her self-confidence, which makes sense, I suppose, since it's uncharted territory . . . much like this marriage I've proposed.

"So, are we doing this tonight?" I ask, leading her toward the box I can already see our parents occupying.

She gives me a decisive nod.

"You and me, Evie," I say, letting my pinky brush against her wrist again as we walk. "Let's do this."

Chapter Eighteen

EVA

"It's like you found the least-cheesy wedding chapel in Vegas," I say softly, glancing around the beautiful room. It's draped in white satin, which fans out from the ceiling to the tops of the walls and then hangs down to the floor. In the center of the peaked ceiling is a gorgeous gold and crystal chandelier. At the front of the room is a small wooden platform with a wall of beautiful white and pink flowers behind it. It feels like we're in a posh wedding tent.

"I didn't think you'd want a cheesy Vegas wedding with an Elvis impersonator," Luke says from beside me, his knuckles brushing against the back of my hand where it hangs beside my body. Electricity zips through me at his touch, but I tell myself it's just nerves.

"Are you sure about this?" I ask, and when he looks down at me, slightly alarmed, I rush on. "It's just that claiming my baby as yours and lying to our parents . . . it's *a lot*. Are you positive you want to take that on? You don't have to. Being my best friend is one thing, but raising a kid together—that's way more than anything you signed up for as my friend."

"Pretty sure it's *exactly* what I signed up for when I suggested this," he says, turning toward me and pulling me closer with a hand that lands on my hip. "There's no world in which I'm not taking care of you in whatever way I can."

"Luke." His name is a whisper when it falls from my lips. This is so far above and beyond best friend responsibilities. But it's also right in line with his tendency to take care of everyone. Someday, we're going to delve into where that need comes from. "Maybe . . . I feel like maybe I'm asking too much of you in this arrangement."

"You didn't ask. I offered." He rests his other hand behind my neck, and everything about this moment feels like it would be the perfect first kiss. *Oh shit.* We're going to have to kiss at the end of the ceremony.

We've been so focused on the details of this marriage, my move to Boston, and a new coach, that I didn't spend any time thinking about the ceremony itself. Oh my god, I didn't even get him a ring!

Is this what they mean when they talk about "pregnancy brain?" This feeling—the overwhelming number of thoughts that enter my head at once, combined with the inability to focus on one of them for any length of time—is happening a lot lately. And the forgetfulness is unreal.

"Hey," he says, his hand squeezing the back of my neck so I'll look up at him. "You're freaking out right now, and I'm not sure why."

"I . . . I didn't even remember to get you a ring. Luke," I say with a sad laugh. "What kind of a future wife am I?"

His shoulders shake with silent laughter before he says, "I took care of it. And you're the perfect future wife *for me.*"

I try not to let that statement go to my heart or my head, because I know he really means this *arrangement* is perfect. I'm about to ask him again if he's sure, when the officiant who we'd briefly met in the lobby walks through the doors.

"Oh, look at you two lovebirds!" His voice has a friendly lilt that makes me smile, even as a knot of nerves grows tighter in my stomach.

"Can hardly keep my hands off her," Luke jokes. At least, I think he's joking, because he drops his hands and takes a step back.

"Hey, it's your wedding night. You *shouldn't* be able to keep your hands off your beautiful bride. Love the green, by the way," he says, looking me up and down. "And the matching nail polish, that's killer."

I laugh, relieved that he's here to break a bit of the tension that I feel heightening between Luke and me. Or maybe it's only heightening *within* me, because Luke seems perfectly at ease.

What are we doing?

Luke takes one look at me and says to the officiant, "My bride's a bit nervous. Do you think we could have one more minute together before we do this?"

The guy glances at his watch. "We have this space booked in ten-minute increments, but sure, if you don't mind an even quicker ceremony. I'll step out into the lobby. You just let me know when you're ready."

"Thanks, man," Luke says. Once the door is shut behind him, he turns to me. "Talk to me, Evie. Are you having nerves because this, right now, is finally real? Or are you thinking we shouldn't go through with it?"

Why does he seem so fucking relaxed, when I feel like I'm going to crawl out of my skin?

"I'm just having some big emotions about this," I say, forcing myself to slowly exhale so I can calm my body down from the state of anxiety that's got a stranglehold on me. "I'm afraid you're going to regret tying yourself down to someone who's pregnant."

He cups my face in his hands. "I'm not worried about that in the least."

"How can you *not* be? You're not worried that once this baby comes, it's just going to be a stark reminder of me making a terrible decision?"

His face softens so much he almost looks sad. "Are *you* worried about that?"

"I don't know. This is *my* baby, though. I'm going to love him or her, no matter what. You, however, are always going to know it's not your child. And I'm just worried that it might be a problem one day."

Shaking his head, he swallows. "I've never been a parent before, so I don't know what that's like. But I know that I'm going to love you and that baby, and take care of you both, like you're mine."

My throat is so tight I can barely breathe, so something between a sigh and a sob escapes. *How is this man so perfect?*

The question I really should be asking myself is *why* he's willing to do this for me. But the only answer that makes any sense is one that would raise my hopes for something that isn't possible. So, I put that out of my mind . . . for now.

"We've never even kissed," I say, suddenly realizing that

this seems like something that should have happened before the wedding.

"I love it when problems have easy solutions," he says, his knuckles meeting my chin as he tilts my head back. Butterflies erupt in my belly as his head moves swiftly toward me. His lips sweep gently across mine, and his other hand snakes around the back of my neck, holding me closer as he gently sucks my lower lip into his mouth.

It's all I can do to hold in the moan as I run my tongue along the line of his upper lip, and he tilts his head slightly, his tongue meeting mine as his mouth parts for me. My hands wrap around his lower back, and I push up on the balls of my feet, needing to be closer, needing to taste him. But he just chuckles and pulls back, saying, "We're in a wedding chapel, Evie."

His voice is teasing, like he's calling attention to how much I clearly want him right now. And I *do*. But I don't know what that kiss meant to him.

"I don't think that's how you kiss your best friend," I say, glancing away and hoping my voice sounds steadier than I feel after having his lips on mine.

But he guides my face back to his until he's able to look me in the eye. His breath coasts along my skin as he says, "I think when I marry my best friend, I get to write the rules about how I kiss her."

A wave of desire snakes up my spine at his words, and I can't help wondering if that means he plans on kissing me a lot. I sure hope so. But . . . no, that would just complicate everything.

That was just practice for the actual ceremony, I tell myself.

"You're positive about this?" I ask.

"I'm positive. Are you?"

"I'm still not sure if what we're doing is smart or crazy or a combination of both." I let out a watery laugh. "But whatever it is, there's no one else I'd rather do it with."

Luke dips his face down and kisses my forehead before he straightens, reaching behind him and pushing the door open. "We're ready."

The officiant wasn't joking about making this a quick ceremony. After a few introductory remarks, which I assume are for the benefit of the witnesses sitting behind us, he asks about the rings. Luke reaches his hand into the front pocket of his suit pants and produces a velvet box. Taking one ring out, he places it in my right hand. And when he takes the other out, it's all I can do not to gasp.

Sweet mother of Jesus. That is not the ring you expect someone to come back from a Vegas wedding with. It looks like a family heirloom. The center emerald-cut stone must be at least four carats, and the two trapezoid-shaped diamonds on either side are equally impressive in size. The entire filigree band is encrusted in tiny, sparkling diamonds.

This is the kind of ring you'd expect to see on the hand of a princess or a billionaire's wife. And that's the moment it hits me. I'm becoming a Hartmann, and there's no way a Hartmann would have a normal ring.

He takes my shaking left hand in his, grounding me as he holds the ring around the first knuckle of my finger. And as he says his vows, I stand there trying not to hyperventilate. Shortness of breath is a fun side effect I've become familiar with during pregnancy, but it's not the pregnancy that's causing it this time.

It's my brain working overtime to process the fact that

Luke bought me the type of ring he'd buy his *actual* wife . . . because that's what I'll be. And it's like my brain is putting all its energy into understanding this fact and has forgotten to also take care of other functions, like breathing.

When Luke slips that ring all the way onto my finger, without taking his eyes off my face, I take what must be my first breath in too long. At least I don't feel like I'm going to pass out anymore.

Okay, I can do this.

The officiant starts in with my vows, and I repeat them on autopilot, not even registering what I'm saying because my mind is reeling so fast.

What does that ring mean? Is this real to him?

Once I slide the ring onto his finger, we're told, "By the power vested in me by the state of Nevada, I now pronounce you man and wife. You may now kiss the bride."

Luke's smile is slow and sure, almost like a smirk. Like he knows exactly how my mind is going crazy and wants to reassure me everything is going to be okay. Except, when he brings his hands to the sides of my neck, running his thumbs along my jaw and tilting my head back, it dawns on me that everything is *not* going to be okay.

Because the way he takes my lips tentatively in his, the way he deepens that kiss, sweeping my mouth open with his tongue, and the way my entire body takes over and I kiss him back like it really means something to both of us . . . I know one thing with startling clarity.

I *want* my fake husband, and I don't think I can hide that desire anymore. And that's the surest way to ruin the trust and the friendship we've spent a lifetime building.

"I think I need to go to sleep," I say, glancing out the airplane window. The lights of Vegas are a good twenty minutes behind us, and there's nothing but darkness below. On the very edge of the horizon, somewhere far out over the ocean, I can make out the pink tinges of the setting sun along the curved surface of the Earth in another time zone. But the sky above and the surface below are completely black.

"I thought you were a night owl," Luke says. He knows me too well.

"Pregnancy makes me tired." At least that's not a lie.

"You don't seem tired. You seem like you're freaking out again."

And here I thought I was hiding it well enough. But the way I'm staring out the window as we talk, refusing to look at him sitting beside me . . . it's a classic avoidance strategy that I'm sure is more than obvious.

"I just need to go to sleep so I can wake up tomorrow and remember how to . . ."

"How to?"

". . . I don't know." I sigh. "How to not be awkward around you."

"Have I done something that's made you uncomfortable?" he asks, his voice tinged with worry and regret.

Clearly, he doesn't realize that his proximity has my skin tingling with awareness, much like it always has . . . but even more than normal. Now we've kissed, now that we just got *married* . . . I can't stop thinking about the way his lips felt on mine. The heat that spread through me when I tasted him for the first time hasn't faded, and I want him more than I ever have.

But that's not what *this* marriage is, so I need to get myself under control. When I wake up, maybe I'll be able to lock these feelings away. Maybe I'll figure out how to just be his best friend again, as if his kiss didn't tilt my entire world on its axis.

Yeah, maybe.

"No," I say, letting out a yawn as I turn toward him, "you haven't done anything. I think I'm just"—I shake my head, trying to clear my thoughts of the memories of his tongue tangling with mine—"feeling awkward about all this pretending."

"Evie," he says, reaching out and slipping his hand behind my neck. Instead of focusing on how possessive his touch feels, I question what it means. Is physical touch his love language? Is that why he's always so affectionate with his friends? "Are you feeling this way because we kissed?"

"Maybe," I squeak, sounding unusually high pitched.

I watch as he swallows, the muscles in his neck moving as his jaw clenches. "I don't want anything about this to be wrong for you, and I'm sorry if kissing you at the end of the ceremony made you uncomfortable. But there's no way anyone will ever believe that we're married if we can't even kiss without you reacting like I'm repulsive."

My head snaps up, my eyes meeting his intense gaze. "Are you . . . being serious right now?"

He's kidding, right?

"I mean, the way you seized up and pulled away when I kissed you, and the way you're suddenly so uncomfortable around me? Yeah, it feels off."

"Luke." I huff a laugh at how wildly off base his assessment is. I seized up and pulled back at the end of the kiss because if I didn't put a stop to it, I was afraid I was going to maul my husband—who's my best friend and nothing more —right there in the wedding chapel. "I'm pretty sure you know that women don't find you repulsive."

"Apparently *you* do." He shrugs with a lift of his eyebrows, and that's when I see it. The way he squints just a little, before his face returns to the placid expression he always wears. That little squint? That's his tell—a sure sign that he's worried or uncomfortable or upset.

And that's when it hits me: he's trying to play this off like he's teasing, but he actually believes that I don't find him attractive, and . . . he's upset by it?

What the hell is happening?

"Okay, Luke," I say, feeling like I need to level with him. "I'm pretty sure you know that you're not the least bit repulsive. And I'm a woman, so obviously I've noticed that. But we're friends, so . . ."

"So . . .?" he prompts.

I consider telling him things I've never told him before. Like how much I wanted him to choose me back in high school, when I thought he was going to ask me to senior prom. There's never been a question that I am *not* his type. He goes for tall blondes, usually with fake tans and light eyes.

But somehow, our senior year, I allowed myself to hope that he felt things for me that he clearly didn't. I mistook his friendship and his affection for something more—just like I did this past winter with Christopher.

It's a mistake I seem to keep making, even though, ever since senior year of high school, I've steeled myself against any hope that there could ever be something between Luke and me. And I'm not going to misinterpret the fact that he's married me as anything other than a mutually beneficial agreement between friends. Even if that kiss felt unmistakably real.

"So even though you're objectively attractive," I say, toying with my ring and hating every word about to leave my mouth, "we're never going there."

He nods in agreement. "There are few things that would ruin a friendship faster."

"Exactly. Which is why we can't kiss like that again, unless absolutely necessary."

He lifts an eyebrow, and his lips quirk up on one side. "Define absolutely necessary."

"Are you suggesting . . ." My eyes narrow as I try to figure out if he's teasing me, or if he really needs the clarification.

"That we should put some boundaries in place so I don't make you uncomfortable again? Yes."

I want to explain that what made me uncomfortable wasn't the kiss itself. It was how badly I wanted it to be real. But I can't tell him that because I'm not sure I could handle the same we're-just-friends-and-this-is-just-an-act conversation I had with Christopher only a few months ago.

I am perfectly capable of reminding myself of this fact.

"Unless there are other people around and we need to convince them that this marriage is real, I think we need to keep our hands off each other."

He tilts his head to the right as he studies me, and eventually his gaze is too much. Looking at Luke Hartmann is like staring at the sun—beautiful and blinding at the same time. If I don't look away, I'll get hurt.

"I guess what I'm trying to figure out," he says, his voice quiet in the cabin of this small private jet, "is if the way I normally touch you, as a friend, is off limits now? And if so, what changed?"

Alarm bells are going off in my head. I've never read too much into or made a big deal out of the way he's always touched me. It's just how he is. It would be weird if I suddenly had a problem with it. It would raise questions, like the ones he's asking right now: *what changed?*

What changed is that he just kissed me like no one else ever has. Like he wanted to take his time and savor me. Like he wanted more, but didn't want to rush things. He kissed me like he cared, like it was a promise of forever.

And that's the kind of thing that could make a girl hope, when she absolutely shouldn't.

"Of course that's fine, Luke," I say with an exaggerated sigh. "Nothing's changed. We're still the same friends we've always been."

And with that lie on my lips, I close my eyes and lean toward him, resting my head on his chest as he wraps his arms around me and I drift off to sleep.

Chapter Nineteen

LUKE

"Uhhh," I say as I stand in Eva's living room, looking down at the loveseat that's apparently replaced the significantly larger couch that took up the middle of this room the last time I stayed here. "Did your couch shrink?"

"I—" Eva sighs. "I didn't even think about that. Yeah, the old one really was just too big for the space, so I got the loveseat and chairs last month. There's actually more seating this way, but it's not ideal for overnight guests. You take the bed, and I'll sleep here."

Eying the loveseat, I try to picture Eva being able to lie on it without being curled up on her side. "Don't be ridiculous. I'm not sleeping in your bed while you're scrunched up on this tiny thing." I glance at the two seat cushions on the loveseat and then each chair. "I could probably take all the seat cushions and make myself a mattress on the floor."

"Yeah," she scoffs. "*That* would be comfortable."

"At least I could stretch out that way."

"Luke," she says, and then covers her mouth as she yawns. "Just take the bed for tonight, and I'll take the couch. It's fine."

"Like hell is my pregnant wife sleeping on a loveseat while I take the bed." I grind out the words and cross my arms over my chest.

Eva lets out a deep sigh that has her shoulders drooping. "It's too late to be having an argument about who's sleeping where." She glances at the alarm clock on her nightstand, and I follow her gaze to see that it's after two in the morning.

"Then stop arguing," I say, reaching down for the loveseat cushions, but before I can pull them off, she flops down on it. She's curled up on her side, with her head on the throw pillows that lean up against the edge.

"I've taken plenty of naps on this thing. I'll be fine."

"You're being utterly ridiculous. That doesn't even look comfortable, and you're going to wake up with a kink in your neck."

"Well, if you try to sleep on the cushions on the floor, you're going to wake up with a sore back."

She's not wrong. Whichever one of us doesn't sleep in the bed is going to get a crappy night of sleep.

Still, neither one of us mentions the possibility of sharing the queen-size bed wedged into the small alcove of her studio apartment.

Previously, we probably could've handled it just fine. Now, I want so much more than the friendship we've had. But sleeping next to her, unable to think of anything but how close we are and how easy it would be to reach out and pull her against me . . .

Don't be that guy, I tell myself. I've spent so much of my life suppressing my feelings and pretending that I didn't want that kind of relationship with her, determined to be the friend she needed, not the guy waiting around for her to change her mind. It didn't occur to me how much harder it would be to maintain that distance once I kissed her ... twice.

I should have just given her a chaste kiss and called it a day . . . but the way she wrapped her arms around me, pressed her body into mine, and parted her lips when I kissed her, I couldn't help myself. And I couldn't stop myself from doing it again.

Which makes me an absolute dick, because if there's one thing in this world I'm not, it's someone who preys on vulnerable women. And in that moment, with her heightened emotions, it's possible her guard was down and I'm an asshole for taking advantage of that. *Fuck.*

"I'm too tired to argue with you," she says, closing her eyes. "For real, just go to bed, Luke. Tomorrow, we can figure out a different solution for the next few nights."

I look down at her where she's cozied up in a ball on her side and sigh. "The only reason I'm agreeing to this is because I don't want to fight with you right now."

She cracks her eyes open and turns her head slightly to look up at me. "But tomorrow you'll want to fight with me?"

"Tomorrow I'm going to find a two-bedroom place to rent for the next few days so we don't have to fight about this at all."

She shoots up to a sitting position. "What? No. I have plenty of room for both of us here," she says, and my gaze roams the studio apartment—all of which could fit in my kitchen back in Boston. "Don't waste your money on that. We'll just . . . get an air mattress or something."

"The only way I'm agreeing to that is if you take the bed tonight," I tell her. I know she always starts on her side when she falls asleep, but I've slept in her apartment before and found her lying crossways on her bed in the morning, so she moves around in her sleep. There's no way I want her falling off this loveseat in the middle of the night, or waking up in pain if she's scrunched in here. "I can sleep anywhere, Evie, you know that. You can't."

She sighs. "I'm agreeing to this for one night only. Tomorrow we'll get an air mattress and I'll sleep on it."

"Fine," I say, even though I have zero intention of letting her sleep anywhere except the most comfortable option, which is her own bed.

With a sigh, she gets up from the loveseat, grabs something out of a drawer in the dresser near her bed, and heads into the bathroom. While she's in there, I take the seat cushions off the loveseat and two chairs and lay them down in a line. I can tell just by looking at them that they're about a foot too short, so I grab the back cushions off the chairs and stick one at each end, for my head and feet. Good enough.

Eva comes out of the bathroom a few minutes later, face washed and in shorts and a tank top. I glance back down at the makeshift bed so I can pretend like I didn't just notice the way she's not wearing a bra. "I'm going to brush my teeth," I say, leaning down and grabbing my toiletry bag out of the top of my suitcase.

"All right," she says. "Goodnight."

"Night."

I take my time brushing my teeth and splashing water on

my face, giving her time to get settled and myself the space to get my racing mind under control. Seeing her in those tiny shorts and a tank top, combined with the memory of how soft she felt as I kissed her—I need to lock that shit down or I'm going to find myself jerking off on her living room floor while she sleeps.

I head back through the dark living room, thankful for the beam of light streaming through the crack in the curtains over the French doors leading to the small court-yard outside. I make it back to my makeshift bed and drop my pants and shirt over the back of the couch, then grab the blanket Eva must have left for me. I toss that over the lower half of my body as I situate myself on the cushions, and then realize I need another pillow to go under my head, so I reach over to the couch and grab a throw pillow. I'm still uncomfortable as hell, but at least I can hear Eva breathing steadily in her bed on the other side of the loveseat.

I'm not sure how long I lie there, but it feels like at least half an hour, before my upper back starts hurting. So, I sit up enough to reposition myself on my side, and as I lie back down, that's when I think I hear her whisper, "Luke."

I consider not responding. Maybe she'll think I'm comfortably asleep? But what if she's whispering my name because something's wrong?

"Luke," she says, a little louder this time.

"Yeah?"

"Can you come here for a sec?"

"This better not be a ploy to switch places," I say with a groan as I stand. There's no world in which I'm letting her sleep on the floor while I'm comfortable on a bed.

"Promise," she says as I walk around the chair and loveseat and head toward her bed.

"What's up?"

I can barely make her out in the dark alcove where her bed sits, but I think she pushes up onto her elbow and pats the opposite side of the bed. "Lay down."

"You want me . . . to sleep in your bed?" Why does my voice sound so damn high-pitched?

"I'm not going to be able to fall asleep if you're uncomfortable on the floor. And you're not going to switch places with me. So just lay the hell down so we can both get some sleep, okay?"

She sounds so annoyed that I chuckle.

"Fine," I say. The bed dips as I kneel at the end and crawl up to lie down, facing her. "Happy?"

I can barely make out the small smile that curves her lips. "Less annoyed. Now go to sleep."

The whole bed shakes with my laughter, and she lets out a little groan in response, but we both must fall asleep quickly because I have no memories after that.

———

The ray of light shining through the window and directly into my eyes isn't what wakes me up in the morning. No, it's the way Eva's wrapped around me like a starfish. I crack open one eye to find her lying on her side with one of her legs draped over mine, her arm across my torso, and her head resting in the crevice between my shoulder and chest, while my arm is wrapped around her back, my hand resting possessively on her hip.

Did I pull her to me in the middle of the night? Or did she roll onto me? Shit. This is why you don't sleep in the same bed as your best friend.

She's your wife now, a little voice in my head reminds me. It's the same voice that would tell me jumping into a pool from the second story of a house when I've had six too many beers is a good idea. I know better than to follow his advice.

But at the same time, as I lie here, listening to the birds outside and the faint sounds of LA traffic in the distance, I can't help but imagine what it would be like if we could wake up together every day. I know Eva's intention when we get back to Boston is to move into my guest bedroom—she has made that *very* clear—but I would love for things to work out differently.

With her, I wish lots of things were different, but this marriage based on friendship is still better in every way than being with *anyone* else.

Eva rubs herself along my side and nuzzles her face into my chest like a cat who wants its back scratched. The cute little moan she lets out has my entire body on notice, but then she lifts her head and looks up at me. Pure panic floods her face and she mutters, "shit," and springs backward so fast I'm afraid she'll launch herself off the side of the bed. Given that there's barely room to stand between the edges of the bed and the walls on either side, I'd probably have to drag her out by her feet. The mental image has me chuckling.

"What are you laughing about? Did I drool on you or something?"

No, you're just as perfect asleep as you are awake.

"I was just imagining how I'd get you out if you fell between the bed and the wall."

"Why were you imagining *that*?" She sounds offended.

Because it's better than thinking about the look of horror on your face when you realized you were cuddled up next to me.

"Because the way you just threw your whole body backward made me think it was a real possibility." I turn on my side to face her. "How are you feeling this morning, Mrs. Hartmann?"

"Oh my god," Eva groans. "Mrs. Hartmann is your mother. Do *not* call me that!"

"When in your lifetime have you *ever* called my mom Mrs. Hartmann?" My parents have always been Uncle Frank and Aunt Elise to Eva.

"Whatever, you know what I mean."

My chuckle fills the space as she rolls her eyes. Based on her reaction to me calling her Mrs. Hartmann, I'm pretty sure I already know the answer to the question I'm about to ask, but I ask anyway. "Okay, what I really want to know is if you're freaking out today like you were last night, or if you're good now?"

"I still can't believe we got married. Oh shit . . ." She lets out a deep sigh. "We have to tell our parents. I wonder if they've been looking for us?"

"We each had our own hotel room in Vegas, so they may not have even noticed our absence yet. Hold on, let me grab my phone." I scoot to the end of the bed and walk over to the couch. My pants from last night are folded on the space where the seat cushions would be if they weren't spread across the floor. I find my phone in my pocket and check the time and my texts as I walk back to the bed.

Luckily, I've got no missed calls or texts. I've never been so relieved to have had no one reach out to me in the past twelve hours. When I turn back toward the bed, Eva's got her phone in her hand and she glances up at me, a look of worry instantly turning into one of annoyance.

"I thought you said you weren't going to walk around in your boxers once we were married?"

I glance down at my body, and there's no mistaking that I'm semi-hard, like I normally am when I wake up. It's actually a miracle I didn't wake up with a raging hard-on, given the way she was wrapped around me. "Sorry, I didn't think about it. Besides, how many times have you seen me in a bathing suit?"

Eva always jokes about how short my swim trunks are, but I hate the way wet material feels when it bunches up between my thighs, so I don't care. I didn't wear longer swim trunks even when that was the style.

"Swim trunks and boxer briefs are a little different," she says, raising an eyebrow. "I'm not going to walk around in my bra and thong, so you shouldn't walk around in boxers—okay?"

The desire to tease her about her modesty is overwhelming, but I can tell she's not in the mood for that, which makes me wonder what's on her phone screen. So, I sit next to her at the head of the bed and make a point of covering my lower body with the sheet instead.

"I don't have any messages. You?" I ask.

"Yeah, my mom texted me half an hour ago, saying she and my dad were going to the breakfast buffet before the flight home, and asking if I wanted to join. And then she texted me, like, ten minutes ago, asking if I was awake yet and reminding me what time the plane leaves."

Eva's family had come on our private jet with us, which

means in an hour and a half, the car will be at the hotel to take everyone back to the airport. "We probably need to tell them before your parents start looking for you and panic when you don't answer the knock on your door, yeah?"

She rests her head back against her padded headboard and sighs. "Yeah. God, I knew that breaking this news was going to be hard, but I wasn't really prepared for how scared I'd feel."

I glance over at her and give her a small smile. "Just remember how much easier this is going to be than if you had to tell them the truth."

"I know," she sighs as her shoulders sag, calling even more attention to the fact that she's not wearing a bra. I don't dare tease her about the double standard—that I can't walk around in my boxers, while it's okay for her to sit here in a skimpy tank top without a bra. Another time, that will be funny. But not right now, when she's obviously on edge about having to break this news to our parents. "I just hate disappointing them."

"So what you're saying is, marrying me is a disappointment?" I say it teasingly so she won't catch the vulnerability in my question.

"No, I'm saying that learning that I'm pregnant and got married in secret without including them will be disappointing to them."

"Listen, Eva," I say, turning slightly onto my side so I'm facing her. "How your parents respond is on them, not on you. You haven't done anything wrong. Yes, you didn't mean to get pregnant, but you're dealing with it in the best way you can—"

She rests her hand on her belly, and her tone is defensive as she says, "I don't regret this baby."

I drop my phone onto the bed and reach out to cup the side of her face. "I know you don't. I only mean that we're doing the best we can in the situation we've found ourselves in."

She tilts her face into my palm and gives me a small smile. "It's weird to hear you say 'we' in relation to this situation."

"That's what it is, though, isn't it?" My thumb strokes the line of her cheekbone and her skin heats under my touch. "Us against the world. We've got this."

"All right," she says with a slight nod. "Did we decide on how we want to break the news?"

"I still think my idea of a picture of our wedding rings is the best option. Unless you've thought of something else."

"No," she says. "You're probably right."

Reaching down to grab my phone, I find the photo we took last night, of my hand with hers crossed on top of it, both our wedding rings clearly visible. I tap the icon to add the photo to a text message and ask, "What do we want to say?"

She bites her lower lip, deep in thought. "Maybe, *About last night . . .?*"

I laugh. "Are you trying to give them a heart attack?"

"I don't know what to say! You write it out if you think you can come up with something better, College Boy." There's laughter in her voice as she uses the nickname she gave me in the four years after high school. Eva's incredibly smart and was a great student in high school. She probably could've had her choice of any college, and I know she feels a tad insecure that she never got her degree. But there was no way she could have managed it while also skating competitively. She's taken a bunch of classes over the years, but never fully pursued a degree.

"I don't think that a sports medicine degree is going to come in particularly handy right now," I say. "But I'll give it a shot."

She laughs and leans in, watching over my shoulder as I type.

LUKE

Eva and I made a big decision last night. We're taking some time to figure out what our lives will look like moving forward, and we'll be back in Boston in a few days. We look forward to seeing you all and sharing this news in person once we're back.

Her body shakes with laughter. "That's 'selling it'? It sounds like we just signed off on a business agreement. You couldn't sound less in love if you tried."

I go back to the first sentence and erase it, then rephrase.

LUKE

Eva and I have been keeping our relationship a secret for too long, and last night we decided to make it official. We're taking some time to figure out what our lives will look like moving forward, and we'll be back in Boston in a few days. Can't wait to see you once we're back.

"Better?" I ask, after I finish adding the last sentence.

"It's fine for a text, but you better be sickeningly in love with me when we actually see our families again."

That won't be a problem.

"Obviously I'll make sure I can't keep my eyes, or my hands, off you. But you can't seize up like a freaking statue, the way you did at our wedding, in front of them either."

"I didn't seize up!" she says as she swats my bare shoulder.

I didn't want to push this last night on the plane, but it bears repeating. "Yeah, you did. Honestly, Eva, you're going to have to get comfortable with me touching you and kissing you in front of other people. Otherwise, no one is going to believe that we're in love."

"Maybe . . ." She pauses, sinking her teeth into her full lower lip again. I can't take my eyes off her mouth. All I want to do is lean in and kiss her.

When my eyes flick up to meet hers, the worried look on her face has me wondering what she's thinking, and what she was going to say. I'm about to ask if she's worried that we can't sell this, but then she says, "Maybe we should send our parents that message and prepare ourselves for the fallout."

Chapter Twenty

EVA

"You know," Luke says as he holds out his hand and pulls me up from my seat. I come to a stand directly in front of him. "This feels like the perfect place to practice acting like a newlywed couple who can't keep their hands off each other."

My breath hitches as my gaze flits around the patio of my favorite Mexican restaurant. The high stucco walls around the perimeter are covered in flowering vines, and wooden tables dot the brick patio beneath string lights. The setting is perfect, except all around us, people are eating their meals.

"I don't think that the middle of a restaurant, out in the open like this, is the right place," I say with nervous laughter. Plus, I'm pretty sure my enchilada breath means it's not the perfect time, either.

Though when, exactly, *would be* the perfect time to practice? At least here, I won't try to take it any further like I almost did in that chapel in Vegas.

His throat bobs with a deep swallow, then he tilts his chin and looks at me. "You're probably right." Still holding my hand, he leads me to the restaurant's exit.

Regret flows through me at the missed opportunity, even though the rational part of me knows that kissing him—any more than completely necessary—is a bad idea. Still, I follow behind him, wondering if I can somehow take him up on his offer without coming across as clingy or desperate. I want to feel those lips on mine again, so much so that the physical yearning overwhelms me.

I don't know if these feelings are a result of lying next to him in bed this morning and pretending like I felt nothing, then trying to quell our anxiety about our parents' reaction by putting our phones on *Do Not Disturb* while packing up half my apartment? Or is it the way we've been sharing my small studio space all day, constantly bumping into each other while trying not to get too close?

Simply *existing* next to him now fills me with a nervous energy I haven't felt around him in a decade. My longing and desire have reached new heights, and I'm starting to ask myself stupid questions like: what's the point of being married to him if I can't kiss him whenever I want to?

Because you're protecting yourself from getting your heart broken, I remind myself. Having that physical connection would make it too easy to convince myself that there were real feelings involved.

But that level of practical reasoning is at war with my desire. When he places his hand on my lower back, and his fingers make contact with the exposed skin between my waistband and the tie across my mid back, electricity shoots up my spine. That feeling should be a warning, but instead, it's a flame that lights an inferno.

"Maybe you're right," I say, turning as he guides me onto the sidewalk outside the restaurant. "Maybe we do need to practice . . . so we'll know how to keep up appearances?"

"Are you asking me, or telling me?" A slow smile spreads across his beautiful face, and I should take it as another warning—he's toying with me. I know it, and he knows it, which means he knows that I want him more than I'm letting on.

Shit. I've worked too damn hard over the years to hide my attraction to him, and here I am, acting all needy. *Don't risk a lifelong friendship for another kiss.*

As if he's following my thoughts and sees me starting to spiral, he wraps his hand around the back of my neck and pulls me toward him, gently but with determination. He dips his face toward mine and traces the line of my cheekbone with the bridge of his nose, until his lips are right at my ear.

"We wouldn't want to be unprepared, would we, Evie?"

I swear I could melt from his voice alone. As if he knows he needs to hold me up, his other arm wraps around my hips, anchoring me to him.

"We wouldn't." I barely squeak out the words because, with him this close, I've suddenly forgotten how to breathe.

"That's my girl," he says, pulling back just enough to look at me. His tongue darts out to wet his lower lip before he pulls it between his teeth, and the longer he looks at me, the darker his eyes become and the heavier his breathing grows.

For our entire lives, I would've described Luke as a nice guy. But absolutely nothing about him looks *nice* right now— he looks like he can't wait to devour me. And as his face descends toward mine, something akin to a strangled moan escapes the back of my throat.

Then his lips are on mine and his tongue is invading my mouth, and I push up on my tiptoes to meet him. His palm is cupping my ass and my arms wrap around his neck. If I wasn't still the tiniest bit aware of our surroundings, I'd lift my legs and wrap them around his hips because my core is positively aching for contact. I need that friction . . . I need *him*.

He threads his fingers into my hair, cupping the back of my head as he owns my mouth with his tongue. And then some guy says, "Get a room!" as he walks around us entwined on the sidewalk.

Luke pulls back, both of us locking eyes as we stand there, practically panting. And then he tips his head to press a light kiss on my forehead. "I think we've got strangers fooled," he says with a subtle laugh. "Maybe with a little more practice, we'll be able to convince our families, too."

———

"The fuck?" Luke's voice comes from somewhere in my dark apartment.

I reach over and tap my phone screen to discover that it's four in the morning. And since I had lain awake for hours, replaying the kiss in my head while convincing myself not to get up and go to Luke, where he was sleeping on the new air mattress, I've probably only gotten two hours of sleep at this point.

It sounds like he's moving furniture. I scoot to the end of my bed and don't see him anywhere obvious. But when I look to the right, I see him moving some of the boxes we packed up earlier and stacked against the wall next to my kitchen table. What the hell is he doing?

"Luke!" I whisper, even though there's no reason to be quiet. Everyone in this apartment is now already up.

His back straightens, and he turns toward me. He's in nothing but form-fitting boxer briefs that show off his muscular thighs and defined abs, because *of course* I'm waking up to this vision after trying, and failing, to convince myself that I don't find him attractive in that way.

"I'm sorry," he says. "I didn't mean to wake you."

"What in the world are you doing moving boxes around at 4 a.m.?"

"There's a noise coming from one of them, and I'm trying to figure out which box so I can make it fucking stop." He sounds so annoyed, I almost laugh, but he's probably exhausted, just like I am. No one should be up at this hour.

"What kind of noise?" I step down onto the floor and head over to what used to be a neatly stacked pile of boxes.

"Found it!" he says, picking up a box and turning to set it on the kitchen table. "This box is labeled 'bedroom supplies.'"

If we weren't standing in a nearly pitch-black room right now, I'm sure he'd notice how the blood just drained from my face. *Nooooo. This can't be happening.*

"Oh yeah," I say, but I'm sure he can tell how strained my voice is. "It's probably one of the massage tools I use for sore muscles after working out."

"Why the hell would that be on right now?" he asks, ripping the tape off the top of the box.

I step closer, putting my arm between him and the box.

"You know what, I packed that all up very carefully. Let me take care of it."

"Hang on, I'll grab my phone and hold the flashlight up so you can find it more easily," he says, stepping away as he heads toward the living room to get his phone.

Oh god, no. I don't know whether to laugh or cry, so instead, I reach into the bigger moving box to find the smaller decorative box that contains my collection of sex toys, which I know are the only things that could be making that pulsing sound.

"I don't need a flashlight, it's fine," I say, hoping that for once his "I need to help everyone" instinct will just chill the fuck out.

No such luck. He starts walking back toward me with his phone, saying, "It'll be easier to find it if you're not fishing around in the dark."

"I'm good," I say as I flip open the lid of the decorative box and wrap my fingers around the offending vibrator.

"Don't be silly," he says, tapping his screen so the back of his phone lights up.

My hand shoots out to block the light. "Stop right there," I say, and he freezes. I'm sure my face is bright red, and my embarrassment is on full display under the bright light he's shining right at me.

"Why?" he asks, his voice tinged with suspicion. I don't blame him; I'm acting highly suspect. But if he takes even two steps closer, he's going to see exactly what's in my hand below the open flaps of the cardboard moving box. Since I'm so lost in panic that I don't respond, he presses, "What's in the box, Evie?"

I can tell by his teasing tone that he's got ideas, and I certainly don't want to confirm his suspicions.

"A lot of stuff you don't need to see," I say, looking down at the silicone dildo pulsing in my hand. I move my thumb over the button at the end, and my anxiety decreases when the sound stops.

"What kind of stuff?"

With a huff, I set the toy down and flip the lid back on. "Let's just go back to sleep."

He turns off the flashlight, and his deep chuckle fills the space. "Maybe you should just tell me what that was so I don't keep myself awake wondering?"

I fold the flaps of the moving box shut and glance up at him. "I told you. It was a massage tool. There was just other stuff in the box I didn't want you to see."

"Uh huh," he says, eyes narrowed on me as he steps closer.

My swallow sounds like a gulp in the space that's now frustratingly silent, and then the fucking vibrator starts doing its thing again inside the damn box. *Kill me now*, I think, wishing the floor would just open up and swallow me.

"Can you take the batteries out?" Luke asks with a laugh.

I wish. "It's rechargeable."

At least I can hide my embarrassment in the darkness.

"Maybe you just need to use it until the battery dies, then? Need anything massaged?"

I can tell he's trying not to laugh as he teases me, and I'm beyond mortified. "I'm just going to throw this whole box in the dumpster in the parking lot." I bend to wrap my arms around the box. "Be right back."

Luke's hand slams down on top of the box before I can

pick it up. "You're not supposed to lift anything heavier than twenty pounds."

I roll my eyes as I stand, leaving the box on the table. He wouldn't let me lift a single box while we were packing, not even the light ones. "You're taking this a bit far," I say, my irritation growing with every pulsating vibration that comes from the box sitting on the table between us. "Stop treating me like I can't do anything."

His voice is gentle when he says, "Hey, twenty pounds is the limit. We can't have you potentially injuring Baby Squash."

I move his hand off the top of the box with an annoyed sigh. I want to be done with this conversation so I can crawl back into bed, bury my head in my pillows, and dream that I live in a world where this entire interaction never took place.

Opening the flaps of the moving box, I pull out the decorative box inside. The pulsing is embarrassingly loud in the silence as we stare at each other. "Fine, I'll just throw *this* box away, then."

I set it on my hip as I use my other hand to close the flaps of the larger box—not that there's actually anything else in there that I don't want him to see—and then head to my front door.

"I'll do it for you," Luke says, coming up next to me as I slip my feet into my flip-flops.

"No!" I don't mean to snap at him, but my response comes out harsher than I intend. I just need to get this box out of here and away from him.

He holds his hands up and takes a step back in response. "I really don't want you walking through a parking lot by yourself in the middle of the night."

"Luke, I've lived here by myself for years. The parking lot is well lit. I'll be fine."

"At least take a sweatshirt. It's cold out there."

"I'm fine," I grumble as I turn the deadbolt, knowing he's going to watch me like a guard dog until I return.

And with that, I step onto the walkway outside my front door and follow it to the parking lot. But damn if he isn't right. Summer nights in LA usually dip into the mid- to low-sixties, and in my shorts, tank top, and flip-flops, I'm shivering by the time I reach the dumpster. Heaving the top open above my head, I toss the box in as far toward the back corner as it will go. Not that I think Luke's going to come looking to see what's in that box, but . . . just in case.

As I turn and run back across the parking lot, sure enough, Luke is standing there in the open doorway. He's leaning up against the frame with his arms crossed against his bare upper body. And if the cut muscles of his abdomen and chest, and the tattoos wrapping around his muscular upper arms, didn't stop me in my tracks, the look on his face would.

"What's wrong?"

His voice is grim. "AJ called."

Chapter Twenty-One

LUKE

Holding my phone out, I show Eva the missed call from about half an hour ago, while we were both sleeping—before the constant pulsing sound from the moving box woke me up—and my ringer was off. Even while we made a conscious choice to ignore the messages from our families we saw coming in yesterday, I can't ignore this one from my boss.

I tap play on the voicemail and AJ's voice fills Eva's small apartment, which, until this moment, had felt like a sanctuary where we could avoid having to deal with real life.

I'm being proactive and sending Morgan out to LA to meet with you and Eva. She's getting on a plane right now and will be there late morning, your time. You'd better be ready to work with her on how you're shaping this story for the media.

Eva glances over at me. "Is this the same Morgan I met last week at the Neon Cactus?"

"I think so?" I'm as confused as she is. Aside from being my agent's daughter, I have no idea what Morgan's connection is to AJ or the Rebels.

"Why . . ." It's like Eva doesn't know what questions to ask and, honestly, neither do I. She shakes her head. "How does AJ know where we are? And do you think this means our parents know, too?"

"There's only one way to find out," I say. "I think we need to listen to our messages." When she gives me a brief nod of agreement, I hit play on the first voicemail that came in yesterday morning after we texted our parents.

Luke, my mom says, *help us understand what's going on. You and Eva got married? When? Why? How? Your father and I are really confused and, quite frankly, hurt that you would keep this from us. Please call me.*

There are several other similar voicemails from both my mom and my dad, and then the voice of Preston, my eldest brother and the new CEO of Hartmann Enterprises, thunders from the speaker of my phone.

What the fuck, Luke? You better have had a prenup in place before you made this impulsive decision. We love Eva, but you're a goddamn Hartmann—you can't just get married out of the blue like this without having certain safeguards in place.

Eva's face falls, and immediately I wish I hadn't played that one out loud. "I'll sign a prenup," she says quietly. "Or whatever you call it after we're already married."

"Fuck that," I say, wrapping my arm around her shoulders and pulling her to my side. "I trust you unconditionally."

"Not that you shouldn't trust me," she says, "but your brother is right. You can't take risks like that, especially not after what happened to Tucker."

Hmmmm. The sound rattles around in the back of my throat, because I hate that she's sort of right. But still, she'd never do something like that to me.

"Should we see what *your* parents have to say?" I ask her.

"Do we have to?"

"Maybe we should see if they know where we are, at least?" It had never occurred to me that they'd realize we were here, though maybe it should have. Going to LA to get Eva's stuff and bring it to Boston now seems pretty obvious.

Eva sighs and walks over to her bed and, as she crawls to her nightstand to retrieve her phone, I try not to focus on the way her ass looks in those short pajama shorts. I look away, because while there's no ideal time to be checking out your best friend, this *certainly* isn't the right time.

She lets out a deep sigh as she walks back to me with her phone in her hand.

"Regretting our decision, wife?" I tease, but it doesn't disguise the genuine worry that compelled me to ask in the first place.

"No." She sighs again. "Just wishing we could fast forward through this part where we have to come to terms with hurting our families."

"It's going to be okay."

"I know." Her shoulders sag as she looks down at the ground. "I just hate disappointing them."

"At some point," I say as I reach out and sweep her hair off her face, tucking it behind her ear, "we're going to talk about why that's always the driving force in your decision making."

She glances up at me, and a look of annoyance flashes across her face—the kind that tells me I've hit a little too close to her insecurities. I'm close to my family, too, and I know many of my decisions are based on "being a Hartmann." But sometimes, it feels like Eva gets stuck in a pattern of perpetually trying to please her parents at the expense of her own happiness. She's a grown woman, and now my wife, and that's something we're going to need to deal with or it's going to get in the way of our relationship.

We can deal with that later, I remind myself.

"I don't even want to listen to these messages," she says, glancing back at her phone. "I just want to keep living in this world where we've made this decision and are dealing with it together, without all the outside factors."

"It's the outside factors that led us here in the first place," I say, immediately regretting my words because they imply that we were forced into this position. In a way, I guess she was. I, however, would have wanted this marriage regardless —not that I can tell her that.

"I know." Her words are clipped, and now I'm certain she took my statement the wrong way.

"Heyyy . . ." I drag the word out as I bring my hand back up to her neck and curl my fingers around the ridges of her spine. "I didn't mean it the way you're taking it."

"Oh yeah? How did you mean it, then?" She glances up at me, looking pissed off. Honestly, with her tired eyes glaring, she's cute as hell.

I pull her against me, wrapping my other arm around her back as I press my lips to the top of her head. "I told you before, Eva. You're the only person I'd want to spend the rest of my life with."

"That's not what you said, actually," she mumbles into my chest, her hot breath skimming over my bare skin.

"It's not?" I'm pretty positive that's what I told her when we were talking about this marriage.

"No, you said if you *had* to pick one person to spend the rest of your life with, you'd pick me. And when I asked you if I was forcing you into this, you never actually said no."

I hate the way her voice is tinged with hurt, and that my word choice caused this pain. "Can you explain something to me?"

She buries her face into my chest like she's embarrassed, but says, "Sure."

"What could I have said differently so I wouldn't have hurt you?"

Obviously, I couldn't have said *If I could pick anyone* . . . because then she'd know how I really feel. And the only thing more awkward than having very real feelings for my best friend would be her looking at me and saying, "You flatter yourself," in response. We've been down that exact road before, and I have no desire for a repeat experience.

"You didn't do anything wrong. It was just a reminder that you felt like you *had* to do this."

"Eva." I pause and wait for her to look up at me. "I didn't *have* to do this. I *wanted* to, and I've told you that all along. I'm sorry if I made you feel like I only made this offer out of necessity or obligation."

"But you *did* make the offer because you had to," she whispers. "If I hadn't gotten pregnant, hadn't been worried about telling my parents, hadn't stressed out about the possibility of losing my healthcare, and—"

"None of that means I didn't have a choice. I very much did."

"Then why?"

I'm not sure what I see in her eyes. It looks a bit like hope, like she wants me to tell her that I'm *choosing* her. "Because there's *nothing* I wouldn't do for you."

She looks down quickly, saying, "I know," as she buries her face against my chest again and squeezes me in a hug. And I'm not sure why, but somehow, I know she's still disappointed with that answer—I just don't know how to make that better, because I'm certain that telling her my real feelings would actually make things worse.

It would make me into the exact guy I've never wanted to be.

———

"Well, if this isn't the cutest studio I've ever seen, I don't know what is," Morgan says, walking across to the open French doors through which fresh air and sunlight are streaming. "And this patio! My god, this is amazing."

"Thanks," Eva says, following behind her. "It was kind of a dump when I first bought it five years ago, but I enjoyed fixing it up."

"Kind of a dump" is an understatement. When she first texted me the pictures, telling me how much promise the place had, I tried to talk her out of buying it. But when she went ahead with the purchase, I helped her find a contractor, then secretly had him charge her only half of his fee—so she could do everything she wanted—and I made up the difference.

Now, it actually *is* adorable, and it's very *Eva*. Dark-green painted cabinets and light wood countertops in the kitchen, floral wallpaper in the dining area with a white table and pink chairs, an upholstered headboard running across the small alcove where her bed is, and the marble-tiled fireplace with a large gilded mirror resting on the mantle. Everything bears her touch, and it's perfect for her.

"What are you going to do with the place now?" Morgan asks, eyeing the boxes packed up next to her kitchen table.

"I'm not sure," Eva says. "It probably doesn't make sense to keep it."

Beyond coming here to pack her things, we hadn't discussed what we were planning to do with her place. It's making me realize just how many things we still need to work out and, for the first time since we made the decision to get married, I'm starting to worry that we jumped too fast. I wish we'd talked through more of these details yesterday when we were packing everything up. I thought we'd have all day today. I didn't realize AJ would be on top of this so quickly or that Morgan would be standing here now.

Her presence is, however, a great distraction from the conversation Eva didn't want to have about the mystery pulsing sound we heard earlier this morning. My mind hasn't stopped imagining the possibilities, and while I'm not planning to go dumpster diving to find out, I'd be a liar if I said the thought hadn't crossed my mind.

"If you want to hold on to it," I say, "we could hire a property management company that could rent it out."

"Maybe," Eva says, and I can tell just by the tone of her voice that she likes the idea of keeping this place.

"It would also mean we could come out here whenever

you wanted," I say. "Or you could, if you just wanted to have a girls' weekend and visit friends or something."

Eva's friend group in Los Angeles is small. Because so much of her life has revolved around skating, and because that schedule is so demanding and unpredictable, most of her close friends have been other skaters. And they haven't always stayed put in LA when they've switched partners or coaches, or retired.

Christopher has been her one constant and, as much as it drives me crazy that she has such an important man in her life who's not me, I'm still glad she has someone. Or at least I was, until he stomped on her heart and she wound up pregnant as a result.

She glances over at me and widens her eyes—a clear reminder that she's about to have a newborn while training for the Olympics. But unlike her, I'm thinking long-term, and I want her to keep this place so she doesn't feel like she's giving up everything that's *her* to become part of *us*.

"We'll figure it out," Eva says and turns back toward Morgan.

"Seems like you guys have several things on your plate to work out . . ." Clearly, Morgan is sharp and observant, just like her father.

Oh shit, does Carson know about this? I didn't even think to tell him, which is exactly the type of thing he'll be furious about. Athletes do impulsive and public shit all the time, and he's always told me how thankful he is that he doesn't have to worry about that with me.

He thinks it's because I'm such a stand-up guy—and that's pretty much true, but I've also had decades of training on what it means to be a Hartmann. If I was ever going to do something inappropriate, I've learned from my older brothers how to keep it from going public. Somehow, though, I was so wrapped up in the details of marrying Eva that I didn't think to plan ahead.

"We do," I say, stepping up behind Eva and wrapping my arms around her waist, pulling her back against me. "We thought *some* parts of our marriage through before tying the knot, but we certainly didn't have time to plan out everything."

"So was this a spur-of-the-moment decision?" Morgan asks. I can't tell if she's just being curious, or if she's collecting information in order to help us frame this story in a way that puts us in the best light possible. When I ask, she just lets out a small chuckle and says, "My job here is to help you craft a message that will reflect well on both of you, personally and professionally."

"So you're a fixer," I observe.

She rolls her eyes and says, "Only when people *need* to fix their image. Is there anything that needs fixing here?" Her gaze lowers, and she notices my hands are splayed across Eva's belly, with hers resting on top. "Oh shit."

The way Morgan sighs those words lets me know that she's connected dots that we'd hoped no one else would without us telling them, and the way Eva stiffens in my arms lets me know she's noticed too.

"Okay," Morgan says decisively and walks over to the kitchen chair where she set her bag when she walked in. "I've got an NDA here, which we can all sign. And then I'm going to need you to level with me about what's going on, because I can't help you spin this story if I don't know *everything* that we're dealing with here."

Eva glances up over her shoulder, her eyebrows raised in question, and I give her a quick nod. I don't see any other—or better—option besides working with Morgan on this. I'm confident that she can identify any holes in our story and help us fill them now, so that they won't come out publicly at some point in the future.

Chapter Twenty-Two

EVA

When I met Morgan at the Neon Cactus last week, I knew I liked her, but I had no idea just how much I would appreciate and value her. She flew out to Los Angeles, wrangled together a believable love story for Luke and me, then insisted that Christopher come over and sign an NDA. She coached him on the best way to corroborate the narrative that Luke and I have been secretly dating, and she worked out a believable timeline for the pregnancy. It was nothing short of a miracle.

Taking her out to dinner to thank her was the least I could do. Plus, after forty-eight hours of close proximity to Luke, I needed some space.

Did I feel bad arranging a girls' dinner and leaving him to fend for himself? A little bit. But I know myself, and if I didn't get some distance from the way he keeps touching me, dropping kisses on the top of my head when he doesn't need to, and looking at me like he's lost the friendship filter, I might start to believe he feels something that he doesn't.

At least once we're back in Boston and Christopher gets settled there, I'll start training again. That will give me *some* physical outlet for this sexual energy that's always coursing through my veins.

I'm hoping my freaking hormones will settle once the baby is born. Then, Luke and I will be so focused on this child that it'll be easier to remember that our agreement is based on friendship and a desire to help each other out, but *not* any *other* kind of desire. Because right now, holy shit, is my body feeling the wrong kind of desire way too often!

Across the table, Morgan laughs, and when I glance up, she's looking at me with the most amused expression on her face.

"I'm sorry, what did you say? I swear to god . . . pregnancy brain has me lost in my own thoughts half the time." *And* I'm feeling a bit hot and bothered, thinking about how much I want Luke. I pick up my glass, hoping a sip of the ice-cold water will cool me off.

"Hey, if I was in a fake marriage to a guy who was clearly in love with me, I'd be all up in my head too," Morgan says, right as I take a sip. A small ice cube slips down the back of my throat, and I cough, spewing water all over myself.

I lift the cloth napkin from my lap, thankful that it caught most of the water, and hold it to my face as I cough into it violently. I'm a freaking delightful dinner companion tonight.

"What the hell?" I squeak out when I can finally manage to breathe again. "He's not in love with me."

She lifts one of her light eyebrows. "Is that the story you're telling yourself?"

"What part of our agreement and our reasons for entering into it weren't clear?"

Oh shit, can she tell that I have feelings for him, and she's just confused about where that energy is coming from?

"Oh, I think your reasons are very clear, and both valid. But you two didn't set an end date for this. This isn't a short-term thing to help each other out and then part ways as friends—"

"How could we do that without crushing our families?"

"Exactly." She shrugs, then glances down to spear a few pieces of pasta. "So you two are in this for the long-term. And no one—especially no *man*—does that if there aren't romantic feelings involved."

"Really?" I ask, my tone laced with sarcasm. "So you're telling me there are actual *rules* about how fake marriages work?"

She looks at me with some combination of sympathy and amusement. "You'd be surprised how often this actually happens. A lot of the time, it's just long-term dating arrangements and stuff between celebrities, but sure, fake relationships, fake engagements, and even fake marriages happen when it's mutually beneficial for both parties."

I think about Luke's brother, Tucker, and his engagement that fell apart so spectacularly last year. I've long suspected that the relationship had been "arranged," but the Hartmanns are tight-lipped about things like that, even with people like me, who they consider "practically family."

"Trust me," I tell her. "Luke does *not* have feelings for me. What you're seeing is just how he is with everyone. He's super affectionate and friendly . . . like a goddamn golden retriever."

She looks at me like she can't quite understand how Luke and I could possibly be best friends. I'm the absolute opposite of a golden retriever. I'm cautious about trusting people and take a long time to warm up to new friends, which explains my incredibly small group of friends. In social situations, I'm pretty quiet and reserved unless I already know everyone—though last week when we met up with Luke's teammates and their fiancées, Jameson and Lauren, and Morgan, I felt much more at ease than usual. Having Luke by my side must have that effect on me.

"Yeah, so the thing is," Morgan says, setting her elbows on the table in front of her as she leans in a bit like she's about to tell me an important secret. "I've met Luke a handful of times before I met you. I've seen him sober, and I've seen him a few beers into his night. I've seen him out with the team and with smaller groups of friends. I've seen women hitting on him constantly. But I've *never* seen him touch another woman. I've *never* seen him lean in and speak to anyone like they're keeping each other's secrets. I've *never* seen him brush a woman's hair behind her ear. And I've *never* seen him unable to tear his eyes away from a woman's lips. Except . . . with you."

I don't know if I want to laugh or cry. Because yes, Luke does all those things with me. But I've *seen* him act that way with other women too . . . haven't I? He's a professional-grade flirt. I've watched it with my own eyes many times over the years.

I wrack my memory, trying to think of the last time I saw him act that way, and I come up short. I can't think of a single time in the last few years that I watched him flirt with someone or saw him touch another woman. I'd half expected to find him in some corner with a woman all over him when we went out with our high school friends, like had happened more than once when we were younger. But . . . that isn't what happened.

"And now you're speechless," Morgan muses, before taking a sip of her wine.

"Can I tell you something?" I ask, suddenly desperate to have someone to talk to you about this. Because there is *no one* in my life who I have *ever* been able to be honest with about my feelings for Luke. Even while Christopher knows more about my life than just about anyone else, I've never even told him the full truth.

"I signed an NDA," Morgan says with a laugh, "you can quite literally tell me anything. Though really, if it's something illegal, maybe keep that to yourself? I have this whole moral complex about doing the right thing." She rolls her eyes with a little shake of her head, like she's laughing at herself.

With her strawberry-blonde hair pulled back in a sleek bun, the smattering of freckles across her nose and cheeks, and her big blue eyes, she comes across as very innocent. But I've seen the way she worked her magic with our situation, shaping our story and helping us spin it into something that looks a lot like true love. I've learned that she works for the famous talk show host Petra Ivanova, and she's done such a great job that AJ brought her on as a "fixer" to help with social media and PR situations for the Rebels. She's the daughter of one of the shrewdest sports agents in the business. So I'm willing to bet that no one should underestimate Morgan based on her appearance.

I take a deep breath and say, "I used to be completely and totally in love with Luke."

Morgan clears her throat. "Wow, I wasn't expecting that."

"Why not?"

"Because his feelings are obvious. Yours are . . . less so."

"That's because I *used* to have feelings for him. Now I know better." Too bad that *knowing better* hasn't truly changed my feelings.

She lifts an eyebrow. "Really? Why's that?"

"How much time do you have?" I joke, and she glances down at the full plates of steaming hot food that we've barely touched since the waiter dropped them off a few minutes ago.

"For this kind of lore? Oh, I have all the time in the world."

———

Eight Years Ago

Across the courtyard, I watch Luke talking to Sadie Montgomery, the blonde cheer captain who's made her recent crush on him well known. She was dating the quarterback of our football team for the first half of the year, but they broke up sometime this winter. It was right in the middle of hockey season, and by the time Luke led our hockey team to the state championship in the early spring, she'd set her sights on my best friend.

I don't know if she just falls for the captain of whatever

team is winning in the current season or if she actually likes Luke, but I've watched her overt flirting become more and more ostentatious as we've crept toward the end of our senior year.

"What do you think he sees in her?" I ask Reese, who's standing next to me, commenting on Luke and Sadie's interaction. If she swats his chest and throws her head back laughing one more time, I might actually throw up. Luke's funny, but he's not *that* funny, and I want to yell across the courtyard and tell her she's trying too hard.

Luke doesn't like girls who come on too strong . . . or try too hard. Not that he's specifically *said* that to me, but every time it's obvious that a girl is after him, he lets her down gently. He's never had a girlfriend and always jokes that I've set the bar too high. *I'll have a girlfriend when I find someone I like better than you, Evie*, he always says.

I've tried to explain that you can date even if you prefer your best friend's company—a point I've also modeled. Is there anyone I'd rather spend time with than Luke? No. But when we hit high school, and everyone started to think we were more than friends, despite the fact that Luke repeatedly explained that there was nothing but friendship between us, I realized that I needed to start dating.

Either that, or I was going to have to admit to myself that he's the guy I measure everyone else against—the one who's totally perfect for me in every way. And since dating him is out of the question, I had to explore other options, or I was going to waste away my high school years pining for my best friend.

Reese snorts his response, and when I glance at him, he says, "I mean, just look at her."

I do, and I regret it, because she's trailing a finger down his breastbone, right between his pecs. Not many guys our age have bodies as built as Luke's. At over six feet tall, he's wrapped in corded muscles that make him look a lot older than he is.

"Okay, what do you think she sees in *him?*"

"You mean, besides the Hartmann name?" Reese asks, sarcasm evident in his tone. "And that he's probably going to be prom king? And that he's the captain of the state championship hockey team with a spot on Boston College's team already lined up? And obviously pretty good looking, and way too nice?"

I elbow him in the side without even looking at him. "Yeah, aside from that."

I get it, I really do. Luke *is* perfect. It's an undeniable fact. Dating other guys over the last four years has had the opposite of its intended effect. Instead of taking my mind off Luke, it's a constant comparison game. *Luke would never say something like that to me. Luke wouldn't be half an hour late for our date. Luke wouldn't cancel plans to hang out with the guys* . . . I could go on and on.

And yet, it feels like something has shifted between us this spring. His glances and friendly touches linger every-so-slightly longer. I've tried to convince myself it's just because we know we're headed in opposite directions this summer— I'm moving to LA to skate with a new partner, and he's heading to a hockey camp before starting at BC in the fall. These are the last months we have together, so it's natural we'd want to spend more time together. It doesn't mean anything.

Yet, I've seen a difference in the way Luke looks at me,

and now I can't unsee it. Now, I read every text he sends, searching for any subtle sign of sexual innuendo. And I've found plenty. Our normal playful banter now sounds and feels a lot like flirting.

All of it is enough to make me hope for something I never dared to hope for before.

And then, there's our prom agreement: if neither of us is dating someone when prom rolls around, we'll go together. It's still just shy of a month away, so I've been nervous to ask him about it—it doesn't feel *quite* close enough to the date to conclude that neither of us is going with someone else, but I've secretly been shopping for dresses online for weeks, so that I'll have the perfect option picked out, should we end up going together.

Then, earlier this week, Sadie made it public knowledge that *she* plans to be Luke's date for prom. And as I watch him wrap his hand around hers, pulling her fingers away from his chest, I note that he doesn't let go. He's standing there, holding her hand in the middle of the courtyard in front of our entire senior class at lunchtime. There's no way to misconstrue this level of public affection, especially as she steps even closer to him, barely a breath apart now.

"Think he's going to ask her to prom?" I wonder aloud. In my heart, I already know the answer. Sadie is exactly his type —tall and blonde, with long legs and a fake tan.

"He definitely is," Reese says. "He said he has this top-secret but very elaborate plan . . ." He pauses, and we both watch as Sadie leans up on her tiptoes and plants a kiss on Luke's cheek.

I don't wait to hear what Reese says next. I don't want to know anything about this plan, and I don't want to watch them together. Instead, I speed diagonally across the court-yard toward the entrance of the math and science building, where my next class starts in ten minutes.

Everything is blurry through the tears filling my eyes. Behind me, I hear Luke call my name, so I put my head down and walk even faster, which is probably why I don't see anyone in front of me until I've run smack into him.

I stumble backward from the impact, but he reaches out and grasps both my shoulders to steady me. When I glance up, Warner James is staring down at me, amusement forming creases near his eyes. Warner transferred here from our rival high school earlier this year and has always had some sort of vendetta against Luke.

He's flirted with me every single day for the past few months in English class and told me, just last week, that if I ever wanted to make Luke jealous, I should come find him. And like a freaking angel, he's appeared right when I need him most.

"You okay?" he asks.

"No."

He glances over my shoulder, then back down at me. "This about Hartmann?"

"Yes. Is your offer still open?"

He smiles down at me like he knows he's about to get his way. "Always."

"How do you feel about prom?"

"I'm not opposed."

He reaches out and wraps his hand behind my neck, at the same time I reach up and fist the fabric of his button-down to pull him closer. "Ask me."

"Go to prom with me?"

"Absolutely," I say and push up onto my toes to kiss him. We're not in the dead center of the courtyard like Luke was with Sadie, but enough people are around that this won't go unnoticed. Which is exactly what I need—a perfectly good distraction so I don't have to face the heartbreak from hoping that Luke had feelings for me, only to find out he was going to ask Sadie Fucking Montgomery to prom.

He pulls back from the kiss and looks down at me with a self-satisfied smile before quietly saying, "This will be fun." And then he's looking past me and pulling me to his side with an arm around my shoulder. "Hey, Hartmann. Did Eva tell you we're going to prom together?"

Luke's gaze shifts to my face, and I'm not even sure what I see in his eyes. He looks hurt that he's hearing this information from Warner and not from me. But I can't focus on that, because I'm too busy pouring all my energy into holding back my tears.

I've never been the sentimental type, but a revenge date to prom, when I really wanted to go with my best friend, was not how I planned to end my senior year.

———

"Oh, honey," Morgan says, her hand covering her mouth as she shakes her head. I can't tell if she's laughing at me or horrified that I'd dared to hope Luke had feelings, only to watch him cozying up with the cheer captain in public. "Did you guys ever talk about that?"

I sigh as I watch her bring her wineglass up to her lips, wishing I could have a drink right now to help me relax. Pregnancy is such a mind-fuck—on the one hand, it's got my *body* convincing me that I want Luke again, and on the other, it's got my *brain* tricking me into thinking he could feel the same way.

The hormones have to be responsible for my heightened sex drive. That, and the fact that sharing my apartment with Luke means I don't have the ability to satiate those needs because he's always around. Even this afternoon in the shower, I could barely make myself come because all I could think about was that it would feel so much better if the man just on the other side of my bathroom door was the one touching me.

Goddamn, the need to have sex feels fucking overwhelming, and knowing that I can't only magnifies the feelings.

"You okay?" Morgan asks, snapping me out of my fantasy of Luke and me in the shower. "You're kind of flushed."

"Sorry, just . . ." I shake my head to clear my thoughts, trying to remember what she asked in the first place. "Yeah, we kind of talked about it, later on. He actually tried to play it off like the only reason he went with Sadie was because I was going with Warner—like that wasn't what he'd planned all along."

Morgan tilts her head, studying me. "How'd you feel about that?"

"I don't remember," I say with a shrug, even though, of course, I damn well remember.

At some point before prom, Luke had said *I thought* we *were going to go together*, as if he hadn't been the one planning to ask Sadie. The only reason I was going with Warner was to cover up how hurt I was that he'd chosen her over me. So instead of being honest about my feelings, I'd teasingly said, *You flatter yourself,* as if the thought of us going together was preposterous. It's a phrase that has stuck with us for nearly a decade.

"It seems like"—Morgan raises her eyebrows—"maybe you guys need to talk about that?"

"Me and Luke?" I practically screech. I can think of nothing more mortifying than telling him the truth.

"Yeah, you and Luke. I think it would be good for the two of you to have an honest, open conversation about how you feel about each other."

"I think we're well established on the fact that we're just friends."

"Who happen to be married."

"Exactly. Believe me, we've talked about all of this, over and over."

She lifts one shoulder and gives me a small smile before saying, "If you say so."

Then she changes the subject, telling me about all the weddings she's in this summer, starting with her cousin, Lauren's, later this month, and ending with her mom's fourth marriage at the end of the summer. And even while I'm listening, I can't brush aside her comment that Luke's "feelings are obvious."

I want to believe her. But I've read that situation wrong with him once before, and getting it wrong this time could ruin our whole arrangement.

Chapter Twenty-Three

LUKE

It's way later than I would have expected when I hear Eva's key in the lock. I watch her from the air mattress as she slips inside and shuts the door quietly behind her, then turns to set her purse on the counter nearest the door.

I want to say something to let her know I'm still awake, but I also don't want to scare the shit out of her. By how quiet she's being, she obviously thinks I'm asleep.

She tiptoes into the bathroom and shuts the door behind her, and all I can think about is the shower I took after she left for dinner. I couldn't get her off my mind while the hot water rained down on me—the way she tasted when I kissed her, how she felt this afternoon when I held her against me, with my hand protectively cupping her belly. This desire I've always had for her feels like it's growing exponentially, and I'm not sure how much longer I'll be able to hide it.

I squirted some of her conditioner into my hand, wishing

that her signature peach scent was filling the shower because *she* was there with me. When I imagined *her* hand jerking me off instead of mine, I felt like the worst best friend ever. But I'm not even sure if that bothers me anymore. I'm trying my hardest to keep myself in check around her, and I'm willing to bet there will be plenty of showers in my future.

I've taken stock of all her toiletries and ordered them for my place so she'll have what she needs when we get back to Boston. I even grabbed an extra shampoo and conditioner for my own shower. Because yeah, I'm that guy now—the one who buys his best friend's scented toiletries, planning to use them to jerk off to all the fantasies of us together.

I'm an asshole is what I am. And if she had any idea, she'd seriously laugh in my face about it. Or would she?

These past few days, I've started to wonder. To hope, even? I didn't miss the way her eyes lingered on my body after we woke up this morning, or the way her breathing gets heavy when I'm close.

Eva opens the bathroom door and turns off the light, and I hear her walking past the kitchen table into the living area, heading toward her bed.

"Shit!" she hisses, and then I hear her jumping around.

I sit up. "What are you doing?"

"I'm so sorry to wake you," she says. "I should've remembered that we moved the chair to make room for the air mattress, but I wasn't thinking. I freaking stubbed my toe on it." She's bent over, with her foot on the opposite knee, clutching her toes in her hand. "I'll just . . ."

She puts her foot down, turns to take a step, but walks directly into the couch. She jumps back like it attacked her, and then starts falling onto the air mattress. I reach out to break her fall as she twists in the air in an attempt to avoid crashing into the coffee table on the far side of the air mattress. She puts a hand out to brace her fall, and it lands right on my shoulder, pushing me back onto my pillow. Her chest slams into mine, but luckily, she holds her head up so our faces don't collide—the last thing either of us needs is a broken nose.

"Oh my god," she whispers, her chest shaking with laughter. "What the fuck just happened?"

I can't help but laugh along with her. "I have no idea."

She lies there for a moment with one of her legs running along my side and her other knee bent by my opposite hip. Then she must realize that she's pressed right against my quickly hardening dick, because she lets out a small gasp.

I couldn't stop my reaction to her proximity if I tried, and I'm not sure I even want to anymore. When she plants her hand next to my head and starts to push herself off me, I wrap my forearm across her lower back without thinking, anchoring her to me.

Her face is inches away, hovering above me, motionless. As her lips part slightly, I can feel her heavy breath on my skin. She slips her tongue out and wets her lower lip as she gazes down at me. I'm about to tell her not to move when her hips flex, pressing her core along me.

I let out a soft groan, and her eyes widen. "I'm sorry," she whispers, eyes wide like she's shocked even herself. "My body just . . . did that without my permission."

I reach my other hand up and slide it along the side of her neck, holding back her waves of dark hair that have fallen forward onto my bare chest.

"And if your body *had* asked your permission?" I can't

take my eyes off her mouth, can't stop staring as her teeth sink into that full lower lip and her nostrils flare with a breath that makes her whole chest swell.

"I don't know." Her words are so quiet I can barely hear them despite the silence of the room. And then her hips press into me again, and we both let out a low moan. I pull her head toward mine. And as our mouths connect, she kisses me with reckless abandon.

I don't stop to think about what this means, or how it will change our friendship or affect our marriage. I'm desperate to taste her, to touch her, to fucking *know* her in ways I've never thought were possible. I want to take my time and savor her, explore every inch of her body and discover her reactions to each place I touch her.

But there's absolutely nothing slow about the way she's kissing me and rubbing herself along my cock like she's desperate for the friction, and I'm struggling to hold my body in check, no matter how hard I try. My hips rock up against her where she's pressed up against me, and she releases a deep moan that reverberates along our entire bodies.

She threads her fingers through my hair and tugs on the strands, while I smooth my hand from her lower back over her ass and push the hem of her dress up to her waist. Sliding my palm back up and skimming my thumb over the lower part of her abdomen, I expect to encounter her underwear. Instead, I find her bare.

I break away from the kiss. "Did you go out tonight with nothing under this dress?"

Her breath is coming in heavy, hot bursts, gliding along

my face as she props herself up on her elbows, looking down at me. "Not exactly."

My thumb strokes the smooth skin along the front of her hip, continuing down until I'm perilously close to her center. I can barely breathe in anticipation of finally knowing what she feels like. "Tell me more."

"I took them off when I got home. They're in the laundry basket in the bathroom." She glances away, but I cup her jaw and turn her face back to mine.

"Do you always take your underwear off when you get home?" I'm not even sure what or why I'm asking, but the fact that she fell on top of me, sans underwear and is obviously horny as hell, has me curious.

"Not always."

"So why tonight?"

"Luke, can you please stop interrogating me and go back to kissing me instead?"

I roll my hips up into her and don't miss the way the head of my dick rubs right along her clit, making her eyes close as her lips part in a breathy sigh. "I'm happy to go back to kissing you," I say, letting my thumb slide farther down her belly. She sucks her stomach in to give me room, but my hand stops just before I make contact with her clit. "But first, I want to know why you took your underwear off."

She lifts an eyebrow. "And if I don't tell you?"

"We can stop."

If this scenario had played out even a week ago, I wouldn't have had the discipline to make this offer. I'd have continued kissing her after she asked, from fear that I'd never have another opportunity.

But her response to me tonight has me more confident

that this attraction between us isn't one-sided at all. Even if she calls my bluff and nothing else happens, I'm relatively certain that we'll find ourselves in a similar situation in the near future.

After years of telling myself this was a lost cause, "we" suddenly feel inevitable.

"I'd love to take care of all your needs right now," I tell her, taking my hand from her jaw and trailing it down her neck until my palm rests on her chest, right between her breasts. Her heartbeat is fast but steady beneath my skin. "But I need to know why you want this."

When she sighs and rolls her hips again, I know she's going to tell me—because it's clear she wants *this* more than she wants to keep her little secret.

"These pregnancy hormones have me . . . *needing* things."

I splay my finger out so my thumb and pinky dip beneath the top seam of her dress, and she whimpers. "What kind of things, Evie?"

"The sexual kind. I just need . . ." She rolls her hips again. I can't stop the way my own hips flex upward, rubbing along her core, and I don't miss the way she's making my boxers damp with her arousal. "I need a decent orgasm. And you said if I had needs—"

"To come to me. Good girl," I say and watch her eyes flare in surprise. I slip my hand farther between us, until my thumb coasts against her clit, and she squeezes her eyes shut, her lips parting as she sighs.

"I need . . ." she whispers, but then stops herself.

I trail kisses along her jaw, knowing I would give her anything and everything she asked for. "Tell me what you need, baby."

"I need this dress off. I want to feel your skin against mine."

"Sit up." I don't mean the words to come so ragged, but I'm so turned on at this point, it's hard to talk.

She straightens up, with her knees bent on either side of me, directly on top of my cock. Sliding my hands inside the stretchy material of her dress, I drag it up her body, and then sit up so I can pull it the rest of the way over her head. But now, her tits are right in front of my face, and I am so fucking distracted by them, I forget what I'm doing. I don't even realize she's finished pulling the dress off herself until I hear her light laughter and look up to find her staring down at me. "See something you like?"

I lick my lips, not breaking eye contact with her while bringing my hands up to cup each heavy breast in my hand. "You're fucking spectacular, you know that?"

She lets out a low rumble of laughter. "So you say . . . now that I'm naked."

"You're always spectacular, Evie. You're just extra amazing naked."

When I run my thumbs over her nipples, she hisses a "Yesss." I pull one of the stiff peaks into my mouth while toying with the other between my fingers, and she rocks her hips back and forth, rubbing her cunt along my length in quick, sharp movements. She's not taking this slow; she's chasing a feeling she can only get from another person. I glance up at her and ask, "Did you already try to make yourself come tonight? Is that why you're not wearing any underwear."

"Yes," she breathes out as she moves her body along mine. "But I need *you* to make me come, Luke. Please."

"I like it when you beg," I tell her with a smirk.

"That's not begging," she says, a flash of defiance on her face.

"Not *yet*." I bring my mouth back to her nipple, swirling my tongue over the hardened peak before sucking it into my mouth with several long pulls that have her moaning.

"Oh my god," she says, her hips bearing down on me harder and faster. "Yes."

I switch to her other nipple while I slide one hand behind her. With her breathy sighs as she rubs her clit against my cock, it makes sense that I find her absolutely soaked when my fingers reach her cunt, slipping right through the evidence of her arousal.

"Oh yeah," she says, her breathing heavy. "Yes!"

I curl my fingers inside her, and the slick, slapping sound of her fucking my fingers as she grinds her clit against me makes the base of my spine tingle. I clamp my lips around her, sucking her into my mouth while my tongue toys with her nipple—and I think the fact that I'm touching her in so many places is setting her off.

"Yes," she cries out. "Oh my god, please don't stop." She sinks onto my fingers over and over, begging me. "Harder, please, oh god, *please* don't stop . . . I'm so close . . . *please* . . ." The last word is nearly a choked sob as it escapes, and I feel the inner walls of her clench around my fingers. "Yes. Holy shit. Yes, Luke!"

That's what does me in—the way she cries out my name when she comes has lightning darting up my spine as I shoot my release against my boxers. When she stops spasming against my fingers, her body falls forward against mine, resting her chin on my shoulder and wrapping her arms around my back as she sighs contentedly against my skin.

"Thank you."

My chest shakes with a deep chuckle, and she pulls back to look at me, the question unmistakable on her face. "Trust me, Evie. The pleasure was all mine."

"I didn't think . . ." She bites her lip. "I wasn't sure we should cross this line. But now that we have . . ." Her hips rock into me again, and then she glances down between us. "Did you . . .?"

"Just find the entire experience of getting my wife off to be the most fucking erotic thing that's ever happened to me? Yeah."

"Sure," she says, her voice teasing, and it's then that I realize—maybe for the first time—that I'm eventually going to have to tell her. Because she deserves to know that the first time I fuck her will be my first time, period.

"Trust me, Evie. I've never seen *anything* sexier than you begging for an orgasm while coming on my fingers."

Even in the darkness, I can tell she's blushing, and I'm about to comment on it when the unmistakable sound of hissing air surrounds us and we start sinking.

"Oh my god, did we break this bed?" Her peals of laughter ring out over the air mattress deflating beneath us.

I look at her with a self-satisfied smirk. "We sure as hell did."

Chapter Twenty-Four

EVA

I wake up to Luke moving around in my kitchen. When I roll over to get a better look at him standing with his back to me in nothing but a pair of shorts, I can still feel the warmth on his side of the bed—and the view from over here is nothing short of spectacular.

The tattoos that run around his upper arms and onto his shoulders highlight the definition of his muscles, but those legs . . . Don't even get me started on how muscular his thighs and calves are. He's got the body of an athlete who's *clearly* never skipped leg day.

What's less clear, however, is why my kitchen looks like a scene from *The Sixth Sense*. Every upper cabinet door is flung wide open, and he's standing still, scanning their contents.

He squats then, pulling open one of the lower cabinet doors, and sighs. I lean over farther to get a better look, and he must hear the rustling of the sheets, because he stands again and glances over his shoulder. With a tentative smile, he says, "You're awake."

I clear my throat. "Yeah."

There's a cloud of awkward energy filling the room, and I hate that. One of the main reasons I've convinced myself that it's probably better that nothing ever happened between us is that I never wanted us to risk feeling this uncomfortable around each other.

He sets a coffee mug on the counter and turns toward me, and then I realize why he'd been searching my cabinets. Since he was last here, I installed pull-out shelves in the lower cabinets and moved my plates and cups there. Yesterday morning, I got a mug out for him and made his coffee while he was in the shower, so he didn't know where to find a mug this morning.

He crosses the living room in a few long strides and sits next to me on the bed. Reaching out, he brushes the hair off my face and tucks it behind my ear. He doesn't pull his hand back, leaving it cupping my cheek. "Are you freaking out?"

"Little bit." I press my lips together and force myself to hold his gaze.

"Okay," he says with a nod that causes his light hair to fall forward before he reaches up with his other hand and brushes it back. It's unfair that all he has to do to get a perfectly styled look is run his fingers through his hair. "Let's talk about that."

My laugh is awkward as I sit up on the bed, facing him, and my mind immediately goes blank, because Luke Hartmann is sitting across from me in nothing but a pair of jersey shorts, still smelling like sex.

Luke chuckles like he can read my thoughts, and all I can

focus on is his smile with perfectly white teeth sparkling between his full pink lips and the way his eyes crinkle at the corners.

Holy shit, get it together Eva.

But it's no use, because when Luke smiles at me like that —like he's remembering what I look like naked and enjoying the fact that I'm struggling to find my words—I can't think of anything but *him*. The way he kissed me like he wanted to become a part of me. The way he knew all the right ways to touch me. The way he made me come harder than I ever have, just from his fingers.

Of course he did. He's had plenty of practice.

It's been hard over the years to watch the women parade in and out of his life, never staying for more than a night or two. Luke doesn't date during the season, and even though we don't really talk about our sex lives, I *know* he's way more experienced than I am. It takes me a while to warm up to people, to trust them enough to be intimate. And the one and only time I let myself get carried away with a one-night stand . . . well, we know how that turned out.

"You're still freaking out," he asks, his eyes scanning my face like he's searching for an indication of what's going on in my head.

"I'm just . . . I'm . . . I . . ."

For the love of god, girl, just say something!

Luke leans toward me, and before I can even register what's happening, he kisses me. It's soft and gentle, his lips brushing mine in a way that has a breathy sigh escaping my lips.

He pulls my lower lip between his teeth, sucking gently, and I fucking melt. I'm a puddle for this man. In just one night, I've learned that he can be tender with me when I need it, but can also take control of my body as if he knows exactly what I need and how to give it to me.

How does he know me as well as I know myself? Better than I know myself, actually?

Just as I lean forward, ready to deepen the kiss and see where that leads us, Luke slowly pulls back.

"What was that for?" I ask, desperate to know why he kissed me. Could he not help himself?

He gives me a smile that's almost sympathetic. "Seemed like you needed something to calm you down."

"And that's how you calm me down?" Does this man have any idea how *not* calm my body is at this moment? How I only want more, every single time he touches me?

I told myself that we could do this whole marriage thing precisely *because* we were friends and nothing more. What does it mean that we've crossed this line now? What does it mean that I don't want to cross back, consequences be damned?

"You still seem worked up. Maybe I need to try again," he says with a sly smile.

"If you try again, we're going to end up with a repeat of last night—because nothing about kissing you is *calming me down.*"

"I'm okay with a repeat of last night." He fucking winks at me, like this is some sort of a game. And maybe it is, to him. I've watched him flirt with women my whole life, and it always looks a lot like this. The teasing comments, the subtle smiles, a wink here or there.

The realization that he's treating me like he treats every single woman he flirts with, that I'm not special, that I'm just one in a long line of women in his life—it's like a glass of ice water in my face. I was so damn *willing* last night, just like every woman is around him.

Fuck! Our friendship is special because it's unique, because there's no one else he's allowed into his life like he's let me in, and the same is true in return. And now I've gone and ruined it by acting like every other woman who has hopped into his bed.

I glance at the clock. "Christopher's going to be here in less than an hour. I need to get ready."

"You can't skip it?" He sounds hopeful, and delusional.

"Luke, this is my biggest endorsement and the main reason I needed to be in LA this week. No, I *cannot* skip filming this commercial."

Endorsement deals for figure skaters are nothing compared to what he makes as a hockey player. The handful of deals I have, and the prize money that Christopher and I have earned at major competitions this year, cover my basic expenses. The athlete-development fund for figure skating and my parents cover the rest. I have enough to get by, but it's not like I'm going to retire rich.

Even winning an Olympic gold medal and landing more coveted endorsement deals, I'd still earn less in a year than Luke makes in a month. Not to mention, he could always fall back on his trust fund he's never needed to touch.

I, however, have no such safety net. Which makes me a little annoyed that he's asking me to blow off something that will contribute to my financial future, just so we can fall back into bed again. It feels like I'm a commodity, instead of a person whose future he's looking out for.

You know that's not his intention, I tell myself. And while, logically, I know that's true, I'm definitely being guided by my emotions right now.

"I'm going to hop in the shower," I say quickly, scooting away from him.

And with that, I rush off to the bathroom, shutting the door behind me.

He didn't do anything wrong, I tell myself as I stare at my reflection in the mirror. He was trying to comfort me, and when I leaned into that kiss, indicating I wanted more to happen, he gladly agreed.

So why am I upset about it? It makes no sense. I'm making no sense. But despite knowing that, I can't stop the tears. I hop in the shower, cursing the pregnancy hormones that made me want to jump my husband last night and have me crying over him this morning.

This isn't me. I'm calm and steady, the opposite of overly emotional. If anything, people have told me I'm not emotional enough. I don't know if I can no longer hide my feelings for Luke because I'm pregnant, or if it's because I'm sensing that he might feel the same way. More importantly, I don't trust myself to know the difference.

———

"That looks great," Christopher tells Luke as he reaches over to return Luke's phone. "I really appreciate you setting me up with a furnished apartment in Boston."

"Anything for Eva," Luke says lightly, before glancing over from where he sits beside me on the couch.

I don't miss what he's really telling my skating partner: *I'm doing this for her, not for you.* And while I appreciate his help in placing Christopher in one of the corporate apartments owned by Hartmann Enterprises, he's only doing it to make our marriage work better. I don't know why, but I keep hoping that he'll eventually come around to Christopher.

At least he hasn't called him Christopher Fucking Steele. Yet.

Honestly, everything would be easier if Luke and Christopher could get along. It was fine when Luke lived in Canada and only saw Christopher a couple of times a year. Now that we'll all be in Boston together, I can see things being a little more difficult.

Maybe I can start by talking to Christopher, whose hostility toward Luke might be easier to tamp down? Christopher isn't the kind of person to be emotional about things—at least off the ice. If anything, he comes off as cool and indifferent, like nothing's ever a big deal to him. And if I tell him to cut this shit out, he probably will. Luke, on the other hand, has some deep-seated animosity toward Christopher that I've yet to figure out. Whenever I bring it up, he deflects.

Christopher chuckles quietly before he walks into the kitchen, opens the refrigerator door, and grabs the orange juice off the shelf. He then grabs a glass from the lower cabinet and sets it on the counter.

Next to me, Luke's eyes narrow as he watches Christopher pour juice into the glass. The glass that was sitting next to the coffee mug Luke struggled to find earlier. And I can sense Luke's frustration over Christopher's familiarity with my apartment—as if it represents a similar familiarity with me.

But I'm not going to feel bad about that. We're friends

who spend a great deal of time together. In fact, he's the one who helped me install those roll-out shelves.

Then again, with the number of times Luke had to listen to me talk about Christopher over this past season, the way I was always hemming and hawing over whether or not he had feelings for me . . . maybe he's a little jealous.

My friendship with Luke has always been the most important thing to me, but I could see how he might think I was putting Christopher before him. Which makes sense because I never shared the insight I finally came to concerning Christopher: the only reason I was desperate for him to see me as more than a friend was because I knew Luke never would.

I just wanted *someone* to choose me.

"Think we should get going?" Christopher calls out from the kitchen.

Thankful for the interruption of my thoughts, I spring off the couch. "Yeah, we'd better go." I glance down at Luke. "Do you want to come?"

His eyes flick over toward Christopher and he says, "Nah, it's probably better if I stay here and keep packing. Plus, I have to drop your car off at the dealership."

My little two-door convertible would be completely impractical in Boston winters, and unsafe with a baby in the back seat, so Luke arranged to sell it to a used car dealership.

"All right. Well, thank you for that," I say as I reach out, ruffle the hair on the top of his head, and turn to leave, thankful for the opportunity for some space.

On the short drive to the rink where we'll be taking pictures for the brand of figure skates that sponsors our team, Christopher is practically gloating about how jealous Luke is with him around.

"Are you intentionally trying to antagonize him?" I ask.

"No, but it amuses the shit out of me to see how jealous he gets. Eva, you can't seriously believe that he sees you only as a friend? He's so fucking possessive of you . . . Even the way he looks at you screams *I want her.*"

"Pfft." I let a hiss of air escape my lips, signaling that his observation is ridiculous. But is it?

I want to push back, to remind him that we've been friends, and only friends, our whole lives. But even I realize that friends don't do what we did last night on that air mattress.

But friends with benefits do, I remind myself. And I guess that's the weird new phase we've let our relationship stray into?

"It'd be a lot easier for me if you guys could get along. He's my *husband*, Christopher. Can you please stop trying to get under his skin?"

"I'm just helping him recognize the wonderful person he has right in front of him." He says it with such confidence that I don't question his meaning, just his understanding of the situation.

"What he has is a pregnant best friend who needed some help covering up how she got pregnant, and better health insurance."

"What's wrong with our health insurance?" he asks.

I'd initially been afraid I'd lose it if I wasn't competing, but when I looked into it, that wasn't the case because my leave would be considered a covered maternity leave. "Nothing's wrong with it. But it only covers 80% of healthcare costs for the athlete and doesn't allow the addition of dependents. So any costs specific to the baby, whether incurred during the birth or afterwards, would have to be paid out of pocket. Luke's health insurance will cover one hundred percent of our family's healthcare costs."

"Hmmm . . . " Christopher says, as if trying to decide whether healthcare is a good enough reason to marry your best friend.

I decide to steer the conversation toward the photoshoot and away from my marriage. "Do you think there's any chance that they'll give us time to break in the skates before they expect us to hit the ice with them?"

Christopher snorts a laugh. "Have you already forgotten about last time?"

"Yeah, no," I say as he pulls into the parking lot of the rink we've practiced at forever. The last time we worked with this company, they were filming a commercial to air during figure skating competitions, and they wanted us in full costume performing our routine in brand-new skates.

You'd think a company that manufactured skates would know that it takes many hours over several different sessions to get the boots to mold to your feet enough that you can confidently jump and spin in them. I've never fallen as many times as I did in the three hours we were filming, and I'm not looking for a repeat experience while pregnant. "Hopefully, since this time it's just photos, we can do more posing and less actual skating."

"Speaking of skating," he says slowly while he unbuckles. "Have you been on the ice much in the past few weeks?"

"No," I admit. "I tweaked my back a week after I got back

to Boston and didn't want to skate until I was sure it was fully better."

"How'd you manage that?" he asks.

"Just bent over, then stood up the wrong way. I'm getting old," I say with a laugh. "Good thing I'm retiring soon."

He turns in his seat so he's facing me and rolls his eyes. "You're not old."

"I feel like I am."

"Are you sure you don't just feel pregnant?"

"I don't think my body is going to feel *younger* after I've given birth."

He presses his lips together, then closes his eyes for a moment before he opens them again and says, "Are you sure you're committed to doing this?"

"The photoshoot?" I ask. But I know what he really means.

He gives me the kind of sigh you'd give an impertinent kid. "For real, Eva. This is our last shot at the Olympics together. I want to make sure you're in this with me?"

There's no way he'd find a new partner and be ready for the qualifiers by December, even if he started now. The synergy that keeps two skaters in sync and the chemistry between the couple that delights audiences takes a long time to develop—four months isn't nearly enough time.

Plus, I want this experience too. Even though training throughout this pregnancy, not to mention coming back after the birth strong enough to compete *and* take care of a newborn, will probably be the hardest thing I've ever done . . . I still want to do it.

I reach over and take the hand he has resting on the gearshift, squeezing his fingers in mine. "I'm in."

Chapter Twenty-Five

EVA

MORGAN

Oh girl, the goddamn tension in that plane
was so thick I almost choked on it.

Would you two just GIVE IN to each other
already? Why are you fighting it?

The three of us spent most of the flight rehashing the commercial Christopher and I shot yesterday, reviewing the story we've crafted about how Luke and I ended up married, and mentally and emotionally preparing to see our parents at dinner tonight.

My parents' voicemail after we'd dropped the "oh by the way, we got married" text made it clear that our presence at dinner tonight was *not* optional. My dad doesn't put his foot down about much, so when he was the one to insist we come to dinner and explain what happened, there was no choice but to agree.

We went our separate ways after the plane landed at the private airport north of the city—Luke and I headed farther north to my parents' house, and Morgan back to Boston in the car the Rebels sent for her. Since she and I couldn't talk candidly about my relationship with Luke on the plane, I'm not at all surprised she's already texting me. She's also probably trying to take my mind off the impending dinner.

MORGAN

Also, let's get together this weekend so we can debrief all this. I have a feeling you'll need someone to talk to after your first few nights at home with your new husband!

"What are you laughing about?" Luke asks, glancing over at me.

"Hey, Andretti," I say, referring to Luke's favorite driver of all time. Even though Mario Andretti had retired before Luke was old enough to be interested in racing, I'm pretty sure he's gone back and watched every race the driver competed in. "Keep your eyes on the road if you're going to drive this fast."

Redirection has always worked best with Luke when I don't want to talk about something he's noticed.

"I'm literally driving the speed limit," he says as he takes a turn down the windy beach road that will lead past his house as we head to mine. I glance at the dashboard to see that, in fact, he is. I'm so used to him driving fast, I just assumed. He reaches over and rests his hand on the very slight curve of my belly, saying, "I've got precious cargo with me."

"Oh god." I laugh. "You're going to be the type of dad who

gets a *Baby on Board* sign for the back of your car, aren't you?"

Luke swallows, like the reality of being a dad is just sinking in. "Sounds like that might be a good idea."

I'm lost in the mental images of Luke being my baby's dad —the birth, all the milestones he'll be a part of, all the ways in which this will change our relationship. And then the road curves past the huge stone entrance to Wellington Manor, and Luke hisses, "Shit," under his breath.

"What's wrong?" I ask, brow furrowing as I look at his expression.

"Preston's and Tucker's cars are both in the driveway at my parents' house."

"Do you think this means your brothers are joining us for dinner?"

"I guess we'll find out," he says, continuing along the road for a few hundred more feet before turning into my parents' driveway. He seems so much calmer than I feel, which is shocking given that he's not just facing our parents—there's a professional component to this for him, since his dad owns the team and my dad is his coach.

As my childhood home comes into view, my stomach flips, and I find myself wondering why I'm so nervous. At my core, I'm a performer, and that's all tonight is . . . putting on a performance that will convince our parents we're so madly in love, we eloped. And as a bonus, they get a grandkid out of it.

"You remember what Morgan said, right? Stick to the script," I say.

"I'm best when I follow your lead," he says. "We'll make sure we sell it."

My stomach does another weird flip as I think about how tonight, after dinner, I need to pack up the remaining things I'd brought to my parents' house when I headed here for the month so we can bring them with us to Luke's place.

As he pulls the car along the side of the driveway and shifts into park, he reaches out to give my knee a squeeze. "We've got this, Evie."

I gulp and my stomach flips again. Am I so nervous that I'm making myself sick? *Get it together, Eva!*

As Luke opens his door and comes around the hood toward the passenger side, I open my door and step out to meet him. With the car door firmly in place between us, I drop my head and sigh.

"Hey," he says, cupping my jaw with surprising delicacy as he tilts my face up to him. "They're going to be happy for us. It's going to be fine." He tilts his head down and presses a kiss right where my forehead meets my hairline, then slides his hands down the side of my neck and over my shoulders. At first, his touch relaxes me, like it always has, but then, it's like my body remembers the way he was touching me the other night and immediately starts to crave that feeling all over again.

Which is terrible fucking timing, given that I see both sets of our parents out of the corner of my eye coming down the stairs of the deck and heading toward us. I look up at him just in time to see his face descending toward mine. The gentle caress of his lips steals my breath and has me wanting more, then he steps back and guides me around the car door so he can shut it.

"Game time," I mutter, and as he turns toward the house, he inhales sharply, as if he's surprised to see our parents walking toward us. But isn't that why he just kissed me? So they'd believe we're blissed-out newlyweds?

"You two have a lot of explaining to do," Dad says, looking back and forth between us. Is that disappointment in his voice? From his neutral expression, I can't tell if he's only looking for an explanation, pissed as hell, or something else altogether. And when Luke brushes his pinky across the back of my hand, I suspect he's wondering the same.

"That's why we're here," Luke says, pulling me to his side and looping his arm around my lower back. His fingers grip my hip possessively, and I'm sure he doesn't miss the way my dad's gaze moves from our faces to Luke's hand.

I hazard a glance at my mom and take note of her pissed-off expression. Which, to be fair, is kind of her default. When I was a teenager, I made the mistake of teasing her about her resting bitch face and quickly learned that she did not find me funny in the least.

I follow Luke's gaze to his parents. Elise and Frank are standing hand in hand, like they almost always are, because they're literally the cutest older married couple. *I hope Luke and I are like that someday.*

I'm not sure where the thought even comes from. There's no guarantee that we'll stay married that long. But god, if there was anyone in this world I'd want to settle down with forever, it's him.

Elise's lips are turned down at the corners and she's blinking rapidly, as though she's trying to prevent herself from crying. It makes me wonder if she's sad about this marriage, or only about having missed the wedding. Could she be this upset that I didn't sign a prenup?

Frank, however, is beaming. He looks like he just won a

bet—as if he knew this was going to happen eventually and has been proven right. It's nice that at least one person here seems happy about this marriage.

"Let's eat before the food gets cold," my mom says, absolutely no emotion in her voice as she gestures toward the house behind her.

Luke drops another kiss on the top of my head and tucks me up against his side as we follow our parents up the stairs and onto the deck, which runs along the entire length of the house. When we get there, I note that Preston and Tucker are nowhere in sight.

"Preston and Tucker didn't come?" Luke asks his mom as we move toward the table.

"No," she says, giving his arm a pat. "Preston stopped by to talk to your dad about some business stuff, and Tucker was kind enough to pick up a dress I'd ordered in the city and drive it up here for me on his way to the restaurant."

Luke nods, and I wonder if he's relieved about their absence or was hoping they could run interference? That is, assuming that they support our marriage and would be willing to back us up? Based on Preston's text about the lack of a prenup, I have no idea how the Hartmann family feels about this. I also have no sense of what it's like to have siblings.

We take our seats around the large glass table, where grilled steaks and skewers of shrimp sit on platters, surrounded by a large bowl of grilled veggies and smaller bowls of potato, pasta, and green salads.

My stomach rumbles loud enough that Luke hears it over the crashing waves below us, and he chuckles. He knows that it's been hours since I ate on the plane and that Baby Squash has probably devoured all the nutrients from that meal, leaving me starving. After a decade of closely monitoring every last thing I put into my body, one of the highlights of the past few days in LA was actually eating what I wanted, when I wanted.

We load up our plates in silence before Frank finally says, "All right, kiddos, tell us what's going on." His white hair is ruffling in the ocean breeze, his pink cheeks glowing from the golden light of the sinking sun, and his light eyes twinkle. I'm pretty sure he's enjoying this, but I'm not certain which aspects of this situation make him happy and which he might be concerned about.

I move my hand from my lap to Luke's thigh, giving him a little squeeze. I know he said he's best when following my lead, but it's like I've forgotten the story we'd concocted in LA and perfected on the flight home. I'm at a total loss for words.

Luke takes my hand in his, gliding his thumb across the monstrous ring on my finger, before he looks at my parents and says, "I've been in love with your daughter for as long as I can remember."

It takes everything in me—every bit of training I've ever had, every ounce of practice smiling for the cameras no matter how I feel inside—to keep myself from gasping. This is so wildly different from the "slowly figuring out we had feelings for each other" storyline we developed with Morgan.

Why is he going off script about this? Did he momentarily forget what we were supposed to say, like I did? Because now it's all come back to me with total clarity, and *this is not it.*

Though honestly, he sounds entirely believable, so maybe this is the right direction?

I'm busy thinking about how we'll probably need to let Morgan know about this, when he glances over, giving me a small and affectionate smile before leaning back in his chair, raising his arm, and resting it over my shoulders. The pads of his fingers toy with the bare skin at the top of my arm, sending goose bumps down to my hand and a wave of longing through my core.

"And recently, I finally started hoping she returned those feelings."

How recently? What is he talking about? Is he trying to tell me something right now, or is this part of the "let's sell this story" plan and I need to step up my faking it game?

"We've been secretly dating for about . . ." He pauses, glancing at me, like he's trying to do the math in his head. ". . . nine months? It started when I was still living in Calgary and went to visit Eva in LA this past fall. Because of her competition schedule and my hockey schedule, we were only able to meet up in person a few times over the winter and spring. We quickly realized we didn't want to keep doing the long-distance thing. So we decided to get married, as quickly as possible."

Okay, at least that part of the story follows the narrative Morgan concocted for us.

"And you couldn't have told us this *before* you got married?" his mom asks, and from her tone, it's obvious she's hurt.

"We knew what we wanted and didn't want anyone to try to talk us out of it," I say, softening my voice so it doesn't come out sounding defiant. We're grown-ass adults and we don't technically need our parents' permission, or even their blessing. But somehow, I know we'd both be happier if they bestowed their best wishes on us. Our families have been super close since before we were both born, and the relationship has remained strong all the way up to this very moment. There are personal *and* professional ties between them, and we don't want to strain that for our parents.

"Why would you think we'd try to talk you out of it?" my dad asks, and by the way Frank tilts his chin as he waits for our answer, he clearly has the same question.

"We weren't sure. We also didn't want a big wedding," I say. "This relationship has grown and changed over time, and because only the two of us knew about it, we wanted it to be just the two of us at the ceremony as well."

"That fact that you got married in Vegas, when we were all there, and didn't even invite us . . ." Elise's voice trails off as she looks out at the ocean and clears her throat.

"We weren't trying to hurt you," Luke says in a rush. "But we talked about it a lot, and this was the wedding *we* wanted. We're about to be parents ourselves—"

Luke stops speaking when the collective gasp sounds around the table. "Shit," he mumbles under his breath. "Forgot we hadn't gotten to that part."

"Surprise," I say, lifting my hands above the table and giving them a little shake—the awkward jazz hands match my equally stilted laugh.

"How far along are you?" my mom asks, and I jump to the shitty, but probably correct, conclusion that she's asking only so she can figure out how much this might fuck up my skating career. I try to give her the benefit of the doubt, because maybe that's not what she means—but the fact that's my first guess speaks volumes about her caring more about my career than about me.

"Almost twenty-eight weeks."

My mom's nostrils flare as she takes a deep breath in an apparent attempt to calm herself, but it makes her look like a horse that's about to rear up.

"How can you be that far along?" Elise asks, looking at me. "You're not even showing."

I run my hand over the barely-there baby bump.

"I was still training pretty hard up until a few weeks ago. I actually didn't know I was pregnant until I was about five months along, and I had a competition season to finish out."

"So this is why you changed up the routine, ensuring you didn't place first in your final competition?" my mom asks. "And why you ended up in the hospital after that flight? Because you're *pregnant*?"

I nod.

"And can you explain how you're planning to continue with your skating now that you've gotten yourself in this situation?" Mom asks, and I instantly stiffen in my seat.

"This isn't something that happened *to* Eva—" Luke's voice is hard, but I squeeze his thigh, signaling for him to stop, and he takes the hint. Fighting with my mom over the specifics of my pregnancy won't make anything better.

"Christopher is relocating to Boston this week," I say, "and we'll continue training here with the new coach we hired last week." When my mom opens her mouth to respond, I continue without letting her interrupt. "That point isn't up for negotiation. I'll train on the ice until my obstetrician says it's no longer safe, and then we'll train off-ice. Our plan is to be ready for the last Olympic qualifier at the end of this year," I say, my hand moving over the slight bump of my growing abdomen, "but obviously, things may change."

"I can't believe you'd ruin your Olympic dreams like that," my mom mutters, quietly enough that it could be an internal thought she didn't mean to say out loud.

"Eva's skating career hardly feels like the thing to focus on right now," Luke says, before turning and pressing a kiss to my temple, and I don't miss the way my dad's eyes track his movement.

"Don't you dare tell me where *I* should be focusing my attention, Luke," my mom says, as Dad sets his fork on his plate and moves his hand to my mom's leg. I wonder if he's giving her a supportive pat, or the kind I just gave Luke, encouraging him to back down? "You have *no idea* the extent of the sacrifices we've made to help Eva achieve this dream of hers."

Well, shit.

"Mom." I keep my voice placating, like I often do when speaking to her. "It's not that I don't appreciate those sacrifices, but . . ." I trail off, unsure of how to justify this when my parents have truly given me everything they could over the years.

"But Eva's an adult," Luke grinds out through his clenched jaw, "and married, and about to become a mother herself. We're not planning to run our decisions about things that affect us, our baby, or our careers, past anyone else—not even our parents."

Mom pushes her chair back, and the sound of metal scraping against the deck is shrill. Before she can stand, Dad grabs her hand and very quietly says, "You're not walking out on *this* conversation."

"I'm not worried about either of your careers," Frank says loudly, like he's trying to draw attention away from the menacing stare-down between my parents. "But this marriage and accompanying pregnancy do present some logistical issues."

Oh fuck. If he tells Luke he's about to be traded, after everything we just did to move Christopher out here so we could train as much as possible before the baby is born, what will we do? Didn't AJ pretty much guarantee that Luke had *at least* one more season with the Rebels? Our whole arrangement is predicated on us being together in Boston.

Luke clears his throat. "What kind of logistical issues?"

"Depending on when this baby's born . . .?" my dad says.

"Early October," I say.

"Okay, so the baby will be born right around training camp and pre-season games," Frank says, looking at Luke. "You really can't miss those, even though you have a new baby at home."

Luke stabs some of the roasted vegetables on his plate. "I know."

"So how is Eva going to get the support and help she needs? You can't just leave your wife and newborn baby like that."

"Obviously, the timing isn't ideal," I say. "But hockey players have babies during the season all the time, and their families manage. We will too."

"We're still working out a plan, but it will depend a lot on when the baby arrives," Luke adds.

The fact that none of our parents has jumped in with an offer of support isn't lost on me. I'd like to think it's just because they're stunned and still processing this news. But

I'd be lying if I denied that it has me a bit worried. But then Frank jumps in, saying, "Make sure you let us know what we can do to help."

Next to me, Luke lets out a small sigh of relief as the conversation shifts more toward the baby. And as we field our parents' questions while we eat, I glance over toward my mother where she's cutting her food and taking bites, without saying a single word.

Eventually, we finish our dinner, and Luke sits back in his chair, slinging an arm over my shoulders. His thumb runs up and down the side of my neck while his fingertips rest along my collarbone. I lean into his touch, resting my head on his shoulder and wishing that this wasn't just for show, to convince our parents that there are real feelings between us.

And the fact that I so desperately want the feelings between us to be real, nearly ten years after I gave up any hope of being anything but a best friend to Luke Hartmann, has sent my anxiety through the roof. Morgan is right that the adult thing to do is to have an honest conversation with him about this, but I'm terrified of ruining the tenuous agreement we have in place.

My mom excuses herself and returns a minute later. "I made some cupcakes," she announces, setting a platter in the center of the table. They're golden with crystalized sugar sparkling upon yellow frosting and a candied lemon slice on each.

I look at that platter and the relief I feel is enormous. I love any and all lemon baked goods, and the fact that my mom made my favorite cupcakes must be a good omen, right? Luke gives my shoulder a quick squeeze, and I know he's thinking the same thing.

"These look delicious," I say as my mom hands out dessert plates.

"You should probably skip dessert," she says in response as she keeps the plate meant for me stacked on top of her own before setting my dad's in front of him and sitting. "You're going to gain enough weight being pregnant, and sugar isn't good for the baby."

There's a moment of silence, and my insides simmer with shame and embarrassment. She's not wrong, but being called out like that in front of my husband and his family feels like she's taking things to the next level. Normally, she keeps those kinds of barbs private, rarely even saying them in front of Dad.

"You know what," Luke says, pushing his chair back suddenly, "we actually already have dessert plans." He stands and effortlessly pulls my chair out from the table, as if I don't weigh a thing. "We're going to head out now. Thanks so much for dinner."

I stare at the deck as we turn to leave and don't even attempt to say goodbye for fear that my voice will crack and betray the fact that I'm about to bawl.

Luke wraps his arm around my shoulders and holds me to his side. As we round the side of the house and follow the path leading to the driveway, we can hear our parents' voices rising behind us, and I'm glad we're not there to witness—or partake in—the argument that seems to be breaking out.

"We have dessert plans, huh?" My voice is quiet, and my laugh is tight.

"If my wife wants cupcakes, she's having fucking cupcakes, and *no one* is going to make her feel bad about that."

My stomach drops at his possessive tone. I like that a little too much. So instead of focusing on that, I say, "My mom's not totally wrong, though . . ."

"Fuck that, Eva. You're growing a baby. Yes, you're also a competitive athlete and need to stay in decent shape. But more importantly, you need to do what's good for you and the baby, and denying your body food—and an occasional treat—is definitely *not* what you need right now."

He kisses the top of my head, and my shoulders shake with laughter.

"What's so funny?"

"The way you just practically growled, *If my wife wants cupcakes . . .*"

As we approach the car, he turns me toward him, and putting his hands on either side of my shoulders, he boxes me in between him and the car.

Dipping his head down next to mine, he says, "If my wife wants *anything* . . . it's hers."

Then he kisses my forehead and reaches down to open the door. As I get settled in my seat and pull on my seatbelt, I feel more than a little dazed and confused from seeing Luke transform from easy-going golden retriever to dominant and possessive in the blink of an eye.

Until a few days ago, I'd *never* seen that side of him. I wish it wasn't just one more thing to love about him.

Chapter Twenty-Six

LUKE

After years of being a night owl, I'm shocked by how Eva can fall asleep instantly like she does now. But the process of growing another human is exhausting, and napping seems like it's practically a necessity. According to the pregnancy app, that's more common in the first trimester rather than the second, but given that she didn't know she was pregnant for so long and then couldn't give her body a chance to rest, it makes sense that she's playing catch-up.

Her practice schedule will start up again once Christopher arrives in a few days, but I'm hoping she can use this time to relax a little. I get that she doesn't want to slow down too much for fear that it will impact her perxformance later, but there has to be a balance or she's going to risk both her health and the baby's.

Yet I'm not sure how much I can push on that issue—it's

neither *my* baby nor *my* career. I don't want to limit her choices; I only want to help her make good ones.

I glance at her sleeping on my couch, and then pick my phone up to reread the text message Charlie sent the two of us after we left.

COACH

I'm sorry about how dinner ended tonight. Please know that we all want what's best for the two of you. While your news tonight came as quite a shock, I just want to say that I trust the two of you to know what's best.

On the car ride home, Eva hadn't been ready to respond so I respected that choice. But now it's been hours since Charlie sent that message, and I feel bad not acknowledging that he reached out.

I'm still pissed as hell about how that all went down, but if it weren't for Helene, the dinner would have actually been okay. Not stellar, but my parents and Charlie came around to our news pretty easily, and if it hadn't been for Helene's comment about the cupcakes, we might have left there tonight feeling okay about things.

None of that is Charlie's fault, though.

LUKE

Thanks, Coach. I appreciate your support as Eva and I adjust to being married and prepare to be parents. I'm sorry we kept you in the dark for as long as we did.

I wait a few minutes to see if he'll respond, even though I assume he's already in bed asleep, but the reply doesn't come.

Then I glance over at the cupcakes cooling on my counter, and back at Eva sleeping on my couch. Even the noise from me mixing the batter and the timer going off when they were done baking didn't wake Eva up. Then again, she slept right through the stops at three different bakeries and a grocery store on the way back from her parents place, so maybe I shouldn't be surprised.

She woke up momentarily as I carried her from the car and into the elevator, but fell right back asleep in my arms before we even got up to my floor. I considered putting her straight into bed and letting her sleep through the night. But I'm afraid that if she doesn't get up for a bit, her body will wake her up in the middle of the night thinking it's already morning.

"Hey, baby, wake up," I say when I kneel next to the couch, where she's fast asleep, covered in a light blanket. She's curled on her side with both hands wedged between the pillow and her cheek, and she scrunches up her nose when I trail my thumb across her brow. "Evie, can you get up for a little bit?"

Startling, her eyes jolt open before they focus on me. "What time is it?" She blinks a few times like she's trying to convince her eyelids they can stay open.

Goddamn, she's adorable. It's not a word I'd normally use to describe her—she's determined, strikingly beautiful, and strong. But when she's sleeping, she's soft, sweet, and utterly adorable.

"It's after ten at night."

Her gaze focuses behind me as she looks around the space like she's completely disoriented. "How did we get up here?"

"I carried you," I say, realizing that she has no memory of waking up in my arms.

"Man, pregnancy is wild. I *never* nap, and now I feel like I could use one every day."

"You should listen to your body. Napping is linked to healthier birth weight in babies, and given how you probably haven't gained much weight . . ."

It's not that she hasn't actually gained weight, it's just that it's mostly all in her tits and her ass, which unfortunately only adds to her physical appeal. And now she's finally developing a baby bump, the sight of which has me practically feral.

I don't know what it is about her being pregnant, but just the thought of watching her body grow and change has me aching with longing. I can't wait to walk this road to parenthood with her, can't wait to watch her body change, and can't wait to meet our Baby Squash. And I want to know if this baby is a boy or girl almost as much as I want its mom to want me like I want her.

I never thought we'd end up here together like this—I gave up that hope a long time ago—but now that I have her, now that I've seen the way her body responds to mine, now that I've watched her start to take down some of the walls she's built up around herself—I'm more certain than ever that there's the possibility of a *real* future between us. And I want that more than I've ever wanted anything.

She scoffs. "You're cute." The sarcastic phrase is followed by an eye roll.

"Oh, come on," I say. "What have you gained? Like, ten pounds, max?"

"Yeah, well," she says, sitting up and stretching her arms over her head before reaching down and straightening out her dress. "I have a skating partner who needs to be able to lift me above his head while spinning around the ice, so even ten extra pounds is a problem."

"Evie, I could lift you above my head with one hand and jump up and down on the ice while spinning around, all without breaking a sweat. So if Christopher is going to have a problem with ten extra pounds, maybe he needs to lift some fucking weights."

She barks out a quick laugh. "It's less about how much I weigh and more about weight distribution. Where I'm carrying that weight affects how and where he holds me, and the extra weight affects how fast we travel across the ice. Every millisecond of our choreographed performances is based on *nothing* changing. Our height, our weight, our speed . . . all of it factors into our routine. It's basic physics, College Boy." She unfolds her legs and stands up before sniffing the air and turning toward the kitchen. "Did you . . . bake?"

"Yeah. I stopped at a few bakeries on the way home, and no one had lemon cupcakes."

She tilts her head, looking up at me over her shoulder. "So . . . you *made* me lemon cupcakes?"

I nod and follow her over to the island where the cupcakes are sitting out on a cooling rack. Google said that was the fastest way to cool them down before frosting them. Her stomach rumbles loudly, and she rubs her hand over her belly. "I think Baby Squash wants some of those."

"Should we frost them first?" I ask.

She gives me a look that lets me know how silly that question was. "Without frosting, they're just muffins."

"Well, even as muffins, these are delicious."

"You already had some without me?" Her mock outrage is cute.

Then she puts her hands on the counter behind her and jumps up to sit on it, right next to the cupcakes. With her sundress bunched around her thighs, bare feet dangling in front of my kitchen cabinets, and long hair hanging over her shoulders as she glances down at the unfrosted cupcakes, she doesn't look at all how I described her earlier. She's not the sweet, sleeping version of herself, or the determined, hardcore athlete the world loves to watch perform.

No, this relaxed, contented version of her is *mine.*

She raises her eyebrows as she glances up at me, an expectant look on her face. *Shit, what did she just ask me?*

"Fine," she says, swiping a cupcake off the cooling rack. "I'm going to have one, too."

"Wait, I have frosting right here," I say, taking the lid off the plastic container bearing a clear sign of my earlier taste test. She laughs quietly when she sees the depression in the yellow frosting from where I dipped my finger in earlier.

Pulling one side of the paper liner back from the cupcake, she takes a huge bite and chews before saying, "It could use frosting."

I dip my finger in the tub, scooping out a hefty amount of the sugary yellow substance. "It *is* your favorite part."

I hold my finger out, expecting her to use her teeth to bite the frosting off the pad of my finger. Instead, and without breaking eye contact, she leans forward and sucks my finger between her lips, swirls her tongue over it as she sucks off the frosting, and then sits back.

I'm literally stupefied watching her, so it doesn't occur to me to pull my hand back, and it falls to her chest, leaving a thin, shiny yellow streak down her breastbone before I pull it away.

My voice is hoarse when I say, "You've . . . got a bit of frosting there." And without even letting myself think about what I'm doing, I dip my finger back into the tub sitting on the counter next to her and use my finger to trace the streak that's already there, covering her in more frosting.

She gulps at the same time I lick my lips, and the sound boosts the tension between us as we stare at each other, only a few inches apart.

If I hadn't smeared more on her just now, we could have laughed about the frosting accident, wiped it off her chest, and then frosted the rest of the cupcakes. Or maybe things shifted the minute she pulled my finger into her mouth and sucked the frosting off while staring me straight in the eye?

Either way, my dick is hard, and the ball is firmly in her court. She can keep saying we're just friends who got married if she wants, but neither of us can deny what's growing between us.

"That's more than *a bit*," she says, glancing down at her chest. Then she looks back up at me and licks her lips. "How should we clean that off?"

I step between her legs, grip her ass, and pull her to the edge of the counter so she's flush against me. "I have some ideas."

"Tell me about them," she says, each word a whisper slipping out on labored breaths.

"Tell you? Or show you?"

"Show me." Her chest is heaving as her breathing becomes more rapid, and the need rolling off her mixes with my own, making the air around us electric with desire.

I lean in, running my tongue from the bottom of the smear of frosting, right near her cleavage, up to almost her collarbone. And then I go back for seconds, sucking up the remains of the frosting as I follow the trail again, the pads of my fingers gripping her ass as I hold her hips still while she tries to squirm.

In general, I'm not a big fan of sweets. But here I am, contemplating smearing frosting over her entire body just so I can lick it off. The inevitable sugar coma would be worth it.

Her small whimper is the sexiest thing I've ever heard, and I groan as she wraps her knees over my hips, links her ankles behind my lower back, and pulls me even tighter, so her core presses right up against my hard length.

I run my hands up her sides, along her ribcage, letting my thumbs ghost the underside of her breasts, and she breathes out, "Yes, Luke."

And then she's threading her fingers into my hair, holding me to her as she nips at my lower lip, sucking it into her mouth. The drag of her teeth along the sensitive flesh and the lingering scent of lemon cupcake on her breath unravels the iron grip I've used to lock down my desire for her all these years.

Or rather, it's been unraveling ever since we got married, especially after that night on the air mattress. Now, I'm ready to throw caution to the wind.

The greedy little moans in the back of her throat as I

invade her mouth spur me on, as does the way she drags her fingers down my spine and around the waistband of my pants, toying with the skin beneath my shirt. Her thumbs trace the ridges of my abs as her fingers curl into my sides, then she stretches her back to push herself deeper into the kiss, her tongue caressing mine as my fingers fist her hair, and she tightens her legs around my hips. All of it has me feeling an overwhelming desperation to be closer to her.

I pull back, just enough to take a ragged breath. I'm pretty sure there isn't enough oxygen in the room, and if the way she's also trying to catch her breath as she stares up at me is any indication, she's feeling that, too.

And then, her eyes locked on mine, she brings her hands up to her shoulders and slowly slides the stretchy straps of her dress down. She leaves them hanging over her biceps as she licks her lips, as if to say, *Your move, Husband.*

Slowly, I move my hands from her hips to her forearms, trailing them upward at an excruciatingly slow pace . . . the kind that makes her breathing grow labored from anticipation and her tits strain against the square neckline of her dress. And then, she glances past me, to the wall of windows on the other side of the dining room.

"Luke, do you have shades or something?"

My condo is on one of the top floors of one of the tallest residential buildings in Boston, but from my corner unit, you can see right into the upper floors of the Prudential Building a couple of blocks away.

"Hey, Peaches," I call out, "turn off the lights."

My kitchen goes dark, the only light coming from the moonlight streaming in.

"You named your AI 'Peaches?'" Eva asks with a husky laugh.

When we were little, she wanted her middle name to be Peaches, after her favorite food, and insisted that she was going to officially change her name to Evangeline Peaches Wilcott once she was old enough. Ironically, I have no idea what her legal middle name even is. It's always been Peaches in my mind.

"I sure did. Might need to change it though, so it doesn't get confused when I use your nickname." My hands continue the path over her elbows until I hook my thumbs in the straps of her dress. "Are you sure you're okay with this?"

It's not like I didn't just have her naked and coming on my fingers two nights ago, but I'm not going to assume that means I have a free pass any time I want. I need to know this is what *she* wants. And I need her to be willing to say it.

She nods.

Keeping my voice low, I remind her, "Use your words, Peaches."

The tip of her tongue sweeps across her lower lip, leaving a glistening trail behind. "Yes."

I tug on those straps, and the neckline of her dress slides down, dragging slowly across her cleavage. Pregnancy has given her amazing tits—the kind that leave me fantasizing about all the things I could do to them.

When the fabric crests her nipples, it falls loosely toward her waist, and she lifts her arms, sliding them out of the straps. "That's better," she says as she puts her hand on the counter behind her, leaning back to give me the full view, which is so spectacular I think I've forgotten how to speak.

It was nearly pitch black that night in her apartment, so

I'm truly seeing her for the first time. She's glorious, a fucking vision to behold. And I must stand there, taking her in for a beat too long, because she looks up at me and chuckles.

"I'm not going to bite, Luke."

I lift an eyebrow as I look at her. "Yeah . . . but I might."

Chapter Twenty-Seven

EVA

A surprised exhale slips out of me, half laugh, half squeak, and then Luke leans forward and gently lowers my upper body to the cool marble counter.

Holy shit. Neither of us is even naked yet, and I might orgasm just from the way he's looking at me. He quickly unbuttons his shirt and tosses it to the side, and I focus on the ink that swirls and dips across his skin, from the bicep of one arm, around his shoulders, and down the other arm. I want to explore every inch of that ink, trace my finger across each design and analyze all the small details—but that's for another time.

He plants his hand next to my head, gazing down at me with naked lust on his face. I'm sure I mirror his expression. I never thought I'd see Luke Hartmann looking at me this way, and I'm fully determined to enjoy every second of this.

Later, we can talk about why I can't be just another notch on his banged-up bedpost, and what this means for our friendship. But right now, need is coursing through my veins, making me desperate for his touch—all I want is his hands and his mouth on every part of me.

Out of the corner of my eye, I catch him reaching for the frosting. His voice is low and husky, fucking downright sensual, when he says, "I fully plan to taste every single inch of you tonight. So if there's any part of you that's off limits, let me know now."

My gasp fills the air as he continues to surprise me. Luke may be the quintessential nice guy, but I'm learning he may have a whole other side to him that I'm now dying to see. "I want to feel you *everywhere.*"

I'm not sure I've ever uttered any words more honest than those. I not only want the feel of him on my skin, and inside me . . . I want to know what he feels like wrapped around my heart. But I shove the last thought away, because I know that's not what he's offering.

The lust may be very real, but this marriage is still fake.

He takes his frosting-covered thumb and smears it over one nipple, and my mouth drops open as my eyes flutter closed. *Holy shit.* And then he's smearing more frosting on the other nipple, and I open my eyes in time to see his head descending.

His lips latch onto my skin, his tongue swirling over the stiff peak before he sucks me deep into his mouth with long pulls to remove the frosting. I let out a guttural groan, matching the way my pussy just clenched against him as he rocks his hips into me, sliding his cock along my clit.

Scraping his teeth lightly along my sensitive skin, he swirls his tongue around my nipple once more, like he's making sure to remove all the frosting, before he moves to the other side. And when he does, his urgent sucking mixed with the pressure against my clit sends heat coursing through my core and up my skin like fire as my climax engulfs me at warp speed.

I can't even make sense of the nonsense that's coming out of my mouth—I don't think I'm even using words; it's just needy gasps and moans and primal sounds filling the air as my body gives itself over to Luke. There are stars clouding the corners of my vision as the orgasm rolls through my body, and Luke doesn't let up. He continues toying with my breasts and rocking against my clit until I go limp.

And then he lifts my hips and slides my dress and thong down my legs before spreading my knees, putting my pussy on full display.

"God, you're fucking gorgeous," he says as he stands above me and runs a thumb along my center, "especially with your cum coating your pussy like this."

My lips part, but no sound comes out, because who the hell is this man? My best friend is some fucking sex god, and I had no idea . . . though I should have figured. I can't even start to think about why he knows exactly what to say to turn me on, or who else he might have said these things to before, because he's sitting on a barstool, leaning in and running his tongue over my clit in a way that has my hips thrashing against him.

He slides his hands under my thighs, lifting my legs as he says, "Put your feet on my shoulders. You made that way too fucking easy, and there's no way you're not coming on my tongue."

"I don't know if I can come again this soon," I say, but as

my entire core tingles, I suspect that if anyone can give me an immediate second orgasm, it's probably him.

He positions my feet on his shoulders and supports my legs with his hands, then chuckles as he kisses my inner thigh, nipping at the flesh before letting his teeth sink into it lightly.

"I'm pretty sure you've got at least one more for me," he says, his voice coaxing as he turns his attention to my other thigh, kissing and nipping at that one, too. And the mere anticipation of his mouth on me again has my hips moving, searching for friction.

He brings his mouth to my center, his lips clamping around my clit without warning as he sucks and swirls his tongue against the sensitive bundle. I'm so tender after my unexpected orgasm that it feels both amazing, and a little too much, all at once.

"Softer," I pant, even as my hips buck against his face. "I'm so sensitive, but I need more."

He lessens the pressure on my clit as he slides a finger into me. No, it must be two, actually, and I've never been happier that he has those long, thick fingers. I ride his hand, meeting him thrust for thrust, but still feeling like I need something more. I've felt Luke's hard cock against me enough times now to know that he'd fill me in a way his fingers can't.

I'm about to demand exactly that when he curls his fingers and hits the part of me that sends waves of sensation rippling all the way to my toes. "Yessss," I groan, and his tongue moves faster over my clit.

I can feel myself teetering at the brink of another orgasm, but it's still frustratingly out of reach. Right now, I want to come more than anything and am shameless enough to do whatever it takes to get me there.

Threading my fingers through his hair, I hold his head in place as my hips rock between his mouth and the counter, his fingers creating a delicious drag against my inner walls as he thrusts into me. And still, it's not enough.

"Harder," I gasp, and his fingers move deeper into me, stroking along my muscles over and over until I'm clenching around him.

He lifts his head long enough to say, "That's right, Peaches, coat my face." And then he runs his teeth over my clit with just enough pressure to have me practically screaming. My hands fly to my breasts and my fingers tweak my nipples as he licks and sucks and bites me.

The sensations are overwhelming, and my muscles clamp down on his fingers as I ride his face and scream out, "Yes, oh my god, Luke, please don't stop. Fuck, yes!" And then my words turn to garbled sounds as my orgasm flashes through me, rocketing my hips off the counter. Luke holds me steady, rising with me as he continues forcing every last drop of my orgasm from me.

I've never felt anything like this . . . Intense waves of pleasure that don't let up, crashing over and over until I am afraid I'll cry because there doesn't seem to be an end in sight. And then, the final wave crests, barreling into me with such force that it leaves me completely sated and absolutely boneless, lying like a heap of nothingness on his counter.

Closing my eyes, I force myself to breathe because I'm pretty sure I just held my breath through that whole experience. But once my eyes are closed, I can't seem to make them open again. Not when Luke stands, trailing gentle kisses up my body until his lips land on my jaw before continuing to my earlobe. "You are amazing, and beautiful . . . and tired," he says with a chuckle. "Time to sleep, Peaches."

———

The soft light filtering through the edges of the light-blocking shades when I wake up shows me that I slept in Luke's bed last night. Naked.

His side of the bed is empty and messy, the sheets folded back in a heap and his pillow sideways. In fact, based on the way it's lined up with me, I'm pretty sure I was snuggling it in my sleep. Did he not sleep in here, too? Or was I cuddled up with him, then used his pillow in his absence?

I glance over my shoulder at the nightstand, hoping my phone is there so I can check the time. It is, but what catches my attention is a clear acrylic tumbler with an orange smoothie. I pick up the folded piece of paper propped in front of it.

I had an early practice and I know you needed your sleep. Hope this is still cold when you wake up. Make sure you drink it all—you and Baby Squash need the nutrients. I'll see you when I get home.
—Luke

The tumbler is still cold, so I unscrew the top to give it a sniff. It's not that I don't trust Luke; I just want to preview what I'm about to put in my mouth. It smells fruity, almost tropical, so whatever it is, I know I'm going to like it.

Sure enough, not only is it delicious, but it's also familiar. I take another sip, trying to place the flavor. It's not until I've finished half the drink while rummaging through the drawers in Luke's closet and finding an oversized Rebels T-shirt to wear, that I realize why it tastes familiar.

EVA

> Thank you for the smoothie. Why does it taste almost exactly like the virgin peach margarita from the Neon Cactus last week?

I know Luke well enough to know this is not a coincidence. And while I hop in the shower and wait for his reply, I realize that the peach-scented shampoo and conditioner in his shower—which are an exact match for mine back in LA—are not a coincidence either.

I'm not entirely sure what to make of these non-coincidences.

Luke's observant, and he likes to be helpful. Is this just his way of trying to smooth this transition for me?

Try as I might, though, I can't convince myself that the multiple orgasms last night, and the one two nights before, are just him trying to be *helpful*. There was no way to miss that he wanted that as much as I did, and enjoyed it as much, too.

At least, back in LA, when he came in his boxers while giving me an orgasm, I know he enjoyed it. Last night, though? I sigh as I lean my head back under the water to rinse the shampoo out. Shit, I feel so greedy that he gave me two amazing orgasms and I fell asleep on the counter without even returning the favor.

Not that I think he'd be upset about that, but the memory

of the way he held me to him on that air mattress, his fingers curling into me as he came with me riding his fingers, has me *wanting* to make him come again.

I want to see his face clearly—not shrouded in darkness, like in my apartment—the moment his orgasm starts. I want to watch him watching me come, and see what he looks like when his own release hits.

Fuck. The thought of Luke coming has my skin singing with awareness, every drop of water running along my body turning me on more. I'm always so damn horny now.

I grab the bottle of conditioner and squirt a big dollop into my hand, determined to think about anything except sex as I pull my hair over my shoulder and use my fingers to work it into the long strands. But as I do, my forearms graze my nipples and desire shoots through my veins, lighting me up.

My hands move to my breasts, smoothing over them with the silky conditioner, and I pinch my nipples hard, trying to mimic the way it felt last night when Luke's teeth were grazing them. It's not enough. So I rinse one hand off and slide it down my body, finding my clit where it throbs. *That's right, you can take care of yourself,* I remind myself as I circle my clit with just the right amount of pressure. But I can't stop my brain from imagining it's Luke's tongue.

Leaning forward, I rest my forehead against the tile wall of the shower and continue pleasuring myself as memories of last night flash through my mind. I need more, though, and I'm frustrated by the emptiness I feel inside me. *I need Luke.*

No, I tell myself, *you just need your sex toy collection—the one you threw in the fucking trash after that embarrassing moment in LA.*

Though now, seeing how willing Luke is to provide orgasms when I need them, I wish I'd just whipped that vibrator out of the box and asked him to use it on me. That could have saved my entire collection!

And that's when I remember that my favorite toy is actually at my parents' house, tucked away in my suitcase in the closet of my childhood bedroom. The suitcase I was supposed to pack and bring back here last night, but then my mom made a comment about my weight and we left early.

I stand frozen in the shower, all traces of the sexual energy draining from my body as I remember the way my mom looked at me like I was a disappointment and said "... you're going to gain enough weight being pregnant."

My hands meet over the growing curve of my belly. It's getting noticeable now—I can still disguise it with empire waist dresses like I was wearing yesterday, but I suspect that in another week, nothing will hide the fact that I'm pregnant.

And then my mind is spinning, thinking about how Christopher will be arriving tomorrow, and we start practicing the day after, and suddenly, orgasms from Luke are the furthest thing from my mind.

All I'm thinking about is the baby and skating, and how I'll manage both things. And right then and there, with the hot water raining down on me, I make this baby a promise.

I promise to listen, to understand, to love—that no matter what this child's dreams are, I'll stand by in a supportive role, never demanding more than they're willing to give or demeaning them if they don't achieve them. And most importantly, I will *make sure* my child knows that my love isn't conditional, that no matter what, I will always love them.

263

Chapter Twenty-Eight

LUKE

"You know this is goalie practice, right?" I say to Zach Reid when he picks his helmet up off the bench. I squirt more water through my mask, letting it spray my face and wash some of the sweat away, before aiming for my mouth again.

"You know someone needs to take shots at you, right?" he replies, then busies himself fastening his chin strap.

"You better be able to block a defenseman's shots, Lover Boy," Colt says from where he sits next to Zach, with one leg sticking straight out to accommodate his knee brace. He's only got another week in this huge brace before he can switch to a smaller one, but I can tell he's over all of this. He wants back on the ice, and is frustrated that he's riding the bench, even though it's only for practice.

"You realize he's one of the highest scoring defenders in the league, right?" I say. Sometimes, I'm surprised Zach's not a winger—he's got the explosive energy and speed, combined with excellent fake-out skills, that have led to a surprising number of goals for him this year.

I don't think he was a big scorer during the seasons he played for Philly, but this year in Boston, he's upped his game. Hockey pundits call that the "Wilcott Effect," and they're not wrong. Charlie has the exceptional ability to push his players in just the right way, getting them to perform beyond what they've accomplished before.

Our team captain, Ronan McCabe, is one of the players always cited as an example. He had a rocky final year when he played for St. Louis and a rough transition to Boston eight years ago, but when AJ hired Charlie as the head coach six years ago, McCabe turned into an all-star player.

"Whatever," Colt grumbles. "Just unfuck yourself, okay."

I turn my head, my lips parted in surprise. Colt has been a really great mentor for the few months we've played together since I was traded, so I'm not used to this type of comment from him.

"Are you pissed about my game, or about your injury?"

"I'm pissed that of all the times something shitty like that could have happened to me, it had to be in Game 7. And I'm pissed now that I know the reason you were so distracted that night was over a girl."

"About that . . ." I say. I hadn't really been planning to tell them today, but there's no real reason to wait—especially when part of the purpose of our marriage story was to explain my performance. "Eva's pregnant."

"The fuck?" Colt says.

At the same time, Zach says, "Congrats, man. And to think you were trying to convince us all that you were 'just friends.' Now you come back from Vegas married *and* expecting a kid?"

"Yeah, well, her being rushed to the hospital right before we walked out onto the ice for Game 7, and me not knowing if she and the baby were okay or not . . . it definitely had me distracted. And that's on me. But it also put some things into perspective."

"What kind of things?" Colt asks, but I can tell from his face that he's picturing what he would have felt like if it had been Jules.

"Having to imagine a worst-case scenario made me realize that I didn't want to wait another second to marry her." As I say it, I realize how true it is. The terror I felt at the possibility of something happening to her and my inability to think about anything *but* her . . . even though I couldn't admit it to myself then, that had to be a sign that I wanted forever with her.

"Is that why you got married in Vegas?" Zach asks.

"Yeah, we thought it would be easier to tell our parents about the baby if we were already married."

"What are you, eighteen?" Colt says and huffs out a laugh. "You're a damned adult; you don't need your parents' permission to get married *or* start a family."

I think about the way Colt's whole family came down from Canada for one of the games early in the playoffs. I'm not sure what his family situation is, but Drew had said it was a big fucking deal that they were all there. Some sort of bad blood between him and his brother that they were finally smoothing over, or something.

"True. But our families are best friends, so that's a consideration, too. We didn't want to do anything that was going to cause a rift."

"Well, I think it's great that you finally owned up to your feelings since they were so obvious to everyone else," Zach says.

"You've never even met her or seen us together," I say, caught off guard.

"Yeah, but just the way you talked about her . . . We all knew."

Colt nods in agreement. "I'm never going to hear the fucking end of this from Jules."

"Why's that?" I ask before I squirt my face with more water.

"Because when we were all at the Neon Cactus, she and Audrey were convinced you two were together. And even when you guys said you were just friends, they concocted this whole story in their heads about how you were in love and secretly dating."

"Guess they're more observant than you," I say, feeling a tad guilty because they were only half right. I'm very much in love with my wife, but it's not mutual. She might like the orgasms I give her, but that doesn't mean it makes the relationship real.

"You done with your water break yet?" Coach Knight calls out from the other side of the rink, where he's standing with a clipboard, having just finished going over some things with Lennington, the goalie for Minnesota, and Kotzu, the goalie for Dallas.

"We're just congratulating Hartmann, because apparently he's going to be a dad," Colt calls out, his deep voice filling the nearly empty rink.

"Asshole," I mutter under my breath to Colt before I turn toward my goalie coach, who's skating across the ice.

"Does Wilcott know you not only married his daughter, but you knocked her up too?"

"Keeping it classy, Knight," Colt grumbles, and I couldn't agree more with his assessment. Sometimes Coach Knight lacks tact. Not that I need him to blow smoke up my ass, but it'd be nice if he wasn't so hostile half the time.

"Hey, he's my boss too, and I just want to know if he's about to fire one of my goalies."

"Wilcott doesn't make staffing decisions." AJ's cool tone carries down to us. Our heads all snap up to see her descending the stairs toward the bench. She's wearing trousers and a sleeveless sweater, and the clicking of her heels punctuates each step.

She's what my mom would call "old money," but Alessandra Jones has fought her way to the highest echelons of professional hockey with her brains and determination, *not* with anyone's help. And the world is finally taking notice.

Evan clears his throat. "Of course."

"And you'd do well not to make suggestions that players should be afraid of being traded, when you aren't even in the know about all the details of their lives." AJ continues.

The hiss of laughter that escapes Colt's mouth is too low for AJ to hear from six steps above us, but I don't miss it. We both like Evan just fine, but he's got a bit of a chip on his shoulder. I would, too, if my professional hockey career ended the way his did.

It's not like AJ to put someone in their place publicly like this, so either she's really intent on standing up for me, or there's something else going on here that I don't know about. I wonder again how she figured out we were in LA and sent Morgan to help us with our story, but I don't have the nerve to ask her.

"I was just giving him shit, AJ," Evan says, looking up at her with a lazy smile.

"Well, don't. Your job is to make him better, not to break him down. That's not what we do here."

It's Evan's second year in Boston, so it's not like he doesn't know the culture of the club, which makes me extra curious about the dynamics at play here. It makes me want to ask Tucker what the fuck is going on, because he'd be more likely to tell me than my dad would.

Dad would say something like, "Leave that up to AJ, Son." But Tucker is just enough of a gossip that he wants *you* to know *he* knows the real story. He'd probably tell me as long as I swore I wouldn't tell anyone else.

Except, the last time I saw my brother, he'd just stood by while Dad told AJ that my Game 7 loss was exactly why he hadn't wanted me on the team in the first place. Maybe *that's* the story I should be asking him about.

Zach steps out on the ice and nods his chin toward the net, and I follow him over there while AJ and Evan continue talking. Zach's voice is quiet, like usual, when he says, "I have to go out of town tomorrow. Ashleigh's uncle is moving and needs our help with some things."

His girlfriend, Ashleigh, is from Seattle, where he met her before a game this past December. Luckily, she was moving to Boston to start grad school in January, and they've been inseparable since. "In Seattle?"

"Yeah. We'll just be gone for a few days. But my weekly

appointment with Chloe is while we'll be flying, so I'm canceling it. Which means she has an open slot tomorrow."

I pull off my mask and use my sleeve to wipe the water from my forehead and eyebrows. "Who's Chloe?"

"My therapist. Well, technically, she's a sports psychologist, but she's actually a fucking miracle worker. Anyway, AJ asked me for her info, so I thought she'd mentioned her to you?"

"Ahhh, yeah, but she suggested I reach out to you for her info."

"And yet you haven't." Zach raises his eyebrows.

After AJ and Drew, Zach's now the third person to mention her to me in the past few weeks. "Talking to someone" goes against everything I was raised on—Hartmanns talk about our feelings plenty, but only to each other. The problem here, obviously, is that there's no one in my family I can talk to about what was going on in my head during our last game, what I overheard my father tell AJ, or why my marriage is so complicated. Though, I'm not sure the latter would be Chloe's area of expertise anyway.

"Will you text me her info?"

"Better yet," Zach says, "I'll text you both and introduce you. That way, you can't just ignore my text with her info when I send it."

"You're a dick," I say, but there's absolutely no heat behind my words.

"I'm a dick who's looking out for you. Meet with her, please. Just give it one meeting, and if it's not a good fit, you never have to talk to her again."

I stick my helmet back on my head, hoping to hide the emotions I'm feeling. I know Zach well enough to know that if he didn't care, he wouldn't be pushing me to do something he thinks will be good for me. Something that might help me be a better player, or at least avoid another situation like what happened in Game 7.

Because, let's face it, now that Eva is in my life in a much deeper and more permanent way, the chances of me letting my worries or my fears about her or the baby overwhelm me in the future have increased dramatically. If that's how I reacted when she was "just a friend," how would I react now that she's my wife? Now that her baby will be my child, too?

"Fine," I say with a sigh. "I'll give it a shot."

"Good man," Zach says, elbowing me.

———

LUKE

Sorry I didn't see your text earlier. My phone was in the locker room while we practiced. I assume that's a rhetorical question, and you're welcome.

I glance at the text as I ride the elevator up to my condo, wondering if I should be worried that I sent it nearly an hour ago before I hopped in the shower, packed up all my gear, and headed home from our practice facility. Maybe Eva fell back asleep?

In my entryway, I drop my keys and wallet into the bowl on the round table in the center of the curved space, and then walk into the open living area. As it always does on a sunny day, the view surprises me in the best way. The curved wall of glass at the corner of this building showcases a huge amount of the city. To the right is the top of the Prudential

Tower with the Public Garden, Boston Common, and Beacon Hill beyond it. Straight ahead is the Charles River, winding between Boston and Cambridge. The river sparkles a deep blue in the bright sunshine, framed by the trees on each side, the brick buildings of Back Bay beneath us, and the soft white stone buildings of MIT across the river. From the other side of my condo, out the bedroom windows, I can see Fenway Park and the greenspace that makes up the connected parks of the Emerald Necklace.

I bought this place in the early spring, as soon as I landed in Boston after learning about the trade. Preston was the one who told me it was on the market, and luxury residences at the top of one of Boston's newest and tallest skyscrapers are hard to come by, so we headed straight to meet his realtor after he picked me up at the airport.

It was a gross, overcast day where the city was covered in a dense layer of clouds and cold drizzle. But up here, we were immersed in those clouds, and there was nothing but white haziness outside. I loved that almost as much as I love the current view, so I purchased it without even seeing another place and moved in within the week.

I glance around the space, and then walk around the corner to make sure Eva's not in the part of the kitchen near the stove, or in the butler's pantry, but she's not anywhere obvious.

"Eva?" I call out.

"Back here, in your room!" Her voice is faint from here, because the bedrooms are down a long hallway off the entryway. I head back there, and when I walk into my room, she's sitting in one of the two swivel chairs in front of the windows. She has it turned to face the view, and her long, wet hair hangs down her back. Her feet are up on the seat, her knees bent with her chin resting on them, and her arms are wrapped around her legs.

I come up behind her, smoothing a hand over the top of her head, but she doesn't look up at me. "What's wrong, baby?"

She sniffles, and I turn the chair, dropping to my knees in front of her. Her face is streaked with dried tears, and her puffy eyes are tinged in red.

"Oh shit, Eva." I reach out and stroke her cheek. "What happened?"

She lets out a choked laugh. "Literally nothing. I'm just emotional."

"Pregnancy hormones?"

"Probably."

"So you just got sad for no reason at all?"

She sighs, then says, "No. I was in the shower and I was noticing the curve of my belly, and it made me think of my mom's comment about my body at dinner last night, and that made me think about the kind of relationship I want to have with my child . . ."

I lean forward and kiss her forehead. What I want to say is that I'm sorry her mom can be such a bitch, but I don't think that will help anything. And I honestly don't think Helene is trying to be a bitch. I think she just has no idea how to be a parent to an adult child and doesn't realize that her role should be as a supportive presence in Eva's life, not as someone trying to micromanage her daughter's career. The problem has always been that Helene is incredibly driven, and she doesn't know how to not push Eva in the same way she's always pushed herself.

But I don't say any of that, because Eva already knows it, and me jumping in with my feelings on the matter won't make it better. Instead, I say, "What can I do to help?"

"I don't know." She drops her head, letting her forehead rest on her kneecaps as she mumbles, "Just don't ever let me be like that, okay?"

I bark out a laugh, and her head snaps up, eyebrows raised.

"Sorry, but first of all, I don't think you ever *would* be like that. And secondly, I don't think you'd like it much if I pointed out any comparison between you and your mom. That would be like walking into a field of landmines."

She gives me a small smile. "Maybe. But I still need you to do it, okay? Unlike my mom, I can take feedback. I might not like to hear it, but I'm not going to act like you're making it all up, or reply with something like 'I guess I'm just the worst mother in the world, then.'"

"I hate that she tries to gaslight you like that," I say, wondering how Charlie deals with that. He's one of the most chill and supportive men I've ever met. It's always seemed like maybe he's exactly the type of person Helene needs to balance her out.

"And I have to go get the rest of my stuff from their house, because we didn't grab it last night, and all my skating gear is there. We have our first practice tomorrow, but I don't even want to go to the house because I don't want to see her."

"We could go right now," I say. It's just about lunchtime on a weekday, so I know Helene will be at the stables with my mom. They just bought a few new horses, and there's always a bunch of work to do when new horses come in.

She lifts her eyebrows. "We?"

Like I'd let her go alone, given how she's feeling. "Well, since we decided to leave your car back in Los Angeles, and we haven't gotten you a new car yet, I guess you'll need a lift up there."

She sticks one foot out, nudging me with her toe. "Don't trust me to drive your car?" Her tone is teasing, and she lets out another small smile.

Don't want to let my wife out of my sight for one second longer than necessary.

"You can drive if you want. But I'm still coming with you. Not only because you're not supposed to lift anything heavy, which I assume a fully packed suitcase will be, but also because I feel like you may want me there for emotional support."

"Why would I need emotional support if my mom's not there?" she asks, brows pinched.

"Because if just the memory of that interaction with your mom last night had you in full-blown crying mode, imagine what packing up your stuff in your childhood bedroom will be like."

Chapter Twenty-Nine

EVA

"You look great," Christopher says, wrapping his arm around my shoulder and squeezing me to him the minute I walk into the rink. "Are you feeling good?"

"Thanks, and yes," I say, before taking the final sip of my morning smoothie. The one Luke adapted from the Neon Cactus drink recipe that he bribed the bartender to give him, and has made for me each morning since we've been back in Boston. Knowing Luke, one will keep showing up on my nightstand daily, which I'm more than happy about.

They're not only delicious, but he's also added protein powder and some nutritional supplements to keep me and the baby healthy. And honestly, he's right about me needing to eat more. Baby Squash has me feeling weaker than I've ever been, and if I'm going to be skating again, I have to supplement my energy levels with some good nutrition and more calories, or I won't be able to keep up.

We make our way into the college ice arena that's only a ten-minute walk from Luke's condo. It would have been a beautiful stroll over here, right along the reflecting pool at the Christian Science Plaza on Huntington, if Luke hadn't been overbearing and insisted on driving me.

I know he's just trying to help, but I don't think he realizes how hard it is for me to remember this is just a friends-with-benefits situation when he's around and doing sweet things all the time.

Yesterday when we got back from my parents' house with my suitcase, for example, I took it into the spare bedroom—or, my bedroom now, actually—and shut the door behind me. But he insisted on bringing me snacks while I was unpacking, and then taking my suitcase and storing it in the hall closet when I was done. He'd already stocked the kitchen with my favorite foods, ordered me dinner, and had peach rings at the ready when he cued up my comfort movie, *Pride & Prejudice*. We'd just watched the mini-series a few weeks ago, and the way he indulges my love of that story frequently makes me wonder if it's not secretly his favorite, too. Eventually, he carried me to bed when I inevitably fell asleep during the movie.

And this morning, I woke up feeling confused about where we stand. Two nights ago, after he'd made me come twice on his kitchen counter, he'd brought me to his bed. Last night, when nothing sexual happened between us, he brought me to the spare room. And now, I'm just trying to figure out what it all means, if it means anything at all.

"You okay?" Christopher asks, and I glance up at him where he stands next to me, his bag slung across his body.

"Yeah, why?"

"You just seem . . . I don't know . . . distant?"

"No, sorry, it's just pregnancy brain. I can be mid-conversation and then suddenly my mind is just thinking about something totally different."

"Is it going to be like that on the ice?" Christopher's dark eyebrows dip, clearly concerned.

I'm about to ask if he's concerned about my safety or the quality of my performance, when Lynette, our new skating coach, sees us and waves us over. As we walk along the first row of seats next to the glass, she nods toward the little kids finishing up their skating lessons and says, "Let's get ready to go so we can make use of every second of ice time once they're done."

As I sit there, lacing up my skates and then pulling the wide bottoms of my pants over the heel of my boot, I get the same nervous feeling in my stomach that I had when we arrived at my parents' house the other night for dinner. Given how things turned out then, I seriously hope this isn't a premonition.

Next to me, Christopher nudges me with his shoulder. "You ready?"

I close my eyes and take a breath, inhaling a scent that's so familiar it feels like home. It's impossible to describe how an ice rink smells—cold air mixed with ice, rubber mats, metal steps, plastic seats—they all combine to create a distinctive aroma.

"Ready."

My stomach flips over again, but I don't feel nervous anymore. I feel anxious to start. I always feel anxious to get back to the ice when I've been off it for a while, and I probably need to think more about what it will be like once I retire from competition. But for now, as Christopher takes my hand and we step onto the ice, listening carefully to Lynette's instructions for our warmups, I breathe in again, determined to enjoy every minute of my last season of skating.

Twenty minutes later, I'm sliding across the ice on my butt for at least the tenth time in a row, and Christopher groans as Lynette says, "Maybe we need to take a break."

Twenty minutes, and I'm fucking exhausted and sore already.

"How long has it been since you skated, again?" Lynette asks, as I plop down onto the bench and grab the water bottle from the side of my bag. When we met, I told her I hadn't skated since the end of our season. I didn't mention the one time I skated with Luke and how I tweaked my back. But it's as if she can't believe I was competing on the international stage just last month. To be honest, I can't believe it either.

"Three and a half weeks." I pop the straw up from the lid and take several long gulps of my water.

"And have you done any conditioning in that time?" she asks.

I glance at Christopher, and he looks pissed. Honestly, I'd be pissed too if my partner showed up woefully unprepared.

"Not much. My body needed a break, but I'm afraid I gave it too much of one. I'm not normally this out of shape."

"You're not normally pregnant," she says. "Go easy on yourself during this re-entry period. You can't expect that your body is going to feel and perform like it did before pregnancy."

My eyes are suddenly full of tears, and I look up at the

metal rafters so they don't spill down my cheeks. This response could not possibly be more different than my mom's was the other night, or than Jessie's would have been if we were still training with her. "Thank you."

Christopher swings his arm over my shoulders and gives me a squeeze, before he looks up at Lynette, where she stands in front of us, leaning against the boards. "I don't think anything involving jumps is happening today."

"No, that doesn't seem like the best use of our time right now," she agrees. "I think we should switch to running through your routine and focusing on the footwork and synchronicity. From watching your performances over and over in preparation for working with you two, the only area —aside from jumps—where there's any room for improvement is on the footwork in the more artistic segment near the end of your routines."

I grab the protein bar from the front pocket of my bag and take a bite. I'm going to need to start eating like an athlete training for competition. No more lemon cupcakes or peach rings. Lots more protein and complex carbs.

Maybe I need to reach out to my nutritionist. Weeks ago, I told her I needed a break and that she could stop coordinating my meals and having them sent to me. I might need to start that up again, but I don't want to go through my mom to do so, even though she's been in charge of that part of my training for my whole career.

I make a mental note to talk to Luke about it, as Christopher and Lynette chat about our routine and I eat half my protein bar.

"You feel like you're ready to try again?" he asks, once I

fold the wrapper over the open end and shove the rest of the bar back into the pocket it came from.

"Yeah," I say with a decisive nod, realizing that I'm wasting our valuable—and expensive—ice time, not to mention our coach's time. "Let's do this."

Christopher and I take a few laps around the rink, going through the steps of our normal warmup again, and this time, it feels much better, much more natural, than it did half an hour earlier. And as we go through the different sequences of the artistic portions of our routine, I settle in. It's as if my body is waking up and remembering that it knows how to do this.

Thirty minutes later, I'm sweating and spent. My legs are lead and I feel like I need a nap in order to have the energy to walk out of here. But we had thirty productive minutes of practice, so that's a win.

"What's he doing here?" Christopher asks quietly as we skate toward the open door at the edge of the rink.

I follow his gaze up into the stands. There are a few families with little kids decked out in hockey helmets, sitting around and waiting for their practice to start now that we're done. I wonder if they realize that above them, an NHL goalie is sitting back in his seat, watching me like a hawk follows its prey.

The possessive and almost jealous look he wears as he notices Christopher's hand on my lower back has my stomach swooping low. I'm not trying to make him jealous, but the thought that he might be is doing funny things to my body.

"He's here to pick me up."

"He doesn't trust that you can make it four blocks back to his place?"

"Given how tired I am right now," I say with a sigh, "it's probably good he can give me a ride home."

The sound that comes from the back of Christopher's throat isn't quite a snort, but almost. "He looks like he wants to devour you," he observes under his breath.

"Maybe he does." As soon as the words are out of my mouth, I roll my lips between my teeth, knowing that I've said too much.

"Oh? Are you *finally* admitting that there's something going on between you two?"

Turning my head, I glance up at him, one eyebrow raised. "Finally?"

Christopher has always insisted that Luke must have feelings for me, but he never indicated that he thought I returned them. "Eva." He says my name like he's chiding me. "Be real right now. You couldn't have possibly thought that marrying him wasn't going to lead you both down this road."

Couldn't I have? "I had absolutely no intention of anything happening between us," I say, so softly I can barely hear myself over the sound of our blades slicing across the ice and the chatter of the kids at the edges of the rinks.

He chuckles. "I love how easily you can lie to yourself."

That stops me in my tracks, and I grab ahold of his arm, spinning us so we're facing each other. "What the fuck does that mean?" My words are still quiet, but they come from the back of my throat.

He just gives me an affectionate smile. "Eva, there was never going to be any other end to your friendship. You were always headed on this path with him, whether you realized it or not. Maybe you never saw the way he looks at you when you're not looking, but I did. And the way you look at him? That longing? You two have it so bad for each other, and I'm happy for you if you're both ready to stop pretending."

My lips part, but the only sound that comes out is a strangled laugh. What the hell is he talking about? Because if my true feelings for Luke Hartmann have been obvious to my skating partner for years, have they been obvious to my best friend, too?

Chapter Thirty

LUKE

"Why don't you tell me a little bit about why you wanted to meet?" Chloe says, and I try not to focus on how awkward it is to be talking to a therapist for the first time over a video call. How are you supposed to build an authentic connection with someone you've never even met in person?

If I hadn't been so determined to be there at the end of Eva's practice so I could take her to lunch and make sure she ate something, I probably would've flown down to Philadelphia to meet with Chloe.

"I'm going to be honest," I say, before I glance over at my door. I'm sitting in one of the chairs in front of the window in my bedroom. Eva's napping right now, and I know she's unlikely to wake up and even more unlikely to barge in here with the door shut and locked, but somehow, I still feel like I need to keep an eye on the door anyway. "I *didn't* really want to meet."

She nods, her blonde hair barely brushing her shoulders, but she says nothing.

"It's not like I'm scared to talk about my feelings or anything," I say, feeling the need to fill the silence. "It's just that in my family, we don't talk about things outside the family."

"Why not?"

"Because we're always in the public eye?"

"Why?" Her eyebrows dip a bit as she asks the question, and I realize that she has absolutely no idea who I am, aside from the fact that I'm one of Zach's teammates.

"My family is sort of . . . well known. I think the fact that we're pretty close-knit and generally stay out of any rich-people drama makes the media constantly curious about us." I shrug.

"Oh, so your family is famous?"

"Kind of." My last name doesn't seem to be registering with her, which is perfectly fine. It's not like we're a household name—a very intentional move on our part. There are plenty of other billionaires out there making complete asses of themselves, and that's not what my family has ever wanted to be known for.

Dad focuses our efforts on the family business, the hockey team we own, and charitable work. Mom's always had her riding program. They raised us in the small town my dad grew up in and sent us to public schools—well, except for Tristan, because he was "exceptional." I'm pretty sure that was code for "much too smart and not nearly humble enough to play well with others."

"All right. So what made you decide to meet, despite not wanting to?"

I glance away again, and then focus on my screen, noting that she's sitting there with a polite but expectant look on her face. "It felt like the right thing to do."

"Can you say more about that?"

I tell her what happened in Game 7. She asks some clarifying questions about Eva and my relationship with the Wilcotts, and suddenly I'm telling her all about both of our families, how my family owns our team, and my lifelong friendship with Eva.

"How did you feel about her being pregnant?"

"It's complicated."

"I'll bet." She adds nothing else, just watches me, waiting for me to keep going. I'm tempted to stare right back, just to prove that I can do that as well as she can, but what would that accomplish? If I'm going to push through my issues on the ice, I need to push through my complicated feelings about Eva and figure out why I'm not able to compartmentalize them while I'm playing, whereas I can do that with everything else.

"We actually got married last weekend."

"Oh?" The slight tilt of her head as she responds is the only indication that this information surprises her, which annoys me, even though I realize this is just her way of keeping me talking. When I don't respond, she says, "What made you guys decide to get married?"

"She wasn't sure about her health insurance if she had to take a break from skating and didn't want her mom and dad to know the circumstances of her pregnancy."

"Those are her reasons. What are yours?"

I lean back in my seat and glance at the door again. "She's my best friend. I'd do anything for her."

"And you did this purely for altruistic reasons, based solely on platonic friendship?"

My laugh is practically a snort. "Maybe not solely."

"So what were your reasons?"

I run my fingers through my hair, pushing it off my forehead. "Well, at the time, I thought I was just being a good friend."

"And now?"

"Now, I realize that I am undeniably, irrevocably in love with my wife." I don't mean to say that, but it slips out of my mouth as soon as the words go through my head. It's not like I haven't known for years that I was in love with Eva. It's just that its something I, up until recently, assumed I'd eventually outgrow, like you outgrow most things from your childhood.

"Normally, that wouldn't sound like much of a problem."

"Except she's not in love with me."

"That's . . . a lot to process. No wonder you're here."

"Yeah," I say on a heavy breath.

"I'm not a marriage counselor—"

"That's good, because we're not really married."

"I thought you got married this past weekend?"

"We did, but just for the reasons I mentioned—not because it's a *real* marriage."

"So, how long are you planning to stay married, then?" she asks.

I shrug in response. "We didn't set an end date."

She just looks at me like she expects me to say more.

"We can't get divorced. We'd never do that to our families."

"Are you sure that's why?"

My jaw tics as I clench it, and I can see in the video how

tense I look. "Why else would we have decided to stay married?"

"I don't know. Why would you have? You said you're in love with her . . . "

"Right, but she's not in love with me."

"And you're sure about that?"

If she'd asked me this question a week ago, I'd have been more confident in my answer. "Yeah."

"And how do you feel about that?"

I pause again, mulling over my answer in my head. "I'm pretty used to it."

"So you know how you just paused and chewed on the inside of your cheek right there before you responded? What was your first thought? The one you had before you said you're pretty used to it?"

I sit back in the chair with a sigh and glance down at my legs where they're stretched out beneath the side table I've pulled in front of me to hold my laptop. "I don't know," I say, shaking my head. "Disappointed, I guess."

"Does Eva know that you have feelings for her?"

"I . . . I don't think so."

"You've never told her?"

I shake my head.

"Why not?"

"Because I didn't want to be that guy—the one who's pretending to be her friend but secretly waiting around for her to want more."

She raises an eyebrow.

"I know it might look like that's actually the type of guy I am. But I assure you, I've done a damn fine job of shoving those feelings aside, reminding myself that wasn't what she wanted from me. But then . . . I don't know . . . things changed when we got married. Now we're spending all this time together, and she's pregnant and the hormones are messing with her, and she's got these needs . . ." I trail off, already feeling like I've said too much. Chloe is a sports psychologist; she's not here to hear about my sex life.

"So the relationship has turned sexual?"

"Sort of?"

She presses her lips together and nods. It's like she wants to say something but doesn't think she should.

"What?" I ask.

"It seems to me that either the relationship is platonic, or it's not?"

"Okay, so our physical relationship isn't platonic, but our emotional relationship still is." When she doesn't say anything in response, I add, "I know that sounds crazy. It's like a friends-with-benefits situation, but we're married."

"She must really trust you," Chloe says, and I consider the way Eva is normally so determined to be independent, but she's allowing herself to rely on me right now—to take care of her financially, to claim the paternity of her baby, to take care of her sexually . . .

"She does."

"I find it interesting that you're hiding your feelings from her, while also acknowledging that she trusts you implicitly."

"Hmmmm." The sound rattles around in my throat as my lips twist, and then I take a deep breath and say, "I don't know how she'd feel about the truth, which is why I haven't told her. I don't want to make her uncomfortable."

"Are you not telling her to spare her feelings, or your own?"

Another hum rattles around in my throat, because *fuck*.

Yeah, I wouldn't want to make Eva uncomfortable, but at the same time, maybe it's more the fear of revealing my deepest and darkest secrets to her that really has me holding back. The fear of rejection isn't something I normally struggle with . . . maybe because no one except Eva has ever rejected me.

"Maybe your wife deserves to know how you feel about her?"

"Maybe." Just the thought of doing that has my stomach clenching.

"Let's bring this back to psychology, just so you understand why I'm asking you these questions, even though we met to talk about your on-ice performance. Research shows that suppressing your emotions—like you've been doing for a decade now when it comes to the most important person in your life—can take a toll on your mind and body, leading to heightened anxiety like you experienced during Game 7, and leaving you feeling much less in control."

Could it really be that the weight of constantly hiding my feelings for her finally took its toll on me, making me unable to deal with the stress of my job?

"If that's the case, and I've been hiding my feelings for her for pretty much my whole life, why hadn't anything like that happened before?"

"Were you ever worried about her safety before?"

"No, I guess not. And it wasn't just that I was worried about her, it was also the baby, and whether Eva's mother was going to figure out she was pregnant. It all just . . ."

She gives me a sympathetic face. ". . . cascaded?"

"Yeah. It was so overwhelming, I couldn't think about or focus on anything but her."

"That's what anxiety is," Chloe says. "It's an emotional and physical response to a stressful or threatening situation."

"Are you saying that keeping these feelings locked down means this could keep happening?"

"I'm saying that the more time and energy your brain spends forcing down very natural emotions, the more likely it is that you won't be able to deal with other stressful situations when they come up."

"That's what being a goalie is, though . . . It's stress. It's taking care of your team. It's protecting the net—using your body to guard a space much bigger than you can physically cover while guys shoot pucks at you at ninety miles per hour."

"Perhaps, then, you need to free your brain up to handle that type of stress?"

"By telling my wife how I really feel about her?"

Chloe shrugs. "That sounds like a logical place to start."

Logical, perhaps. But also terrifying, because there's no way to admit my feelings to Eva without also admitting that I can't remember a time I didn't feel this way about her.

Chapter Thirty-One

EVA

"Oh my god, I knew it," Morgan squeals, a wide smile splitting her face and elevating her cheeks so that her eyes crinkle as she pumps a fist in the air. Heads turn at the tables nearest us, where other diners are distracted by her loud outburst.

She tucks her chin, looking down, as if she's embarrassed, but when she looks back up, I can tell she's not. She's just happy for me.

"So does this mean you're together-together? Like for real?"

I sigh. "No, I don't think so. Like, we had that one almost-hookup, but he hasn't tried anything since." I tell her about watching *Pride & Prejudice* together the other night, and how he carried me into my own bedroom instead of his, and how I've slept alone the two nights since.

"Maybe, since you were asleep that night, he didn't want

to assume you wanted to be in his bed? Luke seems like a full-consent kind of guy."

"Yeah," I say with a shrug, remembering how he told me he needed me to use my words when he was touching me. "But the fact that he hasn't tried anything since then? I don't know. It feels like maybe he regrets it?"

"Aside from not trying to get you in bed again, has he done anything else to make you feel like he regrets what happened?"

I think for a moment before saying, "No. Everything else seems very normal."

"Maybe he's waiting for you to let him know you'd be up for a repeat performance?" Morgan asks between sips of her cocktail. "Because clearly, you haven't told him how you feel." She grinds out the last words, like she's reminding me that I was supposed to talk to him about that a week ago.

"It's . . . complicated. It's clear he's down for this friends-with-benefits situation we've found ourselves in, but—"

"You're *mar-ried*," Morgan says, as if I need help understanding the situation. I burst out laughing.

"Yeah, but—"

"No buts. You need to talk to him. The only thing that's going to happen if you don't is that, eventually, someone's going to get hurt."

"And you're worried it'll be me?"

"I'm worried either way. You saw the way he fell apart in Game 7 when he thought something might be wrong with you. Once the news of your marriage comes out, everyone's going to believe that it's because he was worried about his future wife and his baby. But we know the truth, Eva. We know that he was *that* worried about you before you were even together. No one reacts like that if they don't have serious feelings for the other person."

I chew my lip as I mull over that thought. It's not like I haven't wondered the same thing, it's just that I've never let myself hope . . . until now.

"He cares about you, and only a fool wouldn't see it. And I don't think you're a fool, so why are you intentionally blind to this?" Her blue eyes look almost lavender in this light as they bore into me.

"I just don't want to get hurt. I've been down that road before twice—once in high school when I thought he had feelings for me, and once with Christopher."

"Hold up! What do you mean, 'once with Christopher?'"

Realizing that we didn't tell her that part of the story when we were in Los Angeles, I fill her in on how I ended up pregnant.

"Oh, shit. No wonder you're gun shy." Her gaze flits to her phone, where it lights up on the table next to her empty plate, but she flips it over and glances back at me.

"Last week, when we were having dinner with our parents," I tell her, "Luke said 'I've been in love with your daughter most of my life.'"

Her jaw drops, and she touches the tip of her tongue against her upper lip as she chuckles. "Oh the honesty in that boy."

"I'm not sure if he was being honest, or just really trying to sell it."

"Again with the not talking about shit," Morgan says and rolls her eyes at me. "It's so obvious to *everyone* else but the two of you."

Her words are consistent with Christopher's. "Yeah?"

"After that night at the Neon Cactus, Jules and Audrey were convinced you two were secretly together and they haven't shut up about it since. I haven't told them about the marriage because, you know, NDA and all. But Luke must've told his teammates because Jules had some sort of a bet with Colt, and apparently now she's the proud owner of his Porsche."

I let out another laugh, because he told me about his conversation with Zach and Colt, but I have no idea if he knew there was a bet involved. "Wait, he bet her his Porsche that we weren't together?"

"Uh-huh."

I laugh, thinking back to the way Colt couldn't stop looking at Jules at the Neon Cactus. "That man's obsessed with her. The way his eyes get all gooey when he looks at her . . ."

Morgan just shakes her head. "That is exactly how Luke is with you."

I'm about to respond when Morgan's phone rings, and she snatches it up quickly, swiping the screen and bringing it to her ear. "What's wrong?" Her words are slightly panicked. She pauses, and then says, "I don't know, because you never call unless it's an emergency . . . Yes, I saw that you texted . . . No, I'm not ignoring you. I'm at dinner with Eva . . ." She sighs and moves the phone away from her mouth. "Audrey and Jules want to know if we want to meet up with them. They're at the Neon Cactus, it's only a few blocks from here."

I did tell Luke that I'd be back after dinner, but it's not like we have plans or anything. He might not even be home. When I was heading out a couple of hours ago and asked him what his plans were for tonight, he said he was going to dinner with Preston. So it's entirely possible that he's out, and I'd be rushing home to an empty house when I could be out making new friends instead.

Los Angeles already feels like a lifetime ago. It's time to build a new network of friends here, starting with Morgan.

"I'd love to," I tell Morgan.

"Great," she says into the phone, "we're just going to pay our bill, and we'll be there in a bit."

"I cannot *believe* you guys got married!" Jules says with a bright smile as she holds my hand to get a better look at my ring. "Last time we saw you guys, you were all *Oh, we're just friends.* And all along, you were secretly together?"

It takes a lot of effort not to glance at Morgan. Instead, I shrug, raise my eyebrows, and take a sip of my soda. "I hear you got a Porsche out of it, so . . . you're welcome?"

Jules's laugh is deep and loud and has the two guys standing nearest our table turning toward us. I've noticed them both casting glances her way as we've sat here talking, and I'm not surprised. She looks like Barbie, but she's got a sharp tongue and nice muscles, so my money would be on her in any fight. "I don't even want his car. I just like that I can remind him it's mine."

I bite my lip but can't hold back a smile. I haven't quite figured out their relationship, but anyone who follows hockey knows that Mathieu Coltier was the league's biggest playboy, until about two months ago when he announced his sudden engagement to his best friend's little sister.

Jules doesn't seem like the type to put up with some of the shit I've heard about Colt getting into, so either she straightened him right out, or there's more to the story. I can't help but think of what Morgan said that night at dinner in LA, about how plenty of famous people are in fake relationships. But there's no way what they have is fake . . . She's smitten, and he's obsessed.

"He'll probably buy another one so you can have matching cars," Audrey says and rolls her eyes.

"Nah, he knows I'll never drive it. I like my truck too much. It would be a waste to buy another one."

"Well now that he's sold his condo in the Seaport," Lauren says, "he's probably wondering what to do with all that money."

Jules chuckles. "Between physical therapy and planning the Bali trip, I don't think he's even thought about the condo."

Lauren snorts out a laugh. "So, have you guys decided if you're going to stay in the brownstone for good?"

"We'll see," Jules says, then turns to me. "My brother, sister, nephew, and I lived in our family's brownstone in the South End together. Then Jameson moved in with Lauren, and Audrey and Graham moved in with Drew. Audrey and I run our business out of the office in the basement of the brownstone that Colt and I now share."

"There's no rush to figure it out," Audrey reminds her.

"Figure what out?" a man's voice booms from behind me, and we all turn to find Drew and Colt.

"What are you doing here?" Audrey asks her fiancé, her brows lifted as she rushes on, "And where the hell is Graham?"

"Relax, babe," he says, affectionately reaching out and tucking her hair behind her ear. "Taylor's with him."

"Who's Taylor?" Lauren asks.

"Our downstairs neighbor," Audrey explains.

"She was very happy to babysit for a couple hours, especially since her mom is right there too, so I could accompany my future brother-in-law to this fine establishment."

"This fine establishment where you knew we'd be," Jules says, her dry tone matching the roll of her eyes. But she doesn't look annoyed in the least that her fiancé is crashing girls' night.

"Exactly," Colt says, scooting around to her side of the table and planting a kiss on her head.

"Oh my god," Morgan sighs. "You all are making me sick."

"Hey," Lauren says with playfully narrowed eyes, "it's just *them.*"

"Yeah, until Jameson shows up."

"He's not showing up. He's home with the twins."

"Uh-huh," Colt says, and Lauren's bright blue eyes shift his way.

"Are you serious right now?" Lauren asks, and Colt shrugs.

Morgan glances over at me. "See, I'm happy for you and Luke, but when I first met you, I was initially excited that you two were *just friends*, because I'm perpetually surrounded by people who are sickeningly in love. AJ was supposed to be my new single friend, and now she's with McCabe, so it's just me, I guess." She says it with a laugh, so I know she's not throwing herself a pity party or anything, but it probably does suck to be the only single girl when all your friends are happily in relationships. Even though mine and

Luke's is not real, I don't think she's ever believed that we're just friends, and I'm having a harder time convincing myself of that now too.

"So there's no guy in your life?" I ask.

"Nah. There was this guy for a while, but he ended up being a dick."

"Yeah, most guys are."

Morgan's gaze sweeps around the table, where Jameson's just come up behind Lauren, accompanied by McCabe, who's got his arm wrapped around AJ's shoulders.

"Maybe," she says. "But there are obviously good guys out there, too."

Chapter Thirty-Two

EVA

Out of habit, I almost type out, "You flatter yourself." But then I remember what he said about being in love with me his whole life. Have I been pushing him away this whole time, and he's gone along with it because he thought it was what I wanted? My stomach turns over at the thought that maybe in protecting myself, I've been hurting him.

I glance around this corner of the bar where Morgan and I are chatting with Jules, Audrey, Lauren, and AJ. But there's no mistaking the way Drew, Colt, Jameson, and McCabe are hovering around the table like they can't bear to be away from their significant others. The drag of McCabe's hand across AJ's hip, the way Colt never lets Jules out of his sight, the way Drew can't stop playing with the ends of Audrey's long brown hair. All of it has me wishing Luke was here, too.

"Is there anything else you want me to do this week to get ready for the wedding?" Morgan asks, and my head snaps up to see who she's talking to.

"No, I think we're good," Lauren says.

"Wait, you're getting married *next weekend*?" I ask. I knew she and Jameson were getting married this summer, but didn't realize it was so soon.

"Yeah! You and Luke should come!" Lauren sounds genuinely excited about that possibility, rather than it sounding like a pity invite since I'm clearly the only one at this table not attending.

"Oh, thank you so much," I say. "But Luke and I will be back home for the weekend. There's this big Polo match every July, and then his parents host an event that night at their house."

I've been trying not to think about what it will be like to see our parents for the first time since that dinner. Luke's talked to his mom and dad a few times, and I've exchanged a few texts with my dad, but it's been radio silence from my mom.

"I was there for the team Christmas party this year, and their house is *so* amazing," Audrey says with a dreamy sigh.

"Especially at Christmas. They go all out on decorating." I don't mention that it's just as spectacular in the summer when the expansive lawn and gardens give way to the Greek-bath inspired pool. The outdoor space is just as impressive as the indoors, honestly.

"That I'd like to see," Lauren says. "I love Christmas."

"We'll have to make that happen," I say, then drop my voice lower and add, hopefully, "And we still need to skate together sometime."

"Maybe after the wedding. I haven't skated in so long, I'd probably fall and break my arm and ruin my wedding photos." Lauren laughs it off, but it makes me wonder how long it's actually been.

"I hear it's like riding a bike," I offer. "You never forget how to skate."

Lauren's shoulders lift as she snorts out a small laugh. "Trust me, I've forgotten."

Morgan says something to Lauren then, so I glance down at my phone as it buzzes in my hand with another message from Luke.

LUKE

Or not?

EVA

Maybe I miss you a little bit.

LUKE

Only a little bit? I guess I need to step up my husband game.

EVA

Is that what this is? A game?

LUKE

You know that's not what I meant.

EVA

Do I?

LUKE

You SHOULD know that. But I can tell from that cute little furrowed brow and your frown that you don't.

My head snaps up, my gaze sliding across the crowded space until I find Luke near the door. I know my whole face must light up, because next to me, Morgan's head turns until she finds the object of my attention, and her low rumble of laughter shakes me out of my stupor.

"He can't bear to be away from you," Morgan says as we watch Luke carve his way through the crowd, his broad shoulders easily nudging people aside. Luke's hat is low over his forehead, like he's trying to hide under the shadow of the bill, but his gaze never leaves mine. "That's so cute."

However, there's nothing cute about the way Luke is looking at me—his gaze is full of determination and . . . hunger? My stomach does the flippy thing it seems to do a lot lately, and I don't know where these nerves have come from. I don't get nervous around Luke.

He walks right up to me, ignoring everyone around us, and uses both hands to flip his hat backward. Then, he's taking my face in both his hands, leaning in and kissing me. I wasn't expecting this greeting, the way he's practically claiming me in front of his teammates. I could tell myself the kiss is just for show, but I'm having a hard time convincing myself that's true.

On my other side, Jules says to Colt, "Have I mentioned how much I'm going to enjoy driving your Porsche?"

My chest shakes with silent laughter before one of Luke's hands snakes around the back of my neck and the other turns my barstool so he can step between my legs. I don't miss the way my breasts are pressed against his rock-hard chest, or the way the curve of my belly presses into his abdomen. I'm practically melting into him, but then he gives me one last chaste kiss, pulls away enough to say, "Missed you," and then kisses my forehead once more.

"You got here quick," I say breathily, wondering where he was and how long he's known I've been here.

"I was just finishing up dinner with Preston right near the Common when Colt texted to tell me everyone was meeting up." His thumb sweeps along my cheekbone.

I don't know what I hear in his voice, but it has me worrying that he thinks I should have been the one to tell him. "I thought Morgan and I were just meeting up with Jules and Audrey. I didn't know it was going to be a whole *thing* with your teammates."

Luke says, "I think it was meant to be a girls' night and we've crashed it on purpose. Hope you all can forgive us." He presses another kiss to my forehead and, as impractical as it would be, I wish he'd just keep his hands and his lips on me at all times.

"That's why you came? Because you knew I was here?"

"Yes, Wife. *You're* why I came." He drops his voice on that last sentence, making it sound distinctly sexual and flooding me with memories of the way he came that night on the air mattress. Now, my skin is tingling with the awareness of his proximity and my whole body is leaning in, needing to be closer to his.

Over my head, he nods at his friends, who are calling out greetings. And as he turns me on the barstool, so his thick forearms are wrapped around my belly, I realize that everyone already knows we're married. I know Morgan said he'd told Colt, but I'm super curious about whether they also know I'm pregnant.

But that question is answered almost immediately when the wedding congratulations start flowing and Colt calls the waitress over and orders a round of shots to celebrate, and then says, "Eva, what do you want instead of a shot?"

I order a Shirley Temple, and Luke says he'll have what I'm having.

"You don't even like grenadine," I say.

"Yeah, but not drinking while his wife is pregnant seems like the least a guy could do," Luke says with a smirk, and it's then that I realize he's repeating my words from the restaurant that first night he came up to Newbury Falls.

I shake my head at him, but can't wipe the smile off my face. He's *always* paying attention. Almost like he's saving up all these details about me for . . . I don't even know. But I'm starting to see what Morgan means.

"Are you finally going to tell us?" Jules asks, and Audrey elbows her.

Clearly, they knew I was pregnant and were waiting for me to say something. "Seems like you already know."

Then they start peppering me with questions and squealing with excitement when I confirm that, yes, Luke and I are expecting a baby this fall. But I don't miss the way AJ's sitting back and observing the situation rather than participating, before she looks over at Morgan and gives her a nod.

I try to recall exactly what AJ's voicemail said last weekend . . . *I'm sending Morgan out to LA to meet with you.* And that small nod makes me realize that while Morgan did the job she was sent to do, helping us craft a story that we've decided to release in *Society* magazine next week, she didn't tell AJ any of the details.

And AJ seems . . . impressed by that, as though she's realized that Morgan is someone she can trust. Or, maybe I'm just reading into the situation based on my own feelings about Morgan. I've definitely never felt such an instant connection with another woman, like I'm just certain that we're going to be close friends.

By the time everyone is a few drinks into their night, I'm already yawning. "Sorry," I say to Morgan, because she's in the middle of a story about her mom's wedding in Bermuda next month that she doesn't want to attend. "I'm back to skating in the mornings, and it's exhausting. I'm so out of shape right now."

"You're not out of shape," Luke says, his voice low. "You're growing a human being, and *that's* exhausting."

It's funny how my mind immediately goes from *I'm exhausted* to *that must mean I'm doing something wrong*. Maybe in the past that would have been true, but I'm determined to learn to be nicer to myself about what my body can and can't do while I'm pregnant.

"I think maybe this baby is telling me that I need to go home and go to sleep," I say, and Morgan gives me a smile.

"You go take care of yourself and that baby. You're not going to miss anything here," she says, right as a few more guys from the team who I don't really know show up. The funny thing about my dad coaching the team is that I've heard bits and pieces about everyone, but have met very few of them over the years since I lived across the country.

The bar is getting packed, and the entire place feels downright rowdy. All I want to do is get out of here.

We say our goodbyes, and then, as we walk through the crowd with Luke pushing ahead of me to clear a path, some frat boy with a too-big smile and slicked-back hair grabs my arm and leans in to say, "Hey, baby, you're not leaving are you?"

His beer breath washes over me, making me feel nauseous. Before I can even blink, Luke has the guy's collar in his hand. "If you value your life, I suggest you get your fucking hand off my wife. Otherwise, you'll be drinking through a straw for the rest of your days."

My throat is thick with emotion as I watch Luke defend me. Why is it so hot when he gets all territorial like this?

Frat boy's eyes widen, and he lifts both hands in the air as he steps back. "My bad," he says. "I didn't see the ring."

"You didn't fucking *look* for a ring," Luke nearly growls, his tone deadly in a way I've never heard before and like a little too much. "Maybe next time you want to talk to a beautiful girl, you just use your words and not your hands, yeah?"

Chapter Thirty-Three

LUKE

"You know . . ." Eva says as we step into the elevator after a nearly silent and very short cab ride back to our place. I'd been too keyed up to talk about what had just happened and didn't really want to discuss it in front of the driver, either. ". . . that's the second time you've used the whole 'my wife' line in the past few days."

"You *are* my wife." I keep my voice casual despite the way my body is still simmering with rage at watching that asshole put his hands on my wife. *My pregnant wife.*

"You know that's, like, a thing, right?"

"A thing?" I glance down at her, and the way her cheeks are flushed and her big brown eyes are wide as she gazes up at me makes me relax a bit. *She's fine,* I remind myself. *She was never in any danger.*

But my body reacted like that man was threatening her, and that fact has me a little worried. I kept my cool, but all I wanted to do was end him—and not in the fistfight kind of way, more like I was wondering which of my brothers would be the best one to help me bury a body.

Preston. Most definitely Preston.

"Yeah." Her tongue slides along her lower lip before she pulls it between her teeth, as though she's trying to hide a smile. "It was kind of sexy."

Taking a step closer, I lean in, resting one hand on the wall of the elevator behind her. "Yeah?"

She reaches up and rests her hand on my shoulder, her thumb tracing the line of my collarbone, and it takes every-thing in me not to pin her against the wall with my body in response to her touch. "You were awfully . . . possessive."

I lean in a little closer and her hand falls to rest on my chest. My voice is low and raspy when I ask, "You like me possessive?"

That idea is dangerous, because I have *years* of possessive energy just waiting to be unleashed. All that time I've watched her pursuing other guys, even the years I've watched her skating with Christopher, it left its mark in tiny cuts all over my heart.

I've always felt territorial about Eva, but I've just never had any right to feel that way . . . until now.

Her head is tilted back against the wall as she looks up at me, and I watch the way the steady beat of her pulse beneath her jaw increases the longer she stares into my eyes. Her tone is flirtatious when she says, "I guess I do."

My other hand lands on her hip, but before I can close the distance between us, the elevator dings to let us know we've arrived at our floor. The door opens to the entryway that leads to the two suites on this side of the building, and we turn toward mine.

I don't know what to do with this raw, almost carnal energy that's burning me up inside. I don't miss the way her nipples are hard and straining against the thin cotton fabric of her dress. I know she wears dresses most days because, with the way her body is changing, they're what she's most comfortable in. The way they drive me crazy feels wrong.

I've always tried not to sexualize her because that's not what our friendship was based on, and she deserves more than that.

So instead of acting on the impulse to strip her naked right in my entryway, I head through the living room and into the kitchen. "I need some water. Do you want some?"

"Sure," she says, and I hate the way her voice sounds uncertain and even a little worried. I can tell she doesn't know what to make of my erratic behavior. One minute, I'm about to kiss her in the elevator, and the next, I'm walking away from her, claiming that I'm thirsty.

I don't know what to make of it either, except I don't ever want to take advantage of her in any way. And it feels like every time something has happened between us, I've instigated it.

The other night on my kitchen counter, I was the one who trailed frosting over her body and licked it off, working her up until she needed me as much as I needed her. Back in LA, she might have ground herself against me and claimed it was an accident, but I was the one who egged her on, practically daring her to keep going. At our wedding, it was me who kissed her—both times.

And now, I need her to come to me because that's what she *wants*.

I fill both of our stainless-steel bottles with water and

then turn away from the refrigerator to hand one to her. But as she reaches for it, she gasps, pulls back, and plants her hand on her belly.

Her eyes are huge, but she doesn't look scared or hurt, so I try not to panic as I set our water bottles on the counter next to her. "What's wrong?"

Reaching out and taking my hand, she places it low on her belly, holding my palm flat against her. "Do you feel that?"

Against the pressure of my palm on her abdomen, I feel slight movements pressing back. "Oh my god, Evie. This is the first time you've felt the baby move?"

I don't mention that I was getting worried because normally you can feel the baby move by twenty-four weeks. I've been telling myself that everything with the ultrasound was fine, so we know the baby is okay, but I've definitely been waiting for this milestone and worried that it hasn't happened yet.

"Maybe?" she says, and I'm actually a little choked up that I'm getting to experience this with her. "The other night at my parents' house, something similar happened, but I thought I was just nervous. It happened again at practice yesterday."

"A lot of times, the first movements just feel like normal rumblings of your digestive system."

Her eyebrows dip as she tilts her head to stare at me. "You know this, why?"

"That app I told you about is very informative." I don't mention how much time I've spent doing additional research. If I'm going through this with her, I want to be as informed and supportive as possible.

With the circumstances of her pregnancy, I'm not shocked that she hasn't jumped feet first into learning everything she can about being pregnant. Which is why I'm happy to pick up that slack for her, the same way I picked up some prenatal vitamins and iron supplements when I noticed she wasn't taking them, and I started making her a nutrition-packed smoothie every morning.

"My stomach has been doing these flips a lot lately, and I thought I was just nervous about all these changes in my life."

There's so much I want to ask her about those nerves, but I don't want to ruin the moment. So instead, I focus on the small, fluttery movements pressing against my palm as I lean down and tell the baby, "You're doing such a good job in there."

Eva laughs as I pat her belly, and then we both feel the movement again, and she says, "I think the baby likes you."

"I'm a *very* likable guy," I say, glancing from her belly up to meet her eyes.

Eva stares back at me, and several different emotions move across her face. That lust I saw in the elevator? Gone. And it's replaced by . . . worry?

Maybe she's as confused as I am about the ways our relationship is changing? I need her to want this change as much as I do, because if she tells me that we need to walk ourselves back over that line and remain firmly in the friendship zone, that's going to be an enormous problem for me at this point.

I was done being her friend the moment I slid that ring on her finger, though I was still lying to myself, trying to convince myself that I was only doing this because I was a good friend. And while that might have been my initial intention, that's not what I want with her—it's not what I've *ever* wanted and it's certainly not what I want now that we're married.

"You *are* very likable, Luke," she says, and I hear the *but* coming like a fucking freight train. I let the silence extend and feel like I'm bracing for impact while also needing to understand where her head and her heart are at. Finally, she says, "That's part of what has me worried about how we keep crossing that line together."

Me being a likable guy has her worried about our relationship shifting? That makes no sense. "How is me being a likable guy a *bad* thing?"

She tilts her chin down, staring at my chest instead of looking me in the eye. "Because women love you, Luke. And from what I've seen, there's a constant rotation of them in your life. I can't be just another woman you sleep with."

"Whoa, hold up." It's my own fault she's confused about my reputation, and it's time to set the record straight. I tilt her chin up so she's looking at me. "First of all, you're not just another woman, you're my wife. And second, I'm not sure what you think my sex life looks like, but I can assure you, it's nothing like what you just described."

"Yeah?" she says dubiously, one eyebrow raised.

"Yeah."

"Okay, so how many women *have* you slept with?" She looks like she's steeling herself against my answer, while simultaneously hoping the number isn't as high as she's prepared to hear.

My sigh is deep and long, and the force of it ruffles her hair. I drop my chin to rest against the crown of her head, because I don't think I can handle seeing her face when I give her my answer.

"Zero," I admit as my heart races.

She gasps as her hand flies to my chest and she pushes me away slightly, giving her enough room to look up at me with those dark eyes widened in surprise. "Wait, what? You've . . . *never?*"

Aside from the obvious shock, I can't quite tell how she feels about that. "No."

"But you're in the NHL."

A small chuckle escapes from the back of my throat. "Believe it or not, that's not a draft requirement."

She lets out a small laugh too, before her eyebrows pinch. "But . . . back in LA, and the other night on this counter . . ." As she nods her chin over her shoulder, and then she looks back at me, her face showcases her confusion perfectly. "How did you seem so experienced?"

"I said I've never had sex, not that I've never touched a woman."

"But . . ." she repeats, clearly struggling to grasp how this can be true.

I *know* my reputation, and she obviously does too. However, I've never felt the need to make any kind of a statement, publicly or privately, about my sex life. If there are women out there who want to say they slept with me, that's kind of bizarre, but it's also not a conversation I want to engage in. As far as I'm concerned, people can believe what they want about my sex life.

"Why?" she asks simply, searching my eyes.

I wish I could read her emotions at this moment, because I'm more nervous than I've ever been before. Telling the truth is either going to freak her the fuck out, or it's going to put her mind at ease—and I have *no idea* which.

But I'm also determined to stop hiding my feelings for my wife.

"I told myself a long time ago that I'd have sex with the first person I liked more than I liked you."

Her mouth parts, but no words come out. We stand there, staring at each other, for at least a full minute.

"What? Why?" she finally whispers, dumbfounded, like the shock of this revelation is making it impossible for her to speak.

"Because, Evie . . ." I bring my hands to either side of her neck, making sure her eyes are on mine as I say, "It's always been you."

Her ragged breathing fills the space, but her face doesn't change—it's still a mask of surprise.

"I'm not even your type," she whispers as her eyes fill with tears.

I shake my head. "You are *exactly* my type."

"But every girl I've ever seen you with is tall and blonde."

"And why do you think that is?"

"I don't … I don't know." The words are barely audible as they squeak out of her.

I lean down and press my lips to her hairline, letting myself breathe in her peach scent. "Yes, you do."

If it wasn't obvious before why I only dated women who were her polar opposite, by now, she has to realize it was so that I wouldn't grow attached.

She leans her head forward, pressing her face against my chest, and I rest my chin on top of her head while wrapping my arms around her back. I've held her like this so many times—through disappointment and anger and sadness—at various points in her life.

But something about this is different. I'm not comforting her, I'm reassuring her. And I get the sense that she's going to need answers to all the questions she's never asked.

"How . . ." She sighs. "How long have you had feelings for me?"

I'm so relieved she didn't ask *if* I have feelings for her, because if she had to ask that, then I've failed her. Instead, it's like she's connecting the dots—all the times I dropped everything for her, all the visits to see her in LA, all the times I stayed on the phone with her half the night when she'd had her heart broken, the way I came home for a month every summer when she was going to be back in Newbury Falls, the way I suggested we get married.

Everything.

"Forever."

"But . . . like, *since when?* High school?"

"At least." I honestly don't remember a time when I could imagine my life with anyone but her. In middle school, when all my guy friends started getting interested in girls, she was still the only girl I liked. By high school, I was full-on infatuated with her. "But you always told everyone that we were just friends, so I did the same because that's what you needed to believe about me so our friendship wouldn't change."

"No, that's what *you* told everyone," she says, tilting her head up so I can see the trail of tears streaking down her face. "But if you had feelings for me, why did you want to go to prom with Sadie Fucking Montgomery?"

I bring my hands to her face, brushing my thumbs across her cheeks to wipe away her tears. I wonder if she realizes that the reason I call her skating partner Christopher

Fucking Steele is because she once referred to Sadie the same way.

"I didn't. I wanted to go with *you*."

"Then why did you ask Sadie?" she asks. Beneath my palms, her pulse kicks up a notch.

"Because you were going with Warner."

"No . . . before Warner and I decided to go together, Reese told me you had this whole big plan to ask Sadie."

The way the anger flashes through my body can't possibly be healthy or normal. Fucking Reese. I *knew* he had feelings for her, but he always said he didn't. I wouldn't put it past that asshole to have told her I was asking Sadie so he'd have a shot of going with Eva.

"I told Reese about my plans to ask *someone*. I never said it was Sadie."

"You were going to ask *me*?"

"I was," I say with a nod. "And you should have known that."

She closes her eyes, tilting her head back, and I catch the back of her head with my fingertips. "I'm such an idiot. I was the one who asked Warner."

Well, this is new information.

"Did you ask him because you thought I was going to ask Sadie?" What I'm really asking is whether she was jealous. Did *she* have feelings for me back then, too?

She opens her eyes, and in the low light of the kitchen, it's hard not to get lost in the way the shades of brown in her eyes swirl together, like dark and milk chocolate melting into each other.

"Yeah." She gulps. "When I heard you were asking Sadie, I

needed it to seem like I didn't care—like I hadn't been hoping you'd ask me."

The weight of the missed opportunity hangs heavy in the air. But so does the promise of our future together.

"Maybe it's better that we didn't get together back then?" I say. It's something I've had years to think about. "If something had happened between us in high school, and then I went off to college and you went to LA, we wouldn't have lasted. Especially not once I was drafted and living in Canada. There was no way we could each have achieved our dreams, and still made a relationship work, not for all these years. It's probably better that we stayed friends instead, so we could end up here, now."

"I wish it had been you," she says, and the sigh that follows is edged with sadness.

"You wish *what* had been me?"

"I don't know . . . my prom date. My first . . . everything."

"I'm your first husband," I say with a sly smile.

"About that . . ." As she trails off, my stomach fucking drops like a pit of dread has opened up and swallowed my insides. I'm not sure what she sees on my face, but her eyes widen, and she laughs, saying, "Oh my god, I'm just teasing, Luke!"

"Not something to fucking joke about, *Wife*," I practically growl at her as I pull her closer, erasing the distance between us.

"Sorry," she whispers, right before my lips meet hers. "It . . . was . . . funny . . . in . . . my . . . head." Each word escapes between kisses until I smother them out, because I'm done talking for now.

Chapter Thirty-Four

EVA

"I need . . ." I pull back from his kiss. ". . . a moment."

His chuckle is deep and husky. "A moment?"

"Yeah. I can't . . . process everything you just told me while you're kissing me like this." He just bared his soul—about being a virgin, about having had feelings for me for a decade—and I haven't had space to think about what that means for us now that we're married.

"Like how?"

"Like you own me." God, but he does. He owns my heart and my body.

His rumble of laughter is low and deep. "I don't own you, Eva, and I never will. But I *will* always treat you like you're the most precious thing in my life, because you are."

"Jesus, Luke." I close my eyes and exhale. How is he so . . . perfect?

"I'm done hiding my feelings. We can take this slow, if that's what you need. Take a moment, or take a month—

whatever works for you. I don't expect that your heart and mind are in the same place as mine, but you obviously don't just see me as a friend, even though you keep trying to convince yourself that's the case."

I take a deep breath, trying to calm my racing mind. He's known the depth of his feelings all along, but they're a revelation to me, and it's a lot to wrap my head around.

He sighs, resting his forehead against mine like he so often does. I love it when he's this close to me, when his sweet and woodsy scent overtakes my senses, when I can feel the heat from his skin wrapping me in warmth, when there's nothing but the tiniest sliver of air between our bodies. It's anticipation mixed with comfort—it's Luke showing me every day how he'll take care of me, how he'll meet all my needs in a supportive but not overbearing way.

How did I not see this for the love that it is? How did I convince myself that this man, who never once talked about another woman to me, didn't have any feelings beyond friendship? How did I believe the rumors about his sex life when it was so at odds with the person I've always known him to be?

I could cry when I think about all the times I talked about other men to him. All the first dates that ended in disaster, all the relationships that ended in heartbreak.

"I'm sorry." The words are whispered, but I know he hears the urgency in them.

With our foreheads still pressed together, his warm breath rolls over my lips when he asks, "For what?"

"For not seeing how you felt. It all seems very obvious now."

"I hid it as best I could, because I thought it wasn't what you wanted."

My arms tighten around his waist as I fist the fabric of his shirt between my fingers. "What I wanted was to have you in my life. And I thought friendship was the only way to keep you there. I was terrified that if I told you how I really felt and you didn't feel the same way, it would ruin our friendship."

"Yeah." He nods. "I understand that fear completely. But those weren't wasted years, Evie. Like I said before, we probably wouldn't have made it back then. *This* is our time."

I push up on my tiptoes and trail kisses along his neck and then across the line of his jaw. His hands move up my back slowly until his fingers curl around my shoulders, and right before my lips meet his, he pulls me away from him, just enough that he can look me in the eye.

I'm sure he sees the confusion on my face at him stopping me, because he dips his head toward mine until his lips are at the shell of my ear, his hot breath curling into my hair as he says, "I need you to be sure, or I need us to stop. I can't go down this path with you and have you change your mind. Not when I know what you taste like when you come on my tongue. Not when we're married and going to have a baby." He takes a ragged breath, and I take a moment to absorb what he's saying. "We can do this marriage as friends with a deep but platonic love for each other. Or we can go into this as a real marriage, with no boundaries or escape plan. But I absolutely can*not* go down this road with you, and then backtrack to just being friends. So I need you to be sure."

I let the fear flow through me for one second—let myself feel the worry and the anxiety about something happening in our relationship that might lead to losing him for good. And then I accept the risk, knowing that finally *being with* Luke will be worth it. Because he's not going to let anything happen to us, and neither am I.

"Good," I say, a smile gracing my lips. "Because I think I'm done being your friend."

Without a moment of hesitation, Luke takes total control of my body. He wraps his hands around the back of my thighs, his fingers digging into my muscles as he lifts me so I can wrap my legs around his waist. Then his mouth crashes into mine as he turns and walks us out of the kitchen, through the living room, and down the hall to his bedroom while nibbling my earlobe and telling me how long he's wanted this. When he kicks the door closed behind us before setting me at the foot of his bed, I wonder, yet again, how it's possible that he hasn't done this before.

He kisses me slowly, like we have all the time in the world, like we haven't both been wanting this forever. My body urges him forward, but he keeps his arms wrapped around me so that mine can't slide below his shoulders. Instead, I undo the buttons at the top of his shirt, and he loosens his grip to accommodate my hands as I work my way down his chest. Letting his arms hang by his sides so I can finish unbuttoning his shirt before sliding it off his shoulders, he pulls each arm out of the sleeves and drops his shirt on the floor.

I take a moment to drop my gaze, following the path of his tattoos across his upper arm, onto his shoulder, and continuing down his other shoulder and arm. Most of these are new within the last few years, and I've never been able to get close enough to study them without my interest being obvious, but I've always wanted to see the individual elements that make up the larger montage. I like knowing that I'll have plenty of time to explore them in the future. I want to know what each one means to him, why he chose them, and how he decided where to place them.

When he slips his thumbs under the straps of my dress and raises his eyebrows like he's asking permission to remove it, I nod so vigorously he lets out a small laugh. "Excited much?" he teases, and I love that even in these intimate moments, we still feel like *us*.

Reaching my hand out, I slide my palm across his zipper and let my fingers curl around his hard length. "Maybe not as excited as you."

He slips the straps of my dress off my shoulders, then hooks his thumbs into the elastic band of the built-in bra so he can slide it off my body. As soon as the fabric glides past the curve of my belly, he kneels in front of me and kisses my belly button, letting the dress drop to my feet. And then he looks up at me as he tugs at the lace straps of my thong and pulls it down my legs.

"Jesus, Evie. I can smell you from here." His face is inches from my pussy, so I don't have to wonder what smell he's talking about. I'm so fucking turned on, I'm probably dripping.

"And how do I smell?"

He places his hands on my hips and gently guides me back so I'm sitting on the bed. And then spreads my knees and leans in, running this tongue along my exposed seam. "The same way you taste when my face is between your legs, and the way you feel when you're coming undone on my fingers. *Like. You're. Mine.*"

The way he growls out each word, low and full of both longing and possession, has a moan rattling around in the back of my throat. I lean back, both my hands planted behind me, so I can tilt my hips up and give him better access.

When he glances up at me, his gaze traveling up the curve of my belly, stopping on my full breasts, before continuing onto my face, his pupils are so large that his light irises all but disappear. I've never understood what people mean when they say *his eyes darkened with longing* . . . until now. Because there's nothing but insatiable hunger in his eyes.

And then he's looping his hands under my legs and cupping my ass so he can tilt my hips at the exact angle he wants before he buries his face in my cunt, licking and sucking with absolutely no mercy. If his intention is to overwhelm my senses and bring on the strongest, fastest orgasm I've ever had, he's well on his way.

I lean back onto my elbows, unable to sit up under this assault, but he stops and lifts his head enough to say, "Don't move another inch. I want to watch your tits bounce while you ride my tongue. I want to see your face when you come apart."

Then he brings his mouth back to me, not letting up for a single second as the waves of pleasure start to build. But just like the other night, my orgasm hangs there, just out of reach. "I need you inside me."

"And you can have me . . . after your first orgasm."

"I need *something*, Luke. Your fingers . . . anything."

His cheek scrapes against my thigh as he chuckles, and then he's pushing up on his knees, burying two fingers deep inside me as he presses the heel of his hand against my clit. He wraps his arm around my lower back, forcing me to sit up, and then his mouth is on one nipple as he brings his hand to my other breast, cupping it before sliding his thumb back and forth over the nipple.

The assault on every part of my body has waves of pleasure rolling through me. Every glide of his thumb and tongue across my nipples pulls at an invisible string connected to my core and extending to where his fingers stroke inside me and his hand rocks against my clit. Heat builds in my core and deepens to a burn before spreading so quickly I fear I might explode.

The fire that licks through my veins may feel like it can burn me alive, but I don't care, because the waves of pleasure that follow are worth the pain. I cry out as the orgasm starts to spread. My limbs grow weak as I fall back onto the bed, and Luke groans out, "That's right, baby, give me every last drop of your cum, and then I'll let you have mine."

My lips part as my eyes widen. Who is this man, and what has he done with my sweet best friend? Though I'm not sure I care, because I can get used to this version quite happily.

"Make me," I whimper.

And then one hand is on my breast, rolling my nipple between his fingers and bringing a tiny edge of pain, while he sinks down and brings his mouth to my clit, sucking hard as he continues the relentless thrust of his fingers deep into my core.

I try to make him work even harder for it before completely giving myself over. But in the end, I have no choice because my eyes roll back and my release rips through me like lightning, tearing wanton sounds out of me that I don't even recognize.

My back arches off the bed, my fists curl into the bed

linens, and my legs shake uncontrollably as unintelligible words tumble out of my mouth. And in that moment, I know that Luke can take care of me like no one ever has. But he doesn't let up, continuing to draw every last bit of pleasure from me until my body goes limp.

As I fall back onto the bed, Luke sits back, and I hear the click of his belt buckle and the scrape of his zipper. My whole body feels boneless, but I don't want to miss out on the sight of him taking his pants off. Because if there's one thing I've been wondering for a week now, it's whether my husband is as well-endowed as he felt on that air mattress in LA.

I stretch my arm out toward Luke, where he still kneels at the foot of the bed. "Pull me up?"

He takes my hand and gives me a gentle tug as he stands, until I can plant my other hand behind me to hold myself in a sitting position. Goddamn, that orgasm wrung out every last ounce of energy from my body.

But when he drops his pants and I see the enormous bulge in his skin-tight boxer briefs, it sends a new wave of heat through me. As he hooks his thumbs into the waistband, I can't take my eyes off him. The anticipation accelerates my breathing, causing my heart to beat so hard it feels like my whole rib cage is vibrating.

"Stop ogling me, Wife," he teases.

"No, thanks." I run my tongue along my top lip as I glance up at him, and there's no mistaking the desire in his eyes. Then he slides his boxers down his hips and bends to shove them down his legs, making me groan in frustration that he's blocking my view.

When he stands again, kicking the boxers off to the side

and stepping closer to me, my mouth parts with a small gasp. *Holy shit.*

Luke's a lot bigger than I am, and maybe at 6'3", I should have expected his cock to be proportional to his height, especially given what I felt when I rubbed myself up against him a week ago. And yet, I'm not prepared for the sight in front of me.

I glance up at him again, and his lips curve up on one side in what looks like a smirk—but I don't think that's what it is. I think the anticipation is killing him.

When my attention returns to the silky length of his hard cock, I reach my hand out to grip the base, smiling to myself at the feel of him.

"Just think how good it'll look with your spit all over it," he says huskily, making my thighs clench.

My eyes widen, and my laugh catches in my throat, so it comes out more like a strangled moan, and I wonder again how my best friend has such a dirty mouth.

"I thought you were supposed to be a nice guy, Luke."

"I'm plenty nice when I want to be. But right now?" He slides himself against my hand, sending waves of longing through my core and aftershocks all the way to my limbs. "Right now, I want to watch you gag."

Chapter Thirty-Five

LUKE

I need to hold back a laugh when I see Eva's eyes flare. I would never say that to anyone else, but it's important that I can be totally open with her. I'm done hiding my feelings, and that includes all the things I've dreamed about doing with her—or having her do to me. Because, let's face it, I've never been with anyone else, or by myself, when I wasn't picturing Eva.

That probably makes me a bigger asshole than I'd like to admit, but she's always been it for me.

I watch her stomach muscles contract, and her shoulders roll back as a wave of longing runs through her. She lets out another strangled moan, and then looks up at me, licking those pouty pink lips, and says, "Get over here."

I take a step forward so I'm right in front of her. My dick is so close to her face that when she parts her lips, they brush against the taut skin of my tip, and a groan rattles the back of my throat. She glances up at me, biting her lower lip as she gives me a coy look that makes me wonder whether she's intentionally dragging this out to torture me.

I'm torn between enjoying the way she's exerting control, and wanting to tilt her head back, invade her mouth, and push my cock to the back of her throat.

But then her tongue darts out, licking her bottom lip and the underside of the head of my dick, and my hand is on the back of her head, my fingers threading into her soft, dark hair as she leans in and circles me with her tongue. It takes everything I have, every ounce of self-control I possess, not to push into her—not to rush this moment that I've been waiting a lifetime for.

I want *her* to be in control here. I want her to show me what she likes to do, and how she wants to proceed.

Her lips part as she slides me into her mouth, and her moans send vibrations shooting along my cock. My hips jut forward instinctively, and her free hand moves to my hip as she guides me closer.

I watch her head bob toward me as she takes me deeper, as if testing how much she can fit before she gags. My fingers tighten in her hair as I tilt her head back just a tad, changing the angle so she can take more.

She groans while sliding her hand down my shaft so her fingers rest lightly on my abdomen as she presses my cock between her tongue and the roof of her mouth, allowing her teeth to graze lightly along the sensitive skin. I can tell I've hit the back of her throat because her eyes water and she gags a little. She doesn't stop, though, and she simultaneously rocks her hips against my mattress to create some friction for herself. It's the sexiest fucking thing I've ever seen.

"We're going to have to work on that gag reflex, sweetheart," I say, pulling back until I slip out of her mouth.

She looks up at me with fire in her eyes and says, "After you have the experience of choking on someone's dick, you can feel free to teach me all about managing *my* gag reflex."

I can't help the deep rumble of laughter that rolls out of me. "Just so you know, the more feisty you are, the more I want to fuck you."

Her eyes widen before her lips curl into a smile. "Good."

I set one knee on the bed next to her and, wrapping my arm around her lower back, I slide her closer to the headboard so she's lying in the middle of my bed and I'm kneeling between her legs. On her back with her heavy breasts falling to the sides and her knees spread on either side of my hips, she's a vision. One I wasn't sure I'd ever see.

"What's wrong?" she whispers, her brow furrowed together as her gaze slips across my face.

"Nothing's wrong. I'm just taking this moment in. You're fucking breathtaking, Evie."

She gives me a small smile, then her eyes rake down my chest to where our bodies meet, my dick resting along her belly and my hips pressing into her open thighs. "You're not so bad yourself, Husband."

Hearing her call me her husband has a vise painfully tightening around my heart.

"What was that?" she says, her eyes narrowing.

I hear the worry in her voice, and I don't know if it's better to say nothing, or to tell her what I'm really thinking.

"Honest answer?"

Her hands stroke up the sides of my ribs as she stares at me. "Always."

"I'm a tiny bit scared of you right now."

She laughs lightly, but it's a nervous sound. "Scared of me?"

"Scared of finally handing my entire heart over to you, Peaches," I say, dipping my head and brushing my lips over her forehead. "It's always been yours and, in truth, you've been breaking it, bit by tiny bit, our whole lives without ever knowing it. Now, you could shatter it, if you wanted."

"Or . . ." she says, smoothing her hands from my sides, up my back, and over my shoulders as she pulls me down to her, ". . . I could put it back together again."

Our lips meet tentatively, the kiss softer and sweeter than any we've had. We're both aware of the huge change tonight's revelations have made in our relationship and the significance of taking this next step together.

Wrapping her lower legs around my ass to pull me closer, she deepens the kiss, and I try not to let the weight of the shift in our relationship overshadow this experience. She arches her back, letting her nipples graze my chest as my hips push forward, the base of my cock sliding along her wet seam. Her silken flesh caresses my aching dick, and I can tell by her soft moans that I'm hitting her clit. At first, she meets me thrust for thrust, but then she breaks away from the kiss, whispering, "More."

"I need to grab a condom," I say.

She threads her fingers into the hair at the back of my head, tugging slightly as she breathes heavily. "Do you, though?"

"Peaches," I say, my tone one of warning. "If I'm bare inside you this first time, I'm never going to want to use protection."

Her big brown eyes search my face. "As long as you're clean, which, I assume you are, I'm okay with that."

I close my eyes and rest my forehead against hers. I know I'm clean. Even though I've never had sex, I still get tested regularly because, obviously, there are many ways to contract a sexually transmitted infection.

But damn, the idea of us being together like this has me feeling things I didn't expect to feel. It's not just the anticipation of having sex for the first time, and having it be with the only person I've ever loved, but . . . I'm not even sure how to explain it.

"You still alive up there?" she asks with a light laugh.

Shit, I think I stopped breathing for a minute.

"Yeah. Just processing all this."

"Listen, Luke," she says, tilting her head back so I'm forced to lift mine. "We don't have to do this, or we can use a condom if that makes you more comfortable. I just want you to know that I trust you, and I'm okay with whatever you want to do. It's not like you can get me pregnant."

My chuckle causes our chests to collide, reminding me that my dick is pressed right up against her. "Oh, I *want* to do this. I'm just taking a minute to absorb what this means for us. Taking this step is a big deal."

Her hips rock up into me, sliding her pussy along me again. "I'm ready for this step if you are."

I pull my hips back until I can tell I'm lined up with her entrance, and the slick feel of her against the head of my cock has me groaning with the effort of holding back.

"I'm ready," I say, and she tightens her legs around me, pushing her hips up so I slip inside her.

The way her lips part and her eyes squeeze shut as I push deeper lets me know I need to go slowly. I pause, stroking my thumb along the ridge of her cheek. "You good?"

"Yes," she breathes out, opening her eyes. "Just . . . very full."

"You ready for more?"

She nods, and her eyes flare wider as I slide more of myself inside. She loosens her legs around my hips, stretching to accommodate me, and then her core clenches against my shaft and I can't hold back my moan as I rock my hips away from her and then push in deeper.

Because I'm a goalie, it's my nature to watch people closely to determine what they're going to do next. Everything about Eva's posture tells me she's too tense, that she needs me to keep this slow and controlled. All I want to do is finally unleash everything I've been holding back for the last decade.

But no matter what I want, I'll always give her what she needs.

"Oh my god," she whispers, her lips parting as she sighs. "Are you . . . in . . . all the way?"

I can't help but laugh a little. "Not yet. But you're doing so well, baby. I know you can take all of me."

She trails her tongue along her upper lip and nods, so I rock my hips back and push in again. The drag of my cock along her inner walls seems to ignite something in her, because she plants her feet on the bed beside my hips and says, "Yes, more of that."

And then she pushes her hips up, meeting me thrust for thrust until we're both rocking our bodies into each other as she pulls me down for a kiss. The taste of her on my lips, the feel of her around my cock, and the delicate drag of her skin along mine with each thrust of my body has my balls tightening up.

So I scoop her in my arms, rolling until I'm on my back and she's straddling me. "I want to watch you take me, Evie. I want to see you come apart for me again."

"I don't . . . know if I can . . . again," she says, planting a hand beside my head as she leans her body over me.

I hold my thumb to her lips and my dick throbs where it's fully seated inside her. Then she takes my thumb, her teeth sinking into the pad before circling it with her tongue. And when I move my hand between us, my thumb on her clit and my fingers splayed across the curve of her belly, she lifts and lowers herself onto me. Her full breasts bounce right above my face, and I use my free hand to grab the pillows behind me and bring them under my head and shoulders.

"Your tits are fucking phenomenal," I tell her, before I latch my lips around one nipple. I circle the hardened peak with my tongue, lapping over and around it in a way that has her bucking wildly on top of me. As I tease her other nipple between my fingers, she lets out a breathy, "Yes . . . yes . . . oh my god . . . yes . . . keep doing that."

And so, I do. I force myself to hold back while letting her control the pace of our joined bodies, continuing to graze my thumb over her clit and toy with her nipples until her movements become erratic—almost frantic—as she slams her cunt down on my cock.

"More," she pleads, so I move my mouth to her other nipple and bring my arm to her lower back, anchoring her hips to me as I push up into her fast and hard.

"Oh fuck . . ." she pants, breathing labored. "Fuck yes. Oh my god."

"God's not here, Peaches. It's just me and you. Harder?"

Above me, her lips part, and she nods, so I increase the pressure on her clit as I slam my cock into her until she's whimpering and crying out my name while her muscles clench around me. And then, it's impossible to hold back any longer. I tighten my grip on her hips as I hold her to me. Sparks fly through my veins, and I shake violently as I grunt out my release and pour myself into her.

Her shoulders slump forward, and she hangs her head above me, propping herself up on her arm.

"Holy shit." She tilts her head up slightly to look at me. "Why haven't we done this before?"

I chuckle, looking at her lovingly. "I was just waiting for you to be ready."

Her eyes are half closed, she hums, "How soon can we do that again?"

"Right now, if you want," I say with a shrug that I hope masks how eager I am to fuck my wife again. I want to keep doing this all goddamn night. And probably all day tomorrow. I have a lot of fucking fantasies to work through with her.

"Are you serious? How is that possible?" She narrows her eyes as she looks down from above me.

"Fun fact: about ten percent of men can have multiple orgasms with no downtime."

"And you know this how?"

"Looked it up. Needed to know how special I was."

She snorts out a small laugh and rolls her eyes, like she's saying, *You and that ego.*

But then she cups my face, leans in a bit closer and whispers, "Everything about that was special, Luke." Clenching her core around me and smiling when she finds me still hard inside her, she tilts her hips forward and pushes back again. "But maybe you can be a good boy and give me a third orgasm, just to make it extra special?"

Chapter Thirty-Six

EVA

"Hey, baby." Luke's breath is hot in my ear as consciousness swims around me. I don't want to wake up yet, but his words and my bladder are pulling me from sleep anyway.

"Hey," I mumble without opening my eyes.

The bed moves as he sits up, and then he's pressing his lips to my belly and saying, "And good morning, Baby Squash."

I love that no matter how big this baby gets or what fruit or vegetable that app compares the baby's size to, he or she will always be Baby Squash to Luke.

"I'm dead," I groan, and his rumble of laughter shakes the bed. "But I have to pee. I don't think I can even walk to the bathroom."

"Can you really die from having too much sex?" Luke teases.

"Apparently, if that's all you do for a day and a half, yes." I groan as I sit up and throw my legs over the edge of the bed. Every muscle in my body is sore, because I've used them all. We haven't left the apartment since we got home from the Neon Cactus two nights ago, and I'm pretty sure we've had sex on every horizontal surface in this place.

I stand, but the spots at the edge of my vision have me putting both hands out for balance, and Luke's goalie reflexes must kick in because he springs out of bed and is standing with his arms wrapped around me before I even realize what's happened.

"Okay," he says. "Clearly, it's time to get some food and water in you."

I breathe in deeply as I rest my head back on his shoulder, and the dizziness fades. "First, I have to pee, though," I tell him. "Baby Squash is dancing on my damn bladder."

"Okay. I'll walk you in there, and then to the kitchen when you're done. We're getting you hydrated and fed before everyone arrives for this interview."

"What time is it?" I ask, still feeling quite groggy. I've barely slept the last two nights as Luke and I spent every waking moment exploring long-suppressed desires and confessing all our pent-up feelings for each other.

When we were still just friends, I would've said I've never felt closer to another person than to Luke, but what's shifted between us in the last two days puts the relationship on an entirely different plane of reality—one I didn't believe existed.

And now, I'm borderline hostile about the fact that people from the magazine are showing up here this morning. First to arrive will be hair and makeup, then wardrobe, then Jillian Vance, the celebrity reporter who will interview us.

Morgan's already provided the article we're "allowing" them to publish, but we've agreed to meet with Jillian so she can add in some personal details and observations about us as a couple.

"Eight-thirty," Luke says, and I groan, because I'm pretty sure that means I got about four hours of sleep. If I look half as tired as I feel, it's a good thing a professional makeup artist will be here in an hour and a half.

When he leads me into his bathroom and I catch sight of myself in the mirrors above the vanity, my heart sinks. I look well and truly wrecked—my thick, long hair is a matted mess, the purple bags under my eyes are like welts, and the skin on my face, neck, and chest looks like someone ran sandpaper over it. I look like a woman who just spent the last thirty-six hours being fucked senseless by her husband.

Husband. This marriage has gone from a stark reminder of everything I couldn't have, to everything I've ever wanted, all in the span of a couple of weeks. I'm the luckiest girl on the planet, and I'm too exhausted right now to fully appreciate it.

"All right, Peaches," he says, turning me toward him so I can sit on the toilet.

"I'm not peeing in front of you." I nod toward the door with narrowed eyes.

Luke chuckles, like it's ridiculous that I've been stark naked with him for the last day and a half, had his cum dripping out of me, and let him use my body in nearly every way imaginable—yet I won't pee in front of him. "I'm going to go grab you a T-shirt, and then I'll be right outside the door," he says. "Please don't stand up too quickly when you're done."

"Promise."

Once I'm finished and have washed my hands, I run a brush through my hair and open the bathroom door. As promised, Luke is waiting for me and pulls one of his Rebels T-shirts over my head so I can slip my arms inside. This soft shirt probably clings to every muscle in his upper body, but it's basically a dress on me.

"Let's go make you a breakfast sandwich, and then we're going to shower."

"Luke, if we get in that shower together, we probably won't be out by the time the people from the magazine start showing up." And then I remember. "Oh, shit. Morgan said she'd get here before they did, so we can review our story and she can make sure we don't say anything that we wouldn't want to make it into the article."

"We'll have to save showering together for another time because we need to hustle," he says, giving my butt a little smack that has us both laughing. "Let's go."

———

From my spot on the bench where I'm currently trying not to die after a round of weighted hip thrusts, I look over at Luke. The late afternoon light from the floor-to-ceiling windows in the gym bounces off the thin sheen of sweat across his bare skin, highlighting the dips and valleys of his muscular build. His shorts are low on his hips, and that *V* of muscles headed into his waistband has me wanting to peel off my clothes.

We're alone here now, the last person we were sharing this space with having left just a moment before probably because she was uncomfortable with the way I was openly undressing my husband with my eyes.

"You can't look at me like that when there are other people around," Luke groans as he walks toward the mirrors to rack his weights on the stand.

"Why not? We're newlyweds. No one is going to be surprised if I'm looking at my husband like I want to have sex with him."

Luke chuckles. "You weren't looking at me like you wanted to have sex with me, baby. You were looking at me like you were picturing it happening."

"Maybe I was. Or am," I say with a shrug, loving that I suddenly don't care what people think, when my whole life, other people's opinions of me have mattered as much as, or more than, my own. Maybe this marriage has been good for my self-confidence, too.

His eyebrows dip as he looks into the mirrors behind the weights, watching me stare at him.

"My god," I say. "It's so unfair that you look like *that* after working out, and I look like this hot mess."

"Nothing about you sweaty and panting has me thinking 'hot mess.'" Luke's voice is low and sensual, but then he clears his throat and looks away, and I'm guessing he's trying to stop that semi hard-on in his gym shorts from getting any more out of control in a public place.

But the thought of teasing him gives me a sudden burst of energy, and I stand and cross the space between us, coming up behind him and trailing my fingers up one bicep. "You've never told me about these new tattoos . . ."

Every time I considered asking about them this past weekend, I was too tired from all the sex and fell asleep instead, only to be awoken by my husband either trying to feed me or fuck me again. The hedonistic pleasure of it all is a welcome memory that's spurring me on, wanting more, even though I'm exhausted from this workout.

"Which ones do you want to know about?" he asks.

I trace my fingertips over a few clusters of small flowers up one arm and across his shoulders as I follow the path down his other bicep—some are single clusters, others are a series of clusters on branches. "Tell me about the flowers."

His gaze locks on mine in the mirror, and he runs his lower lip between his teeth. "They're peach blossoms."

My sharp inhale is loud in the silent space. "Why peach blossoms?"

"Why do you think, Peaches?"

Swallowing down the emotions thick in my throat, I wrap my hand around his upper arm and turn it slightly so that I can see the reflection of two scoops of ice cream atop a cone. "The ice cream?"

"I'm convinced we still haven't found the best flavor yet. This is my reminder that I get to keep looking . . . with you."

My fingers trail around his shoulder and over his chest, landing on a full moon with a shadow across most of it. "The moon?"

"The eclipse we watched from the beach in the middle of the night last summer."

"When the clouds rolled in and blocked our view right before the total eclipse?"

He nods his chin. "Keep looking."

And that's when I notice the hazy clouds below the moon, above a beach scene.

"What about these waves?" I ask, trailing my fingers along

the waves hitting the grassy cliffs. It makes me miss the beach, since in summers past so much of our time has been spent there. Maybe while we're up in Newbury Falls this weekend we can make a quick trip down to the water.

"The waves that crash into the cliffs below your house at high tide." As I understand that each of these tattoos is tied to me, my eyes water. Then Luke grabs my fingers and holds them to the waves on his chest as he spins to face me, stepping closer so my forearm and hand are flattened against his body. "The sea was my first love. And then it was hockey. And finally, it was you."

I swallow down the lump in my throat, and instead of showing him how emotional I am, I try to play it off. "Third place isn't exactly the best—"

"You're my last love, Evie, and that's all that matters. After the waves have eroded those cliffs and hockey is a distant memory, it will still *always* be you."

I choke on the sob that erupts from the back of my throat, and then laugh at myself. "I'm sorry, but you can't say things like that while I'm pregnant without me getting overly emotional."

He drops my hand, then rests both of his on my hips as he presses a kiss to my forehead. "I'm okay with Emo Eva. Truth be told, I quite like knowing you have feelings."

I tilt my head back to look up at him as he lets out a low rumble of laughter. "Way to ruin the moment."

"Nothing's ruined, Peaches. But now I see that the way to prevent you from mauling me in public is to start talking about my feelings." He winks at me then, and I can't help but smile back.

"I can't believe you have our memories inked all over your body."

"It shouldn't surprise you in the least," he says, shaking his head.

"It shouldn't surprise me *now*. But you got those tattoos over the last several years—putting permanent reminders of me on your skin, without knowing that we'd ever be here."

"I think somewhere deep down, I always knew we'd end up here."

My cheeks push up as my smile spreads, suddenly feeling warm all over. "Did you now?"

"Well, I hoped you'd finally come to your senses and see what was right in front of you."

I know he's teasing, but in a way, he's right. Whether it was my pregnancy or him living in Boston now, or something else, things shifted between us this summer. And the man who I'd been telling myself my whole life I couldn't have was suddenly looking at me like he wanted me too.

"Good thing I'm nothing if not sensible," I say.

"I'm glad to hear it, because I'd really like you to not kill me when I tell you what I've done."

I lift an eyebrow. "What have you done that's going to warrant murder, exactly?"

"Uhhh . . ." He pauses, then bends to grab the T-shirt he's left hanging off the bench behind him. "Maybe I better show you instead?"

"Ominous," I say playfully, but I follow as he starts walking toward the door while pulling his shirt over his head. He stops at the elevators, but when we get in, he doesn't press the 60 that would take us to our floor. Instead, he presses the P2 button at the bottom, and we head down to the parking garage.

As we step out into the underground garage, I'm about to ask him if we're going somewhere, but then a shiny black mid-size SUV—wrapped in a thick red ribbon and parked right next to Luke's car—catches my eye.

"Please don't be mad," he says as he leads me toward it and presses a key fob into my hand.

"You . . ." A thrill runs through me as I stare at the gorgeous car. "You bought me a BMW?"

"I wanted you to have something safe, that you could easily get an infant seat in and out of, and would handle well in the snow but not be too big for city driving."

"Listen to you being all practical while I stand here drooling over this car. You really didn't have to do this. I could have waited until my convertible sold and then bought something . . . more modest."

Maybe I don't dream big enough, because never in my wildest dreams did I think I'd be driving a car like this. It's so much nicer than anything I've ever owned that I'm almost afraid to touch it.

He wraps his arm behind my back and pulls me to his side so we're hip to hip. There's amusement in his voice when he says, "Evie, what's the point of having money if you can't spoil the people you love?"

I rest my head against him, thinking how easy it is to forget he's so wealthy, given how down-to-earth he is. "You don't have to spoil me, Luke. Just being with you is enough."

Turning to face me, his cool blue eyes are dark in the low light. His lips turn up in a small smile, and the look he's giving me tells me I'm cherished. "I know I don't have to, but

I want to. And when have you ever known me not to get what I want?"

I click my tongue at him and shake my head, but I can't hold in my smile. "So cocky."

"Just confident. You're my future, Evie, and despite everything I might already have, you're all I ever really wanted."

I close my eyes, trying to capture the feel of this moment as he leans in and presses his lips to my forehead. But then my stomach rumbles so loud it's almost like someone started an engine. "You know what I *really* want?"

"Besides me?" he says, his voice husky like he's trying to remind me that not five minutes ago I was about to jump him in the private gym in our building.

"Always you," I say. "But first, ice cream. I hear there's a hidden gem on the South Shore where you can get huge lobster rolls and fries with four types of dipping sauces, followed by amazing soft serve flavors. They have all these different twist combinations—"

"Say less," he says with a chuckle as he guides me to the driver's side of my new car, before reaching to the roof and pulling off the enormous red bow. "We need to make sure Baby Squash is well-versed in ice cream flavors. Let's go."

Chapter Thirty-Seven

EVA

"Is it my imagination, or have you gotten stronger?" Lynette calls out to me when Christopher and I safely land our twist lift.

Our free skate routine includes a triple twist, where Christopher throws me into the air and, with my legs crossed and my arms pulled close to my body, I rotate three times above his head, practically horizontal to the ice, before he does half a turn to catch my hips as I land on the outside edge of one skate.

However, for our practices while I'm pregnant, we're only doing single twists so there's less chance of me risking injury or him accidentally impacting my belly.

I drop my leg down to stop the backward glide that would normally lead me into the next element of our routine. "I'm feeling stronger, that's for sure." Stronger, yes, but my stamina still isn't back up to par, if the way I'm panting out the words is any indication.

"You're doing great," Lynette says, and even though we've practiced almost daily with her for over a week, the affirmation still gets me a tad choked up. Christopher and I spent so long being constantly berated by Jessie that I think I forgot what it was like to have a positive coach. It's not that Lynette doesn't tell us when we need to be better, or what we need to do differently. But she doesn't dwell only on the negative, she also tells us what we're doing well to keep things balanced.

"Is that nutritionist I recommended helping?" she asks.

"The meals begin arriving today, so I'll let you know. But I already started implementing her suggestions, and I'm noticing a difference."

Honestly, I like feeling involved in the process, rather than letting my mom control everything. Understanding what changes are needed, and why, has made it easier for me to make healthier choices—whereas before, I had a strict diet to follow without really knowing why certain things were in place or what their relative importance was to my athletic performance.

I'm not sure why I didn't push back and take more control of my own body and career sooner. Maybe it was guilt, because my parents had done so much to support my skating over the years and I wanted them to be proud of me? Maybe it was doubt that I had what it took to be in control of my own destiny? Maybe it was conflict avoidance because I didn't want to fight with my mom?

And even though I hate the weight of my mom's disapproval hanging over my head, I feel a hell of a lot better about myself and my skating career now that I've removed her strict control over both.

"Good," she says before turning toward Christopher.

"What about you? That toss into the twist looked a lot harder than it should have."

Christopher's neck gets the pink tinge that only happens when he's embarrassed, which isn't often. So I skate forward until I'm right next to him and say, "He's throwing close to twenty pounds more than before."

My belly has finally "popped" into a cute little bump, and my limbs aren't as toned as they once were, even with the extra weight training I've added in. Sure, I'm building muscle, but there's also extra pregnancy-related weight that I can't do anything about—my breasts alone must account for an extra five pounds themselves.

"Okay, fair. But if you can throw a single twist while she's twenty pounds heavier and pregnant," Lynette says to Christopher, "I'm going to expect that triple after she has the baby to look absolutely effortless."

"My part will. We'll see how Eva does," he says playfully, throwing an arm around my shoulders and giving me a quick squeeze.

"If I can do this pregnant, I'm gonna be juuuuust fine afterward," I say with more confidence than I actually feel. Maybe I can manifest this victory if I don't let myself picture anything except a gold medal at the Olympic qualifier?

"Yeah, we'll probably surprise everyone and do a quad twist." Christopher shrugs.

"You two are delusional," Lynette says with a laugh, "but I like that about you. Let's end on a high note and call it a day. I'll see you bright and early tomorrow morning."

As we head off the ice, Christopher glances up at the stands where Luke is typically waiting for me. "Your bodyguard isn't here to pick you up today?"

"He's my husband, not my bodyguard. And my dad wanted to have lunch today, so I'm going to meet him closer to the practice rink in Brighton."

Christopher steps off the ice and bends to slide his guards over his blades. "How are you getting over there?"

"I'm driving."

"Any chance you can give me a ride? I'm meeting Jenn for lunch in Kenmore Square."

"Is Jenn *the girl?*"

So far, Christopher has only referenced "the girl I'm talking to," but never by name.

"Yeah, we're going to grab lunch, because she's flying out tonight for a series of meetings in New York and won't be back until Friday."

"Oh my god," I say, my face etched with mock horror. "What will you do with yourself if she's gone for a few nights?"

In truth, I'm relieved that Christopher has someone to keep him occupied. Given that he left all his friends behind in LA—the only place he's ever lived—I was worried that this would be a hard adjustment for him. But I knew I couldn't spend a lot of extra time with Christopher—beyond the hours we already skate together each day—without adding unnecessary friction to his already tenuous relationship with Luke.

Hopefully, now that Luke is more secure in our relationship, that will be less of an issue. But I also want to respect the fact that I would probably be pretty unhappy if Luke was spending a lot of time with someone he thought he'd had feelings for previously.

Christopher chuckles as he sits to unlace his skates. "Probably a lot of nights spent on FaceTime."

I sink into my seat right next to him. "You really like her, huh?"

"It's only been a little over a week," he says, but he can't wipe the smile off his face.

"Yeah, but didn't you start talking to her before then?" If I remember correctly, he met her on a dating app before moving here. I was pretty distracted with what was going on in my own life, though, so maybe I don't have the details or timeline quite right.

"We've been talking for a few weeks, yeah. Still, this feels quick." He shakes his head like he can't quite wrap his mind around developing feelings for someone in a matter of weeks. Given how cool and detached he can be, this *is* quick for him.

"I think you can meet someone, and sometimes there's just this instant connection." I don't know this from personal experience, because my feelings for Luke have grown and developed over such a long time frame, but I've seen it happen with some of my friends.

"Maybe," he says. "We're trying not to get ahead of ourselves, because we both feel like this is really fast to feel this close to another person. She's just out of a bad relationship and wasn't looking to hop into another one, and I'm . . ."

I elbow him in his side. "Never in a relationship?"

He barks out a sharp laugh. "Pretty much."

"Maybe that's how you know this is good? If neither of you was looking for a relationship, but you want one with each other . . . that feels like something worth holding on to, you know?"

"We'll see how things go. She wants to meet you," he says casually as he sets his skate in his bag.

I laugh uncomfortably without intending to. "Why?"

"Probably for the same reason that Luke's always hovering around the rink after our practices."

"She's jealous?"

"I think it's more like she wants to assess whether or not you're a threat."

I bark out a loud laugh that has heads turning. "Did you not tell her how much I'm *not* a threat?" I mean, this man turned me down many months ago and now I'm married. She should have no reason to be concerned.

"I only told her that nothing's ever happened between us and that you're recently married. I didn't want to share anything that violated your privacy or would lead her to question your marriage to Luke."

"That's . . . I appreciate that. Thank you."

"Maybe if things with Jenn and me continue down this path, she can meet you and Luke. If she sees you two together, I'm confident that she'll realize you have eyes only for him."

"Just like you always knew how I felt?" I'm not asking if this is why he turned me down, so much as confirming that he's always known what I was so blind to.

"Exactly."

———

"That's a really nice car you're driving." Dad nods his chin toward the window next to our table. Somehow,

I managed to snag what Dad always refers to as "rockstar parking" right in front of the restaurant.

"Thanks. Luke wanted to make sure I had something that was safe and would be easy with a baby."

"Easy with a baby?" he asks.

"You know, like the infant seat will be a straight shot in and out without me having to bend down too far, and I can easily get a stroller in and out of the back."

He nods. "I feel like a lot has changed since you were born. Things were . . . simpler back then."

I just nod in response, still waiting for Dad to drop whatever bomb he invited me here to unload. There's no way he just wants to make idle chitchat about my new car.

"It's no surprise Luke is taking care of you." Ah, there it is. I'm gearing up to defend our marriage and our baby, when he says, "I'm glad you two are together."

Wait, what?

I freeze with my spring roll hovering over a small bowl of peanut sauce. "You are?"

"Yeah, considering the bond you two have always had, I kind of hoped you'd end up together." Dad watches my face closely, then asks, "Did you think I didn't approve?"

I sigh, setting my chopsticks on my plate and sitting back. "I don't know, Dad. You sent that text after the shitshow of a dinner, which Luke and I both appreciated, but I still left home that night feeling like . . . I don't even know. Like I just continue to be a big disappointment, I guess."

"What do you mean, *continue to be?*"

"It's not you," I say quickly. "It's just that Mom is always so focused on everything I could do differently, everything I could do *better*. And then for her to tell me that my baby was going to ruin my career—"

"She should never have said that."

"Yeah, no shit."

Dad's eyes widen in the same warning look he used to give me when I was a kid. I *never* talk to my parents like this. But I'm not sure what he'd expect, given Mom's reaction when we told them about our marriage and this baby, and the fact that I've heard absolutely nothing from her since then.

"There's a lot you don't know about your mom, sweetie. And I feel like maybe if I give you some more information, you might better understand where she's coming from."

I'm tempted to say she should be the one reaching out to explain. And while objectively that might be true, I guess the most important thing here is that I actually understand why she treats me the way she does.

I pick up the rest of my spring roll, nodding that he should continue. "Your mom was at the pinnacle of her riding career when I met her."

"I know she was." Mom was fresh off an Olympic gold medal and was the guest of honor at a show jumping competition being held at Wellington Show Park. My dad, a hometown hero, who'd won an Olympic gold medal two years before when the US Hockey team beat Canada in a huge upset, was also attending the event. The Hartmanns, who are at least a decade older than my parents, introduced them. There was clearly some matchmaking going on, and a few months later, my mom moved to Newbury Falls to train at Wellington. She and Elise formed a quick, close bond, my parents got married, and Mom started working at the equestrian center with her new best friend instead of competing.

"The thing is, Eva, she moved here because she was pregnant."

My lips part, but for a moment, no sound comes out. "That math doesn't check out."

Dad presses his lips together and nods. "Not for you, it doesn't."

"I . . . wasn't your first kid?"

"Your mom miscarried pretty far into the pregnancy. By then, she'd already walked away from competing—there was no way she could safely train while pregnant, or compete for England now that she was married and living in the US."

I do some more quick math in my head and realize there were nearly four years between my mom's Olympic medal and my birth. "She didn't want to go back to it after that?"

"She'd already chosen her path, we were married, I couldn't move to England, and she already had a job here. I know she doesn't regret it, because she loves us both very much. But I do think she regrets not being able to continue competing. You may have noticed," Dad says, and his lips turn up slightly at one corner, "your mom has quite the competitive spirit."

"So she threw all that competitive energy into me once I was born?"

"She always said that, no matter what your dreams were, she'd do anything to help you achieve them."

Including micromanaging my career and making me feel like shit. Got it.

I lift an eyebrow as I stare at my dad, and the slight bob of his head tells me he understands. He doesn't have to be a mind reader to know what I'm thinking, because he and Luke's family finally saw the way she talks to me.

"I know you don't always agree with her methods," Dad says and reaches across the table to squeeze my hand. "To be honest, neither do I, and she knows it. I've never known anyone as driven or high achieving as your mother, and that's saying something, considering that my entire career has been spent with hockey players. Your mother could accomplish *anything* she puts her mind to."

I think about her multiple degrees from prestigious British universities, her many equestrian medals, and the way she's helped grow Wellington Show Park into the preeminent equestrian facility in the Boston area.

"Yeah, she accomplishes a lot by sheer force of will," I agree, but there's a slightly bitter note to the words, because we both know that her parenting style is included in that.

"I always tried to temper that aspect of her when she was dealing with you. But I don't think I always knew everything that was going on. The way she talked to you about those cupcakes? I was ashamed of how shocked we all were, and how unsurprised you were by her comment. I'm sorry I wasn't more aware."

"The thing is, Dad," I say, thinking about how much he was gone during my childhood. Before the Rebels, he coached at the college level, and while their season was a bit shorter and the stretches of away games weren't as long, he was still away quite a lot in the winters. "Nothing Mom says is untrue, per se. It's just that she treats me like someone she's coaching instead of like her daughter. Her win-at-any-cost attitude hasn't made me better; it's just become something I have to deal with, to learn to compartmentalize, while training and competing. If anything, it's probably hurt more than it helped."

"I'm sorry." Dad shakes his head sadly. "I need you to know that I'm not trying to justify anything she's done. I just want you to understand why your mom's always been so invested in your career—in making sure you have had every opportunity to achieve your dreams. And I want you to understand the back story, so you can decide what you want to do from here."

"I appreciate knowing the whole picture," I say with a sigh. "But I'm not planning on doing anything. The ball is really in her court now—if she wants a relationship with me, she can reach out. It's time we both stop excusing and apologizing for her behavior."

My dad raises his eyebrows and looks at me like he's seeing me as a capable, independent adult for the first time. "You're absolutely right, honey. Also, in case it wasn't clear enough before, I'm tremendously proud of you, and I know you and Luke are going to be amazing parents."

Chapter Thirty-Eight

LUKE

"The way you're so calm and flawless in practice like this . . . " Colt says, shaking his head as I step off the ice after skills training. "How are we going to make sure you have a handle on the emotional and mental aspect of your relationship with Eva so it doesn't bleed over onto the ice again?"

"I'm talking to Zach's therapist." I have another appointment with her coming up soon, and I guess I'll have some big updates for her.

"Ahh . . . " Colt nods. I'm sure he knows Drew talks to her as well, but it's not my place to mention it. "Good. Because when I retire at the end of this season, you've got to be ready to wear the number 1, okay? Whatever we have to do this year to make that happen, we're doing it. I didn't ask AJ to bring you to Boston to watch you go down in flames."

"What?" I croak out, my throat suddenly tight. I'd assumed that it was either Charlie or Evan who pushed the idea with AJ, and I don't immediately know how to react to this revelation.

"Which part of that wasn't clear?" he says, clearly not understanding why this information is big news to me.

"The part about you asking AJ to bring me to Boston. *Why?*"

"Because clearly, our last goalie, Baker, needed some more time in the AHL, and I had already sensed that AJ was sending him back there. Your first string goalie in Calgary was at the beginning of a six-year contract, so the chances of you advancing much more there were slim. Seemed like coming back to your hometown and playing for the team you grew up rooting for would be good for you. Especially since I only had a year and a half left on my contract."

Knowing that the best goalie in the league personally chose me as his replacement makes me choke up, but I manage to say, "Thanks, man. I appreciate that."

"Well, I'd appreciate one more Stanley Cup before I retire," he says as he claps my shoulder. "So let's make that happen, yeah?"

I nod. "You think Renaud coming back this season will help us get there?"

Colt bites the inside of his cheek. "Depends."

"On?"

"On whether he decides to be a team player."

"He's not already?"

Colt gives a slight shrug. "Hard to say. The team has changed a lot this year. It'll be interesting to see how it all shakes out. Drew's the first line center now, and Renaud's never played with him. He does play well with McCabe and is used to being opposite him on the first line, but now that

Walshy moved up to take his place . . . I don't know. That line was working really well together last season without Renaud. It'll be interesting to see what Wilcott decides to do."

I'm not sure why this whole situation feels kind of ominous, but it does. Because if Charlie decides to keep the current first line together and put Renaud on the second line, that could go two ways: either the second line improves, or Renaud's an asshole about it and things are tense. And from what I already know about Aidan Renaud, it feels like the second option is more likely. Or Charlie could shake things up and give Renaud his spot back on the first line. Who knows?

"Okay, I have to get over to Longwood for Eva's OB appointment, but I'll see you soon."

"Nah, you probably won't," Colt says. "We've got Jameson and Lauren's wedding this weekend. Then Jules and I are headed to Bali for two weeks."

"Oh shit, I forgot about that. Have fun. And don't do anything to fuck up that knee while you're gone." I nod my chin toward his leg, which luckily now just needs a neoprene sleeve supporting his knee.

"I have my whole PT plan outlined, and Jules has sworn she's going to make sure I do it every day," he says with an eye roll. "Like I wouldn't anyway. I'm not fucking up my last season."

Colt heads out, and I finish packing up all my gear, nodding to the other guys as I head to the locker room. Normally, I'd head straight home and shower there, but there's no way I can show up at the doctor's office soaked in sweat and smelling like I do.

Twenty minutes later, as I'm pulling out of the practice rink's parking lot, a text comes over the speakers in my car.

ZACH

Finally back from Seattle. You guys around this weekend? Ashleigh and I want to meet Eva.

LUKE

There's a big polo match in our hometown that we have to go, followed by a family event. Any chance you guys want to watch a polo match? I'm sure I can snag two more tickets.

I'm almost to Longwood before Zach's response comes through.

ZACH

Didn't realize polo was a thing normal people did. Then I remembered you're not normal. Ashleigh and I are in. Is there anything we need to know? I assume we don't show up in shorts and a T-shirt.

LUKE

Dress like you're going to a fancy brunch. I'm driving to Eva's OB appointment but will send you more details soon.

Dr. Lowery knocks on the door before pushing it open, then sweeping into the room in her white lab coat and blue scrubs, before setting her laptop on the counter and turning toward us.

She takes one look at me sitting next to Eva and holding her hand, then her eyes focus in on where Eva lies on the exam table in the cotton gown, her left hand resting under the curve of her belly. She looks back up at us with one dark eyebrow raised and amusement written across her features. "Just friends, huh?"

"Maybe not so much, anymore," Eva says with a soft smile.

Dr. Lowery gives us a nod as she swings one leg over her stool and settles down on it, rolling herself toward us.

Eva tilts her head to the side to look up at me while Dr. Lowery picks up the clipboard the nurse left on the counter, and I lift her hand to kiss the back of it. It feels great to be here as her actual partner, and not just as a friend. A moment later, Dr. Lowery clears her throat, as though she's reminding us that we don't need to be looking at each other like two love-sick fools in her exam room.

"Let's listen to this baby's heartbeat," she says. Her voice is slightly tight, all traces of the amusement from moments before having vanished. What the hell was on that clipboard?

She picks up the small doppler and a tube of gel and sets them on the exam table near Eva's hip. "I'm going to untie this part of your gown," she says as she takes the tie around Eva's waist and tugs to loosen the bow, before pulling each piece of fabric aside to reveal her belly.

I don't know what it is about my wife being pregnant that does things to me, but for some reason, it's a huge turn-on. I can't look at Eva's body and not think about having sex with her. I don't know if this is what it's always like once you've had sex with someone, or if it's because I've waited so long for her, or because she's pregnant—but whatever the reason,

I'm about to be sporting a hard-on in the doctor's office, which is not okay.

Turning my head away from her body, and looking up at her face, I see the same concern etched there that I just felt a moment ago, before I was distracted by her half-naked body.

Fuck, man, get it together. I'm here to support her, not to be thinking about having sex with her.

I squeeze her hand, and she tilts her head to the side to look at me again. I hate the worry I see in her eyes and wish there was something I could do to alleviate it. When Dr. Lowery runs the doppler over Eva's belly, the baby's heartbeat—the distinct *chug, chug, chug* coming through some background static—fills the small room, and we both breathe a sigh of relief.

Glancing at Dr. Lowery, I note that she's still listening intently, but then she nods and says, "The heartbeat sounds good."

"Were you expecting that it wouldn't?" Eva asks, her voice tight with worry.

"No, but your blood pressure is quite a bit higher than when you were last here, and you're measuring small for how far along you are. The former can be risky for the baby's development, and the latter can be a sign that something's wrong. However, you're an athlete and you were barely showing at all the last time I saw you, whereas you're clearly showing now, so that, combined with the steady heartbeat, are both good signs. Still, I'd like to do another ultrasound, just to be extra safe."

Eva's grip tightens around my hand, and her voice is quiet when she says, "Okay."

"Listen," Dr. Lowery says as she sets her hand on Eva's

shoulder. "There's no indication that you need to worry right now. This ultrasound is just a precaution so we can rule out any issues, and then you'll be able to rest easy, knowing that everything is okay with the baby."

Eva nods, and then we move next door to the room with the ultrasound equipment. Together, we watch the baby come into view. Baby Squash is much bigger than the last time we were here and moves around as Dr. Lowery slides the wand across Eva's belly. She uses the mouse in her other hand to click on different parts of the screen, taking measurements just like she did last time.

Finally, she says, "Your baby appears to be growing normally, so there's nothing to worry about. And if you'd like to know the baby's sex, I can check right now."

Eva glances at me, and I try to keep my expression neutral. As badly as I want to know, it has to be her decision. Her eyebrows lift hopefully, and her eyes are full of tears. "Yeah?"

I nod, blinking back my own tears. "Yeah."

"All right," Eva says, turning toward Dr. Lowery with a loud sniff. "Let's find out."

"Okay, Baby," Dr. Lowery says as she digs the wand into Eva's belly, moving it around while looking at the screen, "let's give us that view we need." It takes a few minutes of us sitting there, our fingers threaded together as we squeeze each other's hands in anticipation, before Dr. Lowery sucks in a breath and says, "You see those three faint lines there?" She uses the mouse to circle the area on the screen. "That's our indication that you're having a baby girl."

There are tears streaming down Eva's face, and it worries me that I can't tell whether they're happy tears or not. I scoot closer, leaning in to rest my forehead against hers. "You okay?"

Her chest shakes, but it could be silent laughter or a silent sob. "Yeah."

"Just so you're aware," I tell her, sitting back slightly so I can look at her. "I'm planning to be the best girl dad ever."

She does laugh at that, and the sight of her smile is such a welcome presence. "I have no doubt."

Given her relationship with her own mother, I'm guessing that she's having a lot of complicated emotions about having a daughter. "You know what else? You're going to be an amazing mother. We've got this, Evie. You and me."

She nods, more tears spilling onto her cheeks, and Dr. Lowery says, "I'm going to give you two a moment. Take as long as you need. And then, check in with my nurse, Val, before you leave. She'll give you some instructions for monitoring your blood pressure, and talk to you about things to watch out for. And we'll schedule you to come in weekly, now."

"Oh! Before you leave," Eva says, followed by a deep sigh. "You know that, biologically speaking, this isn't Luke's child. But we are telling people that it—she—is. There's going to be an article in *Society* magazine next week, about our surprise pregnancy and marriage. I know HIPAA regulations would prevent you from saying anything anyway, but I just wanted to make sure you knew our story so you're not caught off guard."

Dr. Lowery glances back and forth between us, and then tells Eva, "It seems to me that—in all the ways that matter, anyway—this baby is Luke's, right along with her being yours."

Chapter Thirty-Nine

EVA

The living room is dark, bathed only in the moonlight streaming through the windows, when I wake up. I'm not sure what time it is or why I'm sleeping on the couch, but when Luke shifts behind me, his hard cock pressing into the crevice between my ass cheeks, I know exactly what woke me up.

Unfortunately, since the doctor's appointment earlier this week, he has refused to have sex with me. He claims that sex will raise my blood pressure, and he doesn't want to risk my health or the baby's. I've been unsuccessful in convincing him that what's really going to raise my blood pressure is being denied sex when I'm always in the mood. Seriously, I've never craved sex like I have while pregnant, and since Luke and I finally slept together, it's all I want.

But now, despite the fact that he's still asleep, his hips are moving of their own volition, and his soft grunts are turning me on so much, my thong is already damp. Reaching behind me, I slide my hand between our bodies and grip his shaft through his soft jersey shorts, running my palm along his length as his hips move faster.

"Yes, Peaches," he whispers, his breath hot as it caresses the top of my head. One of his elbows is tucked under my head, beneath the pillow, but his other arm snakes its way over my hip as he pulls up my skirt, his fingers sliding along the edge of my thong until he pushes beneath the lacy fabric. I lift my top leg, planting my foot on the couch with my knee in the air, to give him better access. And as he slides the pads of his fingers through my slick seam, bringing them up to run over my clit before slipping them inside me, he groans out, "Fuck, I needed this."

"Me too, Luke," I say, moving my hips to meet the thrust of his fingers. "Me too."

He freezes, and his sharp intake of air highlights just how rigid his body has become. I can feel him pulling away, his fingers about to slip out of me, when I press my free hand to his wrist and hold him in place. "Don't you dare stop."

"Eva, your blood pressure—"

"Is going to fucking spike right now if you take this away from me. I'm allowed to feel good, Luke. I'm allowed to have sex. I even asked the nurse on our way out and she said that my blood pressure wasn't nearly high enough to pose a risk."

He curls his fingers inside me while he presses his hips forward so his cock slides right along my palm, the tip pressing into my lower back, and a moan rips from my throat in response. I'm so fucking turned on, all I want is for him to make me come, then fuck me like he can't control himself.

"Do you feel how fucking badly I want this, Peaches?" His

voice is low and rough, sending a thrill of anticipation down my spine. "But I don't want to do anything that might risk hurting you or the baby."

"The risk only exists in your head, Luke," I remind him, as I work one hand along his cock and move my other hand to undo the buttons down the front of my V-neck shirt. I move the front panels of the shirt aside and sweep my hand into one side of my bra, pushing the cup beneath my breast and pulling the flesh up toward my face. Luke's arm slips out from beneath my head, and he props himself up on his elbow, looking down at me as I lie on my side.

"What are you doing?" He presses the heel of his hand against my clit, and my hips buck. I need this freaking orgasm the way I need oxygen—without it, I may actually perish.

"Seeing if my tits are big enough yet that I can reach my nipples with my tongue."

His groan reverberates around me, and he thrusts himself harder against my hand. "And are they?"

"Not yet," I say with a laugh. "But that would be the dream."

"No, baby, that's my job. You can't take it away from me."

"Then do your job, Luke," I say, looking up at him and bringing my shoulder back against his chest so he has a clear view of my breast before I move my hand to the other side and pull that cup away so both my tits are out.

"You're going to drive me fucking wild, Eva, you know that?"

I move my hips to match the rhythm of his hand as he dips his head over my shoulder and pulls my nipple between his lips, sucking to match the pace his hand has set as he fucks me with his fingers. His hips move faster, sliding his cock along my hand as he releases a small grunt that reverberates against my nipple, sending shock waves straight to my core. I'm so fucking close that it's making me greedy.

"You don't get to come yet." My words are soft, but firm as I move my hand off him. "Give me this first orgasm like a good boy," I say, remembering how much he liked me calling him that the first time we had sex, "and then I'll let you bend me over the back of the couch and fuck me from behind."

His moan sends the same shock wave from my nipple to my core, and then he sucks harder, his fingers moving faster and his hand rubbing against my clit with more urgency.

"Fuck yes," I tell him. "More of that." He kicks the pace up a notch, and I can feel my orgasm dangling in front of me, a light that seems to move further away the closer I get. "Harder, Luke," I pant, feeling more desperate and needy than I've ever felt. "Make me come . . ."

He keeps up the punishing pace of his fingers and I gasp when the first wave of my orgasm rolls through me, jolt after jolt of electricity as Luke sucks my nipple into his mouth, each tug matching the ebbs and flow of the orgasm.

I'm a whimpering, sweaty mess of pleasure as I come so hard I see stars. Then, my body goes limp. Luke rolls me onto my back, looking down at me as he pulls his fingers from my cunt and holds them in front of my face. And then he says, "Taste what I do to you, Peaches."

My eyes widen, but I barely part my lips when I ask, "Why?"

"Because I want you to know how fucking sweet you are when you come for me. And I want you to remember that I'm the only one who will *ever* do this to you."

There's a vulnerability to his request, like a plea for me to admit that, although he wasn't my first, he'll be my last.

"There will be no one else, Luke," I promise, and then I part my lips, run my tongue along his three fingers, and pull them into my mouth, sucking them clean.

He stands then, dropping his shorts before pulling me up next to him. Squatting, he slides my skirt and thong down my legs, and I toss my shirt to the side, reaching behind to unclasp my bra. From his knees, Luke looks up at me, his gaze pausing between my legs before traveling over my belly and up to my breasts.

"God, you're a fucking sight to behold. I love the way your body looks when you're pregnant. I know you have the Olympics to qualify for and win, but after that"—he rises to his feet again, skimming his body along mine in a way that sends goose bumps across my skin—"I'm going to fill you with more babies."

I always knew I wanted kids, but never really pictured how many I'd have. "Oh yeah, how many?"

Looking down at me, he smooths his hands up my sides, trailing his fingertips along my ribs. "As many as you'll let me give you."

"All that sex we'll need to have . . ." I say with a long sigh. "It sounds just terrible."

"Yeah." His shoulders shake with a chuckle. "You'd obviously hate it. Now get on the couch and bend over the back so I can see this gorgeous pussy while I fuck you until you're begging for your next orgasm."

How I love the mouth on this man.

I turn, kneeling on the cushions and leaning forward, resting my forearms on the back of the couch, ass in the air facing him, as I gaze out the windows at the view of the Charles River and the lights of Cambridge on the other side. Then I glance over my shoulder at him, raise an eyebrow, and say, "Like this?"

He steps forward, spreading his legs enough to line himself up with me. Then he grips himself, rubbing the fat tip of his hard cock along my sensitive clit as I let out a moan. He slides himself up my seam and pushes into me with one long thrust.

My breath stutters out at the invasion; I'm so full I can hardly breathe. And then he puts his hands on my hips and moves inside me as I thrust back against him, seeking my own pleasure again as I bring him his.

I'm so aroused, I can feel my cum from the last orgasm dripping down the inside of my thigh. Sex isn't normally like this for me, but being around Luke while pregnant has me perpetually on the verge of orgasm. I have a feeling that it'll always be this good, even when I'm not pregnant.

"Put your hands on the back of the couch so you can sit up more," he says. "I want your tits up here where I can play with them."

I roll my shoulders back as I grip the back of the couch and push up, my back arched so I don't change the angle where his body meets mine. His hands slide up my belly, pausing there as he slams himself into me faster.

"So fucking beautiful and strong, Evie. The way you're growing a child like this—"

"Our child," I say, and as I glance over my shoulder at him, I don't miss his throat bobbing as he swallows.

"The way you're growing *our* child makes me want to worship you even more than I already do."

I smile up at him, lift an eyebrow, and say, "And what would that look like?"

"Let me show you," he says, and then his hands cup my breasts, toying with my nipples as he whispers all the things he wants to do to me. His low, gravelly words and grunts of pleasure each time our bodies meet have me so close.

"Touch yourself," he hisses as he bottoms out inside me again, and I gasp at the fullness. "I want you to play with your clit until you're coming on my cock." I spit on two fingers and bring them to my clit right as he says, "I want to watch my cum drip out of you."

Then it's too much pleasure all at once, and I cry out as a second orgasm rips through me, sending sparks ricocheting through my whole body as he emits a primal growl and shoots his release into me.

Just as he promised, I can feel his cum dripping down my thighs, even with his dick inside me, still hard. I drop my forehead down to the cushions on the back of the couch, before he starts to move again and teases, "You didn't think I was going to be done after fucking you once, did you? I think you said good boys always give you that third orgasm . . ."

———

The next morning, everything about practice feels like a struggle.

"You doing okay?" Christopher asks as we finish our camel spin. "That felt like I was holding up both of our legs."

"Looked like it, too," Lynette calls out from the side of the ice.

"Sorry," I say, loud enough for Lynette to hear. "I'm exhausted. Growing a baby is taking all my energy."

But as we move away from where she stands, Christopher lowers his voice and says, "You sure it's not all that newlywed sex?"

"Jealous, much?" I tease. "When does Jenn get back?"

A low groan rattles in the back of his throat, and as he cups the side of my face in his hand in anticipation of a death spiral, he says, "Not soon enough."

Despite the scary name, the backward outside death spiral is actually one of the easier elements for me with my expanding belly. As Christopher enters a pivot holding my hand, I skate in a wide circle on the back outside edge. With my opposite leg straight out, my body is nearly parallel with the ice. My only fear with this one is that my added weight will throw the spin off balance, pulling Christopher down toward me. But as he plants his toe pick into the ice and sits back into the pivot while I drop into my rotation around him, I can tell he's got me.

We come up for the finale, both breathing heavily, even though it was the shorter, pregnancy-friendly version of our free skate routine. And when I drop my arms after our final pose, I can feel my legs shaking and heart pounding as I try to regulate my panting. Christopher wraps his arm around my hips, skating me over to the boards while I cling to him.

Goddamn, I'm tired. I need to get more sleep, which would be easier if I wasn't sharing a bed with Luke. Because try as we might, we can't seem to keep our hands off each other, no matter how exhausted we are. Maybe this weekend, staying at his parents' house after the polo match, we'll both get a full night of sleep? Who knows how thin the walls are in that old house. Probably best if we're not having sex for his whole family to hear.

I glance up at the stands, and sure enough, Luke is waiting for me like he does any day he isn't at his skills practice. It's a relief to see that he doesn't look jealous at the way I'm clinging to Christopher. Instead, his forehead is etched with worry lines.

I rest my elbows on the top of the boards as Lynette talks about what she wants us to focus on next week based on what she just saw in this performance. Then, as Christopher steps through the door onto the mats, she takes her hand and smooths it over my bent head. "You sure this isn't too much for you with your blood pressure?"

I see the same worried look on her face that I saw on Luke's.

"I'm fine. I just tire much more easily now."

"Let's keep an eye on that. We can move to off-ice practice whenever you need to. We have the mats for practicing our lifts, and we can practice the jumps and run through the routines off ice, too."

"My god," I say with a deep sigh. I feel like I can barely keep my eyes open. "Have I mentioned how happy I am that you're coaching us now? Thank goodness Lauren encouraged me to reach out to you."

Her cheeks wrinkle as she lets out a small laugh. "You haven't, but I'm glad, too. You and Christopher are going to do great things this winter. I can feel it."

"I didn't know how much I needed a coach like you until you came along," I tell her, pushing myself upright so I can step off the ice.

"You're in a tough situation, Eva, and anyone incapable of handling it sensitively doesn't deserve to be your coach."

My eyes water, and I don't know if I want to cry from gratitude or exhaustion. "Thanks."

"It's funny what a small world figure skating can be," she muses as I step onto the mats and bend to place my skate guards over my blades. "Who would have thought someone I coached in singles over fifteen years ago would meet a pairs skater in need of a coach and recommend me?"

"It's hard to believe it was that long ago," I say. "I remember watching Lauren skate like it was yesterday."

"It's such a shame." Lynette shakes her head and her lips dip into a small frown. "She had all the potential, but that accident shook her confidence to the core. To think that she was once our number one Olympic hopeful, and then she never got back on skates again."

"Wait!" I say, reaching out and grasping her arm. "Never?"

Lauren had said she doesn't skate anymore, but I didn't realize that meant she had *never* gotten back on the ice after her accident. That's an entirely different thing!

Lynette shakes her head again and lifts one shoulder in a small shrug. "It's a thing that happens, unfortunately. Sometimes, an athlete gets too much in their own head and can't move past some mental block. We know so much more about all of that now than we did when Lauren was a teenager—there are therapists and mental exercises, and . . . just so much more we can do to help now."

I think about Luke and Game 7, about how he felt when it happened, compared to how much better he seems to be feeling now.

His session with Chloe seemed to help, and he's meeting

with her again this week. But I suspect the team aspect of hockey factors into the improvement in his attitude and mental health, too. He's been seeing his teammates more, and Colt's been at the skills practices. Whereas Lauren, as a singles skater, would have shouldered all the pressure herself, not even sharing it like Christopher and I can with pairs skating. And she wouldn't have had a whole team behind her like Luke does. It just makes me . . . sad for her.

She was obviously terrified of getting back on the ice, which makes me worried that maybe I shouldn't have asked her to skate with me. And yet, skating was such a crucial part of her life that was stolen from her . . . and I can't help but wonder if I could help her reclaim it?

Chapter Forty

LUKE

"How do you feel about that?" Chloe asks after I give her the PG-rated description of the changes in my relationship with Eva since we last talked.

My long exhale loosens my shoulders. "So fucking relived."

"And how's hockey going now?" She pushes a pair of tortoise-shell glasses up the bridge of her nose, and I wonder why she wasn't wearing them last time. Does she normally wear contacts? It's such a silly thing to think about, but it's also a reminder that I don't really know her at all. Normally, that would make me way more hesitant to talk to her about anything important. But somehow, she makes me want to keep talking.

"Good, I think. Colt said something to me at practice the other day that I can't stop thinking about."

"Colt's the other goalie?" When I nod my head, she asks, "So, what did he say?"

"Two things, actually. First, he pointed out that I'm flawless in practice. Which got me thinking . . . if I'm flawless there, then the issue isn't that I need to get better, it's that I need to harness that level of focus and performance when the moment calls for it."

Her lips curve up at the ends. "So you need some strategies for maintaining your focus in high-pressure situations. We can work on that. What was the second thing?"

"He said *he* was the one who asked our general manager to get me traded to Boston."

"And why is this significant?"

"I always assumed Charlie, that's Eva's dad and our head coach," I remind her, "asked her to bring me to Boston. Or Evan Knight, our goalie coach, because I'd trained with him in the summers before. I didn't even know Colt when he made the suggestion. And he's the best goalie in the league. So the fact that he chose me to fill his shoes when he retires at the end of next season . . . it's a lot to process."

"Do you feel good about that?"

"Yeah, for sure. I guess it's still a little confusing because of what my dad said." I rub the bridge on my nose to relieve the pressure that forms there every time I rehash

Behind her glasses, her eyebrows dip in confusion. "What did your dad say?"

"Oh, I didn't tell you when I explained why Eva and I got married?" I ask, and she shakes her head. "I was at the Rebels offices for a meeting with AJ shortly after Game 7 and accidentally overheard my dad and my brother, Tucker, meeting with her. And my dad said, 'This is why I didn't want you to bring Luke onto this team.'"

She lifts her chin as she studies me. "What do you think he meant by that?"

I scoff out a laugh. "What else *could* he have meant? He said it put him 'in a really tough position.'"

"I'll bet."

Now it's my turn to look at her with confusion written across my face, but I'm at a loss for what to say. "Why do you bet?"

"Because from everything you said about your dad when you were telling me about your family and the team, he sounds like a supportive, dedicated father who loves his kids, and a fair and respectful owner of your team."

I nod, because it's all true. I didn't just paint that picture of my dad. That *is* my dad. Which is why this all hurts so much.

"So how do you think those two things—loving dad and a fair team owner—might come into conflict after that Game 7 loss?"

My teeth sink into my lower lip as I take a deep breath, considering her question. "I guess how he'd want to respond as a dad could be at odds with how he might need to respond as the owner of the team?"

"That *would* be a really tough position." I don't miss how she intentionally uses my father's words.

"So you're suggesting that . . . maybe he didn't want me on the team because he just wanted to be my dad, not because he didn't think I was good enough to play for the Rebels?"

"I'm suggesting that it's possible. And I'm also sensing a

pattern here. You thought you knew how Eva felt about you, so you didn't tell her about your own feelings, and as a result, you almost missed out on a future with her. You thought your dad meant you weren't good enough to play for his team, so you didn't talk to him about it and have instead let it affect how you feel about playing for the Rebels. But what if he meant something else entirely?"

"Hmmmm." It's all I can respond with. I always thought I was good at reading people—it's an essential skill for a goalie and one I thought I'd pretty much mastered. But maybe my ability to recognize a player's intentions on the ice doesn't necessarily translate into an ability to understand people's intentions off it, in the way I always thought.

"And most importantly," Chloe adds, "why are you more concerned with keeping the peace than with going after what you want?"

"I grew up with three much older brothers," I tell her, "who all have well-deserved reputations for being . . . difficult. I was always the easy one, the peacemaker. My mom used to say I was her gift for surviving Preston, Tucker, and Tristan, so I always tried to be reliable and supportive. Even with hockey, I gravitated toward being a goalie because it's a protective role, where your teammates know they can rely on you to back them up. With Eva, all I've ever wanted to do is be there for her in whatever way she needed me, regardless of what I actually wanted. So . . ." I take a deep breath and let it out slowly. "I guess I've spent my whole life being a people pleaser."

I chuckle softly, and when Chloe doesn't say anything right away, I continue. "I'm trying to wrap my mind around the irony, because I've always claimed not to care what people think and encouraged Eva to care less about others' opinions. But maybe . . . maybe I care a whole lot more than I thought."

"Could that be why you took the Game 7 loss so hard?"

"I took the Game 7 loss hard because I froze in the most important moment of my career. All that training, all the years of practices and games, then when my team needed me, I let them down." I press my lips together, still frustrated with myself. It wasn't *just* a game. It was *the* game.

"People have bad games, Luke," Chloe says. "And it sounds like your coaches, your teammates, and even your GM have reminded you of this on multiple occasions."

"Yeah, but . . . nothing like that has ever happened to me. I guess I'm still not sure how to think about it."

"You've never lost a game before?"

"I've never stood in the goal and let puck after puck get by me because I was too distracted to care about what was happening on the ice. And I don't know how to make sure it never happens again."

I can hear the frustration in my voice, because I need to know what to do differently next time, and I just want her to tell me.

"There are things about the game you can't control—like your starting goalie getting injured, or your defense falling apart. And if either of those things hadn't happened, then you wouldn't have had all that added pressure on you."

"Yes, but that's my job. When the puck gets by everyone else, *I'm* the last line of defense. And I didn't do my job."

"And you're mad at yourself for that?"

"Of course I am." I spit out the words. I didn't realize that talking about all of this would dredge up the same emotions

I was experiencing almost two months ago when it happened.

"Are you mad at Colt for getting injured, or your teammates not doing a better job keeping the puck away from your net?"

That gives me pause, and I chew on the outer corner of my lip for a moment before I say, "That's different."

"How?"

"Because *I'm* the one who needs to step up when the puck gets to me, and I didn't."

"Aren't your forwards supposed to be able to keep the puck on the other side of the ice? Aren't your defensemen supposed to keep the puck away from your goal?"

"Well, yeah. But hockey's a fast-moving game—"

"Where anything can happen," she says quickly. "Where players can be tired because it's the third period of the game, or upset because the best goalie in the league just got taken off the ice at a crucial moment . . . or distracted because the person they love might be hurt. Have none of your teammates ever been distracted?"

I think about how, just in the playoffs alone, Colt was kicked out of a game for fighting over Jules, and McCabe literally left mid-game after AJ was hurt and he thought his baby, Abby, might have been too. And earlier in the season, I know that Drew also left before a game because Audrey and Graham had been in a car accident. "I guess I'm not the only one."

"Then why are you being harder on yourself than you are on your teammates?"

"Because *I* don't mess up like that." My voice takes on an urgent, almost high-pitched quality.

"Or?"

"Or things fucking fall apart, okay?" I sound as frantic as I feel at this admission.

"What kind of things?"

"I don't know. My team, my family."

"And you're the glue holding both those things together?"

"No. But I was always taught that everyone needs to pull their weight, or no one can be successful—that's true for my family, and it's true for a team too. Right before the game, Coach said we were the better team, and there was no reason we shouldn't win as long as everyone went out there and did their job. I didn't do that."

I think about how many people I let down—my family, the coach who's always been a mentor to me, my teammates, the fans. The pressure builds in my chest, the weight of it almost crushing me.

"Sounds like a lot of people fell apart at the end of that game, Luke. You, among others. Here's the thing about relationships . . . " She pauses, waiting for me to focus my attention on her again. "Whether they're with your team or a partner or your family: No one can give one hundred percent all the time. It's impossible. Sometimes, someone gives less and someone else gives more, and it all evens out in the end. I think the question is, why do you feel like you're always the one who has to give more?"

Instead of insisting I don't feel that way—which is my first instinct—I pause, then ask, "What do you mean?"

"With Eva, with your parents, and with your team, you keep describing this need to take care of everyone, to protect them, to go above and beyond. Where does that need stem from? What is its source?"

"I . . . I don't know," I say. But I fear that maybe I do.

She tilts her head again, pressing her lips together, and then asks, "Are you sure about that?"

I close my eyes, lean my head against the back of the chair, and look up at the ceiling. I sit like that for a minute, trying to force all my thoughts from my head to avoid all the fucking emotions that are crowding in. Chloe doesn't push me to talk, but I can hear her breathing, reminding me she's still there, waiting.

"I'm a lot younger than my brothers," I finally say, my eyes trained on the ceiling. "Even in my earliest memories, it was always the three of them. My mom called them her 'Three Musketeers,' my dad called them his 'Triumvirate.' I was always the baby of the family . . . an afterthought, I guess. Not that anyone said that, but . . ." I think about how my brothers were all destined to run the family business, all had positions waiting for them before they even went to business school. "I didn't feel needed."

"Wanting to feel needed—like you've described with your family, with Eva, and with your team—can sometimes be a symptom of a deep fear of rejection."

I think about the way I avoided talking to Evie about my feelings for a full decade, the way I didn't approach my dad about what I'd overheard in AJ's office, and the way I didn't reach out to my teammates after Game 7. "Is avoidance another symptom?"

Her voice is soft when she says, "If what you're avoiding is the potential to experience rejection, then yes."

Another sigh. "I've never not been successful," I admit. "But I've almost always avoided situations where I didn't think I'd be the best."

Not telling Eva how I felt and remaining in the friend zone for way too long, going to Boston College instead of Harvard like my brothers, majoring in sports medicine instead of business . . . Every path was chosen based on the likelihood of success.

"We're unfortunately out of time," Chloe says, and my head snaps up to look at the screen.

"That's it? You're just going to leave me here after unpacking all that?"

"Is it hard for you to sit with your thoughts like this?" she asks.

I look away again.

"You did a lot of hard work today, Luke. I'm not expecting this realization that you have a deep-seated fear of rejection to be easy for you to work through, and I hope you don't expect that either. But you do need to think about it— about why failure is so scary to you, and about how you can get around that so you don't limit your options."

"Isn't that what I'm supposed to talk to you about?"

"Yes, and we will talk about it more. But a lot of this work is internal. You have to dig down and figure out whether this fear of rejection is a reasonable fear to hold on to. And if it is, how you might manage it when it springs up. That's all stuff we can talk about next week, but first you need to spend some time on your own with this newfound knowledge."

I look back at the screen as I crack my knuckles. "I hate everything you just said, even though I know you're right."

"That's a very natural reaction," she says. "Do you want to move our meeting up next week? I have some time earlier in the week."

"I have to look at my calendar. Can you text me your availability and we'll see if it works?"

"Sure. And Luke, for what it's worth, this is hard work, and I'm proud of you for doing it."

On the screen, I watch my lips press together into a flat line, before I say, "Thanks. I'll talk to you next week."

When the window closes on my screen, I let out a deep sigh and get up in search of Eva. I've never needed a hug more than I do at this moment.

Chapter Forty-One

EVA

I'm sitting on a barstool at the counter, thumbing through our article that came out today in *Society* magazine and snacking on a small bowl of almonds, when Luke ambles into the living room. His face is ashen, like he's just gotten terrible news, and there's a thin sheen of sweat across his forehead. Pausing at the wide opening into the kitchen, he leans against the tall cabinets to his left.

"You okay?" I ask, a tad worried about whatever has him looking like this.

"Yeah." He runs his hand through his hair. "I just got off my call with Chloe."

"You look like you've seen a ghost."

He clears his throat and mumbles something unintelligible as he turns and walks to the refrigerator.

Pushing off the stool, I follow him around the island, thankful that I'm home after meeting Amy for lunch. I don't see my high school friends often enough, considering that I live here now, and I'm trying to be better about that.

I cross my arms, resting them on my baby bump as I lean against the countertop and study him chugging orange juice straight from the container in front of the open fridge. "I'm here if you want to talk about it."

"I will. Eventually."

"But not right now?"

He sets the orange juice on the counter, shuts the refrigerator, and steps toward me. "Right now, I just want you in my arms. You're the only thing in my life that feels truly permanent."

I lean into him as he wraps his arms around me. With my head on his chest and my arms wrapped around his lower back, I can feel his shallow, rapid breaths and fast, strong heartbeat. The longer we hold one another, the slower they become, until he feels like my normal, calm, and resilient Luke.

He's always been my rock, but I'm starting to realize that maybe I'm his, too.

I run my hands up and down his back, hoping that the supportive gesture lets him know I'm here for him . . . but if his growing erection pushing into my belly is any indication, he's looking for a totally different type of togetherness.

My shoulders shake with laughter, and he pulls his upper body away so he can look down at me. I glance up to see a confused look on his face. "Sorry, I'm just over here trying to be a supportive wife, and then your dick is poking into my belly . . ."

He moves his hands to my hips and lifts me up, setting me on the countertop and stepping up between my legs. Then he smooths the hair that's fallen from my ponytail back out of my face before leaning forward to press his lips to my forehead. "I missed you today when you were at practice and then at lunch. I always miss you when you're not with me."

"Same," I tell him. "It's going to be hard when the season starts back up."

He rests his forehead against mine and whispers, "I know." Another deep sigh, and then he says, "I wish we got to enjoy this honeymoon phase a little bit longer. Pretty soon, hockey will start, and then we'll have a baby, and after that you'll be training like crazy for the Olympics. We'll never get this much time together, just the two of us, again."

I wrap my legs around his upper thighs. "I guess we'll just need to make the most of the time we do have."

Tilting my chin up, I press my lips against his, and he kisses me back like we've been apart for half a year instead of half a day. I don't know how I once believed I could live with this man just being my friend, and now I can't go six hours without having sex with him. I guess it's because I didn't know what I was missing.

When he lifts me off the counter, I tighten my legs around his hips as he walks into the living room. "Where are we going?" I ask between kisses.

"You're sweaty from practice and I'm gross from my workout with Zach, so I think we both need a shower before we go out to dinner."

"We're going out to dinner?"

"Only if you want to. But I made a reservation, just in case," he says as he turns into the hallway leading to the bedrooms.

"You know I'm always hungry," I say with a smile,

reaching down to find the hem of my tank top and pulling it over my head as he approaches the door to our bedroom.

"Shit, Peaches." With a groan, he looks down at my bare chest as my shirt lands somewhere behind him. "I swear your tits are growing faster than any other part of your body."

"You like that, huh?"

"Just one of the many reasons I plan to keep you pregnant as often as possible," he says, pressing a sloppy kiss to the side of my neck as he turns into the bathroom.

"Oh yeah?" I ask, sighing from the trail of wet kisses that are making their way to my collarbone. "What are the other reasons?"

"Well, your insatiable appetite for sex is certainly another reason."

"Maybe that's because of you and not the hormones," I suggest as he sets me on my feet and looks down at me like he's immensely pleased with himself.

"I guess we'll know eventually. But also, the way you look —like you're glowing from within as you grow *our* baby—it's such a turn-on."

Aside from the way my breasts just keep getting bigger and my hair looks amazing, there's not much I love about my body now that I'm solidly in my third trimester. But if he likes my body like this . . . I'm not going to let the rapid weight gain or the ever-expanding stretch marks bother me.

He drops into a squat, sitting on his heels as he hooks his thumbs into the waistband of my shorts, pulls them over my hips, and lets them fall to my feet. Then he kisses the underside of my belly before he dips his head lower and breathes in my scent. "I fucking love the way you smell when you're turned on."

"I'm always turned on," I say, my breath becoming more rapid.

"Good," he hums, before turning me to face the mirror over the sink and rising to his feet behind me. Reaching his hand behind his head, he pulls his T-shirt up and over his head before dropping his shorts to the floor.

My breath catches at the sight of his broad, bare shoulders and muscular arms. He reaches down to steady my hips while he uses one of his feet to spread my legs, and I can feel his warm breath on my shoulder as he leans over me and tells me to place my hands on either side of the mirror. I'm so keyed up that I don't need him to do anything more to get me ready.

He holds my hips in place as he pushes inside me in one long, slow thrust and leans forward to place one of his hands on the wall above mine, allowing me to adjust to him. Then he tells me, "I love everything about you, Eva," as he starts moving inside of me, holding my gaze in the mirror as he adds, "I think I've loved you my entire life."

It's all so much that I can no longer control my emotions. Tears leak out of the corner of my eyes as I say, "I *know* I've loved you my whole life. I just didn't think you'd ever love me back."

He moves his hand under my belly and across my body so his forearm anchors me to him. "I've never not loved you, and I'm never going to love anyone *but* you."

Tilting his hips, he changes the angle, making contact with a previously unexplored part of me. Shock waves wrack my body and my lips part with a breathy sigh, but words are lost to me as the sensations flood my system.

Luke tucks his chin so he's whispering directly in my ear.

"I'm never going to fuck anyone but you, Peaches." His hand moves beneath my belly and his finger finds my clit, and I'm not sure if it's the way he's touching me that turns me on more, or if it's knowing that I'm the only woman he'll ever have sex with. "And I'm never going to get my fill of you. The way you look when you're about to come . . . it's fucking addictive. *You* are my addiction."

The heat builds in my core, and my body feels like it's burning up, and then Luke growls in my ear, "Now give me that orgasm so I can throw you in the shower and dirty you up with my cum before I clean you off and make you come again."

I'm about to tell him that demanding my orgasm doesn't make it happen more quickly, but then he increases the pressure and says, "I love watching your tits bounce every time our bodies meet."

My eyes follow his gaze in the mirror. The sight of us—of him taking me bent over like this, my belly resting on the counter and my breasts swaying each time he bottoms out—turns the heat within me up a notch. A few more thrusts, the drag of him along my inner walls, has me teetering right at the edge, and that heat turns into lava spreading through me as my core clenches around Luke and my entire body convulses.

I'm a shaking mess of satisfaction as I ride the waves of that orgasm, crying his name as his eyes stay locked on mine in our reflection. The minute my body grows slack, Luke picks me up, one arm under my knees and the other under my back and walks us into his massive shower. Turning the water on, he lets it warm up before setting me on my feet and pulling me under the shower head with him.

Facing him, I reach between us and grasp his length in my hand. He's still coated in my cum, but the water is slowly washing it away.

"Fuck, Peaches," he whispers, his head falling back into the stream of water, as he groans. "I need your mouth." I sit back on the built-in bench with him still in my hand and greedily suck him in. He grunts softly and fists my hair as I take him deeper into my throat until he's moaning with pleasure.

"Fuuuuuuck yes," he growls, like he's trying to hold himself back. His reaction only spurs me on. With my other hand, I reach between my legs and circle my swollen clit as I take him deeper and open my throat so he can press even farther in.

"Look at you playing with yourself while you swallow my cock," he says as I glance up. "There's nothing fucking sexier than this."

And then I slide my fingers into my cunt and fuck my own hand as I take him all the way into my throat, whimpering around him. My hips buck wildly against my fingers and Luke's soft grunts turn ragged as looks down at me.

He pulls out quickly, shooting his release over my neck and chest. The way he's coated me in his cum, the warmth of it trailing down my body amid the hot steam of the shower, is the thing that sends my orgasm ricocheting through me.

Then he pulls me up into his arms and tells me, over and over again, how much he loves me as the hot water rains down on us. I hold my face up to the spray, letting go of the girl I once was: the one who actively pursued other guys, even though she was in love with her best friend, the one who'd convinced herself that finding someone—

anyone—to love her would make up for the fact that Luke didn't.

As I stand under the shower, he adds soap to a bath sponge and caresses every inch of my body with bubbles. Then, he massages my peach-scented shampoo into my scalp and trails the long strands of my hair between his fingers, before rinsing it out. He slowly and methodically repeats the process with the conditioner, running his hands through the strands and giving the occasional tug that sends shivers down my spine.

What should have been obvious all along is more than clear now: this is how Luke shows his love. It's how he's always shown that he loves me—by taking care of me, showing up, being there when I need him. His love isn't transactional, it just *is*.

I follow suit, washing him and hoping my hands carefully moving over every part of his body communicate that I'll always take care of him the same way he takes care of me.

When Luke says that we need to get out of the shower or we'll miss dinner, I reluctantly let him wrap me in a towel. He heads out of the bathroom to give me time to dry off, but he's back in only moments, my phone in his hand.

"You have a text and several missed calls from Christopher," he tells me, handing me my phone, "and from Morgan." And sure enough, my lock screen is littered with notifications from the two of them.

I look at the texts first—Christopher letting me know that he was repeatedly approached by fans asking about Luke and me when he was out this evening, and Morgan telling me that the magazine article has "kind of blown up in a good way," and suggesting that we might want to lay low for a bit.

Luke chuckles and says, "Oh no, I guess we'll have to order takeout and spend all night together naked."

"Sounds like an awful way to spend the evening," I reply with a growing smile as all my concerns from this morning about needing more sleep disappear.

Chapter Forty-Two

LUKE

"Why are you ordering drinks like you're twelve?" Tucker asks as I take a Shirley Temple and a Coke from the bartender.

"I'm not drinking while Eva's pregnant."

"Why the hell not?" Preston asks.

"Because *she* can't drink. It's not exactly a huge sacrifice." I glance over to where she's standing under the shade of one of the tents lining the polo field, her hand resting under her belly as she talks to Zach and Ashleigh. "Unlike what her body is going through right now."

My brothers' heads all turn slightly to follow my gaze. "I still can't believe you bagged *that*," Tristan says, shaking his head.

"First of all, my wife is not a fucking prize, so watch your mouth and stop salivating over her. And second of all, of course we're together, *we* were inevitable."

Tucker chuckles into his rocks glass before tipping it up to his lips.

"You still haven't signed the prenup I gave you when we had dinner," Preston says.

I grind my teeth together at the reminder. "I told you I'm not having her sign a fucking prenup. What's mine is hers."

"That's a dangerous game to play with a small fortune," Tucker says.

"Not when you're this sure." There's no part of me—not even a tiny doubt in the back of my mind—that worries about whether Eva and I will make it. And in the event that anything should ever happen to me, I want everything to go to her and the baby. Or babies, if we have even half as many kids as I want us to make together. My brothers and the Hartmann Family Trust will do just fine without my portion of the estate.

"I think we're all just a bit shocked that Baby Hartmann is the first of us to get married or have a kid," Tristan says.

"Why would that surprise you? You three have avoided settling down like it's a death sentence."

As if on cue, my brothers all raise their glasses, clinking them together and looking at me expectantly.

"What are we toasting?" I ask. "If it's avoiding marriage, I'm not sure why you're looking at me."

"We're toasting *you*," Tristan says, his voice tinged with amusement, "for taking one for the team."

I lift my soda to meet their raised glasses, knowing exactly where they're coming from. Mom and Dad have been vocal about wanting grandkids for a while, and now that they'll be able to focus all their grandparent energy on Eva's and my baby, the pressure is off my brothers. For a while, at least.

"I couldn't get a ring on her finger fast enough," I tell them. "Just wait, you'll see."

Their bellows of laughter ring out, as if I just said the most absurd thing in the world. Some heads turn toward the bar to see what's so funny, but "the Hartmann boys" causing a ruckus at a society event is hardly news, and everyone quickly turns away.

"Not a chance," Preston says confidently.

"Probably true. Who'd want to marry your surly ass?" Tucker says and we all laugh because, as much as women seem to love trying to get Preston's attention, it's impossible to picture him in a relationship. He doesn't have a tender bone in his body. I think some combination of rugby and business—the two loves of his life—hardened him a long time ago.

"Hey, at least I didn't propose to someone who was cheating on me," Preston says, and I watch Tucker's jaw clench.

"Don't make me fucking punch you on the sidelines of a polo match," he grumbles.

Preston just smirks back at him.

"Why aren't you riding today?" I ask Tristan, drawing the conversation away from Tucker's failed engagement. It's still a sore subject for him, even though he didn't want to marry her in the first place.

Tristan glances at the field and says, "My wrist has been bothering me."

"Too much jerking off," Tucker says matter-of-factly.

"Tris needs a woman in his life so he can stop tweaking his hand like this."

"Pfft." The puff of air escapes Tristan's lips as he rolls his eyes and glances at Tucker like he's a bug not worth responding to. That's pretty much Tristan's *modus operandi* when anyone says something he doesn't like. If looks could kill, Tristan would be an assassin. Unfortunately for him, my brothers and I are all immune.

"All right, I'm going to get this drink to my wife before she passes out from heat exhaustion," I say, glancing over at her again. It's hot as hell today, even under the shade of all the tents. There's an oppressive mugginess hanging around after last night's rain showers, and despite the clear blue sky and bright sunshine that dried the field up for the match, the humidity hasn't broken.

Eva's running hot already because of the pregnancy, and as I turn to walk back to her, I see that she's taken her wide-brimmed hat off and is fanning her face with it.

The stretchy navy and white striped dress she's wearing clings to her body, and I'm genuinely worried that she might get overheated.

"Here," I say, handing her the Shirley Temple as I approach. "A cold drink will help you cool down. Or we can go sit in the car with the air conditioning blasting for a bit if you want."

"I'm fine," she says with a sigh, but I worry that she's minimizing her discomfort. She takes a sip of her drink before sliding her hat back on her head. Her hair's in a sleek, low bun, so at least she doesn't have all that heavy, dark hair hanging down her back, but her bright pink cheeks make it look like she just ran a 5K, not like she's been standing in the shade.

Zach nods his chin toward the horses and players returning to the field for the start of the second half of the game. I'd shown him and Ashleigh how to stomp divots during halftime, but Eva had stayed under the shade of the tent. Now, with the start of the fourth chukker, or period, I'm wondering if she's going to make it for the whole match.

"Rich-people sports are funny," he says with a slight shake of his head. "Where I grew up, getting a new pair of hockey skates was a luxury. Meanwhile, these players are switching out their *ponies*"—he says the word almost distastefully, like it's ridiculous that we call these majestic horses "ponies" when they're playing polo—"at the end of every chukker."

"It took me a while to come around to it," Eva tells him. "But normally, when it's not a bazillion degrees, matches are really fun. And Luke's brother, Tristan, is really entertaining to watch—he plays polo like it's hockey, but on a horse. Lots of hooking and bumping. The last match I came to, he actually got ejected."

"That happens in polo?" Ashleigh asks curiously.

"Rarely," I say, thinking about how he got ejected from about half of his soccer games when he was in high school. In games, like in life, Tristan thinks he's above the rules. "But leave it to Tristan to make it happen."

"Your brothers seem . . ." Zach says, furrowing his brow as he glances over to the three of them at the bar, their boisterous conversation still turning heads.

"Impervious to people's opinions of them?" I ask when he doesn't finish his sentence.

He chuckles. "Yeah. Not so different from you, I guess."

His comment gives me a moment of pause, because I know I come off that way—confident and fun-loving—but there's a lot more below the surface. And not for the first time, I wonder if the same is true of my brothers. Do their hardened and aloof exteriors hide something softer underneath? If so, how self-aware are they?

Zach pulls Ashleigh to his side and presses a kiss on the top of her head in a tender way that reminds me of my relationship with Eva.

"Did I hear you're from Seattle?" Eva asks Ashleigh.

"Yeah, I grew up there. My uncle raised me, and I just moved to Boston in January to start a PhD program at MIT."

"You're getting a doctorate at MIT?" Eva sounds genuinely impressed. "What field?"

"It's their AeroAstro program, so basically aerospace engineering."

"Okay, so you're, like, seriously smart," Eva says with a smile. "Got it."

"Just fascinated by space. I grew up as a huge *Star Trek* fan, and everything about space and space travel just captivated me."

We chat for a bit about *Star Trek* and how Zach and Ashleigh originally bonded over their shared love of the franchise, before Ashleigh starts asking Eva about skating. As my wife tells Ashleigh about her partner, and their practices now that she's pregnant, I find that it no longer raises my hackles to listen to her talk about Christopher. Amazing how so much has changed now that we're finally being honest about our feelings.

"Wait, you've never skated?" Eva asks after Ashleigh says she can't skate.

"No, I have." Ashleigh glances at Zach. "I'm just not very good at it. Zach tried to teach me at the last friends-and-family day, and . . . it didn't go well."

Zach huffs a laugh and tightens his arm around Ashleigh's shoulder. "I'm not the most patient teacher."

"Were you on hockey skates?" Eva asks, and Ashleigh nods. "It might be easier to learn on figure skates. The longer, straighter blade provides more stability, and the toe pick can prevent you from falling forward. I'm happy to skate with you if you want to try again."

"Eva taught skating at our local rink when we were teenagers," I tell Ashleigh.

"I'd like that," Ashleigh says, looking genuinely excited.

"Kiddos!" Dad's voice booms as he approaches us wearing khakis, a white button-down with the sleeves rolled up, and a paisley bowtie that's slightly askew. He steps away from my mom, who was walking beside him, and loops one arm over my shoulder and the other over Eva's. Looking down at her, he asks, "How are you doing in this heat?"

She pushes out a breath. "Surviving. Barely."

"I remember when I was pregnant with Luke," Mom says, stepping up to Eva's other side, "we had the hottest fall on record. I think I spent all of September in the pool. I felt like a whale at that point."

"I'm surprised you weren't born in that pool," Dad says to me. "She rarely got out."

"Finally, the rain came, and the heat broke, and that's when Luke was born," Mom tells our friends, "on a stormy late-September night."

We stand there making idle conversation for a few minutes, and I can't stop thinking that it's nice having my friends, parents, and wife here together with me. When Ashleigh and Zach excuse themselves to go grab some water, Mom takes Eva's hand and says, "Your mom and I would really like to host a baby shower for you."

I watch Eva's shoulders stiffen at the mention of her mother, whom she still hasn't talked to since that dinner.

"I really appreciate the offer," Eva says, and I note how she gives my mom's hand a small squeeze. "Luke and I haven't really talked about a shower yet. Can I get back to you on that?"

"Of course, dear. We'll do whatever you two are comfortable with."

Eva thanks my mom and looks up at me with a smile. But I wonder if she's asking herself the same questions I am: Where are her parents? And why hasn't her mom reached out to her since the infamous cupcake incident a month ago?

I reach out and loop my arm around Eva's shoulders, pulling her in front of me and anchoring her there with my forearm across her chest. She relaxes back into me, despite the heat and our sweating bodies. I'd like to think that she feels safest pressed up against me like this.

"Thanks, Mom. By the way, where are Helene and Charlie?"

Eva had spent half the drive up here fretting about what it would be like to see her mom again. I know how hurt she is that Helene still hasn't contacted her, but I'm also proud that she hasn't caved and reached out first—her mom needs to step up and be the bigger person for once. I suspect Helene doesn't know what to do without Eva constantly capitulating to her.

"Helene had a migraine this morning," my mom says, "so

they're home right now, but hoping to join us for the party tonight." Mom looks at Eva, a softness in her gaze. "Your dad will be here tonight either way, but you know how your mom's migraines can be."

Eva nods, her head bobbing against my chest as she does, and I squeeze her a little tighter to let her know I'm here to support her. Because even though it's true that her mother has suffered from frequent migraines for as long as I've known her, this one feels a lot like a copout.

Chapter Forty-Three

EVA

Wellington Manor is decked out for its annual summer soirée. Sparkling crystal and gold baubles hanging from the ceilings create a glittering aura of opulence.

"My dear," Elise says, looking at me appreciatively as she and Frank approach us, "you look spectacular."

"Thank you." I glance down at the pale-yellow satin dress. The bodice is a pleated swath of fabric twisted at the center to create two cups, and a wide satin ribbon anchored in the center travels over each shoulder and secures the dress in the back. The body of the dress is pleated satin below the empire waist, which works perfectly with my belly. "This dress was a lucky find. As you can imagine, it's a bit hard to find formal maternity wear."

If I'd planned better, I could've ordered something and had it tailored, but the event kind of snuck up on us.

It's funny to realize that when I returned home nearly

two months ago, I thought I'd be back in Los Angeles by now. I glance at Luke, immensely grateful that I'm here with him instead.

Maybe the way we entered into this marriage wasn't ideal, but it still feels like I'm getting everything I ever wanted—the family I always dreamed about, with the man I've always loved.

"It looks like it was made for you," Frank says, beaming at us before smiling down at his wife of over forty years.

God, his parents are so freaking perfect. They so obviously love each other. And they've parented their boys, stepping back as their boys grew into men, and accepting the men they've become without trying to mold them into someone else. *That's* the kind of relationship I hope Luke and I have—with each other and with our kids—forty years from now.

And for the first time, I think I understand why his brothers are so resistant to settling down. When this is the type of love you've seen modeled, it must be hard to settle for anything less. Luke and I were lucky to have found our way to each other when we did, because otherwise, I could see it taking a lifetime of searching to find something like this.

Frank reaches into his pocket and hands something to Elise with his fist clasped. When it falls into her open palm, I realize it's a small silver baby rattle.

"Is that . . ." Luke's voice trails off in wonder, and his mom beams up at him before she turns her gaze to me.

"This rattle was a favorite of *all* my boys," Elise tells me, holding it up for my inspection. The small dents are an indication that it's been well-loved, but it's been cleaned up so it sparkles like new.

"I'm passing it on to you, for your baby, with the hope that you'll keep the tradition going through this next generation of Hartmann babies."

Tears spring up suddenly, briefly clouding my vision. But I spent too long getting ready tonight to ruin my makeup, so I take a deep breath and gently wipe at my lower eyelids before stepping forward, taking the rattle from my mother-in-law and wrapping her in a hug.

"Thank you," I whisper as I cling to her.

"You are very welcome, dear," she says. "We're so excited to watch the Hartmann clan grow. It's been way too long since we've had a baby in this family. And the fact that it's *you* giving us this gift with Luke . . . it's just too perfect. We're so happy you're *officially* a part of our family now."

Luke clears his throat, and without even looking at him, I know he's feeling emotional as he watches this exchange. My big, hulking, hockey-playing husband has the softest heart of anyone I know. He hides it well behind the flirtation and the feigned indifference, but I love that he shows *me* how he feels. He's going to be the best dad.

The Hartmanns are called away by other guests, but Tucker ambles up to us with his normal charming swagger. Of all Luke's brothers, I like Tucker the best—but maybe it's only because I know him better than Preston and Tristan.

Luke excuses himself to grab me some food from a table covered with an elaborate display of appetizers. Once he's gone, Tucker says, "He's stupidly obsessed with you. You know that, right?"

I nod and can't contain my smile. "It's mutual."

"Good. Please don't ever hurt him, Eva. I don't think he could take losing you. He's too soft to survive that."

I tilt my head to the side and look up at him. "Why would you think I'd hurt him?"

"I don't think you would on purpose. But sometimes, things happen. And Luke's been in love with you his whole life."

His statement steals my breath away. Not because Luke hasn't admitted as much, but because I didn't know he'd said anything to his brothers. "He told you that?"

"Didn't need to. It was obvious. You're his weakness, Eva. You always have been. And if you take advantage of that—"

"He's my weakness too, Tucker," I say, reaching out to pat his arm in what I hope is a reassuring gesture. Rather than being offended at what sounds a lot like an accusation, I'm thankful that Luke's brother is looking out for him. "And he always has been."

"Good." He nods as the single, crisp word hangs between us.

I'm tempted to ask what happened to *him*. Did that failed engagement break him, the same way he's worried I could break Luke? But Luke's brothers are so damn private. I don't think Luke even knows the whole story—or if he does, he hasn't told me . . . which I find unlikely.

Luke's walking back to us with two small plates in his hands. I'm not sure if he knows that my parents are right on his heels, but Tucker sees them approaching and, giving his brother a brief nod, says, "I'm going to grab a drink."

Luke hands me a plate as he reaches me, and when my parents step up next to him, I can tell by the look on his face that he hadn't noticed them until now. He steps closer to me, the backs of his knuckles brushing against the back of my hand. And when he brushes them across my skin a second time, I realize it's an intentionally supportive gesture—his way of telling me he's right here if I need him.

"You look beautiful, honey," Dad says as he leans in and kisses my cheek, before turning toward Luke and shaking his hand.

Next to him, Mom greets us both with a smile that doesn't reach her eyes. I'd like to give her the benefit of the doubt that she still has a lingering headache from this morning's migraine, but I'm not sure she deserves it.

"I owe you an apology," Mom says, and my gaze snaps up from my plate, where I was deciding what I'm least likely to spill down the front of my dress. "I said things the other night—"

"You mean almost *a month* ago," I say, unable to stop myself from pointing out that this apology is long overdue.

"You're right," she says. "And I should have reached out sooner, but I was embarrassed about how I handled the situation."

Well, that's a hell of a lot more honest and vulnerable than I was expecting her to be.

"It's fine, Mom," I say, but I know the tone of my voice doesn't match my words. I'm simply doing what I always do and trying to smooth things over.

"It's not, though," Luke says from beside me, and Mom's gaze slides over to him. "You're not her doctor. So from now on, you don't need to comment on what she eats or how much she weighs—"

"Which is why I apologized," Mom interrupts. Her voice is hard, with an edge that, no doubt, would leave the equestrian riders she trains quaking in their boots. It's certainly had that effect on me for most of my life. But it seems to have the opposite effect on Luke. He looks like he's ready to lash out to protect my feelings, to protect my heart.

"An apology that should have come *weeks* ago," Luke adds. I reach over and take his hand in mine, hoping a tight squeeze of his fingers will get him to stop talking. I don't want him to inflame the situation, given that she was actually apologizing. Even if what he's saying is true, I already said it and he doesn't need to rub it in just to make a point.

"I'm trying to have this conversation with *my daughter*," she says to Luke.

"That's the thing, though," I say, and my voice wobbles with sadness. Her idea of what it means for me to be her daughter does not match up with what I needed and wanted from her as a mother. "I always wanted a mom, and you just wanted a protégée."

"That's not fair," Mom says. "Everything I've done has been to help you succeed."

"I know it has. And I know what you lost before you had me, and what you gave up to stay and build a family with Dad. I get why that might make you even more driven to see me succeed—" I pause when Mom turns toward my dad.

"You *told* her?"

"She had a right to know . . . to understand why you are the way you are," Dad says, his tone both tired and defensive at the same time.

My mom's head rears back like Dad slapped her. "You had no right to share that story."

His words are low but angry when he says, "I think sometimes you forget that I lost a baby right along with you."

"But you didn't lose your career!"

"Something you remind me of all too often." Dad doesn't

raise his voice, but he's not backing down or placating her like he usually does when Mom's upset.

For the first time in my life, I wonder if my parents' relationship is okay. Dad's always been the steady presence that balances out my mom's fiery personality—and it's always seemed to work for them. But now that I'm an adult, or maybe now that I know more of their story, I'm seeing cracks I hadn't noticed before.

"I can't talk about this here," Mom says, turning on her heel to walk swiftly across the large room and toward the entryway.

"Dad, I'm sorry," I whisper as my heart pounds so hard I can feel it beating in my throat. My head hurts now, too. Luckily, I didn't develop my mom's proclivity for migraines, but I do get headaches periodically.

Luke drops my hand so he can wrap his arm around my shoulders instead. The amount of time this man spends holding me together lately should earn him some sort of an award.

"You didn't do anything wrong, honey," Dad says. "You told your mom how you felt. How she handled it is on her. She's an adult and responsible for managing her own reactions."

"Yeah." The word escapes on a deep sigh. I know he's right, but after a lifetime of trying not to rock the boat—to keep my own emotions in check in order to keep my mom's in check—this feels like a failure.

"I'm sorry too," Luke says. "That was between Eva and Helene. I should have kept my mouth shut, but . . . I don't like to see my wife hurting."

"I know Eva can stand up for herself—and maybe you

need to let her do so more frequently. But don't lose that protective instinct," Dad tells my husband. "I like knowing that you've always got her back."

"You okay?" Luke asks when I press my fingers to either side of my head, just above my temples.

"It's just a headache. I think we should go, though."

I glance up at Luke and see the panic in his eyes, but his face remains calm. I know he doesn't want to alarm my dad. We haven't had a chance to tell our parents about my high blood pressure.

"Okay, I think today's been a lot for Eva," he says to my dad. "I'm going to take her home."

"I thought you two were staying here tonight?" Dad's forehead wrinkles, and his concern over the change of plans is evident on his face.

"We were," I say. "But I just want to go home."

"I'm going to grab our bags from my room upstairs," Luke says to me, then looks to my dad, "and I'll take the back stair-case and come out from the side door in the kitchen, so we don't make a scene. Can you walk Eva to my car, and I'll meet you guys there?"

"Sure." Dad holds his arm out to me, and I take it, leaning on him a bit more than I probably should if I don't want him to suspect that anything is wrong. But my heart is racing, and I feel off-kilter.

Dad presses a kiss to the top of my head before turning and walking me out to the driveway. "You feeling okay?" he asks.

"Yeah, just tired and I have a headache. I'm fine," I assure him, even though I truly do not feel fine.

He gives me a hug and asks me to check in with him

tomorrow and let him know how I'm doing. And then, as I'm getting situated in the passenger seat, Luke opens the liftgate of his Mercedes and shoves our bags inside.

He comes around to the passenger side, shakes my dad's hand, and asks him to quietly let his parents know we left once the party dies down. And then he shuts my door, hops in the driver's seat, and speeds down the long driveway lined with cars.

"You don't have to drive like a maniac," I tell him, speaking softly. "I'm fine."

"Really?" he asks, his voice tight but gentle. "Because when we were checking out after our appointment the other day, a headache was one of the first things Dr. Lowery's nurse told us to look out for as a sign of possible blood pressure issues."

"It's just because I got upset. I'm sure it will subside as soon as I calm down."

Luke heads into town, silent and focused on the road as we drive. When he pulls into the parking lot at the local pharmacy, I look over at him. "What are we doing here?"

"We're buying one of those at-home blood pressure monitors and calling Dr. Lowery if it's elevated."

"Oh my god, Luke," I groan, tilting my head back to look through the glass of the sunroof. "You're overreacting."

"I hope so," he says. "And if your blood pressure comes back in the normal range, then we can laugh about it. If not, we'll be glad we checked."

He opens his door and locks it behind him, returning in just a few minutes. He tears open a small box as he walks and deposits the packaging inside the bag looped over his wrist.

When he slides back into his seat, he hands me the small

device and reads the directions for me to follow. My hands are shaking, probably from the adrenaline rushing through my system after the interaction with my mom. Finally, Luke helps me get the cuff secured around my upper arm, and when the reading flashes on the small screen we both freeze.

"One forty-two over ninety," Luke mutters before glancing at the blood-pressure monitor booklet in his hand. "That's quite a bit higher than at your appointment, and the chart here says it's almost high enough that you should 'call your doctor immediately.' Given the circumstances, I think we should call anyway."

I close my eyes, pressing my lips together and focusing on breathing in slow, deep breaths. Those numbers are scaring me, and my heart rate is kicking up a notch as a result. I know that's not going to help matters.

"Eva?" Luke sounds a bit worried about my lack of response.

I nod, keeping my eyes pressed close. "Yeah. Call."

The phone call connects over Bluetooth, and the answering service takes down our information, telling us to expect a call back within thirty minutes. As soon as he disconnects, Luke is backing out of our parking space.

"Where are we going?" I ask.

"We're going to start driving back toward Boston. We'll pass at least two hospitals on the way, so if she wants us to stop, we can. Or once we're back in the city, we can go to the hospital Dr. Lowery's affiliated with if we need to."

"Okay."

"In the meantime, Evie, I need you to relax. Focus on your breathing, calm your body down."

I shift in my seat, trying to get more comfortable, and

something rolls off my lap. I glance down at the silver baby rattle Luke's mom gave me earlier, which I forgot I'd set there when I got in the car. I pick it up, letting my fingers trace over the engravings along the silver ends. Taking a deep breath, I picture our baby girl holding this rattle, chewing on it with her little pink gums while teething.

We're twenty minutes closer to Boston when Dr. Lowery's call comes through over the speakers in Luke's car. After he explains the situation, she says, "Eva, I don't want you to panic. Your blood pressure is not in the danger zone, but it's higher than I'd like. I'm going to ask you a few other questions."

"Okay," I squeak out.

"Do you have a bad headache?"

"I had a severe headache earlier, but it's mostly gone away."

"Are you feeling dizzy?"

"No. But I was a little dizzy earlier, when I walked out to the car," I say, thinking about how I was clinging to my dad.

"Are you seeing spots at the edges of your vision?"

"No."

"Any increased swelling?"

"No, not that I've noticed."

"Then I don't think you need to rush to the hospital right now," she says, and my whole body sags with relief. "But when you get home and are more relaxed, I want you to take your blood pressure again. If it's higher, then go straight to the hospital. But as long as it stays steady or goes down, we can wait and deal with this tomorrow. I want to see you in my office first thing, though. I'll squeeze you in early. Meet me at my office at eight-thirty."

Chapter Forty-Four

LUKE

In the elevator on the way up to Dr. Lowery's office, Eva faces me, resting her cheek against my chest as I wrap both arms around her.

"God, I'm so tired," she says. I can tell by the slight tremble in her voice that she's not only tired from tossing and turning all night, but she's also scared. And *nothing* in my life has prepared me for this. Hockey players shooting pucks at me at ninety miles an hour? No problem. But my wife when she's scared something might be wrong with our baby? *That* guts me in a way I didn't know was possible. It's worse than the fear I felt in Game 7, and the only thing that tempers it is knowing that I need to be strong for her. I can't break down; I have to hold my shit together.

"I know, baby," I say, running my hands up her back and over her shoulders. "We're going to get a handle on this, though. Promise." I bend my head down to press a kiss to the top of her head, and the elevator dings before the doors open.

Dr. Lowery's office is quiet when we enter. The waiting room is predictably empty, and no one is at the front desk, but we can hear voices quietly talking in the back. We only stand at the reception area for a minute before a nurse appears and opens the door next to the desk, gesturing us in.

"We've got a room ready for you," she says, smiling at Eva.

"Thanks," I say when my wife doesn't respond. She's tense, and I hate that there's nothing I can do to ease her worry—especially when I'm carrying the same fears myself. Hopefully, this visit will put our minds at ease.

Dr. Lowery is in the exam room when we arrive, and once Eva's situated on the exam table, she says, "I'm going to get you hooked up to some monitors just so we can check things out, okay?"

"Sure." Eva's voice is small.

"I know you're worried," Dr. Lowery says, "but there's a lot we can do to help control high blood pressure during pregnancy. We just want to avoid preeclampsia, and you're not there yet, so please, rest easy."

Eva relaxes back into the exam table and nods. Then Dr. Lowery gets her hooked up to a blood pressure cuff and puts the pulse oximeter on her finger. She then attaches a band around my wife's belly. "We're going to continuously monitor the fetal heart rate for a while, too, just to make sure everything with the baby is normal. This band just holds the device in place, but it's essentially the same thing we've done in previous visits, just over a longer period of time."

"Okay," Eva says, but she doesn't truly seem relaxed until Dr. Lowery tells us Eva's heart rate and blood pressure are okay. The baby's heart rate also appears to be steady and normal.

"All right, while we capture this data and double check that all is well, let's talk a bit about what happened last night, and what to watch for in the future. Let's start with what happened right before your blood pressure spiked."

Eva explains about the confrontation with her mom, and even though she doesn't point any blame at me as she tells the story, I recognize my role in escalating that situation. Helene was giving her what was likely a sincere apology, even if it came much later than it should have, and I should've let Eva handle things without getting Helene worked up, which in turn got Eva worked up.

I think back to what Charlie said, about not losing my protective instinct while also allowing Eva to manage things herself. That's a balancing act I'll need to work on, because the second I see my wife in pain, my inclination is to go into attack mode.

"It sounds like it was a very stressful situation," Dr. Lowery said. "And I think that, given your elevated blood pressure, we need to avoid those as much as possible. Has anything else triggered a similar reaction? Like, have you noticed any issues with working out, or skating, or sex?"

"No," Eva says with a shake of her head. "It was just that one time."

"Okay. While your heart rate is normal, your blood pressure *is* still a bit higher than I'd like. I do think we need to start you on some medication to help keep that down."

"It's safe for the baby?" Eva asks, her hand flexing in mine. My thumb sweeps across the back of her hand in a consistent, hopefully soothing pattern.

"Yes, of course. The safest thing for the baby, honestly, is that we keep Mom as healthy as possible. I think you should take some time off from skating, and from exercise in general, this week. Nothing more rigorous than a fast-paced walk."

Eva nods, but Dr. Lowery must see something in her face because she says, "I'm sorry. I know you're training, and I don't think you need to necessarily stop yet, but I'd like to get this medicine into your system and make sure it's working before you go back to skating or working out. I think a week is enough time for us to figure out if it's effective."

"It's fine," Eva says, her tone making it clear that she's worried about losing the practice time, even though she knows her and the baby's safety is the most important thing. "I can take the week off."

At thirty-two weeks, she's not allowed to do jumps or lifts anymore, but she's still training on the ice—something she knows she's going to have to give up very soon, so losing this week is going to be hard for her, emotionally.

"You mentioned warning signs we should watch for?" I ask.

"Yes. Eva, if you get a sudden headache—one that feels like a band wrapping around your head and squeezing—or you're feeling dizzy or nauseous, or you start seeing spots in your vision, or notice increased swelling, those are all signs that something is wrong and you need to seek medical attention immediately. Any of those would be a get-to-the-hospital-as-soon-as-possible event. More than one of them at the same time would be an indication to call 911."

"I'm supposed to go to Minnesota next week, for two

nights, to film an endorsement deal," I tell her. "Should I cancel that?"

"Not necessarily," Dr. Lowery says. "Lots of women deal with hypertension in pregnancy, and we're on top of it. Plus, by that time, Eva will have been on her medication for over a week, and things should be stable. It might be a good idea, though, for someone to stay with Eva while you're gone. If anything were to happen, we'd want someone to be there to help."

Eva glances up at me. "We'll figure it out. I don't want you to miss it."

I'm tempted to say I'll just cancel. It's not like we need the money.

However, the deal is with a national sports apparel brand —the kind that athletes *dream* of partnering with—and the exposure could be amazing for my career. Especially with Colt set to retire at the end of the season, anything that improves my name recognition as a goalie will be a positive thing for both my career and the entire Rebels organization.

"We'll see. I can reschedule if needed." It absolutely would not be easy or professional, but if I had to, I'd make it happen.

"I can always ask Morgan," Eva says, and for the first time since this whole incident started last night, there's a note of hope in her voice. It eases the knot of anxiety in my stomach, just a tad.

I love that she's making friends in Boston, and if me leaving town for a couple of nights helps her cement that friendship, then I'm willing to do it. Bringing her hand up to my mouth, I press a kiss to the back of her it. "Whatever makes you happy, Evie."

Chapter Forty-Five

EVA

The following week, I walk into the Rebels practice facility alone. Public access to the rink, including Rebels practices when they're in season, is a nice perk of having a pro hockey team in your city. But it also means the place is *never* deserted. Except, apparently, at seven in the morning.

As I stand on the upper-level waiting for Lauren, who suggested this ungodly hour, I close my eyes and breathe in the familiar, cold scent of a rink. And when I breathe out, opening my eyes and taking a step forward toward the edge of the balcony, I catch sight of a single skater.

For a quick second, I think it's Lauren, and that she got started without me. That seems highly unlikely though, given that when Lauren texted to invite me here to skate this morning, she mentioned she was only willing to try again because I'd be with her.

But then I notice the long, dark hair, the hockey skates,

the powerful and confident glide of a woman who's so used to being on the ice, skating seems as effortless as breathing.

AJ takes a quick lap, and then slows to grab a stick that's propped inside the players' box. She backskates across the ice and turns toward the goal line, while deftly batting the puck back and forth, before coming to a stop at center ice.

I clear my throat, and she looks up to find the source of the noise. Scanning the seats, she eventually locks eyes with me, standing one level above.

"Well, this is unexpected," Lauren says from behind as she steps next to me. Her red hair is back in a claw clip, and her hoodie hangs open at her sides.

"You didn't know she'd be here?" I know Lauren and AJ are close friends, but maybe she doesn't keep track of her boss's schedule like that.

"I didn't even know she still skated."

AJ skates toward the box and sprays the boards with ice as she comes to a quick stop. "Might as well come down here and talk about me to my face," she calls out.

Lauren's laugh is huskier than I'd expect from someone with such a sweet voice. "You've got so much explaining to do," she shouts back playfully before we head down a flight of stairs to the tunnel leading to the bench.

Once we're at ice level, Lauren says to AJ, "You didn't tell me that you still skate." She sounds hurt, and I wonder why this is something AJ would hide, if she and Lauren are such good friends.

AJ eyes Lauren's bag with the tops of her skates peeking out. "Neither did you."

Lauren coughs out a laugh. "Touché. But I *don't* skate."

"All evidence to the contrary," AJ says, with her trademark no-nonsense tone, before a concerned look passes over her face and she softens her voice to ask, "You're really getting back on the ice?"

"I'm going to put these skates on," Lauren says, lifting her shoulders in a shrug. "And we'll see from there."

As Lauren plops down onto the bench and removes a fairly new-looking pair of skates, I chat with AJ, asking her about how she got involved with hockey. She tells me about playing in college, then coaching college hockey, then working for St. Louis as a scout and eventually moving over to operations. "I was the assistant GM there before Frank brought me to Boston to be the GM."

"Single-handedly rebuilding the organization," Lauren adds, so obviously proud of her friend.

"There was nothing single-handed about it," AJ says. "I just brought the right people in to do the best job they could, and now it's all paying off."

"You *single-handedly* brought the right people in," Lauren adds, before looking at me. "She's way too humble."

"I know I'm good at my job, and I don't need to brag about it. If that's being humble, then okay. Speaking of which, I need to go get started on said job. The rink is all yours. Skating lessons start at eight, so unless you want an audience, you've got the rink to yourselves for the next half hour or so before all the little kids start showing up to get their gear on."

AJ hops off the ice and removes her skates with the speed and precision I'm sure comes from years of experience. Then she says goodbye as Lauren and I continue lacing up our own skates. Once we're done, I ask the question that's been burning in my mind since I talked to Lynette about Lauren's accident. "When you said you don't skate *anymore*, does that mean you haven't skated at all since . . ."

She shakes her head, then sighs. "Well, I did once. With Jameson. But I wouldn't call it skating so much as squeezing my eyes shut and letting him drag me around the ice."

I glance back down at her nearly pristine skates. "Are those skates not broken in, then?"

"They are. He had Morgan break them in for me before he 'surprised' me," she says, using air quotes, "with a trip here one night."

"Jameson brought you *here*?" I ask, and then I remember that he used to play for the Rebels, years before my dad started coaching the team.

"He arranged it with AJ, I later learned," she tells me as she stands, resting her hands on the top of the boards in front of her and surveying the ice. I stand next to her, one hand resting under my belly where Baby Squash has suddenly decided to do somersaults. "I don't know if I can do this," she whispers.

"Maybe you can't," I say lightly, lifting a shoulder in a small shrug that I hope lets her know there's no pressure. "And if not, that's okay. But you won't know unless you try."

"It's the trying that's terrifying."

"Anything worthwhile is usually at least a little bit scary." I start talking about finding out I was pregnant, and having no idea what it would mean for my skating career, as I step out onto the ice and turn to face her, holding both my hands out to her.

She chews her bottom lip as she looks at my hands, and then, closing her eyes, takes a fortifying breath. As her shoulders relax, she opens her eyes and says, "I'm just going to hold on to the wall. I could never forgive myself if I fell and pulled you down with me."

"Whatever you're comfortable with. But also . . . " I pause, waiting for her to look at me. When she does, I tell her, "You're not going to fall."

"You don't know that."

"Just like you don't know that you *will*," I say with a shrug. "Which is more likely?"

Lauren sighs. "Fine." She sets her hand along the top edge of the boards and cautiously steps out onto the ice. I move back slightly to let her glide, so she'll be less likely to fall from a jerky stop.

"How's it feel to be out here?" I ask as I watch her fingers curl against the red plastic edge of the wall.

"Scary."

"More or less scary than last time?" I ask.

"Both. Less, because it's not the first time, and more, because Jameson's not here holding me up."

"Did he hold you up the whole time when you skated with him before?" I ask, holding my hands out to her.

She shakes her head, and then surprises me by taking my hands. I glide backward slowly, letting her get used to the feel of moving along the ice, but making sure that the wall is always in reach in case she feels like she needs it.

As we glide along, I continue talking to Lauren, mentioning things she surely already knows about skating. I use phrases like "remember" and "don't forget" as I point out each technique because I'm trying not to treat her like she's never skated before, even though she truly does seem like a novice.

We're more than halfway around the edge of the rink

before she no longer seems scared stiff. We're all the way around before she relaxes enough that I'm not worried she'll fall. And we've made a full second loop around the edge of the rink before she stops holding her breath.

"You're really good at this, you know," Lauren tells me.

"I used to coach kids when I was younger. I've just started thinking about getting back into that after I have this baby."

Lauren drops my hands, and I watch as she uses her toe pick to push off just enough to move up beside me. "I thought you and Christopher were still going to try to qualify for the Olympics?"

"We are," I say, turning so I can skate facing forward beside her "But this is my last season. I'd already decided that before I got pregnant. So my mind's been on what to do next."

"Do you . . . *need* to do anything next?"

I know what she means. I'm married to a billionaire—and even if he weren't heir to a vast fortune, he still makes more than enough playing hockey that I wouldn't *need* to work.

"For financial reasons, obviously no. But for my sanity, and to feel useful and remain involved with skating some-how . . . yeah, it's probably best that I have something in my life besides being a mother and a wife."

"I absolutely get that," Lauren says. "Staying home with the kids is an absolute privilege, but I feel like the part no one talks about is how easy it is to lose yourself in that process. I applaud anyone who chooses to be a stay-at-home mom. But I'm equally thankful that we live in a time where women *can* continue to work after having kids, as well. I lost that part of me once before, forgot who I was and what I wanted for myself. Forgot that I could exist outside of my children."

I knew Lauren had been married previously, but I didn't know *this*.

"And now," she says, "I love Jameson dearly. I love my children beyond measure. But I am more than just his wife and their mother, and I love that for me."

"How'd you find yourself?" I ask, noting how steadily she's gliding along on her skates. She hasn't strayed far from the wall, but she seems more comfortable on the ice. And as she continues to talk, telling me about how controlling her first husband was, and how she moved with her kids to Boston after his death, it feels like she's overcoming her fear of the ice at the same time.

"Honestly, I'm not sure it would have happened without Jameson quietly helping me rebuild my life," she says with a small, private smile. "He kept doing things behind the scenes —I had no idea he was pulling the strings, and he wasn't looking for credit. He just wanted to make my transition to single motherhood and moving to Boston easier."

"Do you think you would have ended up where you are now, without him?" I ask, curious whether there are any similarities between their relationship and mine with Luke. I feel both thankful and also a tad guilty about all the ways in which Luke has helped me in the past few months. There's no doubt I wouldn't be where I am if he hadn't done everything he could to make my life better.

"Where I am now is *with* him. There was no path *here* without Jameson," Lauren says. "And I'm okay with that. I don't feel like it makes me less of an independent woman that I have a man who I wouldn't want to be without. There's a vast difference between a man who you're *dependent on*, and a man you can *depend on*."

"Oh?" I say, raising my eyebrow as we start another lap around the rink. I wonder if Lauren even realizes how she's put her hands into the pocket of her Rebels hoodie. She's so at ease on the ice now that I'm trying to hide any reaction that might remind her that she was terrified just a few minutes ago. So I ask her questions to keep her talking. "How so?

"A man you can depend on will support you emotionally and encourage you professionally. He has your back . . . you can depend on him to be there for you, without being dependent on him. He doesn't make you feel like you can't survive without him, just that you'd never want to."

"Yeah, a man like that is a definite keeper," I say, thinking that I'm picturing Luke in every way she's described her husband. Luke's always made sure I have *more* choices, not fewer, always had my back, and has always shown me just how much he loves and cherishes me.

"Speaking of keepers, where's Hartmann? I hear that where you go, he goes."

"He's in Minnesota for an endorsement appearance," I tell her. It's probably evident in my tone that I miss him. Last week, I wasn't sure if he'd go unless I tagged along. But after a week on the medication, my blood pressure is controlled, and I'm back to practicing with Christopher. Plus, I'm closer to my doctor here in Boston, and Morgan is staying with me, just in case.

"Oh, you should come out with us tomorrow night, then," Lauren says. "I'm doing a girls' night with my sister, Paige."

"I wish I could. There's a meeting for the international figure skating organization here this week, something to do with planning for the World Championships in Boston next spring. I already agreed to go to a cocktail reception tomorrow night with a few of the organization's international sponsors. When I said I would go, I didn't realize that Luke would be out of town. I hate going to shit like that by myself."

"Could your skating partner go with you?"

"That would have been ideal, but he's leaving town right after our practice tomorrow. Going home with his new girlfriend to meet her family." Part of me thinks that this is happening pretty quickly, because Christopher does *not* settle into relationships easily. The other part of me thinks that what they have must be special if he's willing to be this serious about her. I'm frustrated that we had to cancel our dinner with them last week because of my blood pressure, so I still haven't met Jenn. But Luke and I are supposed to have dinner with them next week after they're back from upstate New York.

"Well, I'll text you wherever we end up," Lauren says, as she casually does a crossover to turn with the curve of the rink, "in case you want to come out afterward and meet up with us."

I thank her, even though I know I won't feel like going out. I've been getting way more tired much earlier in the evenings, and Luke should be back home after I get back from that event.

And, tomorrow is our last on-ice practice, because Lynette's worried about my stamina and potential for injury. Instead, we'll move to off-ice practices next week and continue that way until my doctor says I need to stop entirely.

I smooth my hand over my baby bump, marveling at how much larger it's gotten since Luke and I got married. Back then, you couldn't even tell I was pregnant. Now, you can't miss the size of my belly. It's not like I wasn't prepared for pregnancy to change my body, but I didn't expect stretch marks on my abdomen as evidence of just how quickly that bump has grown. At least Luke doesn't seem to mind . . . he just traces them with his finger and calls them my battle scars.

The morning he left for Minnesota, I woke up to him whispering to Baby Squash through my navel, telling her to be good for me while he was gone. The way that man loves the both of us is something else entirely—it's a depth and breadth of selflessness that I didn't know existed.

"Eva," Lauren says with a laugh. "What the hell are you thinking about?"

My head snaps over toward her, and that's when I realize I got so distracted thinking about Luke that I never even responded.

"Sorry," I say with a slight grimace. "Totally just got lost thinking about Luke."

Lauren laughs. "I'd tease you about it, but that would be like the pot calling the kettle black."

We take one last lap around the rink, and I'm amazed by how comfortable Lauren is now. *That's* what makes me want to coach—witnessing someone doing something they didn't think they could do, and knowing that I helped them get there.

But then the kids start filing into the stands to get ready

for their lesson, and Lauren and I part ways. She heads up to the offices for work, as I head toward the Back Bay for my practice with Christopher.

I'm almost at our practice rink when Lauren's text comes through.

LAUREN

Thanks for this morning . . . I never thought I'd feel safe and happy on the ice again. Coaching seems like a natural fit for you!

Chapter Forty-Six

EVA

*Y*ou *can do this,* I tell myself as the driver takes the turn up Newbury Street toward the restaurant where the event is being held. *One hour of making nice with the sponsors, and then you can go home, crawl into bed, and wait for Luke to get back.*

I glance at my phone again, looking at the last messages we exchanged.

LUKE

Looks like we're going to arrive almost an hour earlier than planned. Can't wait to see you tonight!

EVA

I will make sure I'm home and naked before you get there. 😉

LUKE

That winky face better not mean you're joking. I just spent three nights without you and I miss you like crazy. Don't plan on leaving that bed all weekend.

EVA

It's cute that you think you can tell me what to do.

LUKE

Don't be a brat.

EVA

Why? What happens to brats?

LUKE

Fuck around and find out, Peaches.

Crossing my legs and squeezing my thighs together, I attempt to quell the ache that's building there.

After I'd finally come clean to Luke about having to throw out my whole toy collection in LA, he'd left me a care package with a wide array of toys before he headed to the airport a few days ago. We've had fun on video calls at night as I tested them out—but nothing beats him being here with me. The toys will never be a satisfactory replacement for Luke.

Still, perhaps him being away has been good practice for when the season starts up. I don't know how I'm going to handle the week-long road trips where he's in different cities every couple of days. Maybe after the Olympics, if we even get there, the baby and I can travel with him?

I slide my phone into my purse, hoping that I can control my longing for him for the next hour or so.

After the driver pulls up in front of the restaurant, I walk across the wide sidewalk to the doors, determined to get home even more quickly than I'd originally planned.

An hour and a half later, I'm ready to poke my eyeballs out. I've been caught up in non-stop small talk since walking in the door, answering the same questions over and over.

I feel like an entitled jerk for being so frustrated by people who are genuinely interested in me and my career, but my feet are throbbing in my strappy wedges, and my lower back is aching. I don't know why I thought I should wear anything with a heel while pregnant, and now all I want is for Luke to give me a massage. His sports medicine degree has really paid off during my pregnancy, as he's been exceptionally good when I've needed my back or feet rubbed.

At this point, I'm about ready to turn mid-conversation and run out of here, especially because Luke texted me twenty minutes ago saying they were about to land.

"I'm so sorry," I say to the older gentleman I'm talking to. "I need to run to the restroom."

"Of course, dear," he says. "I'm looking forward to your return to competition later this year. Take care of yourself."

You're being so self-absorbed, the voice in my head says. It's the same one I heard from my mom when I was growing up —the one that makes me feel selfish if I put what I want before what others want from me.

I turn toward the bathrooms, hoping I can duck in for a moment and then make a beeline for the front door. But then I catch sight of an extremely familiar head of perfectly tousled light brown hair and a pair of broad, muscular shoulders. Excitement and relief flow through me as I realize that

Luke must have come here to rescue me instead of going straight home when his plane landed.

I move toward him, not caring that I just told someone I was going to the bathroom. He's talking to a woman I saw earlier from across the room. She's striking, standing nearly as tall as him in killer stilettos, with black hair and bright blue eyes. She's got full lips and a huge smile as she throws her head back with a throaty laugh. The old me would have been jealous as hell that Luke had made someone else laugh like that, especially someone so gorgeous, but the new me is secure in his feelings and our relationship.

She reaches out and squeezes his forearm, saying, "I'll be right back." And after she turns away, I tap him on the shoulder. He spins on his heel, and as soon as I see his face, I feel like someone punched me in the gut.

"Wh—what are you doing here?" I stumble over the words as I stare into the face of a man who would be a perfect stranger if we hadn't spent one drunken night together in his hotel room in Italy eight months earlier.

His chin tilts as he looks at me, and I can tell he's trying to place me. It's then that I notice he really does look like Luke, and not just from the back. His face is incredibly similar. His hair is the same. He's just as tall.

And that's when I realize that, in my moment of drunken despair, I tried to find solace with someone who looked like the one and only person I'd ever loved.

I don't know if that makes it more understandable, or makes me an asshole. Maybe both.

He furrows his eyebrows as his gaze travels from my face to my belly and back up again. And that's when I see the recognition gradually dawning, before he says, "Italy?"

I press my lips between my teeth and give him a quick nod of confirmation.

And then my brain, which has been lagging since the moment he turned around, finally kicks into gear, and I realize I should have fled before he could figure out who I was.

Goddamn it. I just missed the perfect opportunity to say, "How embarrassing . . . I'm so sorry, I thought you were someone else," before turning and walking away.

Now he knows. His gaze flicks down to my belly again, and I wish I wasn't wearing the form-fitting maternity dress that I bought the other day. I can no longer hide the bump beneath empire waists—they just make me look like a pear. But when I sent Luke a picture of me wearing this dress in the fitting room, he video called me in response, insisting that I buy it, and whatever else I wanted, on his card.

"Here you are, darling," says the gorgeous woman he'd been talking to previously as she reaches out to hand him a drink. She looks over at me expectantly, before reaching her hand out to say, "Hi, I'm Adele Becker. Hans's wife." Her German accent is faint, but present.

Hans. His name doesn't even ring a bell, and I wonder if I ever knew it, or if I was too busy wishing he was Luke to even care.

"Hi," I say, taking her hand. "I'm Eva Hartmann."

"So nice to meet you," she says. "I'm sure Hans mentioned we're sponsors for this organization. What about you?"

Sponsors. So he must have been in Italy that night for the same reason I was—the international skating competition.

I wonder for a moment if she would've recognized me as

a skater if I'd said I was Eva Wilcott? Probably not. I doubt sponsors for the large international organization that hosts these skating events really get to know the hundreds of skaters, from dozens of countries, who compete.

"Uhh . . ." I trail off, trying to figure out whether there's some lie that can get me out of this situation. If I wasn't still competing, that might be possible, but if I attend the qualifier or compete in the Olympics, they'll likely see me again. Plus, they could pick up *Society* magazine at the airport on the way home, and I'd be right there on the front of it, next to Luke. "I'm a pairs skater for the US, actually."

"Oh, that's delightful. I love pairs skating," she says, her smile broad as she loops her hand in the crook of her husband's elbow.

Husband. I've been so stunned by all of this, it's just now sinking in that this guy—Hans—is married. Trying to give him the benefit of the doubt, I ask, "So how long have you two been married?"

Maybe, like me, it's a more recent development and he wasn't actually cheating on her.

"Oh," Adele says with a smile as she looks over at Hans, apparently not noticing that my question has come out of left field. "What's it been, about seven years now?"

Oh fuck.

He most definitely was *not* wearing a ring that night. That part I do remember because I checked when he first sat down next to me at the bar—three drinks *before* I went up to his room with him.

Hans gives a stiff nod, and I watch Adele's expression grow concerned. I remember her husband being extremely personable, not the rigid statue standing in front of me, and I suspect she's wondering why his whole personality has changed.

"And you?" he asks, nodding his chin toward my left hand, which currently rests on my belly.

I should tell him I've been married for years, too, so he doesn't wonder if this child is his. But I can't. That fucking article is out there on every newsstand in the country, and according to Morgan, our story has been trending on various social media platforms since it released less than two weeks ago.

I'll just have to hope that because I don't look as pregnant as I am, he'll assume I got pregnant *after* our night in Italy.

"Almost two months, actually," I say.

"That's so exciting! And that ring is gorgeous, just like you," Adele says with a huge, genuine smile. If she wasn't married to the biological father of my baby, I'd adore this woman.

"Thank you," I say, knowing that I need to make my escape before any more questions are asked. "It was so nice meeting you two, but my husband just got home from a trip, and I can feel my phone buzzing in my purse. He's probably wondering why I'm not back yet, so I'm going to run. Enjoy the rest of the night."

Then I spin on my heel and hightail it toward the door as fast as I can, not even caring about the lies I just told. I'm stepping outside when a strong hand grasps my forearm and I'm pulled to a stop.

"What the fuck are you up to, showing up and introducing yourself to my wife like this?" I recognize the anger in Hans's voice, and it pisses me off. *He* has no right to be angry here. *He* is the one who cheated on his wife. And besides, she's the one who introduced herself to me.

My heart is pounding in my throat as I turn to confront him, and the movement has his hand falling to his side where it belongs. "*You* don't get to be angry in this situation. I had no idea who you were or that you'd be here." I practically spit the words at him.

His gaze travels to my belly yet again, and I slide my hand over it protectively. I don't even want his eyes on my baby bump. "Like hell you didn't. I don't know what kind of games you're playing here—"

"I'm not playing *any* games. I didn't know who you were or that you'd be here," I reiterate. "Trust me, I did *not* come here looking for you."

He scoffs, and the sarcasm in his voice is unmistakable when he says, "I'm sure you didn't."

"You are the last person on the planet I'd want to see."

"And yet, here you are. What do you want? Hush money to keep this a secret?"

I'd laugh at the absurdity of this whole situation—of him thinking that I somehow want him involved or want something from him—if only I could breathe. But my head aches and my heart is racing so fast I feel almost lightheaded. "I need to go . . ."

His hand clasps around my forearm again, squeezing harder this time. "We need to talk about this."

I press my free hand to my forehead, hoping to quell the ache. "I can't right now."

He nods toward a coffee shop two doors down. "Meet me there tomorrow morning at eight."

Before I can agree or turn him down, he's gone—back

into the restaurant, back to his wife. I have half a mind to follow him and tell him to fuck right off. To tell his wife what he did and show her the proof. But that would ruin *everything*. And besides, I have a killer headache. I turn toward the street, desperate to get home as quickly as possible, but a wave of dizziness hits me and sends me staggering forward, where I grip the back of a wooden bench that sits in front of the restaurant.

Passersby on the sidewalk give me ample room, probably thinking I just stumbled out of there drunk and am about to throw up. Though come to think of it, I do feel nauseous.

I collapse onto the bench, and that's when I start connecting the signs: the band of pressure tightening around my head, the dizziness, the nausea. What did Dr. Lowery say? Was I supposed to call 911 in this case, or just go to the hospital?

My thoughts are jumbled and confused, so I dig my phone out of my purse to call Luke and ask him. But it never even rings, it just goes straight to voicemail. His phone is probably still in airplane mode. I dial Morgan. She was packing up her stuff at my place, where she'd stayed with me the past two nights, when I headed out for this event. If she's home now, she's only a block away.

"What's up, babe? I thought you'd be home getting freaky with your husband by now?" she says with a laugh when she answers her phone, but I'm having a hard time forming words in response. "Eva?"

"Are you home? I need you." My words are panicked and barely audible. I can't tell if they sound as jumbled as they feel, but now I'm truly freaking out. I press my free hand to my forehead, trying to suppress the ache, but it doesn't help at all.

"Yes, where are you?"

"Restaurant," I tell her, hoping she remembers which one I was going to. "Please, hurry." There are spots clouding the edges of my vision and making me dizzy, so I lie down on the bench. And that's when my phone clatters to the ground.

Chapter Forty-Seven

LUKE

I've never been so glad to get home after a trip as I am tonight. I watch the elevator numbers counting up, each one bringing me closer to holding Eva.

I used this short trip as a test for how I'll do once the season starts up and I have to travel significantly more. It could have been worse, but it could have been a whole hell of a lot better, too. Will I ever get used to being away from her? Will that aching need I have for her ever subside? I hope so . . . and I hope not . . . at the same time.

When the doors open to the vestibule leading to my condo, I breathe easier. I remember what it was like to walk into my condo before she lived here. I loved the space, but there was an emptiness that I never quite got used to. It looked like it had been plucked from a magazine spread, and it felt fucking lonely. Eva's brought a warmth, a sense of home and family, that I hadn't realized was missing until she was here.

"Honey . . . I'm home," I call out, laughing to myself at the silly imitation of a stereotypical, family-friendly TV show.

Silence.

That's weird. I'd texted her when we were close to landing. Although she'd said it might take some time to extricate herself from the event, that was over an hour ago. She should be back by now.

I pull my phone from my pocket, wishing it hadn't died before we landed. The driver who brought me back from the airport didn't have the kind of charger I needed, and mine was buried somewhere in my bag, which I'd stupidly placed in the trunk. But it couldn't have been dead for more than forty-five minutes.

Plugging it into the charging station in the kitchen, I head back toward the bedrooms, thinking Eva's probably back there, showering or changing after the event. I pass the guest bedroom that Morgan slept in while I was gone, but it's empty. That makes sense, since Eva had said Morgan was packing up while she was getting ready a few hours ago. But our bedroom is disturbingly silent too, and I feel a chill running down my spine. Why isn't she home?

I turn and rush back to the kitchen, hoping there's enough of a charge that I can power up my phone to see any missed calls or texts from her.

Impatiently drumming my fingers on the counter, I wait for the screen to light up, and as soon as I enter my passcode, the screen is inundated with multiple notifications of missed calls.

I tap on the first voicemail from Eva, but only hear the sound of a hangup. There are four messages from Morgan, and as my stomach clenches, I click on the first one.

Luke, it's Morgan. I'm in an ambulance with Eva. I think her blood pressure spiked when she was leaving the restaurant, and she got sick. Call me when you get this.

I don't even listen to the others; I just hit the icon to call her back.

"Luke, oh my god," Morgan says the minute the call connects, undeniable fear in her voice.

"Is she okay?" I ask shakily as my heart pounds faster.

"I think so? They brought us through the ER, but moved us up to labor and delivery almost immediately. Dr. Lowery is on her way in."

"Can I talk to Eva?"

"Hold on," she says, and I hear some murmuring in the background. "She's still kind of out of it. It might be better to wait until you get here."

She's too out of it to talk to me? Fear grips my belly, making me almost sick with worry. "Tell her I love her, and I'll be there as quickly as I can."

"Drive safely, Luke," Morgan says. "We don't need you getting in an accident."

I try to follow her instructions, but I still make it to the hospital in about half the time it should have taken me. I toss my keys to the valet and rush inside, where the attendant at the desk directs me to the sixth floor while pointing to the elevators. Feeling like I can't stay still, I clench and unclench my fists as the elevator stops on multiple floors to let people get on and off. I swear it's taking longer to ascend five floors than it did to drive halfway across the city.

"I'm sorry," the nurse at the desk says as I approach the nurse's station, "what did you say your wife's name is?"

I try not to roll my eyes because I literally just told her through the intercom before she buzzed me in. "Eva Hartmann."

"We don't"—she glances over my shoulder like she's looking for backup—"have an Eva Hartmann in this unit."

"Is there another labor and delivery unit?"

"No, just the one."

"Then my wife is here." I can tell I sound agitated, and I'm sure she's thinking I'm unhinged, but holy fuck, *how do people stay calm in situations like this?*

"She's not, sir." The woman's jaw tenses as she reaches for the phone.

"I need to find my wife!"

"And I need you to calm down—"

"Luke!" Dr. Lowery's voice is a sharp bark from my left, and I glance down the hall to see her peeking her head out of a room. "We're down here."

"See," I say, glancing over my shoulder at the nurse as I turn and walk down the hall.

Dr. Lowery steps fully into the hallway and holds her hand out, telling me to stop before I can turn into Eva's room. "Labor and delivery is a locked unit for a reason. Why are you acting like someone who's trying to break in?"

"They kept telling me they didn't have an Eva Hartmann here."

"They don't. Her name in our records is Evangeline Wilcott."

I drop my chin to my chest, shake my head and take a deep breath, recognizing that I really *was* acting unhinged. If I'd stopped and thought about it for two seconds, I'd have remembered that we used Eva's maiden name when we added her to my insurance because we hadn't received our marriage certificate so we couldn't confirm her new last name yet. And *of course* they had her full first name.

I release a heavy breath. "Sorry."

"It's understandable that you're upset, but I need you to get yourself under control before you come in and see Eva."

"Is she okay? What happened?"

"That's what I'm trying to figure out. Now, if you'll *calmly* come in"—she rolls her eyes but gives me a slight smile—"maybe I can finish doing just that."

"I'll be on my best behavior, just let me see my wife," I say with a groan.

When she moves aside to let me through the door, my eyes meet Eva's before I take two quick strides to her side. I scan her body, noticing the wires running from her exposed belly to the monitors beside the bed, the IV in her arm, and the blanket draped across her lap.

I bend to press a kiss to the top of her head, breathing in her peach scent and reminding myself that she's in the best place to get whatever care she might need.

"Stop being so dramatic. I'm fine," she tells me, rolling her eyes at me like she's trying to assure me I'm overreacting. I'm pretty sure I'm not.

"Are you, though?" I cup her cheeks in my palm and press another kiss on her forehead. "I'm so damn relieved that you *appear* fine, but what happened?"

Eva recounts her headache followed by the nausea she felt when she left the restaurant. "I was having trouble thinking because of the headache, so I sat down and called you, and then Morgan. But then I started to feel dizzy, so I laid down. That's all I remember."

"I came running down Newbury Street, as fast as I could in my flip-flops, already on the phone with 911," Morgan adds. "And I found her lying, completely disoriented, on a bench. Luckily, the EMTs showed up within a few minutes."

The mental image of her lying there like that is the stuff of my nightmares, and makes me wonder if I'll ever again be able to force myself to leave her side.

"You did the right thing getting an ambulance there as quickly as possible," Dr. Lowery tells Morgan, before turning toward Eva. "It's clear that your blood pressure spiked pretty significantly, but it doesn't sound like you had a hypertensive seizure, which is fortunate. Preeclampsia, the condition that causes this, is serious, however. We're going to get you started on a magnesium drip and increase your blood pressure meds. I'm also going to run some more tests and admit you, so that we can monitor you and the baby until you deliver."

"Deliver? When?" Eva's voice is tight, her eyes widening.

"We'll see how you do. For now, the baby will need two doses of steroids, twenty-four hours apart, to begin strengthening her lungs should an early delivery be necessary. I'm hoping we can get you through the week—"

"Is it safe to deliver this early?" I can't keep the panic from seeping into my words.

"Premature delivery is never ideal," Dr. Lowery says. "But ultimately, we have to weigh the risk of an early delivery against the risk of waiting, for both mom and baby. We'll keep a close eye on your blood pressure and monitor the baby. We won't deliver unless it's the safest option for both of you."

My wife's eyes well up with tears, but she gives the doctor a nod. I assume that, like me, she had never considered finding herself in this situation. She's young and healthy. She eats well, exercises, and is trying to keep her life as stress free as possible.

What the hell happened in the restaurant to trigger such a reaction?

"The nurse will be back in to get the magnesium and steroids started, and then we'll run those tests I mentioned. It's good that you're here, Eva. You and the baby will be under close and constant observation so we can keep you both safe. I hope that reassures you."

Eva presses her lips together, brushes her tears aside, and nods again. I reach over to brush a wayward strand of hair from her forehead.

"You're safe. The baby is safe. That's all that matters, Evie," I remind her. But I can see in her eyes that there's some piece of the story I still don't know.

As soon as Dr. Lowery is out of the room, I ask, "You said you went rushing out of the restaurant. What happened before that? Did something or someone make you upset?"

I'm wondering who I might need to kill before remembering Charlie's words that night at Wellington Manor: *We both know Eva can stand up for herself—and maybe you need to let her do so more frequently.*

Eva's eyes flick to Morgan, who asks, "Do you want me to give you two some privacy?"

"I think you might need to be here for this story," Eva tells her, bringing both hands to her face to wipe her remaining tears away, as if steeling herself for the upcoming conversation. "There might be . . . PR implications."

That causes a chill to move up my spine, because anything that threatens the story we created—about our marriage and our baby—threatens our family. Because the truth is, it's no longer just a story. It's who we are and how we plan to live our lives forever.

I drag a chair from the opposite wall and invite Morgan to sit down while I settle on the end of the bed and take one of Eva's feet in my hands. Earlier, she'd sent me a picture of her all dressed up for tonight, so I know she'd been wearing heels, which means her feet and back are definitely aching right now, in addition to everything else she's been through.

I stroke my thumbs along the tight ligaments on the bottom of one foot before pressing into the ball and gently splaying her toes. She gives a sigh of relief before explaining how she came face to face with the biological father of our child.

Our child.

Eva winces, her face contorting as she hisses a sound of pain, and it's only then that I realize I'm channeling my frustration into this foot massage. I set that foot down and take the other in my hand, reminding myself to be gentle.

Morgan and I share a glance, which Eva doesn't miss. "Why aren't either of you saying anything?" she asks us.

"It may not be as bad as you think," Morgan says. "It sounds like he's worried that you're up to something and might try to use this baby to extort or blackmail him. If we can just reassure him that you want nothing from him—"

"Except to stay the fuck out of our lives," I growl the words between clenched teeth.

"—he'll probably climb back into whatever hole he came from."

"What if he doesn't?" Eva's voice is small, and it makes my chest ache. "What if he wants to be involved? Or what if he tries to blackmail *us* by threatening to expose this story?"

"Not. An. Option." The words are out before I can even think, and it's at that moment I realize I will do *anything* to protect Eva and the family we're building together.

"How do we prevent it?" she asks, and I glance over at Morgan to find her watching me closely.

"Since you're going to be here for the foreseeable future, and since this is exactly the kind of stress you're supposed to be avoiding, how about if I take care of this? Is that okay with you?" I ask.

Eva sighs and leans back against the bed, closing her eyes while her lips turn up at the corners. "Would you mind? Because I'd really like to never see or think about him again. And *I'm* obviously not able to meet with him tomorrow morning."

"I'll go," I tell her, right as the nurse wheels in a stand with a computer and a bin.

"I need to attach these to your IV," she says, showing two packets of clear liquid to Eva. "That means, I need your two visitors to give us a bit of space around the bed."

Morgan stands and pats Eva on her shoulder. "How about if I go back to your place and get some of your things? You guys can text me a list of what you want, and I'll drop it by in the morning."

"That would be great, thank you," Eva says, before turning her attention back to the nurse. I don't think she sees

Morgan gesturing toward the hallway, so I follow her out there.

I shut the door behind us, and Morgan looks up at me.

"Under *no* circumstances are you to do anything illegal, or lose your cool with this guy," she says, her normally sweet voice sounding a lot like AJ when she's taking a player to task. I didn't know she had this level of bossiness in her. "The last thing we need is for you to blow the narrative because you make a big scene or get caught doing something you shouldn't. And believe me, you do *not* want your agent finding out about this."

"Your dad is my agent," I say dryly.

She folds her arms across her chest, a steely look in her eyes. "Exactly."

"Trust me, Morgan. I'm a Hartmann. If there's one thing we know how to do, it's bury our shit discreetly."

She lets out a laugh as she shakes her head. "That being said, I see how protective you are of her. I know how easily you get *overprotective* when you're worried about her. Just remember . . . this guy doesn't want to ruin Eva's life; he wants to make sure she doesn't ruin *his*. Let that be your guide."

Oh, I'm about to ruin his life, all right. The way he put his hands on her and threatened her? That asshole doesn't know what he just started.

I give her a nod. "Thanks for being here with Eva for the past few days, and for getting to her so quickly tonight. Thanks for keeping our secrets and helping us out."

"I'm here for you guys," she says, reaching out to give my upper arm a pat. "But don't make my life harder than it has to be, because if you fuck up, I'm going to have to fix it. If you want to run anything by me before you meet with this guy tomorrow, you know how to reach me. Otherwise, I'll come back tomorrow with your and Eva's stuff, and keep her company while you're gone."

"Thanks, Morgan. You have no idea how much I appreciate that." Everything about our marriage story and Eva's transition to living in Boston is better because of her. And I'm not quite sure how I'll repay her . . . but I know I'll find a way, eventually.

Chapter Forty-Eight

LUKE

I say Eva's name for a second time, just to make sure she's still asleep. She doesn't stir, so I pull out my phone and call Preston. I don't want any of this in writing, even in a text message.

I've spent the past hour since she first fell asleep figuring out who this Hans guy is. I started with the major sponsors of the international figure skating organization, and from there, it wasn't hard to find the company owned by Hans and Adele Becker.

What I was *not* expecting, however, was to stumble upon several pictures of him that looked eerily similar to me. Could it be that she turned to this guy Hans, in her moment of need, because he reminded her of me?

As much as it drives me crazy that I wasn't there to comfort her that night in Italy, as much as it pains me that she slept with him and that his DNA is a part of our baby, I feel a tiny sense of relief too. Because while I've never voiced it, I've definitely worried that our baby might look nothing like me.

"Luke?" Preston's voice comes through my phone, and he sounds worried.

"Yeah."

"Why are you calling so late?"

Shit . . . I hadn't even considered the fact that it was almost midnight.

"Sorry, man, but I might need your help with something."

"Where are you?"

"At the hospital with Eva."

"She okay?"

"No. She has really high blood pressure, which I guess can happen during pregnancy, so they've admitted her, and we may need to deliver the baby early. That's not why I'm calling though."

"Oh?"

I swallow. "There's this guy, and I need some information on his business. It looks like the company is publicly traded, and I want to know what I'd have to do to procure fifty-one percent of the stock."

"You want to buy his business out from under him?"

"I want to know whether that's an option."

"Who is it, and what's the name of his company? I'll see what I can find out and get back to you shortly."

"Thanks, man." I give him Hans's information and hang up, appreciating that Preston didn't press me for more details. And then I continue researching everything I can find out about him and his wife.

Thirty minutes later, I'm wondering what "shortly" meant to Preston. I know it's late at night, and I'm asking him to gather intel on a person he doesn't know, but even this short wait is killing me. I should have clarified that I *really* needed to hear back from him tonight. The sooner the better.

There's a light knock as the door is pushed open, and I glance over, expecting to see a nurse. In the doorway stand my brothers.

As shocked and confused as I am at their appearance, I motion them in, holding my finger to my lips so they don't wake Eva. The nurse who was here before Eva dozed off said she'd be in every three hours to get her vitals, so I want to make sure she at least gets those few hours of sleep in between visits.

"What are you guys doing here?" I whisper as I give each of them the classic Hartmann one-arm hug. I don't want my confusion to stop them from understanding how grateful I am to see them.

"Seemed like you needed some backup," Preston says with a shrug.

"How the hell did you guys get in here after visiting hours?"

"You're asking the wrong questions," Tristan says.

"Oh yeah? What are the right questions in this situation?"

"Maybe why you thought we *wouldn't* show up if you needed us?" Tucker suggests.

Hmmm. "Who said I needed you?"

"You don't go toe to toe with a guy like Hans Becker alone. Just because you don't work for the family business doesn't mean you don't have our support," Preston says as he takes a seat next to me on the couch.

It's only then that I stop to wonder whether my brothers are closer to each other than they are to me because I'm so much younger, like I've always assumed, or if it's because I've distanced myself—either intentionally or not—assuming they were a triumvirate that I could never be part of.

"Technically, Tucker doesn't work for Hartmann Enterprises anymore either," Tristan says, planting himself in the chair nearest the couch. We don't talk about how Tucker had to walk away from the family business after his failed engagement, but I always wonder if he'd rather still be doing that work than being the CEO of the Boston Rebels.

"And yet, I'm still a Hartmann," Tucker responds, clapping me on the shoulder. "Funny how that works."

"So tell us what's going on, and let us help you fix it," Preston says, nodding to Tucker to take the other chair nearest Eva's bed.

"Okay, but I need you to not ask too many questions. There are some things that I just can't tell you," I say, keeping my voice low, and my brothers all lean in as I fill them in. I don't tell them that he's the biological father of our baby, just that he and Eva had "a thing" before we were together, he's recently popped back up, and I'd like to make sure he stays as far away from our life as possible.

My brothers all pull out their phones, and we get to work identifying everything that this man values, so we can figure out the quickest way to pull it all out from under him.

———

"Hey." I stroke my hand over Eva's hair as I kiss her forehead. I'm trying not to focus on the bruise that's forming around her forearm, no doubt where Hans grabbed her last night. I need to stay levelheaded right now, and the knowledge that he physically hurt her doesn't help.

She blinks a few times before focusing on my face. "What time is it?"

"It's early. I need to go meet with our lawyers—"

"We have lawyers?"

I chuckle at how half-asleep Eva is asking silly questions. "Of course we do. And then I'll head over to meet Hans. Morgan's going to stop by in about an hour, but I didn't want you to wake up and wonder where I'd gone."

"Did I dream that your brothers were here in the middle of the night, or did that really happen?"

She's about as awake now as she was at two in the morning when the nurse came in to take her vitals, and found the four Hartmann brothers with their heads tucked close together, plotting in hushed whispers.

"Yeah, they stopped by."

Her hand coasts over the swell of her belly. "Do they know?"

"No. But they helped me figure out the best way to make sure Hans stays out of our lives forever."

Her eyebrows draw together in concern, and then she chuckles. "Is it legal?"

"Honey, we're Hartmanns. We don't need to do illegal shit. We just stay two steps ahead of everyone else."

She bites her lip and gives me a nod. "Hurry back."

"Of course." I press a soft kiss to her lips and head out to meet our lawyers.

Two hours later, I'm walking into the coffee shop where Hans told Eva to meet him. I move through the crowd of people in line and find him sitting in the back with a cappuccino on the table in front of him. I drop a manilla envelope on the table before I pull out the chair. His head snaps up in surprise.

"That seat's taken," he says.

"Doesn't look taken." I sit.

"I'm expecting someone."

"Well, I'm here instead."

His eyes narrow, and he reminds me a bit of my brothers—confident and accustomed to giving orders, not taking them.

"Where's Eva?"

"My wife was hospitalized last night after you assaulted her outside the event."

His head rears back in shock, but his voice is low when he says, "I didn't *assault* her. I simply asked to speak to her this morning."

"*Simply* asking to speak with her left a pressure bruise around her arm and sent her blood pressure spiking so high she almost had a seizure right outside the restaurant. The hospital has already documented the injury and I'm sure there's ample video footage of the incident on the security cameras of all these businesses. My lawyers are working on getting the recordings as we speak."

His voice is a quiet growl when he says, "I barely touched her."

"The bruising on her arm would suggest otherwise." I rest my elbows on the table, steepling my fingers together as I lean forward, channeling Preston as I say, "I don't take kindly to people who hurt those I love."

He holds his hands up in front of him and says, "I had no

intention of hurting her. I only grabbed her arm to stop her from leaving so I could talk to her."

"Intimidate her, you mean?"

"No. I only requested that we meet up to talk this morning."

I lean back in my seat and lift an eyebrow. "And tell me, Hans. What exactly did you want to talk about?"

"I'm sorry. I don't even know who you are, and you expect me to talk to you about this?"

I hold out my hand. "Luke Hartmann. Eva's husband."

"Hartmann?" he says, staring at my hand rather than taking it. It's clear he recognizes the name. And although it sounds like Eva introduced herself as a Hartmann last night, he obviously hadn't made the connection.

In the early hours of this morning, my brothers and I learned that his wife, Adele, had replaced her father as the head of the family's automobile manufacturing business in Germany well over a decade ago, and grew it into a global operation—not unlike what my father did with Hartmann Enterprises, and what Preston has continued to do since Dad retired.

She met Hans when she decided to hire someone with more international experience to replace her as CEO of her family's business. Now she serves as the president of the board of directors, but technically, the company is hers and he just works for her.

We've done business with them in the past, and according to Tristan, he had to step in when Hans tried to change the terms of a sale of microchips he was purchasing from one of our subsidiary companies. From what I understand, Tristan only gets involved if you've fucked up.

"Yes, *those* Hartmanns." I drop my hand since he's made no move to shake it.

Hans clears his throat nervously.

"So, let me explain to you what it looks like when you fuck with the wrong family." I don't like to be this guy, but I've sat through enough board meetings—and seen Preston at his absolute finest—to know that sometimes you have to remove any possibility of compromise because the stakes are too high, or the people involved are too important, to entertain any outcome but the one you've already decided on. "That private island in the Mediterranean that you and Adele love to spend a month on every summer? I bought it a few hours ago—"

"Impossible. The family said they'd never sell it."

"Maybe what they meant was that they'd never sell it to *you*. And that luxury box you've had your eye on in Munich? My family is really looking forward to taking it over so we can catch a *football* game a few times a year. Oh, and the contract you were about to sign for the new headquarters in Berlin? That space has, unfortunately, just been leased."

"Why are you doing this?"

"Oh, you don't like it when people toy with things you care about? How about people? Eva tells me that your wife is absolutely lovely. How would she feel if she knew that you are worried you might have conceived a child with someone else?"

His face drains of color.

"Let me be very clear. My next move is to buy up fifty-one percent of the stock in your company. Bad move, by the way, convincing your wife to sell so many of her shares. With that much stock available, anyone with enough money can become the majority shareholder and demand the board appoint a new CEO."

"All this because I had sex with your wife?" The absolute arrogance in his voice and look of indifference on his face, as if Eva isn't worthy of his concern, remove any guilt I might have felt about taking such an extreme approach. He's getting exactly what he deserves after messing with the most precious person in my world.

"Let's be very clear. She was not my wife when you were with her, so *she* has nothing to feel ashamed about. I imagine your wife, on the other hand, might not feel so forgiving when she hears about what happened. Especially when she can only sit by and watch as the Hartmanns buy up fifty-one percent of her company, before breaking it apart and selling it piece by fucking piece."

He balls his hands into fists and clenches his jaw, knowing he's been bested. "You wouldn't."

I let out a humorless laugh. "Not only *would* I, but I'd also delight in doing it." We sit there for a moment, staring at each other.

"You may think I'm a shitbag," he says, and I nod in agreement, "but we have an open marriage. It's not like I was cheating on her. But neither of us has any desire to have a child, so I'm *very* interested in making sure she doesn't find out about this baby."

"I'm glad we're on the same page," I say. "Just to be completely clear, this is *my* baby, and you'll be staying the hell away from my wife and my kid."

"Happy to stay far away," he says with a decisive nod.

"Good, then I have some paperwork for you to sign. In

exchange, I'll make sure my family's share of stock in your company never exceeds fifty percent."

"Why would you want *any* stock in our company?"

I don't. I just want him to know I own part of his company, and can buy more if I want.

I lift my shoulders in a shrug and say, "Who knows? Maybe it's a good investment."

Hans reaches for the envelope I hand him and slides the paperwork and pen onto the table. It's simple enough—though my lawyers assured me it would hold up in a court of law in both the US and Germany—that he is able to read it over in a few minutes.

He glances up, one eyebrow raised. "This says you'll sell me the luxury box at cost?"

"Why would I want a box at a German football stadium?" I ask.

His laugh is a snort. "You just throw that kind of money around for fun?"

"Not normally. But there is nothing, and please remember that word . . . *nothing* that I wouldn't do for my wife."

Hans shakes his head and looks back down at the paperwork, picking up the pen. I swear I don't breathe until he returns the pen for me to sign on the remaining line.

Once that's done, I gather up the pages and the pen and stuff them into the envelope. As I turn to leave, I say, "Hopefully, we'll never have to see each other again."

His laugh is surprisingly loud. "Yes, hopefully not."

Chapter Forty-Nine

EVA

"**I** can't believe you made me look presentable," I say to Ashleigh as I look in the mirror she's set up on the rolling table that goes over my bed.

I've been stuck in this hospital room for a week, eating every meal in bed and watching more movies and TV shows than I've ever watched in my life. Since I'm only allowed to leave my bed to go to the bathroom, there's not much else to do unless I have visitors.

I'd feel like climbing the walls, if only I had the energy. The great news is, we've made it to thirty-four weeks and the baby's lungs are now strong enough that she should be able to breathe on her own once she's born. Every additional day that passes before delivery will just make her stronger. As much as I don't want to be tethered to this bed, constantly poked and prodded and monitored, I do want our baby to be healthy.

Ashleigh's chuckle is soft as she runs a comb through the

curls she created in my hair half an hour ago before encouraging me to do my makeup. She suggested that getting myself ready, like I was going on a date with Luke, might help me feel better. She was right.

"You're funny. Or blind," she says. I glance at her in the mirror, and when we lock eyes, she asks, "Has pregnancy affected your brain? Because you're just as gorgeous now as you were before!"

My laugh comes out like a snort. "I haven't had a proper shower in a week," I say, thinking about the one three-minute shower they let me have a couple of days ago. Other than that, Luke's been giving me baths in my bed with a warm washcloth. "I feel . . . I don't even know . . . enormous, and greasy, and gross."

"Well, I hope I'm just as enormous, greasy, and gross as you when I'm pregnant," she says with a smile.

"I do feel better now that my hair is done, I've got a little makeup on, and I'm in real clothes." I look down at the incredibly luxe pajama set Luke brought me yesterday after confirming with the nurses that I could wear something other than a hospital gown. The pale blue pants and tank top are the softest cashmere knit, and I have a feeling I'll be living in them even after the baby is born because the top has a built-in nursing bra and it came with matching shorts.

"I'm glad I could help," she says as she takes the curling iron that's been sitting on the windowsill to cool and wraps the cord around it before sticking it in her bag.

"What else are you up to today?" I ask, suddenly feeling sad that I'm stuck inside on a gorgeous August day. She's probably got fun Sunday plans, and even though I know I'm exactly where I need to be—and damn lucky that Baby

Squash and my blood pressure are both doing okay—I'm still feeling a little sorry for myself. Hopefully, Luke will be back soon to keep me company.

Ashleigh glances at her phone screen when it lights up with a text. "Not much, actually," she says. "Thought I'd hang out with you for a while, if that's okay?"

Just then, there's a knock on the door. "Come in," I call out, wishing that the nurses didn't have to check on me quite so often. It's not so bad during the day, but being woken up every couple hours at night is taking its toll. Everyone keeps saying, "It's good practice for when the baby comes." And while it's true that I'll be sleep deprived once she arrives, I can't help but wish that I could enter parenthood well rested.

I glance over at the alcove where the door is, but instead of the nurse, Jules, Audrey, Morgan, AJ, and Lauren walk in. My jaw drops, and when I get over my shock, I ask, "What are you all doing here?"

They've each visited me individually over this past week, except Jules, who just got back from Bali. Those visits, combined with Luke being here almost non-stop, means I've rarely been alone. But I wasn't expecting to see any, much less *all*, of my friends today.

"We come bearing gifts," Lauren says, and it's then that I notice she's pulling a collapsible wagon behind her, and it's loaded with wrapped presents.

My eyes tear up, but I take a deep breath, trying to not ruin the makeup Ashleigh just encouraged me to apply. That's when I realize that this whole "helping me get ready" thing was in anticipation of my friends arriving. With baby gifts. "Is this . . .?"

"Your baby shower?" Morgan finishes. "Yes."

"Well, a small one, anyway," Audrey says.

"You'll probably want something bigger, with both your families and all your friends, once she's born," Morgan says. "But for now, you get us."

"No, this is perfect actually," I say with a laugh as my friends crowd into the room. Even though I have a really nice private room, complete with a couch that Luke has slept on more than once, it is pretty small. Fortunately, because I'm on a higher floor, I have a good view of Boston out the large window. I guess if I can't *be* outside, the ability to *see* outside is the next best thing. "This is the only baby shower I need."

I glance around the room at these women who have formed a tight-knit family, regardless of biological or marriage ties, and I'm so thankful that they're bringing me into the fold. The tears that were threatening to fall a moment ago start to slide down my face.

"Oh no, what's wrong?" Ashleigh asks. "Why are you crying?"

"I'm happy," I say with a teary smile.

At the same time, Audrey and Lauren both say, "She's pregnant."

"All of that is true." I can't help but laugh. And then I eye the cart with the gifts and notice a bakery box. "Please tell me you snuck in some cake? This low-salt diet they have me on to help with my blood pressure, and the hospital food in general, sucks so much. I could use something tasty."

"We didn't sneak it in," Lauren says. "We got the menu approved by your doctor."

That has more tears spilling down my face because of the

lengths they went through to plan this. "Well, anything is going to be better than what they're serving me here."

The girls set to work unloading the gifts and food from the wagon, and pretty soon, we've got plates piled high with veggies and hummus, a variety of cheeses, deviled eggs, gruyere and filet sliders, and the cutest little dessert cups of whipped coconut cream and berries, and dark chocolate cheesecake bites on the side. Everything is healthy, low-salt, and delicious!

I've never appreciated food more than I appreciate this meal, and when I tell my friends that, Audrey raves about Jules's cooking. "She can make *anything* taste good!"

"I know nothing about cooking," I admit, and tell my friends about how I've had a personal chef my entire adult life.

"I'm happy to teach you the basics, once you're up to it," Jules offers. "A couple quick cooking lessons might be a good distraction from early motherhood?"

"That would be amazing," I say.

"My kitchen is fully set up for cooking with a baby, from when Graham was little," she says. "I still have all the baby stuff in storage in the basement. Until Audrey needs it again." She gives her sister a meaningful look that makes me wonder if Audrey's expecting . . . or will be soon.

"Something you want to tell us?" AJ asks.

Audrey laughs. "No, not yet. But Drew's determined to have like six kids, so we'll probably start trying soon-ish."

I laugh to myself, wondering if *all* hockey players want big families.

"Are you going to start trying before you get married?" Lauren asks. "Is that why you haven't set a date?"

"We've only been engaged for a few months," Audrey says. "That's why we haven't set a date. But yeah, if I get pregnant soon, we'll probably push the wedding off. I don't want to be pregnant when I get married." Her hand flies to her mouth, and she looks at me, wide-eyed, before her cheeks pinken. "Oh my god, I didn't mean . . ."

Shaking my head, I just laugh. "No worries at all. Your situation is different, and *not* being a pregnant bride makes perfect sense! We didn't plan for things to happen the way they have." In so many ways, that's true, yet I wouldn't change a thing because I ended up with Luke.

"You could always go to the courthouse and get married there," Lauren says. "Then have the wedding celebration later."

Audrey nods, like she's considering the idea. "Maybe."

"Speaking of weddings and babies," Morgan says, "maybe we should let Eva open her gifts?"

And for the next hour, that's what I do. Slowly—between meaningful conversations—I open the most thoughtful gifts I can imagine. Things I never knew I needed, but that the moms in the group swear they couldn't have lived without, and some of the necessities I did know I needed but had thought I'd have longer to procure.

Surrounded by my friends, I take a moment to appreciate how truly lucky I am. Not only have I made new friends in Boston, but Luke has made sure Hans will never reappear in our lives. Only a week after coming to the hospital, my blood pressure is under control, and Baby Squash is healthy and still developing, both of which seem truly miraculous given how dire the situation sounded when we first got here.

We're taking a group picture when there's another knock

on the door. Assuming it's the nurse, I marvel at how quickly these past few hours have flown by with my friends.

But as the door opens fully, I get my second big surprise of the day when I see my mom, rather than the nurse, walking into my room.

She pauses in the doorway, and for a moment we just stare at each other. "I'm so sorry," she says, her hand flying to her chest. "I don't want to interrupt. I'll come back later."

She isn't wearing the annoyed expression I've become accustomed to in situations like this—one that says *I've come all the way to the city to see you and you're not available to welcome and entertain me*. Instead, once she gets over the surprise of finding my room full of women she doesn't know, her face conveys a sense of sadness and regret. It's like she knows that she's walked in on an event she wasn't invited to but would have loved to have attended.

"No!" The word springs free before I have time to think. But it's the right move. I don't like fighting with my mom, and she's made the effort to visit, so the least I can do is welcome her. "Don't go, Mom."

"We were actually just leaving," AJ says, before introducing herself and my friends to my mom. It's like she can sense that I don't have the energy to do it. At this point, I'm exhausted, but the only thing I want more than a nap is to know why my mom has come—when she hasn't visited with my dad or Luke's parents the times they've been here—and whether we can mend bridges and restore our relationship.

"Your friends seem really sweet," Mom says after they've stocked the mini fridge in the room with the leftover food and made their way out with my gifts, having already arranged to drop them off with Luke at our condo.

"They are." I rest my head back against my pillows and focus all my remaining energy on staying awake. "They just threw me a surprise baby shower. I didn't mean to exclude you."

"I'm not sure I'd have deserved an invitation, even if you'd known. I've been a real bitch about your pregnancy, and I'm sorry."

"You are?" My surprise at her statement drives away the remainder of my fatigue.

"Yes. I owe you an apology, not just for how I've treated you, but also for how long it's taken me to acknowledge it. I know I've been overbearing and controlling about all aspects of your life, especially your skating career. And I know that I should have given you more independence as you entered adulthood, especially because you've clearly got things pretty well figured out. I knew what I was doing, and I knew it wasn't the right thing for you or for our relationship. I just didn't know how to stop acting like my own mother had acted."

"But you . . . you never even had a relationship with your mom once you moved to the States," I say, trying to figure out why she'd act exactly like a woman she hadn't wanted to have a relationship with once she was an adult.

"Exactly," she says as she wrings her hands together in her lap. "And I don't want that for us."

I want to believe her, but it's difficult not to remain skeptical. Can this one conversation override a lifetime of experience? "What changed?"

"I always knew I didn't want to turn into my mother. I saw it happening—saw myself doing the same kind of things she did to me—I just didn't know how to stop. Now, I've finally started doing the work."

"The work?"

"I've done a lot of reading over the past month about the effects of generational trauma, and breaking negative parenting cycles, even after your child has become an adult. I've learned a lot. I thought I was in a better place when I saw you at Wellington, but when I learned that your dad had told you about the miscarriage even though we'd agreed not to . . . I reacted poorly and lashed out at the two of you." She pauses briefly and shakes her head, and the look of disappointment on her face for once isn't aimed at me, but rather at herself. "Since then, I've had some really open and honest conversations with your dad about how my behavior—overall, not just that night—has impacted our family."

"I—" I press my lips between my teeth and take a deep breath as I process the fact that she's done—and is doing—all this work. It didn't stop her from blowing up at me a few weeks ago, but she's here now, trying to make it better. "I don't know what to say, Mom. I appreciate the efforts you're making."

As if she senses my reluctance, she says, "Honey, I don't expect you to forgive and forget. I know that it will take time to repair our relationship. I just want you to know that I *want* things to get better. I'm willing to work hard to make that happen, and I hope you are open to it, too?"

She's not perfect, but neither am I. I'm not quite sure what we'll need to do or how long it will take to reinvent our relationship, but I want to try.

I open my mouth to tell her that, but then suddenly I'm

sitting in a puddle. I look down, and there's liquid every-where—seeping beneath my new pajama pants and across my mattress pad. It looks like I've peed myself, but since I just used the bathroom before I took the picture with my friends, that seems impossible. I glance around to see if there was a cup left on my bed that got knocked over, but there's nothing.

It's only then that I realize my water has broken.

Chapter Fifty

LUKE

McCabe grunts, one long arm grasping each side of the crib as he lifts and turns to place it in front of the freshly painted accent wall in what used to be my guest bedroom.

"You could just ask for help," Colt says.

"So you can re-injure your fucking knee? Not going to happen," our captain grumbles.

"If lifting that little thing is going to do me any damage, I should go ahead and hang up my skates now." Colt rolls his eyes, but McCabe misses it as he looks up at the ceiling and slides the crib over, centering it beneath the hook for the mobile. "And besides, you could've asked anyone for help."

On the other side of the soon-to-be nursery, Drew and Zach are attaching a changing table to the top of a dresser. Next to them, Walsh is testing out the swanky glider that I hope Eva and I will both enjoy when feeding our daughter before naps and bedtime.

Colt glances at McCabe and says, "You know what's missing here?"

McCabe lifts an eyebrow in response.

"Renaud and his snarky comments."

"You used to be the snarky teammate, too," McCabe reminds him.

"And now I'm a ray of fucking sunshine," Colt says with a goofy grin, and we all laugh.

"It'll be an adjustment having him back . . . for him most of all," McCabe says, and I can't tell how he's feeling about his best friend's return to the team.

"Is he as much of a dick in person as he seems on the ice?" Drew asks.

"No, Renaud's not a dick," McCabe says. "But he's also not in the NHL to make friends."

"Well, training camp ought to be fun then," Zach says, his tone sarcastic.

Again, I wonder what Renaud's return to the team will bring. He's an all-star player, but I'm curious—and honestly a little worried about—how his presence might change the tenor of our team.

"We're not the same team we were when he left," McCabe says. While our team didn't undergo the kind of major shake-up that sometimes happens around the trade deadline, the fact that three of the six of us standing here didn't play for this team before last season says a lot. "He'll need to adjust."

Walsh huffs out an ironic laugh. "Riiiight, because Renaud is so flexible."

"Coming back from injury is humbling, especially when

you missed a whole season," McCabe says. "Let's just give him some grace as he re-acclimates."

"Listen to you," I say with a laugh. "You're such a wise old man now."

"Never thought I'd see the day," Walsh says to McCabe. "Seems like AJ and fatherhood have softened you up."

McCabe lets out a chuckle. "Don't I know it. Now, can you stop relaxing on the fucking glider so we can finish setting this nursery up?"

There's the grumpy captain we all know and love.

"Do you have a chair or a step stool somewhere?" Colt asks, as Zach hands him a mobile with padded white clouds and stars hanging from wooden arches. "I want to hang this above the crib."

I grab a dining chair from the other room, and when I return, Walsh is telling Colt that he should let someone else hang it. "I'm not going to fuck up my knee standing on a chair, and none of you assholes are tall enough," Colt grumbles, taking the chair from me and stepping up on it.

He's leaning over the crib, one hand on the wall and the other reaching up to loop the mobile chain over the ceiling hook, when we hear AJ behind us. "Get your ass off that chair before I have to put you back on the IR, Colt."

I turn to see Jules laughing next to our GM. Colt ignores her and hangs the mobile, before using his injured leg—with the knee sleeve visible below the hem of his shorts—to step down.

"I'm already cleared to skate, AJ," he says, once he's firmly on the ground.

"Yeah, well, you don't need to take any unnecessary risks."

"You realize they have me doing basically this exact thing

at PT, right? We're moving to box jumps next week. I'm not broken."

"Sure you're not, old man," Jules says as she crosses the room to give him a kiss.

It's funny to think that at the beginning of the season, Colt was the wild one—the NHL fuckboy who no one thought would ever settle down. Now, headed into his final season in the NHL, he's engaged to his agent's little sister and is as whipped as the rest of us.

"You guys made great progress while we were at the hospital," Audrey says as she surveys the room.

She and Jules were invaluable in helping me get this room ready for our baby. I'd shared the Pinterest board of nursery ideas that Eva had made, and they'd ordered everything and put us guys to work building it.

Between Audrey's design skills and Jules's carpentry knowledge, which she graciously shared all the way from her vacation in Bali, the two of them have created what I hope will be the nursery of Eva's dreams—a soothing palette of cream, sage, and peach, wooden furniture, and a fun chandelier hanging from the high ceiling.

I can't wait to surprise her when she and our baby come home from the hospital.

My phone rings, and the whole room grows silent as all eyes turn to me. Since our phones are almost always on silent mode, hearing a ringtone is always a little jarring, especially since mine has been on the loudest setting since Eva's been in the hospital.

I slide it out, and sure enough, it's Eva. I make sure our friends keep quiet so Eva has no reason to question why everyone's at our condo, and then answer. "Hey, baby, what's up?"

"My water broke."

My stomach drops. "Wait, what? What does that mean? Are you going to have this baby *now*?"

"I mean, I assume she's not just going to fall out of me at this very moment . . ." she replies, but I can tell from her high-pitched laughter that she's nervous, despite her attempt at sarcasm.

"But they won't need to do a C-section?" That's been a huge concern for Eva since she was hospitalized. Because the recovery time from a C-section is so long, there's a good chance she wouldn't have enough time afterwards to get back into the shape required to compete at the level she needs to.

"They're going to try not to. It all depends on how my labor goes."

"Okay, I'm on my way. Is there anything you want me to bring with me?"

She laughs. "I've lived at the hospital for a week. If I don't already have it, I don't need it. Oh, but my water broke on those cashmere PJs you got me, and now they need to be cleaned. I love them, I hope they're not ruined."

"Baby, I'll buy you ten more sets. And I'll see you in about twenty minutes." Fortunately, the city is pretty quiet in August because so many people are away on end-of-summer vacations, and the college students haven't returned for the fall semester. I don't anticipate it will take me long to get to the hospital.

"Oh!" she says before we hang up. "And . . . my mom is here."

"Uhhh . . . everything okay?"

"Yeah," she says genuinely, with no hint of manufactured happiness I might have expected in her voice. "I'll see you soon."

Once we end our call, I turn to my friends. "We're having a baby!" Despite the excitement in my voice, and the nerves running through my body, I'm frozen in place.

Everyone is congratulating me, and while all I want to do is run out the door to Eva, the room is still in such disarray, and full of people.

"Go," Morgan insists, "we'll finish up here."

———

"You've got this, Evie. One more push," I say as she squeezes my hand so hard I wonder how many new fathers come out of the delivery room with broken fingers.

Her face is contorted in pain and covered with a thin sheen of sweat, and she sounds like a warrior running into battle as she bears down. She collapses against the inclined back of the bed and gasps for breath as the contraction passes.

"Luke," she says, her voice weary as she closes her eyes for a brief rest before the next contraction starts. "I love you *so much*. I love that you're trying to be supportive here. But if you tell me *one more push,* even one more time, I'm going to punch you."

My chest shakes with laughter, and I'm grateful for a break in the tension. I hate seeing my wife in pain. I hate that there's nothing that I can do to help her. I hate that I can't take care of this for her, as I did with Hans. I'd switch places with her in a heartbeat if it meant that I could take her pain away.

"What can I do instead?" I ask, still holding her hand. I hazard a glance at Dr. Lowery, whose amused look suggests that she's seen countless couples in this exact situation.

"Why don't we help Eva get into a modified squatting position, so gravity can help a bit more here," Dr. Lowery says as she glances at the monitor to see how long we have until the next contraction. Not long.

The nurse attaches a bar to the middle of the bed, then drops the foot and we help to get her situated. Eva pushes through another contraction before her head falls back against the inclined bed and tears of frustration leak from the corner of her eyes. "Why isn't she out yet?"

"I know it feels like this is never going to end," Dr. Lowery says, "but your labor is actually progressing really quickly. You're almost there."

"I don't know if I can—" Eva starts, but then her face contorts in pain, and she folds forward as another, longer contraction emerges. Three more pushes, and our baby is out. Dr. Lowery sets her on Eva's chest.

"I'm not sure how to process what I just witnessed," I say, wiping away a tear before wrapping my hand protectively over our daughter's back while she burrows her face into the base of Eva's neck. She's still coated in the white, waxy substance that protected her skin in the womb. I press my forehead to my wife's. "You are the strongest, most amazing person I've ever known."

Her chest shakes with an emotional laugh and our baby startles, her arms flying out over Eva's chest. I gently rub her back to settle her, and she snuggles back in between her mom's breasts.

"It's not like I didn't know how babies are born, but the reality . . . I'm so in awe of you."

"Thank you for staying by my side the whole time," she whispers, and lies her head back, her eyes meeting mine. "And for telling my mom to go home during the delivery."

I'd very gently, but firmly, let Helene know that I would be the only one in the delivery room with Eva, but that we'd call and let our parents know as soon as she was born so they could coordinate when to visit their first grandchild. Helene shockingly didn't make a fuss about leaving, and promised she'd be back as soon as we were ready for visitors.

"I'm sorry," the nurse says a minute later, "but we need to have the neonatal team assess her. We'll be right over there." She nods toward the corner where an additional doctor, two med students, a respiratory therapist, and another nurse stand at the ready.

"Is she going to be able to breathe on her own?" Eva asks, eyes still closed.

"Delayed cord clamping should help," she says, reminding us of what we were told during delivery—that especially for preemies, waiting a minute before clamping and cutting the umbilical cord allows the baby additional access to oxygenated blood from the placenta and increases the baby's blood volume. "If not, we're prepared to help her until her lungs are strong enough."

I nod to let the nurse know that she can go ahead, and watch as they clamp the cord. Our daughter doesn't cry immediately, and I hope that's not an indication that something's wrong. Dr. Lowery holds out a pair of surgical scissors. "You want to cut the cord?"

I take the scissors and make the cut where she indicates, trying to focus on this momentous occasion but finding that I'm wholly focused on listening for our baby's cries. They don't come.

The nurse rushes our daughter over to the plastic bassinet under a heat lamp, and I return to Eva's side while trying to get a glimpse of what's happening on the other side of the delivery room. *Why hasn't she cried yet?*

Eva squeezes my hand tightly in hers, and when I look down, I see her eyes clamped shut and silent tears streaming down her face.

"I need you to rest," Dr. Lowery says, giving Eva's knee a small shake so she'll open her eyes. "Can you do that for me? Because in a bit, you're going to need to push a few more times to deliver the placenta."

Eva nods, then looks up at me with a pleading expression. "Is she okay?"

My chest tightens as I lean back so I can see the neonatal team beyond Dr. Lowery. They're crowded around our baby, speaking quietly. No one seems panicked, and they're not rushing her out of here—both of which I take to be good signs.

"They're clearing her lungs," Dr. Lowery tells us quietly. "Usually that happens during the contractions as the baby moves through the birth canal, but sometimes with quick deliveries, like you had—"

"That was *quick?*" Eva asks. Nothing about the way I just watched her labor in pain seemed quick . . . but since it happened too fast for her to get an epidural, I suppose I have to recalibrate my notion of time.

"Many first-time moms labor for at least twelve hours, and that's before another few hours actually delivering the baby. So yes, having a baby within five hours of your water breaking is extremely quick. And sometimes that means the amniotic fluid doesn't all get cleared from the baby's lungs, so it needs to be suctioned out." Dr. Lowery glances back over her shoulder. "This is all pretty standard with a preemie delivery, so try to relax while the team does their job."

I know she's trying to reassure us, but as I watch Eva force herself to take slow, deep breaths, I know she's worried. So am I. So I focus on the one thing I can control in this situation, which is making sure Eva knows she's amazing.

I lean in, resting my head on the pillow next to hers so my lips are right next to her ear. "I'm not the least bit surprised that you delivered our baby in five hours, you overachiever, you."

Her soft chuckle is exactly the response I was hoping for.

"You did an amazing job keeping her safe this past week and bringing her into the world. She's going to be okay—"

The piercing wail that echoes through the room is such a relief that Eva starts crying again, and I have to wipe moisture from the corners of my eyes.

Thank god.

A moment later, the nurse is back at our side, telling us, "She needs a little extra support breathing, which is normal in this circumstance, so we're going to bring her over to the NICU to keep her on the monitor and watch her for a few hours. You can come by to see her before you go to your room or whenever you want. You'll have twenty-four-hour access."

I can tell Eva doesn't want to be separated from our baby, that she wants the skin-to-skin contact that we know is important post-delivery. "Nothing matters more than keeping her healthy," I remind my wife quietly, and she nods to the nurse, who turns to follow the neonatal team out of the room.

"This isn't the delivery I wanted," Eva whispers, and the sadness I see in her eyes breaks my heart.

"I know. But you did everything you could and now it's up to the doctors to make sure she's okay. What should we name her?" I ask, wishing we'd already decided on a name. It hasn't been that long since we found out we were having a girl, and we both thought we had more time. So far, we'd ruled out names, but never settled on any we both liked.

"I really like Georgia." It's a name she'd never brought up before.

"Because of their peaches?" I tease.

Eva's chuckle is soft as she closes her eyes again. "I just think Georgia Hartmann is a beautiful name. And we could call her Gigi."

My lips curve up into a smirk. "Sounds pretentious enough to keep my family happy."

Eva cracks her eyes open and lets her head roll to the side to look at me. "How'd you end up with the only non-pretentious name?"

"I guess my parents love me best."

She knows I'm teasing. For most of my life, I felt like I couldn't compete with my brothers, so I forged my own path. Now that things between the four of us feel so much more secure, I think it's time to repair the final crack in my relationship with my family and talk to my dad about what I overheard in AJ's office months ago.

"So, what do *you* think of Georgia?" she asks.

"I think after everything you went through to bring her into this world, you can name her whatever you want."

Her brows furrow and she looks almost like she's pouting. "But do you *like* it?"

I do like it. But even more importantly, my wife likes it. So I squeeze her hand and tell her, "I love it."

Chapter Fifty-One

LUKE

"There are our girls," my dad bellows as he walks into the hospital room with my mom and Eva's parents. Making a beeline to the hospital bed where Eva is cradling Gigi in her arms, he asks, "How's my perfect little granddaughter doing today?"

"She's good," Eva says, stroking our daughter's cheek. She sleeps most of the day, but the nurses assure us that's normal for preemies because they require more rest for growth and development than full-term babies. But right now, Gigi's eyes are open and she's semi-alert.

Mom had texted earlier to make sure it was okay for all four of them to show up together. It's the first time we've had this many visitors at a time.

Gigi spent the first seventy-two hours after her birth in the NICU before she was moved to the special care nursery, but she's doing well enough now that the nurses can bring her to Eva's room for a few hours at a time. It's a nice change and means that Eva doesn't have to go to the nursery every time Gigi needs to nurse. We're settling into a nice routine here at the hospital, but Eva and I are both looking forward to bringing Gigi home.

Eva's blood pressure hasn't come down enough for her to be discharged yet, but it's close. At least she can shower and move about normally, and now that her dietary restrictions are lifted, she's thrilled that I can bring her food so she doesn't have to eat the hospital meals.

Eva hands Gigi to her mom, and our parents settle in and take turns holding and fawning over their first grandchild. I turn and gaze at my wife, sitting cross-legged on her bed. Although I can tell that she's tired, she looks as happy as I've ever seen her.

And what's more, each time her parents have visited, the tension between Eva and her mom has lessened. Knowing that her mother meant what she said about doing the work to improve their relationship is a huge relief.

After Eva's parents had left the other night, she looked at me and said, "I didn't realize how reactive I always used to be around my mom. It's like I expected her to be a bitch and jumped on every single thing she said or did, no matter how minor, as evidence to support that narrative. Now that I've accepted that she's trying hard to change, I can see a lot more good in her."

My mom tears herself away from her granddaughter to ask Eva how she's feeling.

"Great, actually. My blood pressure is almost totally normal now, and the doctor said I might be able to go home in a couple days."

"What about Gigi?"

"She should be able to come home soon, too. They're actually going to let her sleep here in my room tonight. She'll still be monitored, but if she does okay for a couple nights, we'll be able to go home at the same time."

"You both must be looking forward to that," Helene says, looking up from where she sits on the sofa with Gigi in her arms.

"So much," I tell her, at the same time Eva says, "God, yes."

We chat for a few more minutes before Eva asks me to refill her water bottle. As I step out into the hallway, my dad follows.

"So, I got a bill from the lawyers the other day," he says, and I freeze mid-stride, turning to look at him.

"I . . . thought they'd bill me directly."

"They're on retainer for the family," Dad reminds me. "Everything comes through me."

It hadn't occurred to me to ask the lawyers to keep my father in the dark about our meeting. But they probably wouldn't have agreed anyway. Dad is where he is in life because he's always been keenly aware of everything that's happening around him—both personally and professionally.

"You going to tell me why you needed to meet with them early on a Saturday morning?" he asks when I fail to say anything.

I consider my options here. I could refuse and just tell him to send me the bill. But I worry that could harm our relationship. On the other hand, if I tell him the truth, he'll know that Gigi isn't my biological daughter. My name is on her birth certificate and her last name is Hartmann. Hans is permanently out of our lives.

Is it worth telling him everything at this point?

I think about all the secrets, lies, and misunderstandings that have brought us to this point, and how heavy it's been to carry them. So I steer my dad toward the alcove that contains the ice and water dispensers. Once we're tucked away, where I hope no one can overhear, I quietly tell him the whole story, going back to even before Game 7, when I first learned Eva was pregnant.

When I finish, he just nods and says, "I'm glad you came clean. Finally."

"What do you mean, finally?"

"I know you, and if you'd been dating Eva secretly for months, there's no way you could have hidden that from everyone. How you felt about her has always been crystal clear to everyone but her. So yes, even though I didn't doubt your *feelings* for each other, I *did* doubt your timeline."

"Do you think anyone else is suspicious?"

He chuckles. "Preston definitely was at first, but Tucker and Tristan convinced him that, of course, you'd been secretly dating the whole time because you're, and I quote, 'whipped enough to go along with whatever Eva wants.'"

I cough out a laugh, then wash it down with a sip of water from Eva's water bottle. They're not wrong about the last part.

"I'm sorry you had to learn the truth this way, though," I say.

"I understand why you kept this to yourself. The old adage is true: two can keep a secret, if one of them is dead."

My lips creep up at one corner. "So who's killing who in this scenario?"

Dad just shakes his head at me, his pink cheeks rounding

as he smiles. "I'm old enough to keep your secret until I *actually* go to my grave."

"Well that's fucking morbid, Dad." My whole body tenses at the thought. Dad's old, yes, but he's a giant of a man, metaphorically speaking at least, and it's impossible to imagine our family without him.

"I'm not getting any younger, so I'm glad to see you settled before I go." He pauses and then says, "And for the record, Eva is family. As far as I'm concerned, you are the only father that Gigi has or will ever have."

I nod and feel some tension that I didn't realize I was holding release.

"I'm glad you leaned on your brothers for help with this," he tells me. "And I'm glad you told me the whole truth."

"You don't mind keeping it to yourself, though, right? We're not planning on sharing that story with anyone else."

"You'd be shocked at the things I know and have kept to myself over the years. Speaking of keeping things to yourself," he says, "let's go back to your story and address what you overheard in AJ's office."

"I know," I say, shaking my head. "I should have said something right away."

"How in the *ever-loving hell* could you think that I didn't want you on the Rebels because you weren't good enough? How could you think it was anything other than what it was: me wanting to be your dad, and not your boss?"

"Dad, you're everyone's boss. Did you ever regret having Preston, Tristan, or Tucker working for you?"

"Working for me and playing for me are two very different things."

"How so?"

"Because if I want to influence the decisions they make in their role, I just do it. If I need them to do things differently, I tell them. Hockey—and the Rebels franchise—is different. I have no power over how good you are at your job, nor can I do anything to help you improve. And unlike Hartmann Enterprises, which isn't a publicly traded company and therefore not subject to stockholders' whims, the decisions made for and about the Rebels players are mostly out of my hands. That's AJ's realm of expertise. She handles hiring, trading, firing, and pretty much everything in between. I didn't want it to look like the Rebels acquired you—or kept you on if you underperformed—because of nepotism."

"But it *wasn't* you who asked for me to be traded to the Rebels."

"Outside the organization, I'm sure most people assume you were acquired because you're my son. And I never wanted my role as your father and owner of that team to come into conflict."

"I appreciate that, actually. And I'm sorry that I jumped to the wrong conclusion."

"Remember how your mom always used to say eavesdroppers never hear anything good about themselves?" Dad teases, lightening the mood.

"Yeah, but I wasn't trying to eavesdrop, and once I heard my name, I hightailed it out of there."

"Thus not getting the whole story."

"What would I have heard had I stayed, or announced myself?" I ask curiously.

"Exactly what I just told you, because that's what I told AJ. You should have at least asked your brother if you didn't want to talk to me about it," Dad says. "The fact that you didn't feel like you could come to your family about this . . ."

I can feel my cheeks heat under his gaze. "I was embarrassed. I was already a wreck over how I'd played in Game 7, I felt like I'd let everyone down—the fans, my team, and, worst of all, my family."

"Son, there's nothing you could do that would make me love you less. You know that, right?"

I swallow the lump that rises in my throat when I hear the words that my dad used to say all the time when I was a kid. If I ever got in trouble, got a bad grade, lost a game, his response was always the same.

"Yeah, Dad, I do. I just . . . I got in my own head about it all."

"Next time, come talk to me first—before you make assumptions about our family, and before you make big decisions. I'm happy to be a sounding board, voice of reason, or shoulder to cry on. And always remember that I am, first and foremost, your father."

My whole body relaxes. "Thanks, that means a lot."

"We should probably get back before they all start to wonder why it took so long to fill a water bottle," Dad says, motioning me back into the hallway, where we run into Christopher, accompanied by a tall brunette.

I introduce him to my dad, and he introduces us to his girlfriend, Jenn. Based on what Eva told me about Christopher, I'm initially surprised he's already labeled their relationship. But when I think about it, Eva and I have gotten married and had a baby in the same amount of time, so I suppose that's long enough for him to go from meeting someone to calling her his girlfriend.

We bring them back to Eva's room, and our parents say their goodbyes as they head out for a dinner reservation.

"I feel so bad that the first time I'm meeting you is in the hospital," Jenn says to Eva, as she and Christopher take a seat. Gigi is now asleep in my arms, swaddled in her blanket after Eva fed her while Dad and I were conversing in the hallway.

"Please," Eva says with a smile. "We're the ones who had to keep canceling on you guys."

"With good reason," Christopher says, as he gently rubs Jenn's back. He hasn't taken his hands off her in the few minutes they've been in this room.

"Do either of you want to hold her?" I ask.

Jenn's eyebrows lift. "Really? Oh my god, yes. I love babies."

I set Gigi in her arms, smiling as Jenn coos about "her perfect little nose . . . those eyelashes . . . her little Cupid's bow."

Eva's still alert and sitting up in bed, but I know she's also exhausted. She makes me go home every night to sleep because "at least one of us should be well rested," but she's up every few hours nursing Gigi, and that's got to take a toll.

Once we're all back home, I plan to get up whenever Gigi wakes. Although Eva will have to do the actual nursing, I can burp and rock her back to sleep, so that my wife can catch a few more moments of rest. I've also been looking into the possibility of hiring a newborn care specialist for the nights, once my season starts up again and I'm back to traveling.

In the meantime, I'm determined to make this a quick visit so that she can get some sleep.

"So the doctors say I can start going for walks to rebuild my stamina as soon as I'm out of the hospital," Eva tells

Christopher while Jenn whispers to Gigi. "They also said in another week or two, I can get back on skates, but literally just skating in circles, nothing strenuous until six weeks postpartum. Given that I gave birth over a month early, it'll mean we have even more time to train before the competition."

Although I know Eva is excited to get back on the ice, it sounds a little like she's trying to reassure Christopher that she'll be able to carry her weight as soon as possible.

"Hey," he says, tilting his chin and lifting an eyebrow, "slow down. You just had a baby. Give yourself some time to recover. We'll work it out."

I've never liked him more than I do at this moment, knowing that he's got Eva's best interests at heart. Maybe it's time to change his name in my contacts to remove the expletive.

"I know," she says with a sigh, "but my mind just keeps going to *how* it's going to work out. How soon I can start lifting weights and rebuilding my muscles, how soon we can start training."

"Sounds like the doctor's already told you, six weeks postpartum. We'll work out a plan with Lynette once you're back home. I know she's dying to meet the baby, too."

"Maybe we can meet up at the rink in a few weeks. Luke's setting up some interviews with nannies once I'm home. After we've found someone and picked a start date, I'd love to come back to the ice." She pauses when she notices the uncertain look in Christopher's eyes. "Just to skate around a bit, nothing more. No spins, no jumps . . . nothing strenuous, I promise."

"You want to hold her?" Jenn asks Christopher, and he

looks so damn uncomfortable. The old me would have insisted he hold her and asked him if he wanted kids, just to mess with him. But I'm no longer interested in being a dick to my wife's skating partner. So, I rescue him.

"I think Gigi needs to go back to the special care nursery, actually. They want to monitor her for a while before she comes back here to sleep tonight. You want to walk her back with me?" I ask Jenn.

"Sure," she says, standing with Gigi and laying her in the bassinet.

As we wheel my daughter out of the room, I'm reassured to hear Christopher reminding Eva, again, not to rush back to the rink. Nothing about Gigi's premature birth was ideal, but them having six weeks longer than expected to train before the qualifiers is at least a silver lining.

Chapter Fifty-Two

EVA

After taking my and Gigi's bags to our rooms, Luke finds me in the kitchen, where I'm arranging some of the many vases of flowers that greeted me when I walked in the door a few moments ago. Everyone's thrilled that Georgia and I are finally home from the hospital.

The week since her birth was one long blur. I'm sleep deprived, but elated to be home and thrilled that my daughter is doing well despite being born a month early.

"Can I convince you to stop futzing with the flowers for a minute?" Luke asks as he comes up behind me, wrapping his arms around my waist and pulling me against him. It crosses my mind for half a second that he can probably feel the fat and loose skin left behind post-delivery, but after the awed way he watched me give birth and all the praise he's lavished on me since then, I can't find it in me to care.

"Sure," I say, leaning my head back against his chest and closing my eyes. I'm so bone tired that I feel like I could sleep for a week. But there's no hope of that. Gigi's still asleep in her car seat in the living room where we set her after walking in the door, but she'll need to eat soon. Maybe next time she naps I can sleep too.

"I want to show you something before Gigi wakes up."

"Oh?"

"Yeah." He unwraps his arms from me and takes my hand. "Come on. I have a little surprise for you."

I follow as he leads me down the hallway toward the bedrooms, and I'm surprised when he stops at the guest room—the same one I was supposed to sleep in once we were married, but only spent a couple of nights in.

Pushing open the door, he leads me into a completely novel space. The room is painted in a soft cream with a sage accent wall, in front of which is an adorable crib with a gorgeous mobile above it. My gaze sweeps around the room, taking in every perfect detail. It's reminiscent of all the photos I'd saved on the Pinterest board I'd been building before I was hospitalized, but it came together even better than I could have imagined.

I'm stunned and place my hand on my heart as I take in everything—this nursery clearly required a lot of coordination and effort. *How in the world did this happen so quickly?*

"Do you like it?" Luke asks.

My laugh sounds a little like a snort, and my eyes fill with tears. "It's *perfection*. How . . .?"

"Everyone pitched in. Jules and Audrey designed it based on the photos you saved. I painted at night when you were in the hospital, and then the guys helped me get it all set up while you had your shower. Then the girls came in and got everything styled afterward so it would be ready when you and Gigi came home."

I sweep my thumb under one eye, and then the other. The fact that all our friends helped make my nursery dreams a reality makes it that much more special. "I wasn't expecting this."

"I know. But Evie, you *should* have been expecting it. You should already know that I'll take care of every need—and want—you have. Not because you can't do things for yourself, but because I will never stop doing whatever I can to make sure you're happy."

I turn and fold myself into his arms as he showers me with kisses on the top of my head. Then he takes a small step back and drops to one knee.

My breath catches when he pulls a ring box out of his pocket. *What the hell is he doing?* "We're already married," I choke out as more tears trail down my cheeks.

"I know," he says with a wink before flipping the top of the velvet box open. "But you deserved a better proposal than what you got. You deserved to have the wedding of your dreams—"

"All I wanted was you, Luke."

He swallows hard and his nose flares as he takes a deep breath. "All I wanted was you, too. And Gigi. And this life we're building together. But I never wanted any of this *unless* it was with you. You're everything I've ever dreamed of, and I will never stop showing you how much I love you."

"With jewelry?" I ask with a watery laugh. My eyes blur with more tears, because even though I've already had our baby, I still have an overload of hormones running through me. Or maybe this is who I am now? A sentimental sap, because I forever have someone showing me what it feels like to be adored and cherished.

"It seemed like the birth of our first child should be commemorated in some way." He pulls an eternity band, encrusted in diamonds, from the box and holds it out to me. Setting the box on the ottoman by the rocking chair, he takes my hand in his. "In fact, I think I'll get you a matching one every time you have a baby. You can stack them together."

I laugh lightly and tell him, "If I have as many kids as you want, they'll be stacked so high, I won't be able to bend my finger."

He shrugs. "You've got plenty of fingers." He slides the ring onto the ring finger of my right hand, which is perfect because there isn't much space on the finger with my wedding ring.

Sinking to my knees, I hold his face in my hands. "Thank you, Luke. For everything. For taking a chance on me—"

"You and me together wasn't chance, Evie. It was fate. There was no other possible outcome than this."

"But to suggest we get married when I was already pregnant—"

"Was the easiest, surest decision I've ever made. And it's one I'll never regret."

"The way you made sure that she could be *ours*," I say, thinking about how he managed the paperwork and got Hans to sign it, all while I was in the hospital. The way his name is on Georgia's birth certificate, the way he's built and protected our family. "I'll be eternally grateful that things turned out the way they did."

He leans forward, wrapping an arm around my lower back and pulling me against him. And then he kisses my forehead and presses his lips to the bridge of my nose, before his lips meet mine. He tentatively sucks my lower lip between his and I open for him, wanting to taste him, to feel him everywhere. I know we can't have sex for weeks still, but my god, I just want his hands and mouth everywhere in the meantime.

There's a knock on the front door, and Gigi lets out a wail from the living room. Luke practically jumps back from me, scrambling to his feet and holding out his hand to pull me up right as she really lets loose. In a split second, Luke's racing down the hallway to get to her.

"You don't have to run," I call after him.

"What if something's wrong? She's all by herself."

"Babies cry, you know. She's probably just hungry."

He turns into the living room, and I stop to open the front door.

"Surprise!" Morgan says, standing in my doorway with my friends behind her. "I hope you don't mind that we stopped by. I was dying to see you and meet baby Georgia."

Behind her, Jules rolls her eyes. "I picked her up at the airport half an hour ago and she insisted I bring her straight here."

"And I figured, if my sister and Morgan were coming," Audrey says, "you wouldn't mind me tagging along."

I glance at Lauren, who's standing next to Audrey. "And when I heard they were coming, I couldn't resist the chance to get some more baby snuggles." She smiles as I step back to let my friends in and then she pauses in the doorway. Dropping her voice, she continues. "I also figured that you could use someone to round them up and get them out of here if having company on your first day home was too much."

"Thank you. For now, I'm very happy you all are here. Hopefully, you can give me some pointers on settling in. It feels like all I do these days is feed her."

"That pretty much *is* all you do with a newborn. And change diapers, of course."

I think about the fact that Lauren was doing this with two babies at once, and I suddenly have a whole new respect for moms of multiples. I feel like I have my hands *more* than full just with Georgia.

Luke heads to the gym for a quick workout as I settle into the living room with the girls. Everyone's spread out on the couch and chairs, and the conversation flows naturally as I feed Georgia. She's so tiny and tires easily, so her eyes drift shut almost immediately.

"You might want to stroke her cheek or something to keep her awake," Lauren suggests. "Otherwise, she'll only snack and never get full, then she'll want to eat all the time."

"Oh, is that why she wants to eat, like, every hour?"

"Probably. She'll eat more and stay full longer if you can keep her awake long enough to finish eating."

"Things you think they would've mentioned in the hospital." I shake my head, realizing that it's entirely possible they *did* tell me, and I was too sleep deprived to remember. "C'mon, Gigi," I say as I stroke her cheek. She doesn't open her eyes, but she starts sucking again so I keep stroking her cheek as she eats. "I'm so glad I have friends who have done this whole motherhood thing before."

"Happy to help," Lauren says. "All three of my best friends from when I lived in Park City have recently had babies, so I'm living my best auntie life at the moment."

"Oh yeah," Audrey says. "You just did the annual trip with them. How was it?"

"Well, now that I'm not the only one with children, we brought *all* the kids. It was great, but Jameson and I skipped going on our honeymoon so we could do this annual trip, and now I feel like I need a vacation from my vacation. Oh, speaking of . . ." Lauren's head swivels to Morgan. "How was your mom's wedding?"

Instantly, the skin across Morgan's cheeks turn pink, making me wonder if it's a family trait since the same thing just happened to her cousin a moment before. They both have the same fair skin, similar eyes framed in dark lashes, and a smattering of freckles across their cheeks, though Morgan's are more pronounced. And whereas Lauren's hair is red and Morgan's is more of a strawberry blonde, the resemblance is still there.

"It was . . . eventful."

"Oh no," Lauren says with a groan. "What happened?"

"We never even heard from you the whole time you were gone," Jules adds.

"Internet and phone were out most of the time I was there because of a huge tropical storm. It was moving toward Bermuda before I left, and my flight managed to get in, but my mom's flight from Atlanta was canceled. So that first night . . ." She glances off toward the wall of windows framing the spectacular view of Boston.

"Oh my god, please tell me you met a hot stranger at the bar and had wild sex with him to get over that douchebag who you were seeing earlier this summer," Audrey says.

"Basically, yeah," Morgan says, biting the inside of her lip.

"And?" Jules asks.

"And then the next morning, my mom's flight came in and the two of us spent the day getting ready for the wedding. And that evening, when I walked down the aisle, guess who was standing there next to my new stepfather?"

"No!" I gasp, just like everyone else, and Georgia startles, her eyes flying open, when my whole body tenses up. I relax and press my hand against her back, soothing her as I help her latch back onto my breast so she can finish eating.

"Yeeeaaah," Morgan says, breathily drawing out the word. "My new stepbrother."

"No fucking way," Audrey says through a laugh.

"Oh my god, Morgs," Lauren says. "Only you!"

"I have the most shit luck of any person on the planet." Morgan shakes her head.

"So what did you guys do?" I ask, trying to imagine navigating that shitstorm of awkwardness.

"Swore it would never happen again, and then tried to avoid each other as much as possible."

"So *did* it never happen again?" Jules asks in a voice tinged with curiosity.

"Uhhhh . . ." Morgan's tongue darts out as she licks her lips and looks away. "There may have been a slip-up, but it's fine. I'll probably never see him again. I doubt this marriage will last any longer than my mom's three other marriages after she left my dad."

"Your mom has been married five times?" I ask.

Morgan nods and says, "Yep."

"But what if they *do* stay married?" Lauren asks.

"You know my mom," she says, waving off that idea. "They won't. The weird thing, though, is this guy—my stepbrother—it's like he doesn't exist. I Googled him on the flight home and couldn't find anyone with his name that looked anything like him."

"That's odd," Audrey says, and asks for his name as she reaches for her phone.

"Believe me," Morgan says, "if he existed, I would've found him. Social media is literally my job."

"Why don't you just ask your mom for more info?" Jules asks.

"And make her wonder why I'm asking? No, thanks. Plus, he'll be easier to forget if I can't stalk him online."

"*Would* you stalk him online?" I ask.

"I mean . . . I might be curious and go looking, which would be bad. It might have been the best sex of my life, but he's my stepbrother. And to be honest, he was kind of an asshole anyway."

"Why'd you sleep with him if he was an asshole?" Jules asks. But from what I've learned over the past couple of months, it seems like assholes are Morgan's default.

"Did I mention how hot he was?" Morgan says. "And he wasn't really an asshole until our parents showed up. Just bossy as hell, which, to be honest, kind of worked in the bedroom."

I chuckle, thinking how much I like it when Luke gets bossy like that. Not that I'll know what that's like for a while. I start imagining what other things we can do that don't involve him actually being inside me, until I notice that all the girls have turned and are staring at me.

"Something you'd like to share?" Morgan asks.

"Uh, no."

"Oh, come on," Jules says. "You're still newlyweds. You should be having good sex all the time. The rest of us are."

"Except me," Morgan chimes in.

"You just said you had the best sex of your life in Bermuda," Audrey reminds her.

"Which is why it sucks that it can't happen again," Morgan says, tucking a strand of her hair behind her ears. "Not that I even know how to find this mystery man."

We start throwing out suggestions, and Morgan just laughs. "You think I didn't already think of all those things? Honestly, it's best if I just put him out of my mind."

"Put who out of your mind?" Luke's voice comes from behind Morgan, and we all look over to see him standing in the entryway, his sweaty workout clothes clinging to his muscles. I hate that I feel so out of shape while he's maintaining his all-too-excellent physique in anticipation of training camp, which starts soon. I know my body needs time to recover, but as an athlete myself, it's hard to convince my brain that I shouldn't be doing some sort of exercise to get back into top condition.

"No one," Morgan says quickly, and Lauren shifts the conversation to the start of the hockey season. Since she and Morgan both work for the team, I'm married to Luke who plays for them, and Jules and Audrey are both engaged to players, everyone in this room is part of the Rebels family.

And that's when it hits me, we're not just united through hockey—these women are quickly becoming my closest friends. I've gotten together with my high school friends here and there, but it always feels forced, like we're trying to hold on to something that's past its expiration date.

But with these women, the friendship flows naturally. Despite our different ages, backgrounds, and current situations, when they're around, it feels like being with family—the kind that loves you no matter what.

And that's what I'm building here in Boston with Luke, not just our immediate and extended family, but friends who are family, too.

I glance over at my husband, where he stands chatting with Lauren and Morgan, and his gaze shifts to me as I hold our daughter against my shoulder to burp her.

Her head is heavy on my shoulder, and the look in his eyes is a combination of love and hunger. It's a look that reminds me that he'll never get enough of us together, which is good, because that's exactly how I feel, too.

Epilogue

LUKE & EVA

LUKE

Four Months Later
Nagoya, Japan

"You'd think you were the one about to skate onto the ice, you're so nervous!" Mom says, placing her hand over mine and giving my fingers a squeeze. It's enough to interrupt the bouncing of my knee, but I can still feel the turmoil inside of me.

From her seat on the other side of my mom, Helene leans forward. "She's going to be fine, Luke. You saw them last night in the short program; it was like they'd never spent a day off the ice."

If you'd told me a year ago that I'd be sitting here tonight with my mom and mother-in-law, with my baby strapped snugly against my chest while cheering on my wife in her bid for the Olympics, I would never have believed it.

Not only because I never dared to hope that Eva and I would end up together like this, but I also never thought Eva and her mom could repair their relationship, nor did I think I'd ever miss three games without being injured or sick. Luckily, my coaches and teammates have been nothing but supportive about my absence.

"You're right," I say, shaking my head slightly to try to clear away my nerves. It's just that so much rests on the next four minutes. I thought the pressure was high in hockey, but we get *seven* games to prove we deserve the Cup. In pairs skating, they get a combined seven minutes over two performances.

"I'm starting to think my daughter-in-law is superhuman," my mom says.

I couldn't agree more. Four months ago, she gave birth, ten weeks ago, she started training again, and today, she's better than ever. As hard as these last ten weeks have been— with her training and me traveling with the team, and neither of us feeling like we're spending enough time with Gigi—watching her skate last night proved that it's all been worth it.

She has *never* skated with such skill and precision, and

she and Christopher are in second place going into tonight's free skate.

"Do you want me to take her," our nanny, Allison, asks from my other side, nodding her chin toward Gigi, "so you can focus on Eva's performance?"

"Thank you, but no. I want to experience this with my daughter." I run my hand down her back and pat her bum. She's wearing the noise-canceling earmuffs I got her for tonight and seems totally content looking up at me with sleepy eyes. I wish I could borrow some of her tranquility. I also wish I could turn her around so she can face the ice and see her mama, but her neck's not quite strong enough for that and she can't see that far yet anyway. Hopefully, she'll be able to watch her in the Olympics two months from now.

The Canadian pair that's just finished their performance finally skates off toward the kiss-and-cry booth to await their scores. My knee starts bouncing of its own will again as I watch the young skaters collect the flowers and stuffed animals that were thrown on the ice after the performance.

Glancing beyond the Canadian pair, I watch Eva and Christopher standing near the door through which they'll take the ice. They're facing each other and her forehead rests on his chest while his hands run along her upper arms. Her shoulders shake, and when she looks up at him, I can see that she's laughing. I can sense their excitement from across the ice. The misplaced jealousy I felt before has completely disappeared, replaced with pure pleasure and pride—for both of them.

Glancing over my shoulder, I look up at Jenn, who's sitting with her parents in the row behind us. She and

Christopher are still going strong, and even Eva is surprised that he's finally settled into a serious relationship. Sometimes, all it takes is the right person in the right place at the right time.

"You nervous?" I ask her.

"I think I'm going to throw up." Her eyes are trained on them, and I'm pretty sure she's let go of any insecurities she had about the nature of their relationship too.

I reach my elbow over the seat and nudge her knee so she'll look at me. "Hey, they're going to do great. They've been working toward this for nearly a decade."

Then the crowd erupts with applause as the Canadian pair's scores flash on the screen, moving them into first place when combined with last night's short program results. We're almost at the end of the competition, and most, if not all, of tonight's medalists will come from this final group of competitors. Eva and Christopher are the second to last pair to skate.

They take the ice, skating hand in hand to their starting position in front of the judges. When their music comes on, I'm completely engrossed, and everything fades away except the two of them. The tempo is upbeat and the crowd claps along as they come up to one of the more difficult parts of their performance—a triple jump combination. I don't realize I'm holding my breath until the crowd erupts in applause after they land all three flawlessly, and I exhale in relief. Eva's broad smile makes it clear she can sense how well they're skating, and she's enjoying every second.

Christopher launches her into a triple twist, and she lands gently on one skate and glides backward so lightly, it's hard to believe she was ten feet above the ice just moments before. They're in the home stretch now. The most difficult parts of the performance are behind them, and the scoreboard shows green checks next to each of the required elements. As they move through the synchronized choreography of the more artistic segment of the performance, they look like they're having the time of their lives.

Entering the final spin, they both plant a toe pick on the ice to stop at exactly the same moment, hands linked and arms up in victory. I can tell that they know that they've done more than enough to qualify for the Olympics.

In the booth a few rows behind where we're seated, I can hear the television announcers saying what I'm thinking.

"With a performance like that, I'm certain that Steele and Hartmann just earned themselves a spot on the US Olympic Team," Alyssa Goodman, a former US gold medalist and an announcer for US pairs competitions, says.

The male announcer, whose name I've forgotten, adds, "The only thing that remains to be seen is if it's enough to move them ahead of the Canadians for a possible gold tonight. But either way, they're definitely Olympic bound come February."

On the ice, Christopher bends to pick Eva up, his arms around her thighs as he holds her in the air so she can wave to the crowd. As the screen zooms in on their faces, it's easy to read his lips as he looks up at her: "You did it."

He sets her down and they move to each side of the ice, taking a bow and waving to the crowd as an unbelievable number of stuffed animals shower down from the stands. And when they turn toward us and take their final bow, Eva doesn't head directly toward the kiss-and-cry booth. Instead, she skates to the boards closest to the stairs near our row and motions me down.

I scoot past my mom and Helene, holding tight to Gigi, before jogging down the stairs with one hand on the rail as the crowd around us stands and cheers. And when I get down to ice level, I reach forward and wrap one arm around her midsection, lifting her to sit on the boards so she can pull Gigi and me into an embrace.

"You did it, Evie," I say, smiling into the crook of her neck.

"I hope so. We'll see." She pulls back, and her smile is huge. She knows she did it, she just doesn't want to jinx it.

"There's no way that performance didn't earn you a ticket to the Olympics."

Christopher skates over then, and we shake hands before he helps Eva down and they skate to the opening, put their skate guards on, and take a seat in the kiss-and-cry booth.

"Your first competition in six months, *and* since having a baby. How did that feel?" the announcer asks before holding the microphone out to Eva. I tilt my head back to watch the interview on the screen, not wanting to miss a second.

"Phenomenal." Eva takes a deep breath, still panting after the intense performance.

"All her hard work paid off," Christopher adds.

"What about *your* hard work?" the interviewer asks him.

"It was nothing compared to what she had to do to come back from a challenging pregnancy and giving birth." He beams down at her with pride, and then their heads tilt up as the judge's scores start populating the screen.

As expected, the performance puts them into first place with only one pair left to skate. They move over to the winner's circle to watch the reigning world champions, a pair from China, take the ice, and I return to my seat.

Six minutes later, as the entire arena awaits the final scores, Eva and Christopher are clutching hands, waiting to find out if it's a silver or a gold for them tonight. The second the scores appear, Christopher tackles Eva in a hug that almost carries them out of their seats because, while their competition put on a great performance, they came up short.

My throat tightens as I consider what this moment means to Eva—to put on the performance of a lifetime, when only a couple of months ago she was battling her own self-doubt while also tuning out the critics who said there was no way she'd be able to compete on an international level so quickly after giving birth. And as I watch my mom and hers jumping up and down and embracing, I know that I'm exactly where I'm meant to be.

Eva and Christopher stand and wave to the crowd in the midst of thunderous applause. Just then, my phone starts buzzing like crazy in my pocket. At first, I plan to ignore it and remain in the moment, but the buzzing continues, so I pull my phone out.

My teammates, who got back from a road trip, are flooding the group chat that I named *Assholes* a while back as a joke. It's not even eight in the morning in Boston, but apparently they all watched the performance after arriving back in town.

WALSH

Holy shit, man. Eva was amazing!

COLT

Right? Jules is all choked up, and she doesn't cry.

DREW

Audrey's already asking about going to watch her in the Olympics.

ZACH

Ashleigh too. Group trip?

MCCABE

Colt and I will be playing, so we'll see you there. You can watch me score on him.

COLT

Right, because that's ever happened.

ZACH

US/Canada rivalry is alive and well. Do we start taking bets on this now, or wait until we're at the game?

WALSH

You know Marissa would be ALL about planning a team trip like this. Should I have her get started on that?

DREW

We have the break in our schedule for the Games anyway, so it feels like an easy decision.

LUKE

You guys are the best. I'll pass all the love on to Eva as soon as she's done with the medal ceremony, and I'll see you in a few days.

Luke Hartmann renamed the group Rebels Fam.

———

EVA

One Week Later
Boston, MA

I stroke Gigi's cheek as her eyes drift shut, trying to keep her awake long enough to finish her bottle. I'd really love for her to sleep through the night tonight. My girl has always been a great sleeper—something I've learned is pretty typical for babies who've spent time in the NICU—but she's waking up more frequently at night now, and we're trying to figure out whether it's because she's hungry or teething or if it's the cold she caught while traveling with us to Japan.

"Come on, beautiful," I coo. "Let's finish the bottle." Her big blue eyes flit open, and she looks up at me before taking a few more swallows from the bottle. Then, apparently sated, she pulls her head away and tucks it into the crook of my arm.

I bring her up to my shoulder to burp her as I glide gently in the chair in her nursery. I hate rushing moments like these, but I really need to get going or I'm going to miss the entire game.

In the open doorway, Allison pops her head in to see whether I want her to take over, but I'm afraid the transfer might wake Gigi. So I shake my head and stand, lightly bouncing as I walk over to her crib.

Placing her on her back, I rest my hand on her abdomen for a few minutes, just to make sure she's really asleep. Then I turn, tiptoe out of the room, and check in with Allison for a moment before heading downstairs to the car I know is waiting for me.

I make it to the game right as the third period is starting. I know a lot of hockey players' wives bring their babies to the games, but we weren't able to do that at the beginning of the season because, as a preemie, Gigi is more susceptible to viruses. Her first real foray into crowded public spaces was our trip to Japan, and she came back with a fever and a stuffy nose. She's recovered quickly, but for now, keeping her away from big crowds so she can stay healthy is our top priority.

In some ways, I feel like everything is in a holding pattern right now: daily practices with Christopher, then time with Gigi and Luke, when he's in town, in the afternoons and evenings. I catch the Rebels games when I can.

This balancing act isn't ideal, but it won't be forever. I'm learning to let go of any expectations of how things *should* be —the notion that there's some ideal "perfect" out there—and instead, I've accepted that, for now, this is the compromise that works for our family.

Tonight though, as I sink down in the seat Morgan saved me in the row behind Jameson, Lauren, Jules, Audrey, and Audrey's son, Graham, I'm immensely thankful this is a home game. Because if the Rebels come out on top tonight, this will be Luke's 100th win. It's a big milestone for a goalie, and if it doesn't happen tonight, the next opportunity will be at an away game that I can't attend.

"How's he doing?" I ask Morgan over the groan of the crowd as one of our wingers takes a shot that's blocked by Chicago's goalie.

"He's having a great game," she says. "Just like the rest of this season. This life and family you two have built really seems to bring out the best in him."

There could be so many reasons that Luke's on fire this season. It could be his continued meetings with Chloe to process and remove the mental blocks that interfered with his game last season, or all the skills work with Coach Knight over the summer. It could be that, after Game 7 last year, he's got something to prove, or that he's getting more playing time than ever now that Colt's retirement at the end of the season has been officially announced. There's no doubt that marriage and fatherhood really suit him, but I'm certain that's not the *only* reason his game has improved.

The puck quickly returns to our side of the ice, and after we fail to block several passes between Chicago's players, I lean forward in anticipation as a shot is taken. Luke easily catches it in his glove, and I breathe a huge sigh of relief. The score is 2-0 for the Rebels, and if we can maintain this score until the end of the game, it'll be Luke's fifth shutout of the year—one more than the league-wide average per season, and we're only in the third month of play.

There's a lot of people saying that this is the best season of his career, but seasons are long and things can change quickly. I know he's trying not to think too much about it, so I never bring it up.

But goddamn, am I proud of him for the way he's come back this year.

With one minute left in the period, Chicago uses their timeout, and as our team approaches the bench, seven rows in front of us, Luke pulls off his helmet and glances up at me. His calm, confident expression relaxes me.

As our first line comes in for the face-off, Luke takes his

position in the crease. There's no doubt Chicago is going to go hard for the last sixty seconds in a final attempt to tie it up and force us into overtime. While it's unlikely they can make that happen in the remaining time, it's not unheard of. And not only do I want to be here for Luke's 100th win, but I also want it to be a shutout.

Lauren reaches her hand back over her shoulder to take mine. Next to me, Morgan takes my other hand, and it's all I can do to stay seated. The nervous energy flowing through me right now is similar to how I feel before taking the ice.

I wonder if loving someone means you feel the same anticipation, and all the highs and lows, right along with them? Probably. Which makes it a tad more understandable why my mom was always so invested in my skating career—she felt every win and every defeat almost as much as I did.

Chicago wins the face-off and Luke crouches into a defensive position, but instead of taking a shot, the player takes the puck behind the goal in an attempt to come in from the other side. Luke anticipates the change and has already moved, and after Chicago makes a few passes, Zach manages to intercept the puck and skate across the center line. He passes to McCabe, who sends the puck across the ice to Walsh as they move closer to Chicago's goal. With the way they're passing the puck back and forth, it's unclear whether they're hoping to score once more or just want to run down the clock. But with seconds left, Drew sees a shot and scores, cementing our win.

With seven seconds remaining, the two teams return to center ice after a line change. Even though Chicago wins the face-off, we quickly steal the puck, and when the buzzer sounds, the entire team spills onto the ice and heads toward

Luke. The crowd is ecstatic, chanting "Shut Out" in sync with the words flashing on the screens running along the perimeter of the balcony.

My eyes fill with tears as I jump up and down with my friends, celebrating the team's victory, and Luke's 100th win. And once he manages to emerge from the dogpile on the ice, he skates over near the bench, motioning for me to meet him at the glass.

It takes me a minute to fight my way down the stairs through the fans who are headed up toward the exit, but when I finally do, he holds his hand up to the glass and I press mine against it.

"Love the way you look in my jersey, Peaches," he yells, trying to be heard over the noise.

I just wink and say, "I know you do, Hartmann." Then I blow him a kiss, tell him I'll meet him at home, and saunter back up the stairs. I'm certain he's watching the sway of my hips as I walk away, and is already picturing me at home, waiting for him in nothing but the jersey.

Maybe we'll get lucky and Gigi will stay asleep for long enough for us to celebrate this win however we want, or maybe she won't. Either way, we'll be okay because we have forever together.

Want more Luke and Eva? Get their sentimental and steamy bonus epilogue, here.

Curious about Zach Reid? He has his own novella, THE TRADE UP, which you can download here.

Want more Boston Rebels? How about more of Luke's brothers? Keep flipping to see what's coming next...

THE END

Join My Reader Group

Not ready to leave the world of the Boston Rebels? Join me in my Facebook reader group, where we're always talking about the Rebels!

PENALTY PLAY
Boston Rebels, Book 5

Aidan & Morgan's story
is coming soon…

HARTMANN BROTHERS

A new new series following three billionaire brothers is coming soon!

BOOK 1

A billionaire and a romance author—both hiding their true identities—have an unforgettable weekend while stranded in a cabin together during a blizzard, only to find out their lives back home in Boston are connected in ways that put them at odds with each other.

Books by Julia Connors

FROZEN HEARTS SERIES

On the Edge

Out of Bounds

One Last Shot

One Little Favor

On the Line

BOSTON REBELS SERIES

Center Ice

Fake Shot

Cross-Checked

Goal Line

Penalty Play

HARTMANN BROTHERS SERIES

Coming in 2026: Book 1

Acknowledgments

Writing *Goal Line* was both a joy, and a struggle. Luke and Eva were the youngest couple I've written, and their childhood best friends to lovers journey was a necessary slow burn . . . and the writing process sometimes felt like a slow burn as well! I love these two with my whole heart, but it took a village to get their story over the finish line, and I absolutely could not have done it without the following people helping push me along:

Rhea – This book is for you. Full stop, that's the message. If it weren't for you, the acknowledgments would end here, because *Goal Line* wouldn't exist if we hadn't had our three-hour car rides where we fleshed out Luke & Eva's journey. Your feedback along the way has been invaluable, especially around changes to the storyline at the end of the book. I'm so glad you're a part of my writing process now, as I have such a deep appreciation for your skill!

Victoria – Sitting at the dining room table at our Airbnb in Houston last fall, you helped bring to life my initial inspiration for Luke & Eva's book . . . you asked the tough questions that helped their story unfurl. Our ongoing chats about plot and characters continue to be an absolute highlight of our friendship, and I'm forever grateful to have you in my corner!

Rachel – Thank you for always being one of the very first readers of every book I write. I appreciate your honest critiques, and the way you're always striving to help make my books better.

Melanie – Thank you for working with me as I wrote this book! Your structured feedback and the way you always kept track of the big picture really helped this story develop into the best version of itself.

Amy – Thank you not only for proofreading this book, but also for stepping in early to beta read it. Your feedback is always so spot on, and I really appreciate you being a gut check for me! And the way you have stepped up to help in other areas of my business has been beyond amazing. I am so glad to have you on my team!

Sierra – Thank you for reading an early version of this book, and giving me feedback along the way. I hope I've done your accidental-pregnancy-obsessed heart justice with this story!

Valentine – Thank you for everything you've done for this book! From reading an early draft and giving me feedback, to helping it find the right readers, you've been there for me along the way.

Elizabeth – Where to start? I just can't. The way you've supported my writing journey, and the way you've gone from proofreading to line editing my books has been amazingly helpful! I can't wait to see where this editing journey takes you.

Kenzie – Thank you for always whipping my manuscripts into shape, and for making sure all the loose threads get tied together in the end! You're the best.

Rachel, Melanie, Alexandra, and Elizabeth – Thank you for

always being there for me. Thank you for not letting me turn into a hermit, and for celebrating my book releases, and for being my safe space, always!

Mr. Connors – Dare I say, we made it through the hardest year of our lives, and survived? I love you. Thank you for being a non-stop source of support!

And thank you to everyone else who has helped, supported, and guided me along the way – my author friends, my ARC, Content, and ALC teams, and my family.

And the hugest, biggest thank you ever to my readers! It never fails to humble me when you show up for me and my books. Without you, none of this would be possible!!!

Afterword

Thank you so much for reading! If you enjoyed the book, please consider leaving an honest review. Reader reviews mean so much to authors, and your time and feedback are appreciated.

Sign up for Julia's newsletter to stay up to date on the latest news and be the first to know about sales, audiobooks, and new releases!

juliaconnors.com/newsletter

About the Author

Julia Connors grew up on the warm and sunny West Coast, but her first decision as an adult was to trade her flip-flops for snow boots and move to Boston. She's been enjoying everything that New England has to offer for over two decades, and now that she's acclimated to the snowy winters and finally found all the places to get good sushi and tacos, she has zero regrets. You can usually find her in front of her computer, but when she stops writing she's most likely to be found outdoors, preferably with a pair of skis or snowshoes strapped to her feet in winter, or on a paddleboard in the summer.

goodreads.com/julia_connors

amazon.com/author/juliaconnors

instagram.com/juliaconnorsauthor

tiktok.com/@juliaconnorsauthor

facebook.com/juliaconnorsauthor

pinterest.com/juliaconnorsauthor